THE
HERON'S CRY

Ann Cleeves is the author of over thirty critically acclaimed novels, and in 2017 was awarded the highest accolade in crime writing, the CWA Diamond Dagger. She is the creator of popular detectives Vera Stanhope and Jimmy Perez, who can now be found on television in ITV's *Vera* and BBC One's *Shetland*. The TV series and the books they are based on have become international sensations, capturing the minds of millions worldwide.

Ann worked as a probation officer, bird observatory cook and auxiliary coastguard before she started writing. She is a member of 'Murder Squad', working with other British northern writers to promote crime fiction. Ann is also a passionate champion for libraries and was a National Libraries Day Ambassador in 2016. Ann lives in North Tyneside near where the Vera books are set.

Ann Cleeves

THE HERON'S CRY

MACMILLAN

First published 2021 by Macmillan
an imprint of Pan Macmillan
The Smithson, 6 Briset Street, London EC1M 5NR
EU representative: Macmillan Publishers Ireland Ltd, 1st Floor,
The Liffey Trust Centre, 117–126 Sheriff Street Upper,
Dublin 1, D01 YC43
Associated companies throughout the world
www.panmacmillan.com

ISBN 978-1-5098-8967-9

1 3 5 7 9 8 6 4 2

A CIP catalogue record for this book is available from the British Library.

Map artwork by ML Design Ltd

Typeset in Plantin Light by Palimpsest Book Production Limited, Falkirk, Stirlingshire
Printed and bound by CPI Group (UK) Ltd, Croydon, CR0 4YY

Visit **www.panmacmillan.com** to read more about all our books
and to buy them. You will also find features, author interviews and
news of any author events, and you can sign up for e-newsletters
so that you're always first to hear about our new releases.

For my BGS friends, with thanks for great memories and looking forward to adventures to come.

Acknowledgements

It takes a whole team to get a book into the reader's hands and I'm incredibly lucky to have the support of the people at Pan Macmillan in the UK and Minotaur in the US. So, huge thanks to everyone who's been involved in the editing and copy-editing, especially Gillian, Vicki, Catherine, Nettie, Charlotte and Lorraine. The PR and marketing teams on both sides of the Atlantic have worked tirelessly to sell novels in very difficult times, so many thanks to them all, with a special mention to Emma and Elle in the UK and Sarah and Martin in the US. My assistant Jill looks after me with a quiet efficiency, and Jean and Roger manage my website beautifully.

I couldn't concentrate on storytelling without the support of my agent, Sara, and her co-agents. I'm hugely grateful to her, and to Moses, Rebecca, Jill, Maydo and Annelie. Indie bookshops have maintained sales, even when they've had to close their physical premises, and I love them all. A special shout out to Helen and James at Forum Books for their kindness and their imaginative events. Libraries too have worked hard in lockdown to supply their readers with books and virtual events, and the staff will always be heroes to me.

Thanks to Cynthia Prior and Sarah Grieve for allowing me to use their names, and to Sue Beardshall, Martin Kerby and Paul Jones for their advice on the first draft of the novel. Jenny Beardshall explained the mysteries of glass-blowing and Bob Crooks showed me how it worked in practice. Dr James Grieve shared his huge expertise so I could use glass as a weapon. Any factual mistakes are, of course, mine. Issy Wheeler continues to be a great model for Lucy Braddick, and in places I've quoted her exactly!

Author's Note

The Heron's Cry is fiction, and I've taken liberty with the North Devon geography to suit my story. There's no Seal Point, no Spennicott and no Gorsedale Hospital. I created North Devon Patients Together, and the Peace At Last website, and I sincerely hope that the Suicide Club is a figment of my imagination. In the UK people with Down's Syndrome are usually described as having a learning disability. The term carries no value judgement here and I've used it throughout the book. I know that in some territories the label is considered inappropriate. Of course no offence is intended. Any resemblance to any organization or individual within the novel is coincidental.

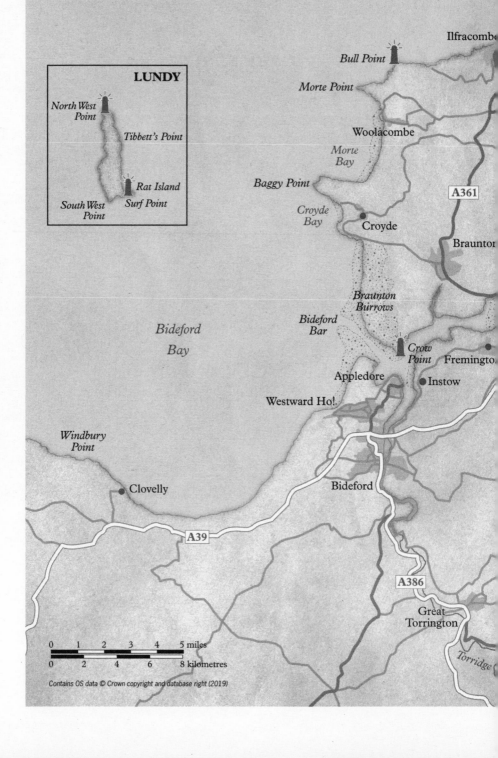

NORTH DEVON

LUNDY

North West Point

Tibbett's Point

Rat Island

South West Point

Surf Point

Bull Point

Ilfracombe

Morte Point

Woolacombe

Morte Bay

Baggy Point

A361

Croyde Bay

Croyde

Braunton

Braunton Burrows

Bideford Bar

Bideford Bay

Crow Point

Fremington

Appledore

Instow

Westward Ho!

Windbury Point

Clovelly

Bideford

A39

A386

Great Torrington

Torridge

0   1   2   3   4   5 miles
0   2   4   6   8 kilometres

Contains OS data © Crown copyright and database right (2019)

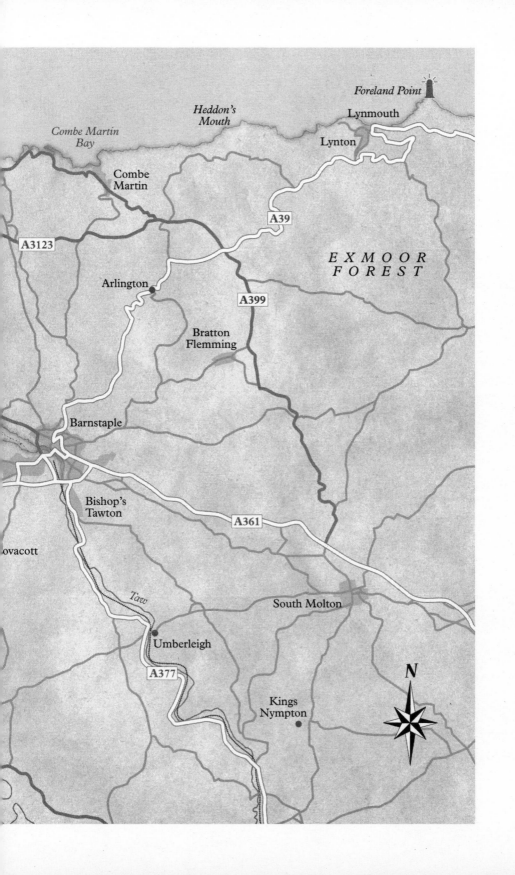

Chapter One

JEN HAD DRUNK TOO MUCH. They were in Cynthia Prior's garden, lounging on the grass, and it was just getting dark. The party had moved outside, become quieter and less frenetic. Jen could smell cut grass and honeysuckle, the scent intense, heady and oversweet. She found herself mesmerized by the rhythm of the flashing fairy lights that Cynthia had strung along the high brick wall and woven between the ivy and climbing roses.

Cynthia's place was the kind of gaff to have a wall around it: a large detached house looking out over Rock Park, only a few hundred yards from Jen's narrow terraced home, but a million miles in terms of class. Jen was a Liverpudlian and carried the idea of class with her like a badge of honour. Her dad had been a docker and her mother still stacked shelves in a supermarket.

Although it was dark, the air remained hot and the fire in the pit was there for effect, and to toast marshmallows, not because it was needed. They'd had an early heatwave. It was only the end of June but already there were calls for water rationing, talk of standpipes if the weather didn't break soon. In North Devon, they weren't usually short of rain.

Earlier, inside the house, there'd been loud music and, despite the warmth, dancing; Jen loved a good dance and could move like a demon. Her husband had disapproved, but she no longer had to care what he thought. Now they'd all drifted outside and Wes, one of Cynthia's arty mates, was playing guitar, something moody and slow. Nobody could do moody like Wes. Jen had fancied him like crazy when she'd first met him, but then she fancied most of the single men she bumped into. She was a tad desperate. Wes was brooding, dark-haired and fit, the stuff of Jen's dreams. Later she'd decided that a weed-smoking musician, who lived with a bunch of hippies in the hills, and supplemented his income by making weird furniture from driftwood, wasn't the best fit for a woman with sole responsibility for two teenage kids. Who was also a cop.

Next to the wall a table had been set up and covered with a cloth. The cloth was Cynthia all over, and showed how classy she was. With the general exodus, Cynthia had brought out all the bottles and put them there, proving to the world that she was still organized and in control, though she must have had just as much to drink as Jen. Jen poured herself another glass of red and sat on the grass too. She told herself, and everyone else within earshot, that it had been years since she'd been to such a great party. Bloody years.

Later, only a small group was left close to the fire. Jen found herself talking to a middle-aged man, one of Cynthia's neighbours. She'd seen him inside earlier, before they'd turned up the music, working the room, chatting politely to the other guests. He was small and sturdy, built like a troll from a fairy story, with a square head and short legs, and a wide smile that just prevented him from being ugly. Jen didn't fancy him in the slightest, but everyone else seemed to have paired off, and she hated that sense of being the only single person in the group. Since her divorce the world seemed made up of happy couples. She even envied the ones who weren't so happy. This man wore a checked shirt and walkers' trousers, lightweight, easily dried. Jen could imagine him a member of a ramblers' club. She thought he might be an accountant or a lawyer. Cynthia was a magistrate, sitting in the lower court, passing judgement on the petty criminals, the misfits and saddos, whom Jen was trying to convict, and she knew lots of lawyers. She and Jen had first met in court. Despite their different roles, they'd always got on. Cynthia's husband was something important in the local hospital trust and she didn't need a paid job.

Now, Jen was at that stage when she knew she'd had enough to drink, but she couldn't quite stop. Her ex-husband had always said she had an addictive personality, the words spoken with a sneer and an edge of pity, just before giving her a good slap, and then blaming her for provoking him.

She thought Nigel had been holding the same glass of dry white for most of the evening.

'So, Nigel. What do you do for a living?' He'd already told her his name, slightly apologetically, as if it wasn't a name to be proud of.

Nigel. Nigel Yeo. Yeo being a local name means he's obviously from the West Country. Nigel ages him though. Who calls their kid Nigel these days?

Now she smiled, her best flirty smile. He might be older than she usually liked her men and was probably a boring sod, but chatting to him was better than sitting here on her own like a Billy No-Mates. Although Cynthia always said she

3

shouldn't try so hard and that the right man would come along eventually, Jen couldn't bear the idea of being lonely for the rest of her life. Soon the kids would be flying the nest and she imagined her little house, as silent and cold as a grave, when she got in from work.

'I work in the health sector.' His knees were bent and she could see his shoes. Good quality, recently polished.

'Oh, a medic?' That made him more interesting. Jen might never want to think of herself as a snob, but she liked the idea of hanging out with a doctor.

'Not any more.' He smiled too, as if he knew what she was thinking, and again, there was something lovely about the smile, something that made up for the troll-like stature. 'You could say I'm in the same line of business as you. Sort of. Though I'm more of a private investigator at the moment. In fact, there was something I wanted to discuss, but I'm not sure this is the right place after all.' He seemed distracted for a moment. 'Actually, it's probably time for me to head home, I think.' Nigel got to his feet, the movement smooth and easy, and wiped a few grass clippings from his bum. It was rather a nice bum too.

He hesitated when he was on his feet. 'Is it okay if I get your number from Cynthia and call you?'

'Yeah,' Jen said. 'Sure.' She thought he might be suggesting a date and was flattered, almost excited, but it seemed he had something more formal in mind.

'Work contact details will be fine if you don't want to give me your personal number.'

She watched him walk away to say a polite goodbye to Cynthia. She felt ridiculously bereft, and that she'd missed an important opportunity for friendship.

The evening went downhill from there. She sat alone for a while with a beer, staring into the flames. When she saw Wes dancing slowly to music that he was humming and nobody else could hear, his arms round a woman young enough to be her daughter, she stumbled to her feet and walked home.

Chapter Two

Jen woke to her daughter banging on the door and shouting. She'd undressed the night before, but not bothered taking off her make-up; she could feel the mascara spiky on her eyelashes, see foundation and lipstick smeared on the pillowcase. So, she'd had a good night, but she hadn't disgraced herself. Going to bed fully clothed was always a bad sign. Waking up with a stranger was even worse, but she only did that when the kids were in the Wirral with her ex's parents. She'd never sunk so low as to bring a bloke home when Ella and Ben were here.

'Yeah, come in, love.' She pulled herself into a sitting position and looked at the clock by the bed. Ten o'clock, but it was a weekend and she wasn't on duty, so no need to panic. She'd even been to the supermarket on her way home from work the evening before, so there was bread and milk for breakfast and they knew well enough by now how to scavenge. At least, she always thought when guilt stabbed her in the gut, more painful than heartburn, her kids wouldn't grow up to be snowflakes.

The door opened and Ella came in. Sixteen, specky and

skinny, at ease in her own skin. A science nerd, already in love with another geek, Zach, a lad from school, who bored the pants off Jen.

'Don't you want to go out and have fun?' Jen would ask. She'd married too early and hated the thought of her daughter settling down too soon.

'We are having fun.'

And they'd disappear off to Ella's tidy room in the attic, not for drink, drugs and illicit sex, but to pore over chemistry homework or to watch some strange fantasy series on Netflix.

This morning Ella looked very young, still in her nightie, but the disapproval was obvious as she crossed the room to open the window. 'It stinks in here. You need some fresh air.' *She* could have been the parent.

'Yeah.' Jen ignored her thumping head. 'Everything all right?'

'You left your phone downstairs. It's been ringing since I got up. Matthew Venn.'

'Shit.' Matthew Venn was the boss. The best boss she'd ever had, but he wasn't much into fun either. He was a man of principle, still haunted, Jen thought, by a strict evangelical childhood. He could do disapproval as well as her daughter. 'I stuck some clothes in the dryer before I went out last night. Can you fish them out while I jump in the shower?'

'It was sunny yesterday. You could have put them on the line.' More disapproval. Not content with saving her mother, Ella wanted to save the world too.

'I know, but they don't need ironing when they come out of the dryer. That saves power, doesn't it?' Jen pulled a face, which she knew would make her daughter laugh. There was an element of ritual to this exchange and El quite liked being superior.

Jen was already out of bed and on her way to the bathroom. She turned her voice into a wheedle. 'And could you stick on the kettle, make some coffee? I bought some proper stuff yesterday.'

She phoned Matthew while she used the coffee to swallow two paracetamol. Ella had made toast too. There was no sign of Ben, who only ever emerged at lunchtime at weekends. Jen buttered the toast while she returned Venn's call. If this was a shout, who knew when she'd next eat? 'Sorry, boss. It's my day off and I've only just picked up your call.'

'We've got an unexplained death,' Matthew said. 'Ross and I are already at the scene. Westacombe. A group of craft workshops in the grounds of a big house.' He gave her the postcode. He hadn't said murder. He was always careful when he spoke.

'I'll be there as soon as I can.' *As soon as I've finished my breakfast.*

'You are okay to drive?' She could hear him trying to keep the judgement from his voice but she knew what he was thinking: *If you had a skinful last night, you might be over the limit.*

'Sure,' she said. 'Sure. See you soon.'

At least Westacombe was inland, and she was driving against the flow of the tourist traffic. She'd lived in North Devon for five years now and she'd become used to the narrow, twisting lanes, the high banks and hedges, which could hide sneaky tractors and oncoming traffic. She'd never quite got used to the summer traffic, though, to the endless streams of huge cars carrying children, camping gear and surfboards. The road climbed away from the coast and at one point, as she pulled into a lay-by to let a Land Rover and horse box go past, she had a view over the whole estuary – the two rivers, the Taw and Torridge, spilling into the Atlantic, glistening in the sunshine. This was her patch now, but she still missed the Mersey, with its ferries and the view from Birkenhead of Liverpool's astounding skyline, with a passion that felt like bereavement. *Classic soppy Scouser*, she thought. *You live as close to paradise as you can get but you're still not satisfied, still dreaming of home.*

The satnav on her phone directed her down a single-track lane; there was no room even for two small cars to pass. Grass grew in the middle of the road. She turned a corner and she was there. The lane fizzled out into a yard. There was a rather grand house, built of warm red brick, the same colour as Cynthia's wall, but older, crumbling in places. It had two storeys and, above them, what must be attic bedrooms, with little dormer windows built out of the slate roof. To one side of the yard a cottage. On the other a large barn. There was a row of smaller outbuildings with stable doors. This was one complex, but with multiple uses, all converted from the original farmhouse and farm buildings. Jen knew this because as she'd driven into the yard, she realized she'd been here before. Westacombe was less than three miles from the busy seaside village of Instow, but felt entirely cut off, a world of its own. That was what she remembered: the sense of having wandered into somewhere a little magical and not quite real.

She'd only visited once, but she hadn't forgotten it. The visit had felt like an act of transgression, but also a celebration of freedom, of getting her life back. She'd never had a wild, irresponsible youth and this was as close as she'd got. Wes had brought her one Easter when the kids had been staying with their grandparents in Hoylake. Jen had been fretful and tense, anxious that her ex's mother and father were poisoning her lovelies with stories about her fecklessness, her inability to look after them properly. Not that Robbie, her former, unmissed husband, had wanted them full-time. He'd never made a claim for custody. He liked his new, single life too much for that. Ella and Ben never stayed in his grand apartment in the old Albert Dock during their increasingly irregular visits, but instead with Reg and Joan in their Victorian villa by the coast in the Wirral. Robbie deigned to call in occasionally to meet his children. When work and his private life allowed. Sunday lunch was a favourite time. Nothing much happened in his world at Sunday lunchtime and his mother was a decent cook.

It was the first time she'd met Wes. Cynthia had invited her out. 'You can't stay at home brooding when you're free from parental responsibility at last.' She'd taken Jen to a bar right on the beach in Instow. 'There'll be jazz. I'll introduce you to a few people.' It had been small, dark, crowded, owned by a middle-aged Scot called George, who introduced the musicians as if they were all his best friends. Checked tablecloths and candles in bottles. A fishing net hung from the ceiling. Kitsch, but in a self-conscious sort of way. Jen had been intimidated by the music and the people, who, in the silences between songs, talked about books she'd never read and films she'd never seen. So of course, she'd drunk too much, become too loud, too chatty. Wes had been in the audience that night, not playing, though Jen had been able to tell he was a regular; he knew all the bar staff, and George treated him indulgently, as if he were a son who'd gone slightly off the rails. When Cynthia and her chums talked about heading back to Barnstaple, Wes had taken Jen's hand.

'Stay for one last drink. We can get you a taxi home.' They'd walked on the beach in the moonlight and her head had been spinning as they'd looked up at the stars. When the taxi had arrived, it had taken them to Wes's place, to this house, where he had a couple of rooms in the attic. Jen, of course, had paid the fare. It only occurred to her now, as she climbed out of the car, that the unexplained death might relate to Wes.

Matthew and Ross were standing in the yard, suited and booted like the CSIs, but recognizable, even in their paper suits and masks. Matthew was upright, almost military in stature, and his eyes were as grey as granite. Ross May was as skinny as a whippet and fidgeted like a child. She joined them, took a suit for herself, and while she was climbing into it, spoke to Venn.

'Male or female? I've been here before and know one of the guys who lives here. Or who used to live here. He might have moved on. It was a couple of years ago.' It was best to let Venn know how things stood before the investigation developed.

'Male,' Matthew said. 'What was your friend's name?'

Jen was going to say that he wasn't a friend, not really, but that would have been protesting too much. Besides, Matthew liked straight answers.

'Wes,' she said. 'Wesley Curnow.' She hesitated for a moment. 'Actually, I saw him last night.'

Matthew shook his head. 'That's not the name.' He looked at her. 'What do you know about this place?'

Jen shrugged. 'I only came here once.' The morning after hooking up with Wes, he'd made her breakfast in a large, untidy communal kitchen on the ground floor. Flagstones on the floor and an Aga pockmarked with grease. Another hangover. More coffee and bacon sandwiches on fresh white bread, dripping with fat. A couple of other people had drifted through, but she'd not taken much notice of them. Wes had been the focus of her attention. He'd been barefoot, in tatty jeans and a loose T-shirt. Even with the hangover, she'd been smitten. He'd been a kind and thoughtful lover, and that had been a novelty for her. Even now, she found a smile drifting across her face as she remembered the night. 'It's a kind of artists' commune. The owner lives in most of the house, but he rents out a couple of flats in the attic to crafts people and they have their work-shops here too.'

Ross sneered, seemed about to say something cutting about artists or communes, then thought better of it in front of the boss. He was learning.

Jen went on: 'The guy I know makes recycled furniture, driftwood sculpture, that sort of thing. He's a musician too. Jonathan will probably have come across him.'

Matthew nodded. Jonathan, his husband, managed the Woodyard, a large and successful community arts centre in Barnstaple. He mixed in such Bohemian circles. The Woodyard wasn't Matthew's natural home, but he was learning too, and making more of an effort to get on with Jonathan's friends. Perhaps because of his evangelical upbringing, Matthew found it hard to consider an activity that was fun, creative or exciting as real work. He'd joined the police service because it provided the sense of duty and community that he'd missed when he left the Brethren. Jonathan sometimes mocked him because he took himself so seriously. He turned his attention back to his colleagues. 'Shall we see what we've got, then?'

Jen tucked her hair inside the paper hood, pulled on her

mask and followed him. A row of farm buildings had been turned into studios and workshops.

'Who found our victim?'

'His daughter, Eve. She lives and works here. She's a glass blower. She found him in her studio at eight thirty this morning.' Matthew paused. 'The cause of death is obvious enough apparently, but Doctor Pengelly is on her way.'

There was a stable door leading directly from the yard into one of the outbuildings, a long, low room. Jen was expecting the space to be dark and claustrophobic, but much of the roof had been replaced by a skylight and sunshine was flooding in. It was almost unbearably hot. The heat seemed to be coming from a furnace in the corner. Jen wondered why nobody had thought to switch it off, but of course, nothing could be touched until the CSIs had finished their work. Getting closer, she realized that the furnace wasn't lit, but must still be hot from the day before. On the wall there were racks from which a series of long metal pipes, a steel shovel with a square, box-like end, and a flat-bladed shovel dangled. There were shelves containing devices and objects which could be instruments of torture: pincers and tongs, and a couple of blowtorches.

The whole place had the air of a torture chamber. Jen thought it resembled an image of hell, as described by one of the more imaginative nuns who'd taught her. A man was lying on his back in front of a polished workbench, caught in the sun's rays. He was surrounded by shattered glass and a shard, as long and sharp as a knife, had pierced his neck. There was blood. A lot of blood, spread all over the floor and spattered on one of the walls.

'So, it seems that he was killed where he was found,' Matthew Venn said.

Jen hardly heard her boss speaking. 'I know him,' she said. 'At least, I've met him. Last night. I was at a party at Cynthia Prior's place and he was there. His name's Nigel Yeo.' She paused. 'He works for an organization that monitors the health authority. Something to do with investigations. He wanted to talk to me, but said it could wait.'

'He wanted to talk to you professionally?' The workshop door was still open and they were standing just inside. Matthew had turned towards Jen.

She shrugged. 'That's what I thought he meant. But it was a party. I'd had a few drinks. You know what it's like . . .'

But Matthew wouldn't know what it was like. He drank very little and certainly would never lose control. Jen tried to imagine him going to bed, too drunk to take off his clothes, but the idea was ridiculous. She looked again at the body, remembered the heavy smell of honeysuckle in Cynthia's garden, the kind smile, and found herself feeling a little faint. 'He seemed like a kind man.'

'His daughter, Eve, is in the kitchen. If you've been here before, you'll know where it is. Go and take an initial statement, while things are still fresh in her mind.'

Jen nodded and went out into the yard. She stood for a moment taking deep breaths. The sun was already hot. The kitchen was cooler, though. There were still stone flags on the floor but the range she remembered from her previous visit had been left to go out. A new electric cooker stood in one corner, and the room seemed cleaner, tidier; otherwise, little had changed. A woman in her late twenties or early thirties sat at the table. She was wearing dungarees and a striped T-shirt, red sandshoes. To Jen's relief she was alone. There was no sign of Wes.

'Eve?'

The woman turned around. She was still crying. Jen thought she'd been crying for hours, since she'd found her father.

'I'm so sorry,' Jen said. 'I met him. Only once – last night, in fact – but he seemed lovely.'

'He was the best.'

'I'm a detective. I need to ask some questions. Is that okay?' Eve nodded.

'Can I get you something before we start? Tea? Coffee?' Jen thought she could do with a coffee herself. There was still a dull ache in her forehead.

'Just some water, please.'

Jen filled two glasses. Even straight from the tap it was clear and cold.

'It comes from a borehole.' Eve looked up. 'Dad said it was the best water in the county.'

'Did he live here?' Jen found it hard to imagine. Nigel had been tidy; he'd stuck out at Cynthia's party because he was so straight, so obviously respectable. And she was certain Cynthia had introduced him as a neighbour, but it was as well to be sure.

Despite her grief, Eve gave a little laugh. 'No way! He had a house in Barnstaple. It was where I grew up. But he visited me lots.'

'Does your mother live there?' Jen had assumed the man was single when they'd met, but it seemed more likely that there *would* be a wife. Someone competent and caring. She knew Matthew would have asked, that the woman would have been notified of Yeo's death and that someone would be with her.

'Mum had early onset Alzheimer's,' Eve said. 'She died two

15

years ago.' The words were flat, hard. *Don't ask me about that. I can't bear it. Not now.*

Jen wanted to reach out and take the woman in her arms. 'Do you have siblings?'

Eve shook her head. 'Just Dad and me. We were so close.' A pause for a beat. 'And now I'm on my own.' She was speaking quietly, but still it sounded like a cry of desperation.

Jen was going to ask about friends, a partner, but she could tell that friends wouldn't be any comfort yet. 'It was quite late last night when I met your father. Were you expecting a visit?'

'Not last night. We'd planned to meet this morning. Dad helped me to make the glass. You need an assistant for most of the work I do. It's skilled and it takes practice, but before Mum died, he asked for an unpaid sabbatical from the hospital and took a course just so he could help out. And have more time to care for her. That's the sort of father he was. The idea was that we'd be at it all day. I've got a commission from a gallery in London, someone Frank put me in touch with, but the deadline's very tight.'

Jen wanted to ask who Frank might be, but thought that could wait.

'He didn't work at the hospital now, though?'

'No, he headed up North Devon Patients Together. It's a kind of watchdog, monitoring the NHS trusts locally, representing users.' She paused. 'He'd been thinking of leaving medicine for a while. The shifts didn't fit with him wanting to spend more time with Mum. But the NDPT is usually nine to five, and more flexible. He could pretty well set his own hours.' She paused. 'Mum died just as he was appointed, but he decided to leave the hospital all the same. A new challenge, he said.'

'You have no idea why he might have come to Westacombe last night? Why he would be in your studio without telling you?'

Eve shook her head. 'None at all. We had planned quite an early start. Seven thirty. I came in at seven to get everything set up.'

A moment of silence. From outside there came rural sounds, still unusual for Jen: birdsong and sheep.

'You live here as well as work here?' Jen asked.

'Yes, I've got a flat in the attic. Small. Two bedrooms – though one's so tiny I'm not sure you'd be able to sleep there – a bathroom and a living room with a little fridge and a hob in the corner. I share this big kitchen with Wes, the other artist on site. But the views are beautiful and it's good to be so close to the workshop.'

'Who else lives here?'

'There are four of us tenants, plus a couple of kids. Wes Curnow has a flat in the attic too. It's even smaller than mine.' Jen gave no sign that she knew the name. 'And then there are Sarah and John Grieve, and their twins, who live in the cottage on the other side of the yard. John manages the farm and Sarah's uncle owns the place. He lives in the rest of the house.'

'What's his name?'

'Francis Ley.' Eve looked up. 'You might have heard of him. The economist. We all call him Frank.'

So that's the Frank who arranged the commission. Jen nodded. She recognized the name. Ley had been all over the news at one time. Not courting the limelight himself – he was notoriously shy – but celebrated by journalists and commentators. He'd predicted the financial crash before it happened, had somehow survived it and made a fortune. *Out of other people's misery,* Jen thought. Somehow the bankers and money-makers came out unscathed. She'd never lost the politics of her child-hood.

'How did you come to be here?'

'Through Sarah, who lives in the cottage. We grew up in the same street in Barnstaple and when the workshop and the flat became available, she suggested I meet up with Frank. He seemed to like me and my work, so I moved in.' She paused for a moment. 'He was actually here yesterday evening. He travels a bit, but when he comes to stay, he invites us all in for drinks. A ritual.'

'This isn't his permanent home?'

'He still has a place in London, but he's talking of selling up. He likes it here best.' Eve's voice was warm, affectionate. She could have been talking about her own favourite uncle.

'Is he still here?' If so, Jen thought Matthew could do that interview. He was good at being polite, even to people he disliked. She'd never got the knack.

'Oh, I don't know. I presume so. He didn't say anything about leaving when we talked to him last night.'

'You haven't seen him this morning?' Jen thought the man must surely have been aware of the fuss in the yard, the cars, the white-suited CSIs.

'No,' Eve said. 'He doesn't come into the yard much. He doesn't need to. He uses the main entrance to the house, looking out over the estuary, and his garage has a separate exit straight onto the lane. Wes and I get to our flats through the back door here and through the kitchen.'

Jen excused herself. 'I'll be back in a moment. We've not finished, I'm afraid.' Outside, Sally Pengelly, the pathologist, was making her way to the workshop. She was short, plump, red-cheeked. Jen had once heard a fancy barrister describe her sneeringly as 'that pathologist who looks as if she works on a farm'. But while Sally Pengelly might look like a farmer's daughter, she was sharp and brave enough to stick her neck out on occasion. The team liked her. Matthew was standing in the yard, checking his phone. He looked up to greet them both.

'One man owns all this.' Jen waited for Sally to move inside the studio before she continued speaking, then waved her arm to take in the yard and all the buildings. 'He lives in the big house but he's not a permanent resident.' She paused again. 'It's Francis Ley.'

Matthew raised an eyebrow, but said nothing.

'I thought you might want to catch him in case he decides to disappear,' Jen said. 'He has his own front door on the other side of the building.'

'Have you done talking to the daughter?'

'Nah, she's deeply upset. They were very close and her mum died a couple of years ago. I'm taking it gently.' Another pause. 'She wasn't expecting to see her dad until seven thirty this morning – apparently he acted as a kind of assistant when she was making glass – and she can't explain why he might have been here earlier this morning or late last night.'

Venn nodded. 'I suppose he could have been here to see one of the other tenants. We need to check possible relationships. Or he could have arranged to meet Ley. I'll find out what the man has to say. If you're still tied up, I'm happy to see him on my own.'

As she turned back towards the kitchen, Jen smiled. That was just the response she'd hoped for.

19

Chapter Three

WHEN JEN LEFT HIM, MATTHEW STOOD for a moment, thinking. He wasn't a man for rushing into encounters without a plan. He liked to be in control of an investigation, in control of himself. His husband, Jonathan, was creative, impulsive, but Jonathan could read people and situations easily; Matthew didn't have that skill. His face to the sun, he trawled through his memory for information about Francis Ley. At one time, the economist had been featured in all the newspapers, set apart from most financiers by his West Country accent, the fact of being an outsider. Ten years after the crash, there'd been a television documentary about him, but he hadn't appeared himself. Former friends and colleagues *had* appeared, speaking of the prophesies that had been ridiculed, the warnings that had been ignored.

'If he'd been to a different school, a first-class university, people might have taken notice of his warnings,' one had said. 'We might have avoided the worst of the crash altogether. But he was never really a City person. He never fitted in.'

The impression was given that Ley was now rather eccentric,

a recluse, disenchanted by the world that had made him a fortune. He'd inherited his father's farm – this farmhouse presumably – and returned to his roots, then set about regenerating the surrounding villages, buying up failing businesses and working his magic behind the scenes. There were a couple of pubs, now thriving and famous for their food; a fish restaurant in Instow with a Michelin star; a handful of village shops, saved from extinction, along with their post offices, but transformed into delis, artisan bakers or potteries and galleries. Not all the changes had been popular. Gentrification, as Jonathan, who'd grown up on a farm on the edge of Exmoor, was fond of saying, especially after a few glasses of wine, wasn't only a problem of the cities. Locals could feel alienated in the countryside too.

Matthew Venn couldn't think what connection Nigel Yeo, who'd worked for an obscure organization linked to the NHS, might have with Francis Ley, but Eve, Yeo's daughter, lived and worked on Ley's property and her father was a regular visitor. Matthew would have liked more time to explore possibilities, to do some research. But Ley was here now, and, as Jen had pointed out, he might leave at any time. Matthew left the row of workshops and walked round the house to find the man.

The door into Ley's part of the building was reached by a gravel path leading around the house, and it faced not inland, but out to the estuary. There was a garden – a lawn with old-fashioned herbaceous borders – and a view of the Taw all the way to Crow Point, and of the Torridge and the towns of Appledore and Bideford. To the far side of the house stood a newly built garage, from which a paved drive led to the lane, avoiding the yard.

Matthew stood for a moment to look at the house and

thought the building was strangely schizophrenic. This side was well proportioned, classic Georgian, with the original sash windows, symmetrical on each side of the door. The brick glowed in the morning sunlight. Once it must have been the home of a gentleman farmer, and it had been restored here to its former glory, the door freshly painted black, the brass knocker gleaming. It seemed very different from the buildings which looked out at the yard, and the flats in the attic. Jen would have put the difference down to class: the cottage and the scruffy outhouses for the workers, and the grand facade, looking out over the estuary, for the owner. Matthew saw it rather differently. He saw one portion as arty and slightly disreputable; this side of the house, from the outside at least, seemed the height of respectability. It was hard to see how the two groups might co-exist. He knocked at the door.

After a while, Ley opened it himself, and stood, framed in the entrance, blinking. He was a big man, round and soft. His size was what people remembered. Before disappearing from public view, he'd made awkward, self-deprecating jokes about being fat. About how his chefs should be less skilful so he wasn't tempted to sample so much of the cooking, and how he would never settle with a woman if he didn't lose a little weight. As far as Matthew could recall from the rumours locally, Ley had never found a woman.

He was wearing an old-fashioned tartan dressing gown over striped cotton pyjama bottoms, and a pair of leather slippers, which flapped as he walked. The dressing gown hardly met across his waist and was held together by a plaited cord. His bare chest was pink and almost hairless. Something about the outfit made Matthew think of a 1950s schoolboy. Billy Bunter or Just William.

'Yes?' Ley seemed flustered, a little anxious, but not angry at being disturbed by a stranger.

Matthew introduced himself. 'Perhaps you've noticed my team in your yard.'

'I've just woken up. I haven't had a chance to notice anything yet.' He was still blinking. His eyelashes were sandy and fine. The voice was slow and pure North Devon. It was hard to imagine him doing hard-headed deals in a high-pressure financial market.

'One of your tenants found her father dead in her studio this morning.'

'What?' He stared at Matthew as if he was talking a foreign language. 'I don't understand. Eve's the only woman with a workshop. Are you talking about Nigel?'

'I'm afraid I am.'

There was silence. Ley shook his head as if he was still struggling to make sense of the words. Again, Matthew wondered how someone so slow to respond could have become so powerful.

'How did he die?' Ley asked at last. He stepped back into the hall behind him, assuming that Matthew would follow. 'He seemed so fit. Some sort of heart attack?'

'He was murdered. We can't discuss the details yet.'

Ley seemed to stumble, and put a hand against one wall to steady himself. He turned back to face Venn. 'I can't believe anyone would want him dead. Nigel was a good man. You'll discover that for yourself when you make your inquiries. You'd better come in. Give me a couple of minutes to make myself decent and I'll be with you.'

The hall was shady; impressive but not intimidating, with a scratched oak floor and faded rugs, a large chest against one wall. Ley opened a door and showed Matthew into a big sitting room. More wood, more rugs. A fireplace with a vase of flowers on the hearth; the vase so wide at the rim that it was more of a bowl. A window seat with cushions in hand-woven covers. The furniture might have been there since Ley's childhood: a worn leather chesterfield and a couple of sagging armchairs. The art on display was quite different, though. There were huge abstracts, shocking blocks of colour. In one corner a life-sized sculpture of a curlew made from driftwood. Venn supposed these had been created by the Westacombe tenants, past and present. He looked again at the vase containing the flowers: blue swirling glass, made perhaps by the murdered man's daughter. It seemed Ley wasn't only the craftspeople's landlord; he was also their patron.

The only sign that he'd hosted a drinks party the night before was a single glass on a coffee table. The other debris must already have been cleared away. Venn wondered if there was a housekeeper, or if Ley managed the place by himself.

The man returned more quickly than Matthew had been expecting, but still he'd found time for a shower. His hair was wet. He was dressed in large, wrinkled grey trousers, which made Matthew think of an elephant's legs, and a baggy black T-shirt. Surely, he thought, Ley wouldn't have dressed like that when he was a City trader. Matthew liked to hide behind the uniform of a suit; even his casual clothes were freshly laundered and well pressed.

'I'm making coffee,' Ley said from the door. 'I'm afraid I can't function without it. Would you like some?' He seemed diffident, as if he was the visitor, not the host.

Matthew could smell the coffee and was tempted. The kitchen must be close by. 'Please.'

Ley disappeared and came back with a mug in each hand. 'No milk,' he said. 'I don't take it. I can probably borrow some from the tenants' kitchen . . .'

'Black's fine.' Matthew stood up to take the coffee, then returned to his seat by the window.

Ley stood for a moment, looking out of the window, before landing on an armchair close by. 'You're saying that Nigel Yeo's been murdered?'

'Yes.' Matthew paused. 'I'm afraid that I am.'

'Shit!' The reply was explosive, more personal than might have been expected if Yeo were simply an acquaintance, the father of a tenant. The word and the emphasis were unexpected. Ley gave a quick, shy smile. 'I'm sorry . . .'

'Dr Yeo was a friend?'

'No.' A pause. 'Well. I suppose he was in a way; becoming one at least. Eve came here a couple of years ago after finishing her Master's degree.'

Matthew said nothing. Silence, he'd found, was an ally and a weapon.

At last, Ley continued: 'Nigel worked for North Devon Patients Together, NDPT. It represents patients' views to the trusts. It's a small organization but very efficient, I thought. Important and well respected. Since Nigel took over as boss, he's widened the brief to look into anomalies, and to explore patients' complaints.'

Venn nodded. That chimed with what Jen Rafferty had said.

Ley looked up at him, weighing his words. 'A young friend of mine suffered from depression. Nothing major – at least, that was what I thought. Not life-threatening. I've had bouts myself. It didn't suit me being in the public eye, and then I was low again when my mother died – but I took the drugs

25

and came through it. We talked about it, the two of us, and shared experiences. I thought Mack's illness could be as easily treated.' Ley was staring at the flowers in the fireplace. 'I blame myself for not realizing it was more serious, perhaps a different illness altogether, and then I was away in London when the real crisis happened.' He paused and pulled a grubby handkerchief from his pocket and wiped his eyes.

Matthew said nothing. He knew there was more to the story. In the garden, blackbirds were singing. Joyous. Inappropriate.

'Mack killed himself. He was talented, bright and he had a family who loved him. But he went out late one night, walked along the cliff path above Seal Bay and he jumped. He left a note by the path. In a little plastic bag, in case it rained, weighed down by a stone. Everything planned. A couple of ramblers found it the following day. His body wasn't discovered until three days later, what was left of it, washed up on the north end of Lundy Island.'

'When was this?' Matthew asked. He couldn't remember the case, but he wouldn't have been involved officially in a suicide.

'The autumn. The end of October.'

'And his full name?'

'Alexander Mackenzie. Known to us all as Mack.' A pause. 'His parents, George and Martha, run the bar on the beach at Instow. The Sandpiper.'

Matthew nodded his head slowly. Details of the case were coming back to him. Jonathan knew the family and had been horrified by the boy's death.

'It should never have happened.' Ley's voice was raw with emotion now. 'His parents knew how ill he was. They called the hospital, but nobody would do anything. He was just nineteen and, caught between children's and adult services, he seemed to fall into the gap. They ended up calling the police because Mack was paranoid, imagining all sorts. The police took him to A&E, and he was sectioned, taken to the psychiatric hospital in the grounds of the General, but after a night, there wasn't a bed or for some reason the clinic let him out. There was supposed to be community support, but that didn't happen either. Mack was desperate, still paranoid apparently, dreaming of conspiracies and strange men following him. He even believed that his family were against him. In the end, I suppose, he couldn't stand it so he just walked off the cliff and into the sea. A way out. Some kind of peace.'

'You were very close to him.' It was a statement, not a question.

'I know the family. Mack was almost like a nephew, or maybe a surrogate son. I understood him because he didn't fit in. As I said, we confided in each other. There's a daughter. Lively, pretty. Very bright. Not long out of university. Mack was more challenging. More troubled.' Ley looked up. 'More like me.'

'And Dr Yeo was involved in the case professionally?' Matthew was trying to see how this all hung together.

'Yes. George and Martha made a formal complaint against the health trust. Nothing was happening. All they got was a standard response. It could have been written by a computer. It probably was written by a computer. I talked to Nigel, and he got involved.' Ley paused. 'The family are not going to sue. Nothing will bring their boy back. But they need to know what happened. To know that it won't happen again.' Another pause. 'We trusted Nigel. He was conscientious. No stone was left unturned. I'm not sure any of the medics or officials within the trust will be so diligent.'

There was a moment of silence while Matthew processed the information. Outside the window, the morning light made the colours in the garden shimmer, turned the view into an Impressionist painting.

'Had Nigel reached any conclusion about what might have happened?'

'I don't know. He was very careful about what he told me. Very professional. I saw him recently about another matter entirely. I asked him how his inquiry was going, but he didn't say anything. Of course, I could understand that, the need for confidentiality.'

'Do you know why he was here last night? It must have been late when he arrived. We know he was at a social event in Barnstaple until ten thirty.'

Ley shook his head. 'I assume he was here to see Eve.' A pause. 'I didn't see him; we hadn't arranged to meet.'

'You had a party yourself, yesterday evening?'

'Not really a party. I'd been away for a few days and I invited the tenants in for drinks. I like to keep in touch with them. But that was earlier. We kicked off at seven o'clock and everyone had left well before nine.'

Ley sounded rather sad. Matthew wondered if he was lonely here, without his mother. Did he resent the young people, who'd come for the free drink and then disappeared?

'Did everyone come?' he asked. 'All the people who live here?'

'Yes, they all showed up. I think they see it almost as a duty. Wesley didn't stay for long. He said he had another engagement in Barnstaple.'

'That would be Wesley Curnow?'

'Yes.' Ley got to his feet and pushed open the window, letting in a burst of birdsong.

'Can you give me details of the other residents?'

'Sarah and John Grieve have the biggest space, the cottage, which you'll have seen at the other side of the yard. They've got twins. No one else has kids. John manages the farm for me. Not that there's much land these days, we rent most of it out, but we have a small herd of dairy cows.'

'Sarah's your niece?'

'Not really a niece. I don't have brothers or sisters.' The thought seemed to sadden him. 'I suppose she's a kind of second cousin, but she's my only relative. We've grown very close. She's turned one of the outhouses into a dairy and makes traditional clotted cream and ice cream.' Ley gave a slow smile and patted his stomach. 'Delicious, but not so good for the figure. She looks after my house while I'm away too. There are two smaller flats in the attic. Wesley has one and Eve the other.'

'And they also have studio space?'

Ley nodded. His attention seemed drawn to the scene outside, the lush garden and the sea beyond.

'What made you decide to open your house to these young people?' The question came unbidden, without Matthew's usual consideration. It had been at the front of his mind since walking through the door. If he had a property as beautiful as this, he wouldn't want to share it with so many people. And if Ley was as rich as everyone said, he didn't need their rent.

At first, Ley didn't answer the question directly. 'They're not so young,' he said. 'Wes must be forty, even though he behaves like a teenager.'

'All the same. You know what I mean. Do you enjoy the company?'

Ley turned back into the room and gave Matthew his full

attention. 'No,' he said. 'I don't need the company. I've always been happy enough on my own.' He paused, took a breath. 'It's guilt. All that money just dropped into my lap. I didn't have to work for it. Not really. I've always enjoyed figures. Logic. I didn't mix with the flash young traders and didn't get swept up in the hype. I could see which way the market was going and sold at the right time. It was luck as much as anything. But I know what it's like to struggle. The house looks very grand now but it was falling to bits when I was a kid. We only lived in the kitchen and a couple of the bedrooms. It makes me feel a bit better about myself to share my good fortune.' He smiled. 'I expect you think I'm bonkers.'

Matthew shook his head. He knew the power of guilt. He'd lived with it throughout his childhood and was still haunted by it.

Ley continued speaking. Now he'd started, it seemed he felt the need to continue. Matthew had the sense that this was a sort of confession and the man had nobody else to confide in.

'When I first came home,' Ley said, 'I thought the answer was to build more thriving communities, to rescue post offices and shops, take over pubs and restaurants. But it hasn't really worked. Not everywhere. In some of the villages, it pushed up house prices, brought in the tourists and the second homers. And it made me money. More money. More guilt.' He smiled again and again Matthew was reminded of an honourable schoolboy, naive and struggling, attempting to do the right thing and somehow always failing.

'So now you support individuals?'

'I still give to charity,' Ley said. 'Of course I do. But somehow this is more meaningful. Less demeaning. Investment, not handout.'

'And more of a sacrifice?' Matthew said. 'To be sharing your beautiful home with people who need the space, even though I'm sure you'd rather have it to yourself.'

'A sacrifice?' It seemed he hadn't considered the idea before. 'Yes! Of course, you're right. After all, I'm not really being altruistic. Providing homes for other people just makes me feel better about myself.'

Matthew would have liked to ask Ley if he had a faith, but that was none of his business. How could it possibly be relevant to finding out who had killed Nigel Yeo? Instead he pulled himself back to the investigation. 'What did you do after your guests left the house at nine?'

'I sat in the garden for a while, watching the sun setting over the water.' He paused. 'And I drank too much. It's become rather a habit, I'm afraid.'

'Did you hear a car in the lane?'

He shook his head. 'I didn't stay outside for long. Once it was properly dark, I moved inside.' He paused. 'And carried on drinking. Hence, the lateness of getting out of bed.' He turned back to face Matthew. 'I told you that I don't need company, Inspector, and in general that's true, but last night, when the others had gone, I felt overwhelmed by a sense of loneliness. It was almost unbearable.'

Again, Matthew felt that he was listening to a confession, almost in the religious sense. Few people would share their pain with a complete stranger. He didn't know how to reply. But it seemed that no response was needed. Ley became suddenly more formal, distant.

'If that's all, Inspector, I'm expecting a call from London. But of course, if I can help in any way at all, do come back to me.'

They walked together to the front door. From somewhere inside the house there was the sound of a phone ringing. Ley nodded sadly and turned away.

Chapter Four

EVE LOOKED ACROSS THE TABLE AT the red-haired detective with the nasal, grating northern voice and wished she'd just fuck off and leave her alone. At this particular point in time she didn't care who'd killed her father. All that mattered was that he was dead, that she'd be alone, with nobody to hold her when she was miserable, or make her laugh when she needed cheering up. Her anger was undirected, or perhaps more directed towards him, for leaving her, than at the person or persons who'd made it happen. But Eve was polite. She'd been well brought up by her parents. So, she sat at the big table in the shadowy, cool kitchen and she drank tea, and she answered the intruder's questions.

'Tell me about the other residents,' the detective, Jen Rafferty, said. 'I've met Wesley, but I don't know the others.'

'John and Sarah Grieve. They've got twins. Daisy and Lily. They're very cute. The girls, I mean, not the parents.'

'How old are the kids?'

'Just seven. They had their birthday a couple of weeks ago. We had a party.' *My dad came with balloons, different presents for each of the girls. I made a cake.*

'What role do the parents play here at Westacombe? How do they fit in?'

'John's a farmer and Sarah runs the dairy. She also looks after Frank's house now his mother's dead, does his laundry, stuff like that. Things are tight for them financially and he pays her well to do it. She never stops working, even though she's pregnant again.' Eve paused for a moment. Sometimes Sarah's energy made her feel incompetent, idle. 'Even now, she's making plans. She'd like to open a tea shop alongside the dairy. That would bring more people in and give Wes and me a chance to sell more of our stuff.' Eve wondered why she was even mentioning that. She'd been excited when Sarah had first thrown out the idea, but now, what importance could it possibly have?

'Were Sarah and John at the drinks party with Mr Ley yesterday evening?'

'Yeah, and the kids for a while. Halfway through, Sarah took them away and put them to bed. She came back later and John went to babysit. He's not exactly sociable, and I think he was glad to escape.' Eve paused for a moment but decided to continue. Better to give the woman all the information she needed and then she might be left in peace to cry and howl without an audience. Sometimes, she felt like glass, which was pliable and easy to mould when it was hot. She could be amiable and pleasant, until the stress built up, then, like glass, she became cold and hard and she'd crack under the slightest pressure. She didn't want to crack in front of the detective. 'Wes was there too, but just for a while. He'd obviously had a better offer but felt the need to show his face. To keep Frank sweet.'

'Frank is Francis Ley?'

'Yeah, of course.' *Jesus, what's wrong with this woman? She's supposed to be a detective. I've already told her that.*

'What time did the party break up?'

'It wasn't really a party, just a few drinks. If anything, it was a kind of business meeting.'

'In what way?'

'Sarah brought up her idea of opening a tea shop. Obviously, we'd have to get Frank's approval. There's spare space by the side of the dairy, which would be ideal, but we couldn't go ahead without him.'

'What did he say?'

'It was a bit disappointing, actually. He said he'd never envisaged this place becoming so commercial. He was worried about access and parking. It's okay for him, though. He's minted. He doesn't need to be commercial.' The detective was scribbling in a notebook and Eve felt compelled to add, 'Of course, it's Frank's place and we're lucky to be here. He doesn't charge anything close to the going rent. It obviously has to be his decision.' She wouldn't like to come across as ungrateful. Even now, she realized, with her father stabbed, looking like a slaughtered animal, his body still on the studio floor being mauled by strangers, she was worrying about what people thought of her.

'So, there was this discussion over drinks?' Jen Rafferty said. 'How did it end?'

'With Frank asking Sarah to draw up proper plans. He said he'd think about it. And we all drifted away about nine. Sarah went back to the cottage.'

'And you?' The woman looked up from her notebook. The red fringe almost hid intense brown eyes.

'I went to the studio for an hour, then I went home too, to my flat in the loft. I was in bed by ten thirty.'

35

'You didn't hear from your father at all during the evening? He didn't say he planned to come over?'

Eve shook her head. 'There's no phone reception in the studio, but there were no missed messages or calls. I checked before I went to bed.'

There was a moment of silence. The detective seemed to be choosing her words carefully. 'You saw how your father was killed.'

Eve couldn't speak. The image of bloody glass flashed like faulty neon in her head. It occurred to her that she might never be able to work with the material again. But there had to be a response. She nodded.

'That piece of glass. Did you recognize it? Was it something you made?'

The picture appeared again, like something from one of the arty films she sometimes dragged her father to see at the Wood-yard. All flashbacks and jerky cuts.

'Yes. I'd been commissioned to make a couple of vases for a smart new shop in Ilfracombe. Tall. Green. Big enough to hold lilies. The shard came from one of those.' She'd been so proud when they were finished, just the shade of green she'd been looking for. Supremely elegant.

'I assume it hadn't been broken when you last saw it?'

'No, they were both on the shelf in the corner when I left the studio. I'd agreed to deliver them on Monday.' Again, she pictured the scene. 'One of them is still there. They were as identical as pieces of hand-crafted glass could be.'

The sun must have shifted, because a beam was shining through the window, lighting dancing motes of dust.

'I'm sorry.' And Jen Rafferty did sound genuinely sorry for these questions, for making Eve relive the moment of finding her dad. It seemed she understood the anguish she was causing.

Eve thought that in different circumstances she and Jen Rafferty might even get on. Eve had done her MA in the Glass Centre in Sunderland, and had liked the northerners she'd met there. Something about Jen took her back to that space on the Wear, perhaps the most creative, and happiest, time in her career. But she didn't want to start crying again and she tried to rekindle her earlier resentment. Anger was easier than overwhelming grief. 'Have you finished?' The question was so sharp that it was almost rude.

'Nearly.' Jen paused. 'Can you think of anyone who would have wanted your father dead?'

'Of course not!' This was close to laughable. 'He was kind, gentle, understanding. He'd spent most of his career as a doctor specializing in end-of-life care.'

'And more recently for an organization which investigated his former colleagues and poked around in their business,' Jen said. 'That could have been tricky, if he was investigating *them*. He hadn't made enemies through his work?'

'He never spoke about work.' That was true, Eve thought, but not quite the full story and perhaps this detective deserved the full story. 'He found it stressful. More stressful than medicine. I don't think he found managing a small team of bitchy women easy! When he took it on, he said the job was important. Another way of saving lives. But challenging.'

'And recently?' Jen prompted. 'Had it become more challenging recently?'

'Something was puzzling him.'

'Just puzzling? Or worrying?'

That was when Eve realized that this woman wasn't stupid

as she'd first thought, because, of course, Jen was right. Very recently, her father had been worried. He'd tried to hide it but she'd felt the unusual tension, seen the dark rings under his eyes, which suggested he hadn't been sleeping well. There'd been moments of joy too and she'd wondered about the strange mood swings. Eve nodded. 'Yes,' she said, 'I think something at work was troubling him. He'd become obsessed by it. But he wouldn't talk about it. He couldn't.'

'Confidentiality,' Jen said easily. 'Of course. He'll have kept records, though, and I assume he'll have discussed it with his colleagues at Patients Together. You can leave all that to us.'

Eve didn't say anything, but it seemed to her that it might have been the team which had triggered her father's anxiety. That was guesswork, though. Instinct. And she wasn't sure how she'd put her feelings into words. In the end she didn't need to speak, because the kitchen door flew open, letting in a blast of sunshine, and Sarah, earth mother extraordinaire, and possibly her closest friend.

After a couple of miscarriages, this time all seemed to be well with Sarah's pregnancy. She was round and short, and she was wearing a cheesecloth smock over a patchwork skirt of her own design with an expanding elasticated waist. Eve always thought Sarah looked as if she'd stepped straight out of the seventies.

'Oh Evie,' she said. 'I've just heard. I mean, I saw the police cars when I came back from taking the girls to gymnastics and all the fuss, but none of them would tell me what was going on. Frank came to the cottage to fill us in. He'd been talking to a policeman.' She sat beside Eve and put her arms around her. Eve smelled the henna Sarah used to dye her hair and a faint base note of cow.

Eve pulled herself gently away, and thought that Sarah was a bit like a cow herself: placid and wide-eyed. Soon, she would be full of milk. 'This is Detective Sergeant Rafferty.' She nodded across the table towards Jen. 'She's been asking me some questions.'

'Oh.' Sarah turned her attention to Jen, and Eve was aware of her friend's ritual hostility to the police. She was already bristling. 'Don't you think this is a bit soon to be hassling her? She's only just lost her father.'

Jen didn't quite roll her eyes. Eve had a moment of amusement and then felt guilty to be enjoying the stand-off between the women.

'It's okay,' Eve said. 'Really. I want to help find out what happened.'

'And besides, we're finished for now.' The detective smiled at Eve. 'If you think of anything, though, give me a shout. Anytime. Here's my card.' Jen got to her feet, stood for a moment silhouetted in the doorway, the bright light behind her, and then she disappeared.

'Come into the cottage.' Sarah could have been bossing around one of the twins. 'I can get you tea, wine, whatever you need. You can't be alone at a moment like this.'

Eve was tempted to go along with the idea. Politeness was a habit. But really, she couldn't stand the idea of Sarah's cluttered house, kids' toys and shoes everywhere, half-finished craft projects, half-eaten plates of food. The dairy was always immaculate but the cottage was her idea of a nightmare.

'To be alone is absolutely what I need,' she said, her voice firm. 'It's kind of you to offer, but it's been a shock and I need some time.'

'Are you sure?' Sarah hated to be alone, but knew her friend well enough to understand how different they were.

'Certain.' To make her point, Eve stood up and made her way into the main body of the house and to what had once been the servants' stairs, leading to her attic flat. She climbed slowly and pushed open the door, which was never locked. She'd left all the windows open and a breeze blew the curtains into the room. She lay on her bed and began to cry again.

Chapter Five

MATTHEW WAS STANDING IN THE YARD, in the corner, which was as far away from Eve's studio as he could get. He'd always been an observer, on the outside looking in, and hated the thought of getting in the way of the CSIs just to make his presence felt. The investigators would pass on all they knew at the evening briefing. Jen came out of the kitchen and walked towards him.

'How did you get on?' Matthew said. 'Anything useful?' He'd still been thinking of the conversation with Ley and was attempting to process the information about Yeo's investigation into the treatment of the boy who'd killed himself. Now he tried to clear his mind so he could listen properly to anything she might have to say.

'I have a better idea of what's going on here, how the place runs.' Jen paused. 'I can't see a reason why anyone here might have wanted to kill Yeo, but according to his daughter, there was something worrying him at work. That would explain why he wanted to speak to me.' She looked up. 'If I'd been more together last night, he might have told me then. All this . . .'

– she swept her arm to take in the CSI vehicles and the blue and white tape – 'might have been avoided.'

Matthew shook his head. 'If he had a concrete suspicion, he'd have reported it to one of the bosses in the health trust, the organization that runs all the North Devon hospitals, or he'd have come to us officially. I don't think he'd have discussed it with you at a social gathering.'

'Perhaps it wasn't concrete. No proof, but a suspicion, a sense that something wasn't quite right.'

'Maybe. We'll certainly need to speak to his colleagues.'

'Do you want me to do that now? I could go to the hospital.'

'Dr Yeo wasn't based in the hospital; he was quite independent of the trust. I've discovered that the NDPT worked out of a small office in Ilfracombe.' Matthew had tried phoning but the call had gone straight to an automated voicemail. 'They work office hours.'

'He must have worked closely with the health trust, though. I could talk to them.'

Matthew thought about priorities. Jen always liked instant action, but he wanted to know more about Yeo's role before confronting the man's colleagues or any health service officials. He shook his head. 'Our focus should be here for the moment. Ross and I are about to talk to your pal Wesley. Francis Ley thought he heard him come back early this morning, but he hasn't emerged yet. Obviously, that's not an interview for you because he's a friend. Can you talk to the Grieves? We need a statement from them.'

Jen nodded. 'I met the woman briefly when I was talking to Eve.'

'And?'

'Very hippy dippy. Not a huge fan of the police.'

Matthew smiled. 'I'm sure you can persuade her that we don't eat babies.'

Jen seemed about to reply, but she said nothing.

Ross had been chatting to Brian Branscombe, the crime scene manager, and sauntered over. 'Ready when you are, boss.' As if he'd been waiting for Matthew and not the other way around. There were times when he still managed to come across as cocky, arrogant.

'Well, thank you, Detective Constable. Sorry to keep you.'

Ross only nodded, not recognizing the sarcasm. Matthew couldn't help smiling.

Matthew had checked the layout of the house with Ley. They went through the kitchen and climbed narrow, wooden stairs to a corridor, dimly lit by a dusty skylight. At one end was a door to Eve Yeo's flat, and at the other the entrance to Wesley's. Matthew knocked and heard a faint groan inside. He took that as an invitation to enter and pushed his way in. Ross followed.

They walked straight into a sitting room, with a sloping roof and two small dormer windows. There was a sink, a fridge and microwave at one end. The rest of the room could have been a student pad, from the sixties or seventies; a couple of sofas were covered by Indian throws, there were posters on the walls, celebrating bands Matthew had never heard of, rush mats on the floor, a guitar propped against a chair. The faint but unmistakable smell of cannabis. Matthew was struck by the fact that Ley's tenants seemed stuck in a time and a place that would have seemed unreal to Ross and his generation. This would be ancient history, where the values were entirely different. Ross had worked hard for his mortgage, his tidy house, the two cars on the drive and the annual holiday in the sun. He would despise the chaos and the lack of security. Matthew's husband Jonathan would understand it, though. He'd feel at home here. For a moment Matthew felt caught in the middle, in a time warp, tugged two ways.

'Hello!' Matthew shouted.

'Who is it?' The voice from the bedroom was muffled, groggy.

'The police.'

'Shit.' A pause. 'Just a minute.'

He'd obviously pulled on the jeans and T-shirt he'd been wearing the night before, just because they were the first things that had come to hand. They were crumpled, looked as if they'd been snatched from a pile on the floor. Through the open bedroom door, Matthew could see the heap of unwashed clothes. The bed was low, covered again by Indian cotton, this time unhemmed, frayed at one edge. Without Wesley, it was empty. That made things less complicated. Matthew had thought the man might have brought home a companion, someone he'd met at Cynthia Prior's party.

'What's going on, man?' Wesley Curnow pulled back his long dark hair into a ponytail. 'I had a heavy night.' He gave a smile which Matthew took as an instinctive attempt to charm or ingratiate. 'It must be my age. I never got a hangover when I was younger.'

'We're investigating a murder.'

'What!' He stopped in his tracks, arms still raised to pull the hair through an elastic band. 'You're kidding, right?' He moved to the kitchen bench and flicked a switch on the kettle. 'Coffee? Tea?'

'No thank you.' Matthew didn't give Ross a chance to reply. 'Look, you'd better sit down. I'm sorry. It was a late one last night and I'm not really with it.' A pause while he made instant coffee, before turning back to them. 'Who's dead?'

'Nigel Yeo. Eve's father.'

'No!' He sat heavily on the sofa opposite them, his mug of coffee in his hand. 'Fuck. I thought you were going to say some stranger. I don't know, an ancient body, hidden in the woods or on the common. Not someone I actually knew. Oh God, Eve! How is she?'

Matthew ignored the last question. 'How well did you actually know Nigel?'

'Quite well. He came to visit Eve most weekends, helped her with the glass and had become almost a partner. He bought a few of my pieces. I liked him a lot.' Wesley paused, noisily drank coffee, then looked up, shocked. 'I saw him last night. He was at a party in Barnstaple. It was a surprise to see him there. He's not the partying type. A bit like Eve, who can't think of anything except her work. But it was thrown by a neighbour, so perhaps he was just there to be polite.'

Or to speak to my sergeant about a case that was troubling him.

'What time did you get home?'

'I'm not sure. Not super late. One? One thirty? I took a while mooching back up the lane.'

Matthew nodded. He was in bed by eleven unless he was working. Jonathan would have considered one not super late too, and he was learning to adjust his ideas, to be more open-minded about other people's habits.

'Did you notice anything unusual when you were on your way in?'

'Nige was killed here?' Again, the man seemed horrified by a murder so close to home.

'Yes, in his daughter's studio.' Matthew thought there could be no harm in passing on this information; the man only had to look out of his window to see what was going on.

Wesley sat with his hands cupped around the mug. He had the body of a young man, but this close, Matthew could see he was approaching middle age. There were lines on his forehead and around his eyes. He looked tired, washed out.

'I got a lift back to Instow with a friend and walked up the lane from there. It was dark, of course, but there was a bit of a moon and I enjoyed the exercise. Still a bit pissed, but in a good way, you know. Euphoric, full of plans. Music in my head. I wandered off the track for a bit and just sat at the edge of a field. It had just been cut for hay and there was that wonderful smell. I could have got drunk, just on that. I was looking out at the estuary and the lights on the opposite shore, putting together some words for a song.'

'We'll need the name of your friend.'

'Sure. Janey Mackenzie. Her dad runs the bar by the beach in Instow. We're old pals, play some music together. Hook up every now and again when she's bored or she doesn't have a better offer.' Wesley found his phone in his jeans pocket, looked at it and gave Matthew the number.

Another connection. Janey must be Mack's sister. The pretty, lively one everybody likes.

'She didn't offer to give you a lift all the way?'

'Nah.' Wesley gave a wry smile. 'She'd had enough of me by then. Janey's not the sort to do favours.'

'So, you walked all the way back from the main road?'

He shrugged. 'It was a beautiful evening and I'm used to it.' He paused. 'It's only a mile or so. There was a car, coming in the opposite direction, down from the farm. I was in the middle of the road. That time of night, you don't expect to

46

see anyone. It must have freaked them out too. I jumped into the hedge and they slammed on the brakes. Missed me by inches.'

'Can you tell me anything about the car?'

Wesley shook his head. 'I was blinded by the headlights. It was going fast. Too fast for the road, even though there was no other traffic about. It disappeared down the hill and I pulled myself out of the hedge, covered by bloody nettle stings.' He held out his arm, but the stings seemed to have faded.

'And this would have been about one o'clock?'

'Even later than that. I was nearly home.'

'Anything unusual when you got here?'

'I didn't notice anything, but I was still a bit shaken after my close encounter with mortality.' He leaned back and closed his eyes. Matthew thought he was trying to picture the scene, the late-night, starlit farmyard. Ross was restless and seemed about to throw in a question of his own, but Matthew motioned for him to stay quiet. Wesley's eyes opened. 'I'm pretty sure there weren't any lights on in the building. I'd have noticed. Sarah is like the planet police and gives us grief over any wasted energy. Eve follows the rules, so it would have struck me if she'd left a light on in her studio. Everything was quiet. I let myself into the kitchen and came up to the flat.'

'You and Eve have keys to the kitchen door?'

'Yes, that's how we get into the house. Frank has the rest of the space and uses the front door overlooking the garden.'

'What about the studios? Are they kept locked?' Matthew thought Jen would have asked about that, but it was worth checking.

'Yes. Even though most of my work uses stuff that people are trying to get rid of, my tools cost a fortune. Nobody much finds their way here, but I wouldn't take the risk. And Eve's the same about her place. Some of her commissions take hours to make and her equipment is worth a bomb. Her dad bought the furnace as a twenty-first birthday present.'

Matthew thought that made sense. 'Would Nigel have had a key?'

'Yeah, almost certainly. He kept an eye on the place when Eve went away. She's got uni mates in Exeter and spends weekends with them sometimes.'

'Did you see Dr Yeo's car in the yard when you arrived back from the party?'

Wes shook his head. 'But that doesn't mean it wasn't there. We all park in the far corner so John can get his tractor through and that's in shadow.'

Matthew would have liked to close *his* eyes now, to run through various scenarios. Nigel's car had been found in the yard, so he'd driven here. Jen had said that he'd hardly had anything to drink at the party. Had he arranged to meet someone? Why here and not his home in Barnstaple? But a detective inspector couldn't look as if he was sleeping in the middle of an interview, so he kept his eyes open and stood up.

'I think that's all we need for now. I'm sure we'll have other questions.'

'Of course. Come at any time.'

He seemed very relieved that they were leaving. Matthew wondered if that was because of the cannabis. Or because the man had something more important to hide.

Chapter Six

IN THE LOW, WHITE HOUSE BY the shore, Jonathan was enjoying a lazy Saturday morning. Matthew was at work; he'd been woken very early by his phone. Jonathan had got up too, made coffee for them both while Matthew showered, then as soon as he'd heard his husband's car drive away down the toll road, Jonathan had gone back to bed. He'd woken again to full sunlight streaming through the open window, the long call of herring gulls and the sound of waves on the beach. Somewhere in the distance, a dog was barking. At this time of year Crow Point attracted *lots* of dog-walkers.

Now he was in the kitchen planning. The following day, Matthew's mother would be coming for Sunday lunch. Such a simple event was fraught with difficulties. They'd invited her before, but she'd always refused. Too proud or too bigoted to meet her son's husband. Or too anxious, Jonathan thought, about what her friends in the small, tight, uptight religious community to which she belonged might think. More worried about appearances than her son's happiness. Matthew had grown up in the same community, and despite rejection, seemed not to have a strong sense of resentment against the Brethren. There was more a cold reluctance to engage, either with his former friends or with his mother. Tomorrow would be her birthday. Jonathan had issued the invitation in writing, in a card, and a small formal note of acceptance had been sent back. That was when he'd told Matthew what he'd done, and Matthew had been worried about it ever since. Matthew was a worrier in every situation. He'd rushed off to his murder scene this morning almost with a sense of relief. Work would be a distraction.

Jonathan would cook, of course. He loved cooking and sometimes had dreams of leaving the Woodyard and setting up a restaurant, something unpretentious and welcoming to celebrate local food. He knew he'd never do it, though. The Woodyard, the arts centre and community hub on the banks of the Taw, in Barnstaple, was his baby, his creation. He'd found the funds, set it up and from the magical opening evening, he'd managed it. Now, he couldn't imagine life without it.

Lunch would have to be a roast, because it would be a Sunday and Dorothy Venn would expect it. She'd be traditional in her tastes. He'd never met her, but he thought he knew her. And a roast would make Matthew happy. Jonathan was almost entirely veggie these days, and because he did most of the cooking, so was Matthew, at home at least. A large slab of meat, a rib of beef perhaps, would be a treat. And it would give Jonathan the chance to show off his Yorkshire puddings. Afterwards there would be cake. A special birthday cake, still to be decided on. Something spectacular with a lot of whipped cream and the first strawberries from the garden.

He made more coffee and went outside to sit and drink it,

lazing on the wrought-iron bench with its view of the estuary. He was wearing shorts and sandals, and the sun was already hot on his bare legs. He was writing a shopping list, planning his trip into town, when his mobile rang. It was one of the young craftspeople he'd encouraged to exhibit in the Woodyard when it had first opened and he was looking for the support of younger artists. Soon afterwards, Eve Yeo had become more than another work contact. They'd become friends when her mother was in the final stages of Alzheimer's disease, close to death. Eve had come into his office one day and burst into tears, spilled out her grief and her guilt and her rage. He'd comforted her and she'd come back a few weeks later with a jug made from cloudy blue glass with a clear twisted handle. 'Just to say thank you.' He'd gone to Helen Yeo's funeral a fortnight later.

Now, Jonathan was pleased to hear from her. He was proud that she liked to keep in touch. He wasn't quite old enough to be Eve's father, but if he'd had a child, he'd have loved them to be someone like her: passionate, creative. He loved her energy and her dedication to her art.

'Hi, Eve.'

'Can I meet you?'

They got together occasionally on Saturday mornings for coffee in George Mackenzie's bar in Instow, but plans for the meal were still at the forefront of his mind. He never liked to rush when he was creating.

'Sure,' he said easily. 'One day next week?'

'I was hoping you'd be able to see me today. Something rather dreadful has happened. I need to get away from Westacombe for a while.'

Only now could Jonathan tell how upset she was. She was

just about holding it together. He didn't want to pry over the phone, though. Eve had always been a private young woman. The only time he'd seen her break down was the time she'd cried in his office. Even at her mother's funeral she'd been controlled, almost calm.

'Of course,' he said, thoughts of the meal forgotten. 'Lunch at George's, in the Sandpiper?'

There was a moment's hesitation. 'That's still a bit close to home.'

'I'm planning to go into Barnstaple anyway. Why don't we meet in the cafe in the Woodyard? It's not too busy at the weekend.'

'That would be perfect.' He could sense her relief. 'Half an hour?'

'That might be a bit optimistic with the traffic,' he said. 'But yeah. I'll get there as soon as I can.'

Once, the place had been a timber yard, putting together door and window frames and shipping them all over the country. When it had first become a part of Jonathan's life, the yard had been derelict for years, the warehouses crumbling behind a high security chain fence. There had been plans to clear the empty buildings and replace them with a new retail park, but the shops on the high street were already struggling for survival, and Jonathan had seen the site's potential. His vision had created the Woodyard, an arts centre with spaces for performance and exhibitions. It housed a community choir and a youth theatre, and a day centre for people with learning disabilities.

The cafe had a view over the river. The sliding doors to the terrace had been opened and most customers were sitting outside. Lucy Braddick, a woman with Down's syndrome, who worked part-time as one of the waitresses, was clearing tables. She gave him a little wave and a huge smile. Eve was there before him. She'd chosen a table inside, in a corner, hidden by a pillar. As soon as he saw her, Jonathan could tell that she'd been crying. He gave her a hug; her shoulders were rigid, could have been formed from twisted wire.

They sat for a moment in silence. There was no need to ask her what was wrong. She'd tell him when she was ready. Staying quiet was one of the skills he'd learned from Matthew.

'I think I met your husband today,' she said at last. 'You did tell me he's called Matthew and that he works as a detective?'

'Yes. He was called out to a case earlier this morning.' This wasn't at all what he was expecting.

'He's at Westacombe. At the farm.' She looked up. 'I only saw him briefly, but he seems very nice.' Her voice was horribly controlled. 'It was a woman who spoke to me.'

'That will have been Jen. Jen Rafferty.'

She nodded. 'Somebody killed my father,' she said. 'Stabbed him with a piece of my glass. I found him in my studio early this morning.'

'Oh love.' The shock seemed a little like a stab. It was as if the blood was draining from his face and he felt almost that he was about to faint. How must Eve have reacted to finding Yeo? To a horrific scene in the place where she was at her most creative? She was closer to her father than he'd ever been to either of his adoptive parents; he'd envied the relationship she and Nigel had shared. He pulled his chair closer to hers and held her in his arms again. He couldn't believe that an hour earlier he'd been obsessing about the ingredients for Sunday lunch; that choosing the right menu had seemed the most important thing in the world. 'Do you want to tell me what happened?'

'I don't know,' she said. 'That's the worst thing. Not knowing what happened or why. It seems so random. Everybody liked my father; he was a good man. And yet, a piece of *my* glass killed him, caused all the blood. I know it's irrational, but I feel somehow responsible.'

Jonathan didn't know what to say. Usually words came easily to him. He held her hand for a moment. It felt tiny, the bones thin, like a small bird's, and it fluttered, as if it were separate and alive.

At last, he spoke. 'Matthew will find out. That's what he does. It's almost who he is.'

Gently, she pulled her hand away. 'I should go back. I can't run away forever.'

'Do you want to come and stay with us for a while?' The words came out on impulse.

She thought for a moment. 'Not today,' she said. 'I need to be on my own now. But I might take you up on the offer. In a couple of days maybe.'

'Anytime. Really, anytime.'

Chapter Seven

JEN STOOD OUTSIDE WESTACOMBE COTTAGE, rang the bell and waited. The cottage was like something out of a child's picture book, with low eaves and a thatched roof, but Jen didn't appreciate its beauty. It was early afternoon and she was starving; breakfast seemed an age away. Sarah Grieve opened the door, and stood, blocking the way, silent and implacable.

'I'm sorry to disturb you,' Jen said, 'but I do need to ask some questions.'

'It's not convenient.'

'Eve's dad is dead. Someone stuck a piece of glass in his neck. He bled all over her studio floor. That was more than inconvenient.' Jen stopped speaking, and thought she'd ruined any chance she'd had to build a relationship with the woman. Even Ross would have done better and Matthew would be furious. But something about this woman, and missing lunch, and the remnants of a hangover, had got under her skin. She was about to apologize when Sarah Grieve stood aside.

'I suppose you're just doing your job.'

'The first few hours are important,' Jen said. 'We need to talk to you all.'

There was a dark hall, coats piled onto hooks, boots and shoes spilling out of a rack.

'You'll have to excuse the mess.' The words were automatic; there was no sense that Sarah really cared what Jen thought about the state of her house. There was an open door leading into a kitchen. A tall, good-looking man with an impressive beard, and two small girls in shorts and T-shirts, sat at a scrubbed pine table. They'd been eating lunch and the remains of the meal were crammed at one end. At the other stood a pile of files, a basket of knitting wool, a doll with one arm and stray pieces of Lego.

The man stood up, stared. Jen picked up hostility. Was this how he always reacted to strangers in his home? 'This is one of the detectives,' Sarah said. 'She wants to ask us some questions.'

'I need to get back to work.' But John Grieve hovered where he was. He didn't move towards the door.

'It won't take long.' The window in the room was small and there was no direct sunlight. After the brightness of the court-yard, it seemed very dark. Even in this heat, there was a faint smell of damp. The cottage might be idyllic from the outside, but it was cramped for a family of four. Jen was still struggling to make out all the detail in the kitchen. There seemed to be nowhere for her to sit.

'Why don't you go and play?' Sarah said to the children. 'You can use the laptop in our bedroom. Just half an hour.'

This seemed an unexpected treat and the girls ran off.

'We don't usually allow them screens.' Sarah sat on one of the chairs and nodded for Jen to join them at the table. Jen thought briefly that if she'd been any kind of mother, she'd have limited her kids' access to the internet, but it was too late for that now. Ben could barely make it through dinner without recourse to his phone. John Grieve returned to his chair. No move was made to clear the bread board, the rinds of cheese, the wilting salad. The woman leaned back in her chair. 'So, what do you need to know?'

'Did you hear or see anything unusual last night? Or the early hours of this morning?'

The couple looked at each other. Jen couldn't work out what was going on. Some secret message passing between them? But they must have known the question would be asked and they would have had time to work out a story.

'I was in bed by ten,' John Grieve said. 'I have to be up early for milking.'

'I was later,' Sarah said. 'Frank wanted something in writing on the changes we're planning to make to the dairy. I thought I'd make a start while it was clear in my head.'

'What time did you finish?'

'Midnight. Maybe a bit after.'

'Did you hear a car in the yard? We know Nigel drove to Westacombe last night. At least, his vehicle is here.'

Sarah shook her head. 'I was listening to music and had headphones on so I wouldn't wake the kids.'

'You didn't see headlights?'

'No, sorry. I was pretty focused on the screen.'

Grieve looked up. 'I noticed Nigel's car when I went out to the cows this morning. I thought he'd had an early start.'

'You didn't see *him*?'

'No, I thought he'd be in the flat with Eve.'

'Nothing unusual at all?'

'Sorry.' John Grieve got to his feet. 'Look, I've got to go. It's a busy time.' He gave a brief nod to his wife and left the room. Through the kitchen door, Jen saw him pull on his boots in the hall and there was a sudden flash of sunlight as he went into the yard.

In the cluttered room, there was silence. Jen waited. She thought the woman might have more to say. Everything was still. She felt for a moment like a character in a gloomy Dutch painting. All brown interiors and rotting fruit. Her friend Cynthia fancied herself an expert in art, and dragged Jen round visiting exhibitions occasionally.

The silence stretched, until at last Sarah spoke. 'Everyone thinks it's paradise living here. We're almost rent-free because I look after the big house for Frank when he's not around, and he gives Wes and Eve a great deal too. But it's not without its difficulties, living practically on top of each other. This place might look pretty, but it's a bit low on mod cons. And Frank isn't always easy.'

'In what way not easy?' This wasn't Jen's idea of paradise. She could imagine it in the winter when the westerly gales came hurtling off the Atlantic, the place all draughts and mud. And wouldn't that attract vermin? Mice? Rats even?

Another silence, only broken by laughter from the girls upstairs.

'He's full of principles, which is great if you're minted, but not so easy for the rest of us.'

'You're thinking of the tea shop idea?'

'Well yeah, but there are other things too, which get under John's skin. It makes for a tense situation, and John's not the best at coping with stress. Frank's passionate about animal welfare and the whole organic thing. We are too, but there needs to be some flexibility. It's as if he actually wants to lose money on the venture. We can't have that sort of attitude. We've got the girls to think about and this new little one.' She patted her belly.

'Is Mr Ley a relative of yours?'

'His mum was my gran's sister. I called her Aunty Nancy. I visited the farm when I was a kid. Frank was already working in London then and the place was falling apart. His dad died not long after the crash and Frank came along with all that money to bring it back to life.' She paused. 'Nancy only died a few years ago. She was in her nineties, still sparky, still active. She had a heart attack after a day of gardening and died in her own bed. Frank was devastated, but I know that would have been how she'd want to go. That was when I took on the role of housekeeper, as well as working in the dairy.'

'You must be knackered, with the kids to look after too.'

Sarah gave a little grin. 'Yep, that's my world. Permanently knackered.' She didn't seem thrown by it, though.

'What does your husband make of it all?'

Another silence. 'John finds it tricky,' Sarah said at last. 'He'd rather we were more independent, able to do our own thing. He doesn't have an arty bone in his body, so the whole set-up here – Wes treating the place like a commune and bringing his mates to stay, impromptu gigs in the yard when we're trying to sleep – that's not really his bag. Like I said, he's not good with stress.'

'And you? Is it your bag?'

'Honestly? It is really. I love the buzz and the company. I'm not sure how I'd cope doing the traditional wife thing, miles from anywhere in a hill farm on the edge of Exmoor. And that's John's dream.'

Jen thought about that. She could see how that might cause problems for the couple. She'd be with Sarah every time.

Before she could speak, the woman continued. 'I'd give it a go, though. Only fair. We've done my thing since we moved here and now we're saving like fury to find our own place. That's why the tea shop is so important.'

Jen nodded to show she understood. 'How well did you both know Nigel?'

'I lived in the same street as Eve when I was growing up. I was a few years older but she was brighter and we were best mates, in and out of each other's houses. Both only children. So I've known Nigel since I was a kid. He still lives in the same house in Barnstaple. John met him a few times when we first married – he came to our wedding – but only really got to know him when we moved in here.' For the first time, Sarah seemed to notice the food left on the table. She pulled herself to her feet and began, haphazardly, to move plates towards the sink. 'In a way they were very similar. Both quiet men. Both competent. No need to show off. None of that macho crap. They liked each other. John might not show it, but he's upset.' She turned to face Jen. 'I loved Nigel. He was like a second father. When I was growing up, I could tell him stuff that I could never tell my parents. Just find out what happened. For Eve and for us.'

No pressure, then. Jen nodded and got to her feet.

Chapter Eight

IT WAS LATE AFTERNOON AND MATTHEW ordered Jen and Ross back to Barnstaple. 'Get something to eat, then make notes of initial witness responses to share with the team. Ross, please could you do an internet search of all the residents at the farm. Any criminal convictions? And let's see if we can have a first report on our victim's phone records. Eve has given us the details of his mobile provider. Jen, any social media activity or news reports around Dr Yeo? His work could sometimes have been controversial, occasionally high profile if he'd started taking on his former employers in the health trust. We'll clear out of the way at Westacombe now, and leave the place free for the CSIs and the search team.

'Let's meet in the office for a briefing at six. Sal Pengelly has agreed to fast-track the post-mortem and will carry that out later this evening, if it's at all possible. I'll be there for that.'

He paused, and looked at them both to check they'd registered the instructions. 'Ross, can you get a lift back with Jen and leave me the car? I'll just call into the Sandpiper, where

Janey Mackenzie works, on my way back to town and check Wesley's alibi.'

And find out a bit more about Mack, the young man who killed himself. The case Nigel was working on when he died.

When he arrived, there was nowhere to park on the street close to the Sandpiper, and the only place he could find was outside the Glorious Oyster, the fish shack and kitchen behind the dunes. A customer was sitting at the picnic table outside, carefully poking the flesh from a crab's leg, completely absorbed. Matthew knew Lindsay, the owner, because this was one of his and Jonathan's favourite places to eat, and she waved agreement when he asked if he could leave the car.

'I'll be packing up soon, anyway. It's been manic and we've almost sold out.'

He walked back to the bar through hordes of families, people greasy with sun cream or pink with the heat. At the Hocking's ice cream van there was a queue which led over the low wall and down to the beach. Suddenly, Matthew was shot back in time to his childhood. His mother had disapproved of any form of processed food:

'The good Lord created my body and it's a sin not to take care of it.'

But his father, who'd only converted to the Brethren to be married to her, had been less rigid. If they were out walking together, they'd both enjoy a vanilla cone with a flake, whenever they came across a Hocking's van. His father would wink: 'Our secret, eh?' Matthew had been a bit of a prig when he was a boy and hadn't quite approved of the deceit. He'd never turned down the ice cream, though, and now he regretted that he hadn't been more relaxed, that he hadn't been able to enjoy those shared moments with his father more. The man had died a few months before and the opportunity had been missed.

As soon as he reached the Sandpiper, he realized that he'd made a mistake. He'd thought there might be a quiet spell between the afternoon teas and the first beers of the evening, but the place was heaving. People were sitting on the wall that separated the pavement from the beach, already drinking. Inside, there was a queue at the counter that reached out into the street. The noises from the coffee machine, raised voices and raucous laughter battled against each other and made his head ache. He was bombarded by a sensory overload and felt completely out of place. Like the Glorious Oyster, this was somewhere he'd come with Jonathan, but only in the evening when it was quieter, more intimate, to listen to the music. He stood at the door, thinking he'd go away and make a proper appointment to come back, when George Mackenzie saw him. He waved at Matthew and yelled so his words were quite clear, even from the other end of the room and over the background noise of the bar.

'I heard about Nigel. Come round to the yard.'

Matthew reached the yard via an alley at the side of the building, and through a wooden gate. The bolt was on the other side and even he had to stretch to reach it. This wasn't a place for punters. It held empty kegs and crates of wine bottles, and the concrete floor was scattered with cigarette ends. The yard must be an unofficial staff smoking area. Through an open window, Matthew saw the kitchen, heard shouts for service and the banging of pans. George was already there, leaning in the shade against the high wall.

'Sorry about the surroundings.' He hadn't lost the Scottish accent after years working in the south. 'This is the only place we'll make ourselves heard.' He looked up at Matthew. 'I can't believe it. Who would have done such a thing?'

'We don't know yet. None of the details are very clear.' Matthew was deliberately vague. 'Everybody speaks very highly of Dr Yeo. Did you know him well?'

'Not personally. Not as a friend. He was investigating the circumstances surrounding my son's suicide.'

'I heard that.' Matthew paused. 'Frank Ley told me.' Another silence. 'I wondered why Frank was so closely involved with your boy.'

'Two oddballs together, maybe.' The words came out quickly and immediately George seemed to regret them. 'I loved my son. Of course I did. But I never understood him. He was different even as a child. Intense, given to obsession, anxious.'

'And Martha? What did she make of him?'

'Ah, my lovely Martha.' George sighed. There was something theatrical about every response. 'She's not what anyone would call maternal and when Mack was growing up, she was hardly ever here. She was in that soap opera about the doctors' practice. It was shot in Bristol, and she spent most of her time there. Sometimes, I felt that her life was all about filming schedules and wrap parties.'

'She's retired from acting now, though?' The last time Matthew had been at the Sandpiper for an evening of music, Martha Mackenzie had been front of house, still glamorous, propping up the bar, inviting attention. More attention, it seemed, than the singer on the low stage.

'Well, let's say that acting has retired her. If an offer came through, I know she'd jump at the chance.' A pause and a wry smile. 'I know where I come in her list of priorities. But she's too proud to go begging for work.'

'Was she here when Mack died?'

'Yes, and she was devastated, of course. We all were.'

'I did wonder . . .' – Matthew chose his words carefully – '. . . if there might be more than friendship between Frank and Mack.'

'You thought they might be lovers?' George said. 'Or that Frank might have groomed him? Mack was only nineteen when he died after all. No, I never suspected anything of that sort. Frank's a kind man and they were kindred spirits. Both loners struggling to make sense of the world. We would have been happy if Mack had found a partner. There were girls he fell for, but the relationships never survived. I think he scared them off by being too intense, too demanding. Too unstable.'

'Is your daughter around?'

'Yeah, Janey's behind the bar. Working. Can you talk to her when it's not so busy? You can see what it's like in there.'

'Was she working yesterday night?'

George shook his head. 'Nah, she asked for the night off, and I thought she deserved a break. This weather's great for business but it's been relentless. She was at a party in Barnstaple. Wesley up at Westacombe took her along.' He gave a little laugh. 'When she got home, she said that she'd have had a better time staying here. The party-goers were all closer in age to her mother and me. She likes a real bash, our Janey. Something a bit livelier.'

'She gave Wesley a lift home?'

'Well, as far as the turn-off to the farm. She made him walk up the lane. To serve him right, she said, for the boring evening.'

Matthew nodded. So far Wesley's story was confirmed. 'What time did she get back?'

'I'm not sure. I was still in the bar when she got here, so

twelve thirty maybe? I'd just finished the last of the clearing up. Janey hadn't been drinking because she was driving, so we shared a nightcap.' He nodded towards the house on the other side of the wall. 'You know we live next door.'

Matthew nodded again. 'One of my officers will be back tomorrow to take a statement from her. When's the best time to come?'

'Early afternoon maybe. We do brunch on a Sunday instead of lunch, and things should be quieter by then.'

Mention of Sunday lunch gave Matthew a jolt. The following day was his mother's birthday. She would be coming to the house and Jonathan would be cooking. He experienced the sense of dread, of social anxiety, that had been part of his life since he'd left the Brethren. He'd lost his faith suddenly and publicly, and had been cast out by the people he'd thought had cared for him most: his parents and his friends. The group talked of 'un-fellowshipping' and despite knowing, rationally, that he'd only been honest, there had been times when he'd felt unworthy of human contact.

The sense of loss had haunted him when he was a student, and at the beginning of his working career. Only Jonathan had given him the confidence to face the world. It occurred to Matthew fleetingly that the investigation would give him an excuse to cancel, but he imagined what Jonathan would say if he called the meal off. He'd face accusations of cowardice. Murder or not, he'd have to be there. He turned his attention back to Mackenzie.

'How do you and Frank Ley know each other? You didn't grow up here. How did he get so fond of Mack?'

The question seemed to surprise Mackenzie. He'd thought the conversation over.

'Frank helped us out.' George, usually so urbane and relaxed, was almost embarrassed. 'Three years ago, we were going through a difficult time financially. We were more of a traditional cafe then: breakfasts, lunches and afternoon teas. Martha had just been dropped from the telly show, so no regular income, and no savings. She spent everything she earned as it came into her account. It was desperate, actually. There was a chance we'd lose the business. Ley had bought up a restaurant two doors away and they were taking all our lunchtime business. I was furious and got in touch with him. He asked me up to Westacombe, came down specially from London for the meeting.' George paused. 'It wasn't what I was expecting. I had my pitch all ready, had managed to stoke up the righteous indignation, but in the end he just listened.'

'And he invested?'

'Yeah, he invested. But more than that, he came up with ideas. Or he got me to come up with ideas. "You don't seem that enthusiastic about the place. Not passionate. Ideally, what sort of business would you like to run?" I'd expected a half-hour confrontation, but I was there all evening, drinking his very good wine on the terrace, watching the sun go down over the estuary. I started talking about music, Martha's experience of the theatre, all her contacts, and he came up with the plan: "Seems to me you should turn the Sandpiper into a performance space. I'd put money into that." And he did.'

'He was right,' Matthew said. 'It's what makes this place unique. How does it work? Are you partners?'

George shook his head. 'He gave us a loan. Interest-free. We paid it back after the first year, but we became friends. And he's still there if I feel I need advice or to share ideas.'

'And that's how he got to know Mack? Through you?'

'That first night, we didn't just talk about the business. As I said, he was a great listener. He could have been a shrink or a priest. I talked about the family, about Mack and his problems. Mack was sixteen, and struggling at school, in danger of permanent exclusion. Frank said he needed someone to look after the garden. Maybe Mack would be interested in the work? Only weekends and it wouldn't need anyone skilled. Someone to mow the lawn and keep the beds weeded. His mother, Nancy, had designed it all and Frank wanted to keep it going in her memory. Their friendship started like that.' George paused. 'When Mack died it was as if Frank had lost part of his family. He was as upset as we were.' A pause. 'He asked to speak at the funeral and had us all in tears.'

'So, he got Nigel to look into the circumstances surrounding the suicide?'

George nodded. 'Frank has a way of making things happen. Perhaps money can do that. It helped that someone was taking our concerns seriously. We knew we couldn't bring Mack back, but there were all those unanswered questions about his care.' His voice tailed off.

Matthew understood how stretched the community mental health teams had become. His police officers seemed to be the first point of call for troubled people these days. Time which in the past had been used to investigate burglary was now spent tracking down a response from the community mental health team or driving to A&E. He wondered if Mack's care had been any worse than that of other young people similarly struggling with depression or addiction. He looked at his watch. It was getting late and soon his team would be gathering for the briefing. And still, he hadn't eaten.

'Thanks,' he said. 'I'll let you get back to the fray.' He was about to ask if George could get him a sandwich to take away, but that would have meant jumping the queue at the counter, and his principles, as strange and as rigid as those of his mother, couldn't quite allow him do it.

They were gathered in the ops room in Barnstaple police station. The building was brutalist concrete and scheduled for redevelopment. The civic centre had already moved on to other premises and sometimes Matthew felt as though they were stranded, forgotten by superiors nearer to the centre of things. North Devon still felt isolated and miles from the mainstream. He'd picked up a sandwich and bad coffee from a service station on his way back into town, consumed them too fast in his office, and was almost the last to get to the room.

Matthew stood at the front and waited for the team to settle. It didn't take long. They'd learned by now that he wasn't a man for shouting to get attention. He was patient, and most police officers weren't. They nudged the colleagues still talking until everyone was quiet.

He didn't shout when he was addressing the team either. They had to sit close to him and they had to listen carefully.

'Our victim is Dr Nigel Yeo, a former doctor at the North Devon Hospital, who worked with a small organization which represents patients' views and experiences to the health trust, the governing body of the hospital. He seemed to have broadened the brief and had started following up complaints about care. North Devon Patients Together is based in Ilfracombe and he headed up a small team of four people.' Matthew had gained the last piece of information from the organization's website. 'His body was found by his daughter, Eve, in her studio at Westacombe Farm. Eve's a glass blower and she'd expected her father to come early on Saturday morning to help her work. But by early she meant seven thirty. It seems likely that death actually occurred at about one in the morning, because a witness says he saw a car driving at speed down the lane towards the coast. The lane only leads to Westacombe. As yet, we have no idea what might have taken Nigel to the farm late yesterday evening or in the early hours of this morning.'

In the front row, Ross May had stuck up his hand. He looked young and eager, a schoolboy trying to impress a teacher. Matthew thought the constable had realized that his mentor and guardian, superintendent Joe Oldham, would soon be forced into early retirement, and was trying to curry favour with his more immediate superior. As soon as this idea came into his head, Matthew thought he was being unfair. With more experience, Ross would make a good detective.

'Yes, Ross.'

'Might we have more of an idea of the time of death after the post-mortem?'

The irritation deepened. This was going over old ground, a lesson not properly learned. 'Most unlikely. Can anyone tell me why?'

Jen answered immediately. 'Research shows that it's impossible to pinpoint time of death with any accuracy.'

Matthew gave her a little smile. 'Quite right. As Dr Pengelly never fails to tell us. So, we have to rely on old-fashioned policing, not a pathologist's magic or guesswork. Jen, you were actually the last person we know to see Dr Yeo alive. What time was that?'

'It was at a party held by Cynthia Prior in Newport. I can't be positive about time but I'd say between ten thirty and eleven p.m.' She looked at Matthew for understanding. 'I'd had a few drinks. I wasn't looking at my watch.'

'Can you talk to any of the other guests? See if we can pinpoint it more precisely? Or find out if he told anyone what his plans were for the rest of the evening?'

'Yeah, sure.'

'Although Wesley Curnow, another of the Westacombe residents, claims to have seen the vehicle leave the farm in the early hours, we can't assume that the killer was someone from outside. Curnow could have made up the story, or the car might have strayed up the track by mistake. So, we need more information on the residents. Ross, you were going to do a background check.'

Ross stood up and faced the room. Practising, Matthew thought, for the promotion he felt he deserved. Then he chided himself again for his meanness of spirit.

'Wesley Curnow. Aged forty-two. He's been cautioned once for possession. Cannabis, a small amount. The officer assumed it was for personal use.' A moment of silence to express his disapproval. 'No other offences, apart from road traffic violations, one for speeding and one for bald tyres. As far as I can see, he's never married and never had children. Eve Yeo, our victim's daughter, hasn't been involved with us in any way. Neither has the couple who live in the cottage, John and Sarah Grieve, or the house owner Francis Ley.'

'Thanks, Ross.' It was much as Matthew would have thought, and didn't take them any further forward.

'I have managed to prise some info out of his mobile provider. Calls and texts were much as you'd think. Lots to his daughter. I haven't had a chance to look at all the others in detail, but there's one recurring number, which appears even more frequently. To someone called Lauren Miller.'

The name seemed familiar to Matthew. He remembered he'd seen it on the NDPT website. 'She was one of his colleagues at Patients Together. You'd expect that.'

'Some of them were very long calls. Made late at night.' Ross allowed the implication to sink in, before taking his seat.

'Ah, that is worth following up, but of course, we won't jump to conclusions.' Matthew paused. 'Did Yeo take any calls yesterday evening? Something must have prompted him to go to Westacombe that late at night.'

Ross shook his head. 'Last one was to Lauren Miller late afternoon.'

Matthew thought about that. So, there'd been no urgent, last-minute call summoning him to Westacombe. He turned to his sergeant. 'Jen, did you dig out anything interesting?'

'There's loads of archive news material on Ley. You just have to google and you come up with pages of the stuff. He made his fortune by selling the shares he'd bought cheaply in the years immediately before the financial crash, but there's no evidence of him breaking any rules. He doesn't seem to have been involved in anything dodgy. He just recognized the risks before other people. I had an interesting conversation with Sarah Grieve this afternoon. Her husband's desperate to move away from Westacombe to some Exmoor hill farm, but she's not so keen. She likes the arty set-up and would miss her mates, especially with a new baby on the way.' She caught Matthew's eye. 'I'm not sure how relevant all this is, but I know you like background.'

'Oh, I certainly do. Gossip is our friend.' He scanned the room. 'I'm tied up over lunchtime tomorrow. Important family occasion. Jen, can you talk to the party-goers, see if we can get a precise time of Nigel's leaving and some idea what took him to the farm that late? Ross, I'd like you to head round to the Sandpiper. Apparently, early afternoon is best. I talked to George Mackenzie today, but his daughter wasn't available. We need a statement to confirm Curnow's story, but also anything she might have on the Westacombe residents. I'll see what I can make of Nigel Yeo's home. He might have kept work records there.'

I can do that early in the morning. Leave Jonathan the kitchen to himself. Still be back for lunch.

The nauseous sense of dread about his mother invading his home ground returned. He smiled at his team, sent them on their way and made his way to the hospital mortuary, where Sally Pengelly and the corpse of Nigel Yeo were waiting for him.

Chapter Nine

Eve didn't go straight back to the farm after meeting Jonathan at the Woodyard. She couldn't face Sarah's smothering love, Wes's awkward pity. She had another coffee after the centre manager left, then chatted for a moment to Lucy Braddick, whose smile could light up any room. Eve started crying again, despite herself.

'Are you all right?' Lucy asked.

'Not really. My dad just died.'

She saw a shadow pass over Lucy's face and the smile fade. Because Lucy's dad was in his eighties and Lucy was aware that nobody lived forever.

Eve gathered up her bag and made her way to the car. There'd been no shade left to park in and it was roasting inside, the seat burning even through her dungarees, the steering wheel almost too hot to touch. On impulse, she went to the woodland burial site, where her mother had been put to rest in a willow coffin. It was inland from Barnstaple, on the back road to Ilfracombe, a small copse of newly planted trees close to the river. She and her father had planted a sapling on top of the grave, and their friends had given a lusty rendition of 'Yellow Submarine', led by Wesley. She and her father had chosen the song. It was what they'd always sung on journeys when she'd been a child, and this, they'd decided, was a journey of a kind. There were no stones or memorials, but she knew where the grave was. The last time she'd visited, she'd been with her father and there were pools of bluebells.

Sitting in the shade, with the noise of the river running low over pebbles, it was her mother she thought about now. Helen had been a medic too, a GP, passionate about her patients and a furious activist, fighting for the NHS. Spiky and funny, given to bright unprofessional clothes and angry letters to the papers. It was Helen who'd first suggested her husband should consider taking on a new role, her tone flippant, only half serious. Eve had just come home from Sunderland after completing her MA and she remembered the discussion. They'd been sitting at the dinner table, eating boeuf bourguignon cooked in her honour, drinking smooth red wine. After a student house in the north-east, it had felt wonderfully luxurious.

'You need a new challenge,' Helen had said to her husband. 'You're starting to get bored.'

'You're not suggesting management, are you? Can you imagine?'

They'd all laughed, but perhaps that conversation had sown a seed, given Nigel permission later to give up medicine. Not long afterwards, Helen had started to notice the first signs of early onset Alzheimer's. She'd gone secretly to a specialist for tests, kept the panic to herself until she was sure of the diagnosis. Excluding them both.

Then there'd been another dinner. More good food. More wine. The revelation which would change all their lives: 'I could tell I was losing it,' Helen had said. 'The first tests weren't conclusive, but I knew.'

And there'd been another discussion about Nigel's future.

'I'm thinking of applying to head up Patients Together.' He'd taken Helen's hand across the table. 'You said I needed a new challenge.'

'You're doing it because you think I'll need a carer.'

'I'm thinking of it because I want to spend more time with you. That was what we always planned for this stage in our life. This'll be office hours, no ridiculous shifts.'

There'd been a silence. Eve had felt herself holding her breath, waiting for her mother's reply. Certainly, she'd been trying to hold back the tears.

'Your decision,' Nigel had said, his attention completely focused on Helen. For the first time in her life with her parents, Eve had felt in the way, that she was intruding.

Helen had nodded. Decision made.

'Of course, there's no guarantee that I'll get the job.'

'You'd better fucking get it.' At that point, Helen had still been very much herself.

The illness had taken hold very quickly and soon Helen had become frail and confused. There'd been occasional flashes of her old self, but they'd become scarcer. Her mood had swung between frustration and good humour, but Nigel had always been there, patient and uncomplaining. Eve had often visited, of course, and Helen had seemed pleased to see her. There'd been moments of laughter. One day, however, she'd arrived and Helen had treated her as a stranger. She'd died soon after, only months after Nigel had taken over his new role at Patients Together. A relief, everyone agreed, that it hadn't dragged on, that she hadn't had to go into care, but Eve knew her father hadn't seen it like that. She'd wondered if he'd go back to a post in the hospital, lose himself in medicine again, but Helen had wanted him to take the job in NDPT and so he'd stuck to it.

Now, as a slight breeze brought some relief from the heat and moved the leaves above her, scattering light across the undergrowth, Eve wondered if that decision was what had killed him.

Chapter Ten

SALLY PENGELLY WAS WAITING FOR MATTHEW in the mortuary, gowned and booted.

'Thanks for doing this so speedily at a weekend.' Matthew knew she had a family: a husband who was head teacher of a village primary school, and at least three children. He and Jonathan had been invited once to a barbecue at their home, a rambling place with a garden and orchard, a paddock with ponies. There had been a lot of children there, all running wild, and he hadn't quite worked out which of them belonged to Sally. It had been a chaotic and good-humoured evening. Jonathan had loved it; Matthew not quite so much. There had been insects and they'd had to sit on the grass.

'This suits me better than tomorrow morning,' she said. 'Finn's got running club and Jo's at youth orchestra. Freddie says the surf's looking good, so he *has* to be at Croyde. Bloody kids rule our lives.' A pause. 'And we didn't want to leave Dr Yeo at the locus longer than necessary. That poor young woman, with her father's dead body on her doorstep. In her workplace.'

Matthew nodded.

'You don't need to stay throughout.' Sally was already focused on the body on the stainless-steel table. The mortuary technician moved quietly and efficiently beside her. 'Cause of death is pretty clear and, of course, we have an ID.' She looked back at Matthew. 'You've had quite a day. You'll be glad to be home. So, let's get on with it, shall we?'

Her assistant started cutting away Nigel's clothes and Sally provided the running commentary:

'In the trouser pockets, we have a handkerchief and two sets of house keys. No car keys.' She turned again to Matthew, a question.

'They'd been left in his car,' Matthew said. He wondered if that was significant. Had Yeo been distracted when he arrived? Did he trust the Westacombe residents not to steal the vehicle? But wasn't locking a car automatic? Matthew kept a running log throughout an investigation, and now he opened the blue, hardback notebook and wrote a reminder to check with Eve if her father usually left his vehicle unlocked when he was at the farm.

Sally was still speaking. 'The cause of death is a stab wound to the neck, and severing of the artery and critical nerves controlling cardiac and brain function. Bleeding will have been brisk, at least until the blood pressure dropped, and we noted the pulsatile nature of the spatter on the workshop wall.'

Matthew closed his eyes for a moment and pictured the crime scene, the blood. It was hard to imagine that one man could produce so much.

Sally continued. 'The murder weapon was this piece of glass. The axial strength meant that it didn't shatter, though there is evidence of deformation where it hit the bone.' She turned to Matthew. 'Really, this is all as we thought at the locus.'

'I did wonder,' he said, 'if the glass was window dressing, there for effect.'

She shook her head. 'Glass can be remarkably strong. I did part of my training in Aberdeen. Plenty of glassings in pub brawls there.' She paused for a moment. 'Go home to your husband. I'll get my report to you as soon as I can, and I'll be in touch immediately if I come across anything unusual.'

For a moment he hesitated. Duty had become a habit, almost reassuring, an excuse to avoid the personal. But Sally was right. There was nothing more for him to do here.

It was dark when he got home, but Jonathan was still in the kitchen, music playing. Something cool and bluesy that Matthew didn't recognize. Jonathan was at the sink, peeling vegetables. He turned and took Matthew briefly into his arms. No words until they'd separated.

'I met Eve today. She told me what had happened.'

'Will she hold it together, do you think?' Matthew took a seat at the long table.

'Yeah, in the end. But to lose her father so soon after her mother . . .' Jonathan paused. 'I invited her to come and stay. I don't think she should be on her own there, so close to where her father was killed.'

Matthew looked up sharply. For a moment he couldn't quite believe what Jonathan had said. 'She's a witness to a murder. A potential suspect. You can't see that it would be impossible to have her here?'

'You really believe that Eve could have killed her father?' Jonathan's face was set, stubborn. 'And that protocol is more important than kindness?'

'The rules matter!' Matthew was aware of his voice rising, that he was almost shouting, and made an effort to remain calm, reasonable. 'Sometimes they're the only thing between us and chaos.'

They stood staring at each other in silence. Matthew broke it first. He nodded towards the sink. 'I'm sorry but I'm really not that hungry.'

'This isn't for tonight,' Jonathan said. 'I'm getting prepped for tomorrow. Your mother's grand lunch.' His voice was brighter. In his mind, at least, the tension between them was over; he was clearly looking forward to the occasion. He put his arm around Matthew and kissed him lightly. That was Jonathan all over. He hated confrontation and never saw the point of letting an argument drag on. He thought that a moment of tenderness could make everything better. Matthew felt the old dread settle like a headache, but said nothing.

Chapter Eleven

ROSS AND MEL HAD A ROUTINE for Sundays if neither of them was working. Sometimes she had to go in; she was manager of an old folks' home and took her job seriously. It wasn't fair, she said, for the care staff to work shifts if she didn't take her turn. She'd started working there when she was sixteen, fitting it in around taking the care qualification at the FE college on the edge of the town. They'd already been going out then. Childhood sweethearts. She'd worked her way up from care assistant, from wearing the ugly pink tabards to her own clothes. Always smart. Ross hadn't liked to think of her wiping the old men's bums, had been a bit embarrassed about her job, but he was proud of her now.

Mel and Ross had met at school. She had always been the prettiest in the class and not just good-looking, but easy-going and even-tempered too. Not one of the stuck-up girls who thought it was clever to bad mouth or tease. Not pushy or overly academic either. Despite her looks, he had never found her intimidating. They'd first started going out when they were fifteen and had been married in their early twenties.

Ross's parents had been through hard times, and he didn't want that for himself. He'd already mapped out his life before Mel walked down the aisle to be his wife. Security was important. He and Mel had bought their own home while their friends were still renting or spending their cash on travel and flash cars, instead of investing in their future. Ross had grand plans for *his* future: promotion, a bigger house. That would be the time for fancy holidays.

Sunday morning started with the Park Run. Ross liked his sport. In the winter it was rugby; Joe Oldham had introduced him to the club when Ross was still a boy, and the superintendent came along to cheer at most of the important matches. Though he usually retired to the bar at half-time. This time of year, Ross still wanted to keep fit. He had a horror of ending up like his dad: flabby, his belly hanging over his belt, taking no pride in his appearance.

Mel was a good runner too and went out with her mates some mornings, coming back glowing, laughing just with the pleasure of the exercise. Ross thought that was when he loved her most. She was a credit to him. He'd tried to persuade Jen Rafferty along to the Park Run, but she'd looked at him as if he was crazy. *Are you joking? On a Sunday morning?* Ross wished Jen would take him more seriously – everything was a joke to her – because he only had her best interests at heart. At her age, she could use more exercise and it wouldn't hurt if she cut down on the booze. Not that he said anything about that. Jen had a way with words that made you wary, that could cut into you like a knife. With one sentence she could slice away his confidence and his self-belief. If he'd known her at school, she'd have been one of the girls he'd have avoided like the plague.

After the run, Mel always did a cooked breakfast. It was the high point of his week. Some of their running mates went out for brunch in a cafe close to the park, but Ross could never see the point. It all cost money and, anyway, the food wasn't great; there was nowhere decent to eat in Barnstaple. And Mel was a great cook. Today, it was scrambled eggs and smoked salmon on sourdough toast. Afterwards, she made a pot of real coffee – on weekdays, they made do with instant – and they took their mugs out into the garden. He sat with his face to the sun and thought this was all he'd ever wanted: to be a good cop and a good husband. Maybe a good father when the time was right. Mel got up from her deckchair and began to pull a few weeds from the flower bed next to the path.

He looked at his watch. 'I've got to go in to the station. We're working on that murder out at Westacombe and the boss has decided he's got something important on at home. Who knows what Jen will be up to?' He rolled his eyes. 'One of us has got to be there.'

She was still crouched, and turned to face him, her eyes screwed up against the sun.

'No worries,' she said. 'I'll do the washing-up, shall I?'

He thought he caught an edge to her voice, a touch of sarcasm. 'Is that okay?' He wouldn't want to upset her for the world.

'Yeah.' She stood up and smiled. 'I know how important your work is.'

There was a moment of relief. He should have known she wouldn't have a go at him. He was overreacting. 'I won't be back until late-ish. I've got to take a witness statement out at Instow, then there'll be the briefing.'

'That's all right. I might go out for a drink with the girls.'

Again, he thought he caught an undercurrent of resentment, but when he looked at her face, she was still smiling.

The police station was like a sauna; the sun was streaming through windows that had never been opened and, of course, there was no air con. Ross looked again at the list of the calls Nigel Yeo had made in the previous week. Besides those to Eve and to Lauren Miller, everything seemed work-related. He must have been a sad bastard. Not much social life at all. There *was* a text sent at six o'clock on the evening before his death by Cynthia Prior: **Look forward to seeing you later.** Nothing else that day. So, Ross thought, any meeting at Westacombe had been arranged previously. Or Nigel had been contacted on his landline. Or he'd turned up on the spur of the moment. That was speculation, of course. Ross had learned from Joe Oldham to be suspicious of speculation, but Matthew Venn thought it was a useful tool. *Our job is all about* What if? *No harm creating a number of scenarios and seeing if the facts fit. The danger comes when you twist the facts to fit the theory.*

It was still a bit early to be heading out to Instow, but Ross left the station anyway. He thought he'd call in at the house, surprise Mel. They might go to bed. Sex in the afternoon had always been his favourite, and, somehow, they'd got out of the way of it. Too busy both of them. He was excited, a schoolboy again, planning illicit jaunts with his girlfriend, as he drove through the new executive estate, past the men washing cars and the kids playing out. But when he got there, Mel's car wasn't in the drive. Perhaps she'd popped round to her parents'. He rang her, but when she didn't reply, he decided not to wait. The moment of uncharacteristic spontaneity had passed.

There were more cars heading away from Instow as he drove there than were making their way to the coast. Family Sunday afternoons were a time of preparation for the week ahead: homework, hair wash, the ironing of school uniform. At least, that was how it had been when he was a boy. And this wasn't yet prime grockle season. A few people were still in the Sandpiper, but they were lingering over coffee, relaxed. Ross had never been in here. It wasn't his sort of place. Most of the customers were his parents' age. A young woman was drying glasses at the counter. Blonde hair. A white blouse, the cotton thin enough that he could see her bra. She moved out to clear a table and he saw she was wearing skinny jeans and Converse sandshoes.

'Janey Mackenzie?'

'Yes.' She seemed to see him for the first time. 'Oh, you must be the detective. Dad said someone would be coming.'

'Yes, I need to talk to you about Friday night.'

She was still carrying a tray. 'Just a minute. I need to get rid of this.' She disappeared into the kitchen and returned soon after with a middle-aged man. 'This is my dad. He'll cover while I talk to you. Do you mind if we walk on the beach? I've been stuck in all day.'

She looked at him, waiting for his agreement.

'Of course, if that's what you'd prefer.'

She gave him a smile and he followed her out of the door.

Outside, it was early afternoon, even hotter, and despite the cars heading back to Barnstaple, the beach was still heaving. Kids were running in and out of the water, splashing and screaming. Janey took off her shoes and made her way to the sea's edge, then walked away from the worst of the crowd towards the far end of the beach. He wasn't sure what to do. He was dressed for work, not for the shore. In the end he followed her, but stayed on the dry sand, just about close enough to speak to her without shouting.

'Friday night you were at a party with Wesley Curnow?'

'Yeah. Not exactly my idea of fun.' She pulled a face that made him smile.

'Why did you go then?' Ross wasn't sure where the question had come from. How could this be relevant to the investigation? But something about her intrigued him. He'd expected her to be confident, arrogant even. She'd been to a fancy university, was good-looking in a way that would catch attention wherever she went, and she had a mother who was a minor celebrity. Ross was always suspicious of people who were better educated than him. He sensed they were judging him. Janey didn't give that impression, though. There was something of the little girl about her: nervy but precocious. He thought she'd say the first thing that came into her head, no filter, no matter how that might seem to the listener.

She shrugged. She was wearing big sunglasses now and he couldn't really see her face, couldn't tell what she was thinking. 'I was bored. I thought anything would be better than staying in or working. And Wes is a mate. He asked. He didn't quite tell me what I was letting myself in for.'

'Did you see Nigel Yeo there?'

She turned her back to the sun. It was white and bright and she was almost a silhouette.

'Yes. He didn't stay very late.'

'Long enough for you to speak to him?'

'We had a quick chat. He and I were probably the only

sober people at the party.' She gave a little laugh. 'Middle-aged drinkers. What are they like?'

'I know!' They walked on for a moment, in almost companionable silence. 'How well did you know him, Dr Yeo?' Ross was trying to put himself into Matthew Venn's shoes, to ask the questions the boss might ask. He hadn't wanted to like Venn when he'd first arrived, but the way the new detective had dealt with the body at Crow Point, and all the drama of the aftermath, had earned a grudging admiration.

'Not well at all,' Janey said. 'He was a friend of my parents. At least, a kind of friend. He was trying to find out what happened to my brother, why he was allowed out of hospital to commit suicide.'

'What do you think happened to your brother?' Another Venn-like question.

It seemed to surprise her and she paused for a moment. 'I think he was ill and he killed himself. He had pretty shit treatment from the NHS, but I don't think anyone could have stopped him if he'd wanted to do it. He was really quite stubborn. I think my parents feel guilty because they couldn't love him. Not really. He was so fucked-up and so different from them. So, they're looking for someone else to blame.'

'Could *you* love him?' For a moment Ross was afraid she'd laugh at him. If anyone had asked him a question like that, *he'd* have been embarrassed and covered it up with laughter.

But Janey considered it seriously. 'Yes,' she said. 'I loved him. He was demanding and self-obsessed, and there was no protective wall between him and the universe, so he made everyone around him believe they had a duty to look after him. But he could be joyous and gentle, and he looked after me too. He was my little brother.' She seemed lost in thought.

'We came on holidays to North Devon, before we moved down for good and took over the business. Mum spent her first big repeat fees from TV on a little chalet in the dunes at Seal Bay. It was magical. Like something out of a kids' book. Mack and I ran wild, rock-pooling and surfing. Picnics and ice cream. Long walks on Seal Point. Mum was never really a hands-on parent, and most of the time she was learning lines for the next ep. Dad wasn't there much. He still had his permanent job in IT. So mostly it was just the two of us. Mack was a weird little scrap even then, but I don't remember any arguments or sibling rivalry. Nothing like that.'

'Seal Point was where he killed himself?'

'Yeah. I guess it was his happy place.' She looked at Ross. 'Somewhere he felt at peace.'

They walked on. Ross could feel sand in his shoes, gritty between his socks and his skin, but it didn't seem the time to take them off. What would that look like, when Janey was so at home on the beach?

'On Friday night, you gave Wesley a lift home, but not all the way?'

'I dropped him at the end of the lane leading towards the farm. He was pissed and I thought the walk would do him good. Besides, he didn't have anything to wake up for and I knew I'd be working on breakfasts.'

'This is your full-time job? Working in the cafe?'

'For the moment.' She walked out of the shallow water and joined him. 'I've got a degree. From Oxford. But there's not much call for students of Victorian fiction in contemporary Britain.'

Ross didn't know what to say to that.

'Wesley says a car passed him, going very fast, coming down the lane from Westacombe, but he was quite vague about it.

As you say, he was drunk, so he wasn't terribly convincing. No details. Something about that might come back to him, but it's not very helpful at the moment. You didn't see a speeding car going *up* towards the farm when you dropped him off?'

'Not then, but later there was some maniac driving through the village much too fast.'

'Can you describe the car?'

'Black. One of those MTBs.'

'MTB?'

She smiled. 'Much too big. For the lanes and the roads round here.'

He smiled too, though he wouldn't mind something solid when he could afford it. A Range Rover. Something of that kind.

'Did you catch the registration number?'

'No way. It just flashed past.'

'Is there anything else you can tell me about Dr Yeo? Any reason why someone might want him dead?'

She didn't answer immediately and he thought Janey might have something, some little bit of information to make sense of the killing. But as they walked back to the road, she shook her head again.

'No,' she said. 'Nigel was a lovely man. Everyone will tell you that.'

Chapter Twelve

ON SUNDAY MORNINGS, IF SHE WASN'T working, Jen usually stayed in bed until lunchtime. In the past, she'd tried to do the good mum thing and attempted a roast – meat, veg, Yorkshire puddings, the whole deal – but it hadn't seemed worth it since Ella had decided she was mostly veggie, and Ben made it clear he'd rather be talking to his friends online, playing some computer game. All that effort, she'd thought, for a meal nobody really wanted to eat! She'd given up, and now Sunday was her day for a lie-in.

Today, though, she was up before the kids, and on the phone to her friend Cynthia, who was always awake early. In a way, it seemed to Jen that Cynthia's party had been at the start of the whole investigation.

'You'll have heard about your mate Nigel. Can I come around for a chat? It's official.' *Though, as Matthew says, gossip has its place too.*

'Of course.'

Jen heard Cynthia take a breath, and knew she was about to fire off a load of questions, so she cut off the conversation quickly. She didn't want to get into details on the phone. 'Get the coffee on then. I'll be there in twenty minutes.'

Cynthia's husband opened the door. Sometimes Roger Prior joined them when Jen went to visit, but more often he hid himself away in his office. He was a tall, dignified man, unremarkable except for a head of very dark, almost black hair, which Jen was convinced must be dyed. It seemed a strange vanity for someone so reserved. Only now did it occur to Jen that, when it came to the investigation, Prior might be an even more useful contact than Cynthia. He worked as something vague but important for the local NHS trust, and, of course, she should have made the connection before.

'Cynthia's waiting for you in the garden,' he said. They were standing in an entrance hall bigger than Jen's living room, all pale wood and family photos. 'We're both rather shaken. The man who died in Westacombe was a neighbour of ours.'

'I'm on the team investigating his murder.'

'Oh,' he said. 'I suppose you can't discuss it then. I understand all about confidentiality.'

'Nigel must have been your colleague at one time. And he was still looking into a case which involves the trust. You might be able to help.'

'I don't think I can,' the man said. 'You'll need to contact the hospital about that.' He gave a tight, sad smile. 'I'm governed by confidentiality too, I'm afraid.' There was a moment of silence. 'Why don't you go on through? Cynthia's waiting for you.' He disappeared through a door. Jen had a brief glimpse of an office, a desk, a wall of bookshelves, then the door was firmly closed. She'd been to the house many times, but she'd never been inside that room.

In the garden, Cynthia was sitting on a white wooden chair,

her head tilted back, her eyes closed against the sun. She was wearing a long silk tunic in blues and purples over white linen trousers. Silver sandals and silver toenails. This week her hair was purple too.

Jen had never thought of herself as a jealous woman, but she envied Cynthia her garden. It could have come out of one of those magazines she read occasionally in the dentist's waiting room. Everywhere there was colour, and the lawn was as smooth as a carpet, without moss or weed. The beds a mix of exotic flowers and vivid shiny-leaved shrubs. Of course, the Priors could afford a gardener and Cynthia merely super-vised. A jug of coffee and two mugs stood on a white wrought-iron table. Cynthia heard Jen approaching and turned to face her. She looked as if she'd hardly slept. The purple circles under her eyes were real, not cosmetic to match the hair.

'I can't believe it,' she said. 'Wesley phoned me yesterday evening. He thought we should know.' There was an implied criticism. *Why didn't you tell me?*

'I'm part of the team investigating his murder,' Jen repeated the words. 'We were pretty tied up.' Sometimes Cynthia forgot that other people had kids and full-time jobs.

'Oh, I can understand. But it was just such a shock.'

'He was here on Friday night.' Jen poured coffee. 'The party didn't really seem his kind of thing.'

'It wasn't! He was only here to see you.'

'What do you mean? I'd never met him before.'

'He called in on Friday afternoon. He knew we were friends.' Cynthia looked up and for a moment she was herself again. 'It's quite something having a mate who's a detective sergeant. A bit of a talking point, a kind of vicarious celebrity. He asked if I'd be able to set up a meeting. Rather urgent, he said. I told him you'd be coming to the party, and he'd be welcome. I wasn't sure if he'd come along, but there he was.' A pause. 'I thought the two of you might get on. He lost his wife to early onset Alzheimer's, so he was on his own too.'

Jen ignored Cynthia's implied matchmaking. After the man's death, the idea seemed hugely inappropriate. Grotesque, as if Cynthia was suggesting she should hook up with a corpse.

'What time did he arrive here on Friday?' It might not be important but Venn would want to know.

'I'm not sure. Five-ish. Maybe a bit later.' Cynthia paused. 'He seemed a little out of sorts.'

'Did he say why he wanted to talk to me?'

Cynthia shook her head. 'No, it was all very mysterious, very secret squirrel.'

'How well did you know him?'

'Well enough to have had him round for dinner a few times. His wife, Helen, was my real friend. I got closer to Nigel when he cut back his hours to care for her. When he started at Patients Together, he could work a lot from home. I went sometimes to sit with her, to give him a break, and so he could work with Eve on the glass. He was taking some kind of course.'

'He and Roger must have been colleagues, though, when he was still working at the hospital. That must have been another point of connection.'

'Oh.' Now Cynthia seemed deliberately vague. 'I don't think so. Roger's just an admin person, really. Nigel was on the front line.'

'Until he took up his new investigative role with Patients Together. He must have come into contact with Roger then. Nigel had taken up the case of the Mackenzie boy, hadn't he?

He had some idea that negligence by the trust had led to his suicide.' A pause. 'That must have been difficult for Roger.'

There was a moment of silence. Jen had always thought that she and Cynthia were close friends. Very different in lifestyle, of course, and Cynth, with her monthly trip to the hairdresser and her exuberant, expensive clothes didn't seem to have a clue about the real world until she sat in the magistrates' court. Then she seemed to have an unusual understanding of the offenders who stood before her. Occasionally, Jen wondered if Cynthia's family had been dysfunctional too. Perhaps the woman's empathy came from her own experience.

'Honestly, Jen, I can't talk about Nigel's role in the Mackenzie case. I think there's an ongoing investigation within the hospital and you'll have to ask Roger about that.' Now the woman sounded uncomfortable.

'I just did. He ran away into his office without answering.'

Another silence. In the distance a neighbour was mowing a lawn. There was the scent of roses and cut grass. It was all very perfect. At this moment, Jen didn't quite believe in perfection.

She hoped she hadn't offended Cynthia, but she *had* warned her friend in advance that this conversation would be official. Jen thought her work would always come before personal considerations. Her husband had never quite realized that; it had been one of the many matters of contention. It was his view, often stated, that she should be a wife first. For a woman, work should come way down the list.

'Actually,' Cynthia said at last, 'Nigel was becoming a bit of a thorn in the authority's side. A bit overreaching. The brief of Patients Together was traditionally quite narrow, but he extended it.'

'In what way?'

'In the past it represented patients in a more general sense. They advised on policy, provided feedback on services. Nigel seemed willing to become involved in more personal disputes between patients and the health authority. Roger thought it was a little unprofessional. He felt it almost as a betrayal. He said that Nigel was acting like a sort of private detective, not a former employee of the NHS.'

'And it was the Alexander Mackenzie suicide that was causing the particular problem?'

Cynthia, usually so composed and confident, seemed to squirm a little in her seat. 'Nigel had taken an interest in other cases previously, but he appeared to have got a bee in his bonnet about the way George Mackenzie's son had been treated before he committed suicide.' She looked directly at Jen. 'You can see how awkward that was. For me, as well as for Roger. George is a friend. I've been going to the Sandpiper since he started doing music there. I sympathized. But Roger's my husband and he needed my support through it all too. The last thing he wanted was a press witch hunt about the trust's mental health provision. Nigel wasn't a psychiatrist and he should never have involved himself in something so close to home. There was a definite conflict of interest.'

'Is that why Nigel wanted to see me on Friday night? To discuss Alexander Mackenzie's death?'

'I don't know.' Cynthia gave a quick glance back at the house. *To make sure her husband isn't listening in?* 'To be honest, I didn't *want* to know.'

'I didn't speak to Nigel for very long.' Jen had never seen Cynthia quite so jumpy, not even when a guy out of his head on spice had threatened her with a knife when she was coming out of court. 'Did you talk to him before he left?'

'He came to say goodbye,' Cynthia said. 'Of course he did. He was a gent. He wouldn't have just wandered off.' She was speaking very quickly, like a kid rattling off an excuse to a teacher. Too much coffee? She'd already topped up her mug and she liked it black and very strong. Or was she hurrying to move the conversation on in a different direction?

'Did Nigel say where he was going when he left here? We found his car at Westacombe, so we presume that he drove himself there, either that night or early the next morning.' Jen tried to keep her voice even, but she was losing patience. And she was hurt because she'd thought they were friends. Proper friends. And here was Cynth treating her like some sort of moron who could be lied to.

There was no answer.

'Cynthia. Someone stuck a shard of glass, half a metre long, into his neck. We're not fucking about here. This isn't a couple of lasses shoplifting from Markses.'

'He said he was meeting someone. Polite as always. "Brilliant party, Cynthia, but I've got to go, I'm afraid." It seemed a bit weird. I mean, why would you arrange a meeting so late?'

Perhaps, Jen thought, *he'd realized I was in no fit state for an intelligent conversation, and he just made an excuse to leave.* 'So,' she said, 'he was expecting someone at his house?'

'That's what I thought he meant. He might have had guests coming to stay; he's close to Helen's parents. I suppose he could have been waiting for a phone call.' Cynthia looked up, part defiant, part pleading for Jen to believe her. 'You know what it was like here on Friday night. Music, background noise. I can't really be sure what he meant.'

'He didn't mention going to see his daughter? A trip out to Westacombe?'

'I don't think so. Honestly, Jen, you spoke to him as long as I did that night. There were lots of other guests and I wanted to make sure everyone had a good time.'

The lawnmower in the neighbour's equally perfect garden chugged on. A blackbird sang. But Jen thought Cynthia wasn't being straight. She was keeping a secret – or secrets – and things would never be the same between them again. Jen pushed herself out of the chair and stood up. Cynthia stayed where she was, eyes closed.

'Where was Roger on Friday night?' The question came out more loudly than Jen had expected.

The eyes opened. 'He stayed out for the evening, keeping out of the way. You know he has to be in the mood for a party.'

'But where was he?'

Cynthia stood up too, slowly and carefully, making a point, and they stood, staring at each other. 'What's this about, Jen? Do you think he needs an alibi? Should I be phoning for our lawyer?' Her accent was even more upper class than usual. *Don't mess with me, pleb!*

'I only asked, Cynth.' Now Jen just felt tired. She wished she could have had her usual lie-in and a proper breakfast. 'I just need to know where everyone who had any dealings with Nigel Yeo was that night. It's my work. Like it's Roger's work to protect the health authority.'

'He stayed in the office at the hospital,' Cynthia said, each word spoken a bit too clearly, a bit too slowly. 'He was working late. It's a stressful job, keeping the show on the road with too little money, too few nurses, too few doctors. He often works late.'

'What time did he get home?'

Cynthia shrugged. 'I haven't got a clue. I was out in the

garden with half a dozen guests who stayed on until about twelve. Wes was playing music. Janey joined in singing, until she got bored. It was all very chilled, all very ordinary. When I went to bed, Roger was already there. Fast asleep.' She turned to face Jen, and her words became hard, sarcastic. 'I suppose he would just have had time to drive to Westacombe and stick that piece of glass in Nigel's neck, if Nigel headed for the farm as soon as he left here. But I'd have thought there would have been blood. Roger's work suit was hanging in the wardrobe and his shirt was in the linen basket. I put it in the washing machine this morning. There were no stains. I can promise you that.' She gave a harsh little laugh. 'You do see how ridiculous this is?'

Jen didn't answer. She thought there was nothing faintly funny about the violent death of a good man.

Normally they would have hugged before they left each other and made some arrangement to meet up soon. Today Cynthia marched ahead of Jen, around the side of the house to the front gate, assuming that the detective would follow. It seemed Jen wasn't even to be allowed to take the shortcut through the house, through the kitchen with the shiny granite worktops and the hall with the pale-wood panels, past the firmly closed door where Roger was working. Or hiding. She was being treated like a tradesman, the gardener or the window cleaner. At the fancy wrought-iron gate, they paused for a moment. Awkward, both of them prickly. Two strong women facing off.

Ridiculous, Jen thought. She opened her arms. 'It's just my work,' she said. 'It gets in the way of friendship.'

Cynthia hesitated, and Jen thought she would come in for that hug, but in the end, she didn't move any closer. 'Let's hope this gets quickly sorted. Then maybe we can be friends again.' The magistrate turned and walked away, the long silk tunic floating behind her, leaving Jen standing, her arms still outstretched, waiting for the embrace.

Chapter Thirteen

On Sunday morning Matthew Venn woke early, as he always did. There remained the sense of unease that had nothing to do with the investigation. He'd always found work easier, certainly less complicated, than the personal baggage which weighed him down. This was his mother's birthday and she would soon be sitting at their long kitchen table eating Sunday lunch. He still couldn't quite believe her change of heart and wasn't sure if he'd be hurt or relieved if she called the meeting off at the last minute, making some excuse about a sick sister or brother. Not talking about a relative, but a member of the Brethren, the community into which he'd been born.

By the time he'd showered and dressed, Jonathan was up too. There was music playing and Jonathan was singing along, loud and tunefully, and starting to pull out the ingredients he needed for the grand birthday cake. A rib of beef had already been taken from the fridge and would cook slowly, Matthew was told, until it melted in the mouth. Jonathan loved entertaining, everything about it, the preparation and the cooking, and the sitting down with friends. Matthew still couldn't quite enjoy it, but he was starting to get there. Not with his mother, though; not with the crabby, anxious woman whose life was fixed with certainty, and who despised everything that her son had become.

They had coffee and toast together, with the music still playing. Outside, the sun was shining, but they took that for granted. They'd all come to expect it now, the clear skies and the heatwave.

'We could have lunch in the garden,' Jonathan said. 'I can set the table out there.'

'Oh God, no! She'd hate it.' As she'd hate anything adventurous and different.

'Okay, in here then, but I'll bring in flowers. Loads of flowers.' Jonathan set down his coffee cup. 'And give me a ring just as you're about to pick her up. I'll have everything ready.' A pause. 'You *will* be on time, won't you? This is more important than work, for today at least.'

Matthew nodded. Now all this was started, he had to see it through to the end.

It was a relief to be on the road and heading to Barnstaple. The traffic wasn't too heavy yet, and without needing the satnav he found the house where Helen Yeo had died and where Nigel Yeo had mourned her. It was a pleasantly proportioned house, substantial not grand. It backed onto the road out of the town, but was close to the shops and pubs of Newport, not far from Jen's little terrace, a part of the community, not separate from it. There was a high wall to keep the traffic noise from the garden and Matthew struggled at first to find a way in. The entrance was from a side street and led into a shadowy garden, an oasis away from the town, with the muffled rumble of cars and lorries in the distance. Eve had given him a key. The crime scene team had been through the house, but hadn't yet done a detailed search. They'd found no indication of violence there. It was clear that Yeo had been murdered where he was found.

Inside, it was cool. Matthew moved through the house to get a sense of the place before looking at it in any detail. This was a family home, but no longer lived in by a family. It was tidier than it would have been when Eve was a child; they already knew that Nigel had employed a cleaner, a woman who'd worked there for years, coming in on Thursday mornings for three hours, to clean the bathrooms and the kitchen, but there was none of the clutter that had probably been there when Nigel's wife was alive and when Eve was still at home. One mug, rinsed and ready to go in the dishwasher, on the draining board in the kitchen. A pair of slippers carefully placed together close to the entrance to the hall. A copy of Friday's *Guardian*, neatly folded on a coffee table in the living room, which looked out over the garden. There was a small television, the controls tidily arranged on the shelf beside it.

It seemed that when the illness had taken over Helen's mind and her body, Yeo had moved her downstairs, to a pleasant little living room with a view of trees. The bed was still there, with its mattress cover and three pillows piled at one end. The nightstand had a cassette recorder on a shelf and a pile of audio books and music. Perhaps he couldn't quite bring himself to clear the place.

Matthew wondered how he'd cope if Jonathan were suddenly ill, if he'd have Nigel Yeo's dedication and patience to look after his husband this well. He hoped that he would. Then he thought ill health would probably hit his mother first. When he asked himself the same question about caring for her, he had no reply.

He moved upstairs and into Yeo's study, which had been converted from the smallest bedroom. It faced the road and a row of smaller houses opposite. Matthew saw a gaggle of people going into the Baptist church on the other side of the road. He started opening drawers in the desk, not quite sure what he was looking for, and came across a large diary, with a page for every day. The diary contained both work and personal appointments. The writing was tidy, a little cramped. It seemed to Matthew that this was a man in control of his life.

He checked the entries for the week before Yeo's death. There were a number of appointments marked. One said *Team meeting*. Beside it, he'd drawn a face with a down-turned mouth. It seemed he hadn't been looking forward to that one. Others all seemed to be work-related: sessions with community groups and one with a social worker, a visit to a care home in a rural village.

On the Friday of Cynthia's party, it seemed he'd had two meetings in the hospital. The first seemed more significant. Three names were listed, but one jumped out. Roger Prior. Matthew knew Cynthia Prior through court and this must be the husband who worked for the health trust. Another connection.

Further down the page there was another entry: *Party (Jen Raff)*. This was another indication that he'd engineered an invitation to Cynthia's gathering just to meet the detective. What a shame, Matthew thought, that Jen hadn't spent more time with the man and listened to his concerns. But he knew Jen would already be thinking the same, would be haunted by guilt, and he didn't intend to make her feel worse.

On the same page, hardly legible and scribbled at the last minute, it seemed, in different ink, Yeo had written a number: 8531. Or 8537. Matthew wasn't quite sure. Some sort of reference or PIN? He put the diary in his briefcase and moved into the bedroom overlooking the garden, which Yeo must have once shared with his wife.

The room wasn't at all what Matthew had been expecting. It had none of the bachelor austerity of the downstairs rooms, and was quite different in tone. There was a faint smell of fresh paint, and one wall was vivid red. A huge black and white photograph of a lighthouse with cliffs beyond hung there. The style seemed more Eve's than Nigel's and Matthew wondered if this had been the daughter's attempt to cheer him up, to move him on from the period of grieving.

He then went into the attached bathroom. There were candles on a shelf near the bath. And on hooks on the door, two dressing gowns. Two electric toothbrushes over the sink. Perhaps Nigel Yeo hadn't been the grieving widower everyone had thought him to be.

Matthew looked at his watch. It was still only ten thirty. He checked the number Ross May had provided for Lauren Miller and punched it into his phone. A woman answered and when he introduced himself, she said:

'Of course. You want to talk about Nigel. I saw the news yesterday evening.' The voice was ageless, pleasant, educated. 'I live in Appledore.' She gave him the address and the post-code. 'I'll be waiting for you.'

★

105

When Venn was a boy, Appledore had been known as a rough place, a centre for drug-dealing and teenage violence. It had the shipyard, as close to an industrial enterprise as anything in this part of the county. His mother had discouraged any social contact with the boys who lived in the town. Now the shipyard had closed and Appledore, at the mouth of the Torridge, North Devon's second river, had transformed itself into an arty place of immaculately painted cottages along the narrow streets, artisan coffee shops and expensive restaurants. Former council houses on the edge of the town were now mostly in private ownership. There was an annual book festival and galleries exhibited local artists. Few locals could afford to buy properties here, and in the winter many of the houses – second homes and holiday lets – were empty. Matthew supposed it was an improvement, but on a sunny Sunday morning he knew it would be a nightmare to find somewhere to leave his car, and he felt some nostalgia for the past.

In the end, parking was no problem because Lauren lived a little out of the town, in a settlement of smart new houses. If she could afford to live here, with the landscaped gardens and the view over the Torridge to the estuary beyond, she hadn't started working at NDPT for the money.

The house was minimalist, almost bare. Matthew couldn't imagine children here. There was one enormous seascape on a white wall. Matthew found his gaze pulled into it; the wild sky and the space made him feel dizzy, vertiginous.

'Brilliant, isn't it?' Lauren was standing behind him. She was almost as tall as he was, elegant, silver-haired. Not elderly, but not feeling the need to dye her hair to prove that she was still stylish. Perhaps because of the name, he'd been expecting

somebody younger, and there'd been a moment of awkward-
ness when she'd opened the door to him. He hadn't been quite
sure that he'd found the right place. 'I got it from a student's
degree show, when I was living in London, but the artist is
Cornish. I think you can tell.'

'When did you move here?'

'Just over a year ago. I grew up in Bideford and was here
until I went to university.' She turned, gestured for him to take
a seat on one of the sofas. 'I came back because of my mother.
She's almost blind now. We live together. It's not that she can't
manage on her own, but after my father died she became more
isolated. She'd always been such a lively, companionable soul,
and I couldn't bear the thought of her being lonely. We sold
her cottage in the town and moved in together.' There was a
pause. 'But of course, I had selfish reasons for running home
too. A messy divorce. We'd never had children and my share
of the flat in Highgate easily bought me this place and gave
me enough to live on until retirement.'

'And yet you decided to go back to work?'

'Ah, that was to keep me sane.' Lauren smiled. 'And because
Nigel asked me to.'

'You were friends?'

She didn't respond at first. 'Rather more than friends, I
hope. In the last few months at least.'

'You were lovers?' Although he'd already suspected that there
was more to the relationship, Matthew felt himself blushing.
The puritan upbringing could come back to shock him when
he was least expecting it.

'Only recently. We'd been close friends for a while. Why are
you so surprised, Inspector? Is it our age that makes it so
unlikely?'

'Eve didn't mention a relationship,' Matthew said. 'I thought she would have done.'

'Eve didn't know. I've met her, but only a couple of times and then with other people. Nigel and I were very discreet and had decided to wait to go public. It would have been very tricky because of working together and Eve was so close to her mother. Besides . . .' – she gave another sad smile – '. . . there was something exciting about the secrecy. It made us feel young and foolish. Romantic. We wanted the chance to be selfish for a while. I hadn't even told my mother.' She looked directly at Matthew and he could tell how wretched she was.

'How did you meet Nigel?'

'It was at a dinner party at Frank Ley's place, Westacombe. I'd worked with Frank briefly in London and I liked him. Perhaps we had things in common, coming from the same part of the country, not quite fitting in with the brash young money men. I sent him an email when I moved back down and he invited me along. We all sat round the table in his grand dining room: Frank, Eve, Nigel and another guy who worked there.'

'Wesley Curnow?'

'Yes. That's right. I was sitting next to Nigel.' She paused. 'I remember everything about that night. It was a first step in moving on from my previous life. Nigel said that the woman at his work who looked after the accounts had taken early retirement. I volunteered to take over until they could employ someone.'

'And you're still there?'

'Yes, it keeps my brain active. The accountancy's basic, but it's a good cause and the financial situation was pretty chaotic before I took it on.' She smiled. 'The pay's hardly more than the living wage, but that's not why I'm there.'

There was a moment of silence before Matthew spoke. 'You seem very composed.'

'On the outside perhaps. I've been trying to hold things together in front of my mother. It's hard, grieving on my own. In one sense, I don't believe I have a right to grieve, certainly not publicly. To the rest of the world we had nothing special, and I'd hate to appropriate feelings that seem out of place, and which might offend his daughter. I'd be grateful if you'd respect my confidence about our relationship.' A beat. 'What *is* going on here, Inspector? I can think of no reason why anyone would want Nigel dead.'

'I'm hoping that you might be able to help with that,' Matthew said. 'You worked with Nigel and you were very close. Do you know what took him to Westacombe the night he died?'

She shook her head. 'I knew about the party. He'd invited himself to a gathering at Cynthia Prior's house, hoping to meet one of your officers.'

'Why did he need to speak to her?'

Lauren shook her head. 'I don't know. It was a last-minute thing and we didn't have a chance to discuss it. We'd talked about my staying at his house that night but he sent me a text to cancel. It was very apologetic. It said he was hoping to get informal professional advice about something he was working on.'

'The Mackenzie suicide?'

'I assumed so.'

'Was he working on anything else that might have needed input from a police officer?'

'Oh, I don't think so. Much of the stuff he worked on was pretty routine.' She looked up. 'He asked if I'd like to go to the party with him, but I couldn't quite face it. I wanted Eve and my mother to know before we went out in public as a couple.' She got to her feet and moved towards the window. 'If I'd been there, he would probably still be alive.'

She was still standing there when an elderly woman came in through a door at the far end of the room. She walked with a cane, but her back was straight and her white hair was as beautifully cut as her daughter's. 'I was thinking it was time for a pre-lunch sherry, darling, and I wondered if you'd like one.'

'We've got a visitor,' Lauren said. 'Inspector Venn. He's investigating Nigel Yeo's murder.'

'Good afternoon.' Matthew got to his feet. It seemed a politeness, even if the woman couldn't see him.

She turned in his direction. 'I don't suppose you'd join us for a sherry, Inspector?'

'I'm sorry,' he said. 'I'm afraid it's a busy time. And of course, I'm working.'

'Of course.' She hesitated for a moment, as if choosing her words carefully. 'I never met Dr Yeo, but my daughter's a fine judge of character and she says he was a good man. I have a sense that she's missing him more than she wants to acknowledge to me.' There was another hesitation. She moved towards Lauren and reached out with the hand that wasn't using the cane to touch her daughter's arm. A gesture of tenderness. 'My sight is very poor but there's nothing wrong with my hearing. A mother hates to hear her daughter weeping in the middle of the night. She's been so happy in the past couple of months and I was delighted for her. And now there's this. Please find Nigel's killer. I know that won't bring him back, but it'll give us a story. Something to help Lauren understand this terrible nightmare.'

'Of course,' Matthew said. 'We'll do all we can.' He wanted to promise a result, to provide some reassurance, but in the end, he thought there was nothing more he could say.

When he let himself out, the two women were still standing by the window at the far end of the room, their arms around each other.

Chapter Fourteen

WHEN JEN LEFT THE PRIOR HOUSE, she was tense, restless. The encounter with Cynthia had upset her and she found herself brooding about it as she walked into the town centre. It was still not quite eleven o'clock. The River Taw was low – the tide was out – and it smelled of mud and rotting vegetation. In the police station Vicki Robb, a uniformed PC attached to the team, was poring over CCTV, but Ross and Matthew weren't there.

Vicki looked up. 'I'm trying to find a record of Dr Yeo's car leaving the town on Friday night. There's a camera in Bickington and you'd think he'd have gone that way.'

'Nothing yet?'

'Nah, I'm stopping to grab a coffee. The quality's really poor and I'm going boggle-eyed.'

At her computer, Jen looked up everything she could find on Roger Prior. No criminal record, but she'd been expecting that. Some press coverage, though, and some brief mentions on social media, which she found interesting, and which she decided to follow up on. It seemed the Priors had moved to

North Devon not long before Jen. They'd been living in London before that and Roger had been director of mental health services of a large health trust in Camden. The move to a much smaller trust, even when he was taking on the new role as CEO of combined services, seemed hard to explain. Had Roger, so controlled and private, suffered from some stress-related crisis or burnout? Perhaps it was simpler than that. Perhaps Cynthia had had a romantic notion for a life away from the city and had persuaded him to move? She was a woman who liked to get her own way.

Jen pulled up past copies of a local north London newspaper for the time nine months before the Priors' move from the capital. Soon she was finding it as hard to keep focused as Vicki, who'd returned from her coffee break to stare at the CCTV footage. But Jen persisted. In the end the piece was easy to find: a front-page article with a photo. Roger looking dignified, standing outside a hospital at a press conference. The article reported the finding of a serious case review into the death of a young man. The headline read: *Review finds no individual to blame.*

Jen read on. A sixteen-year-old lad had hanged himself in his hospital room. Staff, only metres away, had been chatting by the nurses' station. The young man, whose name was Luke Wallace, had been suffering multiple mental health problems and had been brought into the hospital by the police. They'd been called out by the family after the boy had become violent at home, smashing furniture and threatening a younger sister. The family had earlier asked for community health support but nobody had turned up to help.

The same newspaper, six months later, reported Prior's resignation. Despite having been cleared by the serious case review, it seemed his position had become untenable. While the facts surrounding Luke Wallace's death were substantially different from the Alexander Mackenzie case, Jen could see why Roger had become jittery and had wanted to close down Nigel Yeo's investigation. The last thing he'd want would be another big press story about the death of a vulnerable young man.

Once Jen had tracked down the original story, it had been easy to find the social media gossip and chat around the case. There was a 'Love Luke' Facebook group, sharing memories of the boy. It seemed he'd been warm, friendly, until he'd hit early adolescence, when he'd become withdrawn and moody. The impression given was that his family was close. His father worked in a library and his mother was a social worker. His younger brother was bright and popular. The mother had posted a plea to other parents:

We'd thought he was a classic moody teen and that he'd grow out of it. We were complacent. We thought bad things didn't happen to people like us. He was ill and we were too busy with our own lives to notice. We allowed him to spend too much time on his own in his room. Too much time online. Don't be like us. Be aware of your children and what they're doing.

She'd taken all responsibility for her son's death. All the guilt. But Twitter had found a different target. The hashtag #LoveLuke accompanied tweets blaming the trust and Roger Prior in particular.

Don't let this man wreck more young lives.

Jen could understand why he'd resigned and made the move to Barnstaple.

Jen sat back in her chair and considered the implications. Her first thought was personal: she'd considered Cynthia her best friend, yet the woman had never discussed the background to the Priors' move from London. It seemed that Prior had been horribly harassed by social media, even though he'd been cleared of all blame by the official review. Jen felt real sympathy for the couple. No wonder Cynthia had been so prickly and tense.

But this must be relevant to their investigation and she had to work out the best way to move forward. Jen didn't want to talk to Luke's mother without checking with Venn first, and Venn had said he shouldn't be disturbed unless it was urgent. She was too close to the Priors to challenge them about this now. That would be down to somebody else.

Jen's thoughts returned to Cynthia, so loud and proud, with her size and her coloured clothes, and considered what an effort it must have taken her friend to put on such a show each day. Because the move from London to Barnstaple felt close to disgrace. Perhaps over the years it had become easier. Perhaps the couple were beginning to forget the reason for their move to the south-west. Then Alexander Mackenzie had killed himself and it would have seemed that the past had come back to haunt them. They'd escaped the Luke Wallace story by moving, but surely it wouldn't have remained hidden if Nigel Yeo had had his way.

There was a real temptation to go back to Cynthia's grand house, not as a police officer but as a friend. To say she understood. To share a bottle of wine and let Cynthia pour out her worries. But she was a cop, so in the end she stayed where she was, and she pulled together all the facts she'd gleaned into a report, to pass on to Matthew Venn when he returned to the office.

She was still staring at the computer screen, checking what she'd written, when she heard Vicki Robb give a whoop from her end of the room. It was a relief to get up, to stretch her back and her legs, and to walk to where Vicki was sitting.

'What have you got?' Jen kept her voice as upbeat as she could.

'His car. At last. Not from the street camera in Bickington, but from the petrol station just outside Instow. It's a late-night one. Closes at midnight. He was there at eleven thirty.' Vicki was jubilant. She'd almost given up on finding anything.

'Wouldn't he have turned off for Westacombe before hitting Instow?'

'Maybe he was just low on fuel and wanted to stock up before heading out into the wilderness.'

'Yeah, that was probably it. At least it gives us some sort of time frame.' But Jen made a note in her briefing report. It was just another detail to pass on to Matthew Venn. She was think-ing she might go home, check up on the kids. She thought of Ben, a moody teenager, who spent too long in his room in front of a computer screen.

Ross May came in then, and he wanted to tell her about his talk with Janey Mackenzie. That was classic Ross. Impatient, wanting to spill out everything he knew, like a kid coming home after the end of a school day, full of what had happened in class, forcing his parents to hear every detail. She sat down again and thought she'd give him ten minutes. No longer. That was when the phone rang.

Chapter Fifteen

On Sunday morning Eve woke early after a restless night of odd, unremembered dreams. She'd surface from sleep at intervals, her heart racing, her limbs rigid, only to drift back into the nightmare. At seven, she got up, stood by the window and looked out at the farmyard and the hills beyond. There were the sounds of birdsong and distant sheep. The background noises to her life since she'd moved here. She picked up her phone and saw a list of missed calls and new emails: friends asking after her, offering hospitality, condolence, wanting a chance to be a part of the drama. She felt swamped by the attention. What she really needed was a day in the studio, to lose herself in the rhythm of glass-making. The constant movement of twisting the pipe, the concentration needed in heating, melting and blowing would fill her mind and let her escape, at least for a while. She had the sense that today she might create something fine: a pleasing shape, an eruption of colour. Something entirely unique. But the studio was still a crime scene with a police officer standing outside it, looking bored. She made coffee and thought she should take a mug down to him. In the end, though, a kind of lethargy took over, and even walking down the stairs and through the big, cool kitchen seemed far too much effort.

She looked at her phone again and scanned through the messages. There was one from a woman called Lauren Miller, a colleague of her father's, asking if they might meet. *No way!* That was the last thing she needed: someone else wanting a part in the drama of her father's death. Eve poured more coffee and returned to her seat by the window. John Grieve was releasing the cows from the parlour. She watched him walking them back down the lane to their field by the common.

Sometime later, Sarah Grieve came out of the cottage. She was wearing green overalls, so she looked like a gooseberry, round and plump, juicy. From this angle, her head seemed very small, like a gooseberry's stalk. Sarah looked up at her, waved and made a gesture to suggest that Eve was being invited into the cottage for a drink or something to eat. Eve shook her head. She knew then that she had to get away from Westacombe for the day. What could be worse than sitting in the flat while the police officers and crime scene investigators in their nightmare white suits and masks pulled apart her studio and her father's life?

She switched on her phone and sent a text to Sarah. **Need to get out for a while. Sure you understand. Don't worry. If anyone asks, I'll be back at teatime.** She was pleased with *teatime*. It was flexible and could mean anything from late afternoon to well into the evening. Sarah's husband John called dinner tea. She switched the phone off again. She was tempted to leave it in the flat, but at the last minute she picked it up. How dependent everyone had become on these devices! Even in the midst of this crisis, she couldn't imagine leaving home without it.

Her car was in the yard and a different police officer on the gate stopped her as she pulled out. This was a woman with a round baby face and short blonde hair.

'Hi, I'm Sharon. Just here to keep an eye out for you all.' A pause. 'Have you let DI Venn know where you're off to?' Her voice was kind enough, but the question rankled.

'I don't think I'm under house arrest.' The comment shocked Eve – it was as if someone else had spoken – and she felt her hands gripping tighter on the steering wheel. She wondered if she should have taken up Jonathan's invitation and moved in with him for a while. But that would have meant living with the detective who was investigating her father's death and how weird would that feel?

'Course not. He'll just want to make sure you're okay. He's a bit of a mother hen, our Inspector Venn.'

And you're talking to me as if I were an eight-year-old. But the words remained unsaid. Eve had never been good at confrontation and today she was too exhausted to make a fuss. 'Sorry if I was rude. I just need to be away. You'll appreciate that. And I've got my phone with me if anyone needs to get in touch.'

'Of course, my love. Just take it easy, okay?' The officer gave her a little wave and sent her on her way.

Eve drove. The car, a Mini, felt like a place of safety. Her parents had given it to her when she'd graduated. Her dad had offered to replace it with something a bit newer a year ago, but she'd said she'd keep it, maybe wait to replace it until the electric model came out. Do what she could to save the planet.

She had no direction in mind. When she hit the main road near Instow, she headed towards Bideford, the town on the River Torridge, and then out towards the coast. She parked up at Northam Burrows, put a random amount of cash into the pay and display machine and walked along the top of the pebble bank, which separated the estuary from the golf course. The sun was behind her as she looked across the two rivers to Crow Point. It was still too early for the horde of tourists to descend on the beach, but there were dog-walkers, and families hoping to find a good spot before the crowds arrived. Then she picked up the car and went inland, down narrow lanes with tall overgrown hedges and grass growing in the middle of the road, not caring that she was lost. Being lost was good, the equivalent of escaping into making glass. It stopped her from thinking.

Eventually, she felt hungry, came to a junction and followed the sign to South Molton. She got the last parking space close to the cattle market and felt ridiculously pleased with herself. The town was Sunday relaxed. It was early afternoon, the pubs and cafes busy with people taking a late lunch. She found a table in a coffee shop with low beams and ordered tea and sandwiches, revelled in the anonymity, the fact that nobody was asking how she was, that there were ordinary conversations going on all around her. There was a moment of stabbing guilt then, like the shard of glass in her father's neck. How could she feel this content when he had so recently died? She began to cry, pretended to the waitress who brought the bill that she was suffering from hay fever, and went out into the street.

She drove on, up towards Exmoor, in search of a breeze, and only stopped when she came to a place close to a river, shaded by trees. There was a fisherman on the opposite bank, but he took no notice of her. That was when she switched on her phone. Habit. The curse of her generation needing always to be in touch with the world.

There were texts from the same friends who'd been in contact the night before. She ignored them. Today she had the right not to care about them. Grief gave her that freedom, the permission to do as she pleased for one day at least. Then a text from Wesley, which seemed strangely formal, quite unlike him. She was never entirely sure what she made of Wes. Sometimes he seemed like an eccentric older brother, wild and unreliable, but keeping a lookout for her all the same. Sometimes he just irritated her, with his lack of responsibility and focus. How could he still live like this? He must be at least forty. Forty-five even. He would make a fine musician or a good artist, if only he worked a bit harder at either craft.

The message said: **I'd like to talk to you if you're free. It's urgent. I'll be in my shed at the Woodyard. Four thirty.**

It was three thirty. Plenty of time to make it into Barnstaple, if she decided to go. Wesley had his studio in Westacombe, but his work was made with found objects, mostly material scavenged from skips, pallets and large pieces of driftwood. He made furniture from them as well as art: twisty garden benches, coat racks, coffee tables fashioned from discarded bedroom doors. There was no room to store all his scavenging in his studio, which was the same size as hers, so he'd conned a space at the Woodyard. A large unused shed at the back of the building. The deal was that he was supposed to give the occasional workshop in lieu of rent, but that seemed to have been forgotten after the first couple of sessions.

If it had been one of Wesley's usual texts, all misspellings and random emojis, she might have deleted it with all the others. But here, he seemed so serious and the meeting sounded important to him. Besides, she'd driven aimlessly for long enough. The Woodyard was somewhere to aim for and it would put off the moment when she had to go home. Maybe she'd be able to meet up with Jonathan too. She'd always thought of him as a much older brother or a kind younger uncle. But now, she seemed to be clinging to the thought of him as if he were a substitute dad. She sent a text back to Wesley: **Okay.**

Chapter Sixteen

MATTHEW LEFT LAUREN MILLER'S HOUSE IN Appledore and drove back to Barnstaple. Dorothy Venn was waiting for him at her home. Matthew could see her peering through the window of the bungalow where he'd grown up as a child. It had always felt like an old person's house, even when his parents had been in early middle age. It was as if his mother, at least, had always been anxious, always planning for some disaster, which had never occurred until her son, her only beloved child, had renounced his faith publicly at a meeting of the Brethren and brought shame upon her whole family.

It had been a murder which had brought them together again, a body on a beach and the kidnapping of a woman with a learning disability. Matthew supposed he should be grateful for the resulting awkward reconciliation, but sometimes he thought life had been easier when there'd been no contact. Contact brought responsibility and he could see now in the gaunt, sharp face looking out at him that his mother was getting old. He was the only son and the only person who would care for her.

There was no sign of weakness, however, when she opened the door. 'I thought you were going to be late.'

He was five minutes earlier than they'd arranged but he said nothing. He opened the car door for her and helped her in. 'Happy birthday!'

'It's only another day. Nothing to make a fuss about.'

'Have you been to the meeting?' He meant the meeting of the Barum Brethren, held in a dusty community hall on the edge of the town. He remembered the smell of rising damp, disinfectant and elderly women.

'Of course! Brother Anthony gave me a lift and brought me home.'

Of course. The Brethren might have been riven by scandal and corruption, but she'd chosen to maintain her loyalty. Matthew could understand that. It had been hard enough for him to break away as a young man and the community was all that his mother had known. Like him, she'd been born into it.

They drove the rest of the way in silence. She sat with her handbag on her lap, her knees firmly together. She was still in the clothes she would have worn to the meeting: a green skirt and a long-sleeved white blouse. Despite the heat, she had on a green, hand-knitted cardigan. She had removed the hat, something woollen and mushroom-shaped, which seemed to be required dress code at Brethren worship.

She spoke first. 'Where exactly do you live?'

'In the house close to the shore at Crow Point. Do you remember, we had picnics on the beach there sometimes?'

She nodded and for the first time gave a little smile. 'Your father loved a picnic.' A pause. 'I could never see the point. Sand gets everywhere. But he loved the open air.'

'You must miss him a lot.'

For a while, Matthew thought he'd overstepped some virtual mark, become too personal, but at last she answered. 'I do. All the time. If it weren't for the brothers and sisters, I think the loneliness would kill me.'

The comment took his breath away and a wave of guilt swept over him. He'd thought his mother had stuck with the Brethren out of stubbornness, or because her faith had remained despite the drama surrounding it earlier in the year. But of course, these people were her friends. They'd been there for her when her husband died and when Matthew had stayed away.

They came to the traffic lights in the centre of Braunton. There was already a queue of cars leading to the coast and the lights changed twice before they could get through. A group of bronzed, scantily dressed young women crossed the road in front of them and he sensed his mother's disapproval, but she didn't speak. They crawled along the road until the turn-off by the Great Marsh. This was a place for locals; most holidaymakers didn't realize that it was a way to the beach, to the other end of the long sweep of Saunton Sands. Matthew threw change into the basket at the toll keeper's cottage, the gate lifted and he drove through. He pulled into their drive and switched off the engine.

'This would be a bleak sort of place in a gale,' his mother said. He opened the car door for her and offered her a hand to get out. She stood for a moment looking around her. 'You've made a lovely garden, though.'

'That's Jonathan's work,' Matthew said. 'He's the practical, creative one.'

Again, she took a while to answer. 'I don't know about that. You were always creative when you were a boy.'

Matthew smiled. The words felt like a vindication. Of himself as a boy and of the relationship with his husband. Perhaps, after all, this would work out. 'Come on in. You'll see he's a brilliant cook too.'

She sniffed. 'No need to have gone to any trouble.'

Jonathan had heard the car and was at the door to meet them, arms wide in greeting. 'Come in! And happy birthday, Mrs Venn!' He gave Matthew a light kiss on the cheek.

His mother pretended not to notice and was looking round the kitchen. 'This is very fancy.'

'We love it,' Jonathan said.

The table was laid and there were two vases filled with deep red roses from the garden. The window was wide open and the curtains stirred in the breeze. It was as close to eating outside as Jonathan could make it.

Jonathan took off his apron and hung it on the back of the cupboard door. He was wearing black shorts and a black T-shirt with the name of a craft brewery on the front. Dorothy wouldn't recognize the name. On his feet he wore flip-flops. His toes were wide and flat. Matthew called them hobbits' feet. A silliness and intimacy he'd allowed himself with no other person. His mother stared at Jonathan for a moment, as curious as if he were a being from another planet.

'Are you ready to eat?' Jonathan asked. 'Or would you like a tour of the house first?'

'Why don't we have lunch now?' Matthew couldn't bear the idea of showing his mother around the house: another bedroom with two dressing gowns and another bathroom with two toothbrushes. And Jonathan wasn't the tidiest person. Who knew what might be left out? Matthew wanted to check first. 'I might be called back to work. We're in the middle of a murder investigation.'

'That makes sense.' Jonathan rolled his eyes at the mention of work, but only Matthew could see. 'And of course, I have champagne!'

Dorothy still hadn't spoken. The room with its flowers, the copper pans hanging from a rack on the ceiling and the art on the wall – mostly posters for exhibitions Jonathan had held at the Woodyard – seemed to overwhelm her with its space and its colour. She appeared almost breathless.

Jonathan went to the fridge and pulled out a bottle. Only the supermarket brand, but real champagne all the same. 'Let's have this with the starter.'

Matthew expected his mother to refuse. Alcohol wasn't forbidden by the Brethren and his father had enjoyed a whisky most evenings after work, but Dorothy never participated. More, Matthew suspected, because she enjoyed the martyrdom of denying herself pleasure than through religious conviction. Now she stood in the middle of the room, gripping her handbag, looking around her, and he saw that she was nervous. He'd never known his mother be anything other than confident in her certainty.

'There's orange juice if you prefer,' Jonathan said very gently. She might have been one of his clients at the Woodyard day centre. 'It's your day. Whatever makes you happy. Why don't you sit here with your back to the window, then you're not squinting into the sun?' He took her arm and led her to the head of the table.

Matthew watched, moved, as she took her seat. She smiled. At Jonathan, not at him. 'I might try a glass of champagne,' she said. 'I had some at a wedding for the toasts and I did quite enjoy it.'

Jonathan turned, winked at Matthew and opened the bottle.

The phone call came late in the afternoon. Dorothy had complimented Jonathan on the tenderness of the beef, the way the Yorkshire puddings had risen. 'I was never very good at batter. Not for Yorkshire puddings or pancakes.' The cake, with its candles and elaborate decoration, had been a huge success. After a lifetime of healthy eating, it seemed to Matthew that his mother actually had a very sweet tooth and she had been persuaded to have a second slice. He and Jonathan had sung happy birthday, Jonathan taking the lead. The whole afternoon had a strange surreal tinge to it. It was hard for Matthew to believe that this woman, who had haunted his life and had been the subject of earnest discussions with his therapist, had become elderly, lonely and powerless. Someone who was willing to compromise in return for kindness and company.

By now she was rather pink and had removed the cardigan. Her handbag had been put under her chair. She looked younger, more relaxed than Matthew could remember. Jonathan had been collecting plates. There were two empty coffee cups on the table. Dorothy had asked for tea and Jonathan had made it for her in a small pot. She'd liked that; she still disapproved of teabags. Matthew had switched off his phone, but he could hear it vibrating in his pocket.

He looked at it. 'Sorry. I really have to take this.' He walked out into the garden and heard gulls, the tug of the tide on the shore.

'Boss.' It was Jen Rafferty, calling on his mobile. 'I'm sorry to disturb you. I know you were busy today.'

'What is it?'

'I think you need to come in. There's just been a 999 call. The report of another body.'

Chapter Seventeen

EVE HAD TAKEN HER TIME DRIVING back to Barnstaple. When she arrived at the huge, converted sawmill on the River Taw, which had become the Woodyard arts centre, the place was almost empty. The day centre for adults with learning disabilities was closed at the weekend and there were no classes on a Sunday. No Pilates or community choir. No middle-aged women learning to paint with watercolours. The cafe opened to serve Sunday lunches, but soon that would be closing too. In the quiet of a hot late afternoon, she imagined the timber yard as it had once been, the workers and the machinery, overpowering with its noise. Today, the silence sang out.

There was a marked car park at the front for the centre's visitors, but she made her way through the big open wooden gates to the back, to the rough concrete yard where the staff left their vehicles. This was close to where Wesley stored his found and scavenged material.

Wesley's shed was as large as a good-sized barn, built from wood, but solid. He'd once held a party there, after hours, and Jonathan had gone ape. Someone must have told him it was happening, and the centre manager had turned up, genuinely furious, yelling about Wesley taking the piss. 'We're not insured for this kind of thing. Someone gets hurt or you start a fire and we're fucked. Not just me, but my day centre clients and the women who sing in the choir and the artists who are supposed to be your mates. Just fucking grow up, Wesley!'

Yet, Wesley was still here, still using the place. Eve thought he slid through life on charm and the goodwill of others. He was amiable, good to be around. He lightened the mood wherever he went, so they all put up with him.

The shed had double doors, wide enough to let a forklift in. Wesley usually left them open if he was inside, but today they were closed. Not locked, though. The padlock had been left on the hook. She slid the doors open. The windows were small and high in the walls, too dusty, smeared with decades of grime and countless spiders' webs, to let in much light.

'Wes!' It would be typical of him to summon her here and then to be late. But he must be here, otherwise the doors would still be padlocked and, besides, she'd noticed his white van, parked in a corner away from the sun. She walked further into the space and her eyes got used to the gloom. One of the windows had a clear patch in the middle and the sun shone through like a spotlight. There was a pile of pallets, roughly stacked at one end. Wes used them a lot in his art. He painted on them, produced shop signs and quirky notices to go into restaurants and bars, frames for menu blackboards. Presents for friends. He'd made a painting for her of a vase that had been selected for an exhibition at the V&A, with the date. It hung now in her flat. Perhaps, after all, it was those moments of kindness that forced them to tolerate the fact that he used them. This was more than a storeroom. He made his larger furniture here and there was a workbench in the centre of the space.

She could see the man now, and moved slowly towards him, frightened already of what she might find. Because Wes wasn't a quiet man. He'd have responded to her shout, jumped to his feet, called out a greeting in return. Put his arms around her. And she was scared because she still had an image of her father, lying on her studio floor in a pool of blood.

There was blood here too, and a shard of glass, *her* glass, not green this time, but blue, was sticking in his neck. A blue vase had been shattered here – she remembered making it and giving it to Frank Ley as a present – and there were pieces of glass scattered across the bench, reflecting the single beam of the sun. Blood had spattered across the bench and as far as the nearest wall. She pulled her gaze back to the pieces of glass, which looked almost decorative in the shaft of sunlight, and wondered how they had got here – anything rather than to look at Wesley, who was still and white, stark against the red pool of blood, already dried and dark in the heat – and was deciding she should phone 999 when there was a sound outside. The screaming of sirens and the thumping of boots, loud and rhythmic as soldiers' drums, on the uneven concrete, and half a dozen police officers ran in through the doors, yelling for her to get on her knees and put her hands on her head.

Chapter Eighteen

WHEN MATTHEW VENN ARRIVED AT the scene, Jen Rafferty was already there. He'd left Jonathan to get his mother home in a taxi.

'You can't drive,' Matthew had said. 'You'll be over the limit.' Always the cop, but then Jonathan *had* finished most of the bottle of fizz.

Jonathan had nodded, was already calling the local minicab when Matthew left. 'After we've dropped her off, I'll come on to the Woodyard. I'll see you there.'

Matthew's mother had been confused by the change in mood, the sudden rush to action. There'd never been much drama in her life. Not that she'd been aware of, at least, until the kidnapping of her friend's learning-disabled daughter, and she'd seen little of that investigation. Before that, even his father's death had been expected and managed, a slipping away, not a sudden event. But when Matthew had hurried away, she'd created no fuss; there was no recrimination that the birthday celebration was being cut short. In old age, she was making fewer demands. Loneliness had changed her.

Matthew was confused too. He'd received garbled stories about the 999 call and the discovery of the body. Initially, it seemed that the first officers at the scene had assumed they had their perpetrator. A woman crouched over the body, a piece of glass in her hand. Blood on her clothes. But the glass in the woman's hand hadn't been the murder weapon. That was still in the victim's neck. And this was Eve Yeo, who had just lost her father. Matthew couldn't see her as a serial killer. The idea was ludicrous.

When he arrived at the Woodyard, Jen got out of the car to talk to him. Matthew thought she looked drained and white. This had hit her personally. He wondered if she'd had a closer relationship with the victim than she'd let on.

'No way could it have been Eve,' Jen said. 'The caretaker saw her drive in at four twenty. The 999 call was made ten minutes before that. Curnow had been dead for a while before she got here.'

Matthew saw now that Eve was sitting in the passenger seat of Jen's car. She was frozen, her face too drained of colour. Was this another woman who'd been taken in by Curnow's charm? He considered the logic behind Jen's statement. 'I suppose she could have made the call before coming to kill him, but I agree that it's unlikely.' He paused. 'Was the call made by a man or a woman?'

'You can hear the recording. Hard to tell apparently. The voice is muffled, disguised. We'll need to get it analysed.'

Matthew nodded towards the car. The glass maker was as still as stone, staring ahead of her. 'What did you get from Eve?'

'Not much. She's still in shock. I'll take her home and we can chat again there. I asked if she'd prefer to go back to her dad's house now the CSIs have finished there, but she said she'd rather be at the farm. The house in Barnstaple has too many memories. That's about her mother, I guess.'

Matthew nodded. He looked at the group of uniformed officers standing close to the main building of the Woodyard. Ross May was with them. 'I suppose our eager young DC led the charge.'

'Yeah,' Jen said. 'You can't blame him, though. I was in the office when we got the shout from emergency services. You get a call, apparently from a witness, saying that someone related to the Westacombe murder has been attacked, you don't hang about. The guy could still be alive, the attacker could still be at the scene.'

Matthew didn't respond immediately. *You could hang about long enough to consult the officer in charge of the case.* But then Matthew had said he shouldn't be disturbed unless it was urgent. His team. His responsibility. 'Did he talk to you before gathering the troops and setting out?'

Jen gave a quick grin. 'Yes, but he took charge on the ground. I stayed behind for a moment to call for back-up and to phone you.'

Matthew nodded to show that she, at least, had got it right. 'Did Eve tell you how she came to be here?'

'She got a text. Apparently from Wesley asking her to meet him here. But his phone's not on his body.'

'So, someone set her up. The killer sent her the message using Wesley's phone?'

'Looks like it.'

Matthew was suddenly furious. These changes of mood hit him sometimes, scaring him with their ferocity. Not a red mist, but a clear flash of white light, a lack of control, a rush of energy and aggression. Calling Eve to the murder scene seemed wilful, almost playful. The killer must have known that the police would check the voice on the 999 call and the timing of the text. This wasn't setting the woman up as a realistic suspect. It was cruel. A child pulling the wings off a living fly. Matthew took time to breathe slowly, counting the seconds, trying to release the tension in his body. 'Did the caretaker see anyone else in the yard this afternoon?'

Jen shook her head. 'No. He had the afternoon off and only came back to check the place was empty before locking the main gates into the centre car park. This yard is always left open in case staff want to use the place after hours.' A pause. 'There'll be CCTV, though.'

'Maybe.' Matthew wasn't so sure. Jonathan was running the place on a shoestring. He'd maintain the security in the main building and the areas surrounding the day centre, but perhaps not here. He was about to pull on his scene suit, then thought he should give Eve some reassurance, and the last thing she'd need was some anonymous figure in a hood and mask. The suits made his kindest officers look sinister. He opened the car door and sat beside her, perched sideways, his feet still on the cracked concrete, not wanting to crowd her. 'I'm so sorry,' he said, 'that you had to go through this again. I can't imagine what it must be like.'

Eve turned to face him. 'It doesn't hurt yet. It's unreal. As if I've wandered onto a film set.'

'Of course. One shock too many. We'll need to hang on to your car, just for the moment, but we'll get it back to you as soon as we can. It's just routine. Nothing to worry about.'

'The blue glass vase, the one that was in there.' Eve made a vague gesture with her hand, but couldn't look at the shed.

'It was one of mine. I gave it to Frank Ley as a birthday present. He'd filled it with flowers on the evening we spent with him, the night before I found my father in the studio.'

'Are you sure?'

'Oh yes!' She sounded offended. 'They're all slightly different, my pieces. Individual. I can recognize each one.'

Brian Branscombe, the crime scene manager, walked Matthew round the locus. He was middle-aged, diffident, unwilling to commit himself without reason, meticulous. He had a reputation for being slow, but Matthew would rather have slow than impulsive. They stood for a moment at the wide sliding door into the shed and looked in. The pathologist hadn't yet arrived and Wesley's body still lay in the middle of the space next to the workbench. Shattered blue glass glinted in the shaft of sunlight. The room could have been a piece of installation art.

'So, we assume he was killed here?'

'Oh, I think so.' Branscombe was local. The accent somehow comforting. 'All that blood.'

'It looks staged somehow. More staged than the Westacombe stabbing.'

'Maybe they had more time.' Branscombe stepped through the doors and stood next to the wall. A CSI was moving through the space, a fingerprint powder brush in his hand. Matthew assumed it was a man, but it was hard to tell. More would turn up soon, but this was a Sunday, the county was big and the team was small.

'I don't think I've heard back from you.' Matthew thought he should be used to wearing the mask by now, but it felt uncomfortable and the scene suit seemed to trap the heat and made him feel unbearably hot. 'Did you get any workable fingerprints from the green glass, the piece used to kill Yeo?'

'Only a smudge, which came from the daughter.' Branscombe moved closer to the body. 'And you'd expect that. She made the thing.' He sounded distracted. All his attention now was on *this* locus. 'I think our victim was standing here at the bench. Look, he's wearing headphones, so he was probably listening to music. He might not have heard the killer approaching. Not until it was too late at least.'

'But he'd have heard if the perpetrator smashed the vase on the bench, and seen what was happening too.' Matthew was trying to picture the scene. Wesley had been focused on his work. There was a plank of timber, which could have been part of an old roof joist, lying across the bench and held by a vice. A handsaw lying on the floor looked as if it had fallen out of his hand when he was killed. In headphones he might not have heard the attacker approaching, but the shattered vase was in his line of sight.

'The vase could have been prepared in advance,' Branscombe said. 'Smashed elsewhere and brought in in pieces. One used for the stabbing and the rest left here for effect.'

And to point us back to Westacombe.

'Wesley would have been listening to music on his phone' – now Matthew was talking to himself – 'and we haven't found that.'

'There's a chance of DNA. In this weather our killer could have been sweating. Even if he was wearing gloves, droplets might have fallen from his forehead onto the surface or the glass.'

'If it's there, I know that you'll find it.' This wasn't flattery. There was no need for Branscombe to answer. He knew how good he was at this.

Matthew went on, putting his first thoughts into words. 'I have a sense of someone overconfident, willing to take risks. The general public don't come to this part of the Woodyard, but he could have been disturbed at any time. The killer might not have been so cautious or careful this time.'

'Let's hope.'

'If your theory works,' Matthew said, 'and the killer came up behind Wesley and surprised him, we're looking for someone who's right-handed, aren't we?'

'Yeah.' Branscombe was definite now. 'They must have been.'

'Thanks. I'll leave you to it. You'll give me a shout if there's anything important?'

Branscombe remained silent as if the answer was too obvious to be worth speaking.

Outside, there was a slight movement of air, but still it was hotter than they were used to. Matthew stripped off the scene suit. A taxi pulled up in the road outside and Jonathan was there, dressed as he had been at the lunch, in shorts and T-shirt, flip-flops on his feet. For a moment, Matthew wondered what that must be like: to dress for comfort, to be so loose and easy. But he felt more comfortable in a shirt and tie, real shoes, highly polished. His clothes gave him confidence, support. He went over to Jonathan, partly to stop him wandering into the area, which still hadn't been completely taped, partly because his husband's presence was always calming, a reassurance that in the end all would be well.

'I got your mother home okay.'

'Thanks.' He paused for a beat. 'And thanks for looking after her so well, for making her feel special.'

Jonathan shrugged. 'It's easy, isn't it, when you're not too close. You're better around my parents than I am.' He nodded towards the activity, the officers in their white zombie suits. 'Who is it?'

'Wesley Curnow.' Matthew waited for a reaction, but there was none. 'Of course, you'll have known him, if he rented the shed from you.'

'We never saw much in the way of rent!'

Matthew was surprised by the coldness of the response. This was Jonathan, who had sympathy for losers, drifters and dropouts of every kind. 'You didn't like him?'

'Perhaps I liked him too much and that was the problem. I should have turfed him out ages ago.' Jonathan paused. 'I knew he was taking the piss. He used people, but somehow, they didn't mind. He was like a spoiled kid, desperate to be loved. Charming, but in the end entirely selfish.'

Matthew didn't say anything. He knew his husband well enough to realize there was more to come.

'An example. Wes would wander into the day centre some-times if he'd been working here at the Woodyard, and he'd chat to our learning-disabled chaps there. He'd sit and listen to them and make them laugh, appear to be giving them all his attention. I thought it was kind. Then I saw he only came in the afternoon, and on the days when they were baking. He came for the tea and cake. It was that simple.'

'Maybe he came for both.' Matthew wondered how such a small act of selfishness could have got under his usually tolerant husband's skin. Had Wesley provoked such a response in everyone who'd known him?

'Yeah, perhaps I'm just being cynical.'

Matthew knew that was unlikely. Jonathan thought the best

of everyone. The insight was useful. 'I'll be late back,' Matthew said.

Jonathan turned and saw Eve in Jen's car. 'What's Evie doing here?'

'She found Wesley's body.'

'Oh no!' Jonathan said. 'Not again. Not after finding her father. Can I take her back to our house? Really, she can't go back to Westacombe on her own tonight.'

'Of course not!' Now Matthew was impatient. 'I explained. She's a witness. A possible suspect.'

'It's a strange sort of job you have. Eve wouldn't hurt anyone.'

There was a moment of silence.

'When this is all over,' Matthew said, 'we'll have her to stay then. You can work your magic, feed her up, bring her back to life. That's when she'll need a friend.'

'She needs a friend now. I'll go with her back to Westacombe and stay with her there until she's ready to be alone.'

Matthew thought for a moment and nodded. 'Jen can drive you both.'

Chapter Nineteen

ALL THE WAY BACK TO WESTACOMBE, Eve remained silent and still. Jonathan sat next to her in the back of the car. He put his arms around her and pulled her in close to him. He was surprised by the warmth of her skin. He'd almost expected it to be as cold as ice, because she sat white and motionless as if she was frozen. He had a sudden picture in his head, as strange as a surrealist sculpture, of Eve thawing, of the grief flowing out, filling the car and drowning them both.

They were driving against the flow of traffic, a stream of cars on their way back to Barnstaple after a day on the beach, or a long, lazy afternoon in the bars and cafes. Jen made no effort to talk either. Jonathan thought she would become as fine a detective as Matthew one day; she understood emotional trauma and knew that victims had to be allowed their own time frame, their own healing process. Everyone was different.

Jonathan had never previously been to Westacombe, and when they pulled into the farmyard, he was struck by the beauty of it all, distracted for a moment from his reason for being there. The low sun made the place glow, seem magical.

Every colour was heightened, more intense: the red of the brick and tile at the big house and the green of the field next to the lane where black and white cows grazed. From a distance, the thatched cottage could have been a poster for the North Devon Tourist Board. It was all too perfect and not quite real. It seemed flat to him, like a painting or a stage set. In this odd light, it had no depth. The car came to a stop, but Eve made no move to get out.

Jen sat still too. 'You ready?' she said at last. 'No rush, though.' But she unclipped her seat belt and made to step out of the car.

'I'll go in with Eve,' Jonathan said. 'No need for you to come.'

'I really should talk to her.' Jen's voice was kind enough, but she seemed prepared for battle. *This is police business. Nothing to do with you.*

'Not yet,' he said. 'You must have got all you needed from Eve at the Woodyard. For now, at least.' He saw she was about to argue again. 'An hour,' he went on. 'Surely you can give her that to come round, to come to terms with what's happened?'

Jen seemed to think about it, and Jonathan wasn't sure what he'd do if she didn't agree – Matthew would be furious if he upset one of his core team of detectives – but finally she nodded. 'Okay.'

Jonathan leaned over and undid Eve's seat belt, then helped her out of the car. 'Come on, my love,' he said. 'Let's get you home.' He still had his arm around her shoulders as she led him through the big kitchen and up the stairs to her flat.

★

They sat together in the airy sitting room, with the window open and a breeze blowing the curtain. Eve still seemed numb. She allowed Jonathan to settle her on the sofa, a cushion at her back, as if she were an invalid.

'What can I get for you?' he said. 'Might you like a cup of tea?'

She smiled and the muscles of her face seemed to be working for the first time since he'd arrived at the Woodyard. 'I'd much rather have a glass of wine. There's a bottle in the fridge.'

He fetched it, found a corkscrew in a drawer and glasses in a cupboard, and opened the bottle. He sat on the floor, a low coffee table holding the glasses between them. 'I was never sure how things were between you and Wesley,' he said. The words had come out without his thinking about them in advance.

'I was never sure either.' She gave another little smile and took a drink.

Jonathan waited for her to speak again.

'I liked him,' she said, 'but not as much as he wanted. Wesley needed adoration, or at the very least a captive audience. I think that was why he couldn't settle to anything. He made interesting art, but he didn't believe in it unless somebody told him it was amazing. It was the same with his music. He was less interested in his work than in the reaction it created.' She looked up. 'I suppose he just wanted to be loved and perhaps we're all like that.'

'Did *he* love anyone?'

'Certainly not me, if that's what you're asking!' Her glass was empty. She stood up, went to the fridge in the corner and filled it. She waved the bottle at Jonathan, but he shook his head.

'Maybe he was a bit in love with Janey,' Eve said. 'I saw the way he looked at her and I'd never seen him like that before. He was always hanging round the Sandpiper and he kind of lit up when she was there.'

'Did she reciprocate his affection?' Jonathan knew the Mackenzie family. Sometimes there were artistic links between the Sandpiper and the Woodyard. They had different audiences and musicians coming to the region played both venues. He'd always dismissed Janey as hardly more than a schoolgirl, pretty but immature, a bit of a show-off, and he found it hard to imagine the pair as a couple.

'Oh, I don't think so. I'd have thought she was well out of his league.' Eve paused. 'I don't know her very well. She's not been back from university long. I always thought I should make more effort to become friends with her. It can't have been easy, losing her brother and then being stuck, working in the family business. But somehow the glass always seemed to get in the way.'

Jonathan stood up and paced around the room. He didn't want to stay where he was, staring at Eve across the table. Even though he *was* sitting on the floor, it still felt like an interrogation. Besides, he was always restless and could never sit without moving for long. There was a big family photograph over the mantelpiece and he settled in front of that. He recognized Nigel and Eve and assumed that the attractive middle-aged woman smiling out at him was Helen, her mother. In the background there was a line of dunes, the spikes of marram grass. He wondered where it had been taken.

'I slept with Wesley once.' Eve's words broke into his thoughts and pulled his attention away from the picture. 'I'd been dumped by a bloke I'd been going out with since university. I was lonely, wretched and Wesley listened. At least, he came here and helped me drink the very nice bottle of whisky Dad had brought back for me from Islay. I thought he was listening. And we went to bed. But it didn't mean anything. Not really.'

'A comfort shag,' Jonathan said.

She gave a little giggle. Perhaps she was already on the way to getting drunk. 'Something like that. Then I realized that crap telly and chocolate worked much better. I regretted it in the morning and neither of us mentioned it again.'

'Wesley used to come into the Woodyard cafe,' Jonathan said. 'He was always with a woman. Not the same woman each time but the same *type*.'

'Older, a bit arty? And I bet they always paid for the meal.'

'Yeah!' Jonathan realized then that he'd never seen Wesley at the counter with cash in his hand.

'Sarah and I called them the groupies. His fans. He kindly allowed them to take him out and buy him dinner.'

'Who's Sarah?' Jonathan thought he was starting to sound like Matthew. Asking questions. He should just let Eve talk.

'Sarah Grieve. She lives in the cottage on the other side of the yard.'

They sat in silence. Jonathan realized then that Eve was crying, that tears were running down her cheeks. He stood up, fetched a roll of kitchen towel from the bench, tore off two pieces and handed them to her.

'It was my glass that killed him,' she said. 'Just like with Dad. Why would somebody do that? They had to go into Frank's part of the house and steal the vase and break it. Then they set me up to find him. Who would hate me that much?'

'I can't believe that anyone hates you.'

'Why use my glass then? Why try to point the blame at me?'

Jonathan didn't have an answer to that. He sat beside her on the sofa and put his arms around her again, stroking her hair away from her face as if she were a child.

Chapter Twenty

WHEN MATTHEW DROVE INTO THE FARMYARD, he saw Jen still sitting in her car, the windows open. By now, it was evening, all long shadows and silence only broken by bird calls. He got out of his vehicle and walked towards her, then nodded up towards the attic.

'How is she?'

'I don't know. I haven't talked to her yet. Jonathan asked for an hour with her, before I started the questions.'

Matthew felt a spark of fury. How dare Jonathan interfere with his investigation and order his staff around!

'I was just about to go up.' Jen seemed awkward, uncomfortable, a child caught in the middle of rowing parents. It wasn't fair, Matthew thought, to have to put her in this position, to have compromised her authority. Jonathan had used his relationship with Matthew to get his own way. 'The hour's about up.'

'I'm sorry you were put in this situation,' Matthew said. 'Eve's a witness and you had better things to do with your time. Jonathan should have known that.'

147

'He was just being kind. She's been through a tough time. She needed the support.'

'We're police officers.' He knew his voice was sharp, hard. 'Not social workers.'

'What do you want me to do now?'

Matthew thought for a moment. 'Go home. It's not your fault you've been hanging around here with nothing to do. Show your face to the kids. I've called an early briefing in the morning. Seven thirty. Lots to discuss.' He paused. 'In a while, I'm going to talk to Frank Ley.'

'To see if the glass vase is still in his living room? Or if Eve is right and it was used to stab our victim?'

Matthew nodded. 'And to see what he's been doing with himself all day. I'd like to know what he made of Wesley Curnow too.'

He stood until Jen had driven away, trying to calm himself. He was tempted to climb the narrow stairs into Eve's flat and tell Jonathan to go, but a public row wouldn't help now and would only embarrass her. That conversation would have to wait until later. He walked round the farmhouse and into the red light of the setting sun.

He saw Frank Ley through the living room window. From this angle, Matthew couldn't tell if the blue vase of flowers was still sitting on the hearth. Frank seemed to be working, to be going through the pile of papers that he'd placed on the arm of his chair. He was wearing little round spectacles, which made him look even more like Billy Bunter. At one point the work seemed to overwhelm him. He took off his glasses and put his head in his hands. Matthew knocked at the door. Frank saw him and beckoned him in. The door was unlocked.

'Inspector, do you have any news? Have you found out what happened to Nigel?'

Matthew's eyes were drawn to the hearth. No flowers. No vase. He looked back at Ley. 'I'm afraid I have other news. Another tragedy, involving Westacombe Farm. Wesley Curnow is dead.'

'How did he die? Accident? Suicide?' The words were explosive, the tone so out of character that Matthew was shocked.

Matthew didn't answer. He kept his voice even, conversational. He knew some of his team considered him dull, but sometimes he used lack of drama as a tactic. A weapon, even. He'd never found that shouting produced results. 'Was Wesley the type of man who might commit suicide?'

'I'd never thought of him in that way. But when you mentioned his death, I wondered if the two events might be related.'

'You thought Wesley might have killed himself because he'd murdered Nigel?' Matthew thought that was a strange conclusion to jump to. 'A fit of regret. Conscience. Do you think Mr Curnow was capable of murder?'

'I think most of us would be capable of murder, Inspector.'

Would I? Perhaps when I lose my temper, when my reason drowns in the stark, white light, when my control shatters into pieces like Eve's hand-blown glass.

'We don't think Wesley killed himself,' Matthew said. 'We believe that he was murdered too.'

Frank looked away. 'What's going on here?' His voice was low, almost mumbling. 'This is like some second-rate horror film.'

'He wasn't killed here. He was stabbed in the Woodyard

Centre, in the place where he stored the materials for his work.' Matthew paused. 'Eve found him there.'

'Oh no!' He stared back at Matthew in apparent disbelief. 'Not Eve again. How is she?'

'Very shaken, of course. A friend is with her.' Until now, Matthew had been standing but he took a seat on the sofa. 'We have to inform Wesley's next of kin. I wonder if you know who that might be and how we might get hold of them?'

'I do!' The man seemed glad of the chance to help. 'Their names are Martin and Liz. Martin was a financial journalist and I knew him through my work. I'll get their phone number. They moved to France when they retired, to live the good life in the Dordogne.' Francis fumbled for his phone, his hands trembling, and passed it to Matthew so he could make a note of the numbers.

'Is that how Wesley came to be living here? Because you were a friend of his parents?'

'The family were from Cornwall. That gave Martin, Wesley's father, and me something in common when I was in London. We worked in different fields, of course, but we were both West Country boys. Both interested in the politics of money. Wesley was always happier staying with his Cornish grand-mother than in the city, and spent all his holidays there; he ended up at school in Truro.' Frank paused. 'He tried all sorts when he left, but he couldn't settle. He dropped out of art school, ran a bar in Newquay for a couple of seasons, but couldn't make it pay, joined a band for a summer. All the time his parents were subsidizing him. Not really doing him any favours. By then he was in his thirties, almost middle-aged, and he'd never really earned his own living. In the end, they decided to cut him loose.'

'And you took pity on him?' Matthew wondered if that was down to guilt again, to Ley's sense that his comfortable living had been achieved through luck and at the expense of other people.

'I didn't want him out on the streets,' Frank said. 'He paid rent, just like Eve. He made some beautiful objects. He really seemed settled, happy.' He paused. 'I liked to believe that I'd helped in that a little.'

'Did he know Nigel Yeo?'

'Only through Eve, I think.' Frank considered for a moment. 'After Helen, Nigel's wife, died, I'd invite Nigel to dinner along with the others. Wesley certainly met Nigel here.'

'You asked Lauren Miller along once too? She went on to become Nigel's colleague.'

'I did! A lovely woman.' He paused. 'I had hoped we might get to know each other better . . .' His voice tailed off. 'But in the end, I was too shy to ask to see her on her own. Besides, I'm sure I wasn't her type. She might have gone out with me through pity, but I could tell there was no real attraction. Not on her part.'

Matthew didn't say anything. It seemed Nigel and Lauren hadn't mentioned their relationship to Frank. At this point, he couldn't see any need to do it.

'I understand that Wesley was friendly with the Mackenzies,' he said. 'I presume he knew that Nigel was investigating the son's death. The family would have discussed it with him.'

'The family perhaps, but not Nigel. He wouldn't have gossiped. He was always very discreet. He never told me what he'd discovered about the circumstances surrounding Mack's death, and I doubt if he told George and Martha either. The complaint might have come from them, but Nigel said from the start that any findings would be in a report to the health trust.'

'It wouldn't be made public?' Matthew thought that was interesting.

'Oh, I think it would, but the trust would be given the opportunity to respond first.'

'Do you know if the report had been completed?'

'No, you'd need to ask Nigel's colleagues in NDPT. Of course, Lauren might know.' Frank paused. 'I don't see that there was any way Wesley could have learned about Nigel's findings.' He turned to the window and stared into the garden. 'Besides, Wesley was always self-centred. I'm not sure he'd have cared much about it. Unless it related to him.'

It was getting late. The colour had seeped out of the sky. Frank hadn't switched on any lights and the room was shadowy.

'I have to ask this. What were your movements this afternoon?'

It was too dark now for Matthew to see clearly the expression on the other man's face.

'I was here, working, mostly in my office in the house. I sat outside for a while this afternoon, but I didn't go anywhere else. You had an officer on the gate, I think. He'd be able to see my drive where it joins the lane. You'll be able to check.'

Matthew nodded. He thought there was probably a way from the bottom of the garden to Instow, but he couldn't imagine Frank scrambling through bramble and gorse to get there. He stood up. 'When I came yesterday there was a vase of flowers on the hearth. It was large, round, more like a bowl than a conventional vase. I think Eve had made it. What happened to it?'

Ley looked at the space, as if noticing the absence for the

first time. 'Sarah must have come in earlier to do a quick tidy. I imagine the flowers were dying, so she threw them out and put the vase away.'

It seemed odd to Matthew that the man wasn't more curious about his reason for asking the question, but he said nothing and let himself out.

Matthew stood for a moment in the farmyard. There was a police van parked and a light on in Wesley's flat, so he assumed the search team were already in and working. There was still no sign of Jonathan. Again, he was tempted to go into Eve's flat to see what was happening there, but his anger had dispersed a little and he hated the idea of making a scene.

Joe Oldham, his boss, had left him a voicemail, saying they could push the budget a bit on this one. '*The PCC is under pressure to get it sorted quickly. They don't want tourists cancelling because they think we've got a serial killer on the loose. The press has already got wind of the second murder.*'

Classic Oldham, shifting responsibility to the officers below him, piling on the pressure, taking no real action to respond to the situation beyond giving him a little extra money. Oldham was close to retirement, ineffective, and all he wanted was a final year without confrontation or controversy. Matthew couldn't really blame him.

He thought it would be churlish to drive home, leaving Jonathan here to get a taxi, and was about to text his husband to offer a lift when his attention was caught by a view inside the Grieves' cottage. The curtains hadn't been shut and through the window, he saw the couple inside, framed. They were sitting at the kitchen table, coffee mugs in front of them. He tapped at the window, surprising them. Sarah waved for him to come in.

'I'm sorry if I made you jump. I should have thought . . .' Matthew introduced himself.

'We spoke to your sergeant earlier.'

'I know. But that was before your neighbour had been killed.'

'Of course.' She paused for a moment. 'I can't believe that Wes won't just wander in, saying the whole thing was some kind of tasteless joke, and trying to con a drink from us. The whole thing is a nightmare. So scary.' Sarah had got to her feet and automatically switched on the kettle. 'We've been trying to work out what to do for the best, wondering if I should take the girls and stay with my mother for a bit. But they've got school, and everything we have is invested in this business.'

Matthew could see that she was exhausted. 'Just one question. Did you go in to clean for Frank today?'

'Good God, no! I haven't had a moment. Things have been bonkers for the last two days and we've just been trying to catch up, do the essential stuff.' She looked up. 'Why? Did he say he needed me to go in?'

'He told me you'd been in to do a quick tidy.'

She shook her head. 'He must be mistaken. I dropped off a tub of cream in his fridge – he's a bit of an addict – but that was all. Is it important?'

Matthew shook his head. 'Probably not. We're just trying to work out where everyone was. Did either of you leave the farm?'

'I went into Barnstaple to do a supermarket shop,' Sarah said. 'I took the girls and we went to the park first. They've got all this space to play in, but they do love it and I just wanted to be away for a bit. You do understand?'

'Of course. Mr Grieve, where were you today?'

The man looked up. 'Here,' he said. 'Working. There's all this drama, but the place doesn't look after itself.'

Matthew nodded. He wished he could speak to the man on his own. Grieve carried about him a sense of resentment. And if the rest of the family were in Barnstaple all afternoon, perhaps he could have slipped away. He'd know the land, might have access to a vehicle away from the farm. But now wasn't the time for that conversation. Matthew was tired and he felt his concentration wandering. He wasn't in the right mood to listen and often, he thought, his work was all about careful, intense listening.

Back in the farmyard, Jonathan was waiting for him, leaning against the car. His hair looked very white in the dusk. It glowed like a halo.

'Is Eve okay?'

Jonathan shrugged. 'As well as she could be in the circumstances. Halfway through a bottle of Pinot, but there's no other booze in the place. I checked. The last thing she needs is to wake up with a hangover.'

'You should have left Jen Rafferty to do the interview. It wasn't your place to interfere.' Matthew unlocked the car and got inside. Jonathan followed.

'I wasn't interfering. I was being a friend.' He paused. 'I'd have left as soon as Jen came up. But I wanted to make Eve comfortable. She was so stressed. Rigid with shock.'

Matthew started the engine. He said nothing and let the tension stretch.

'You don't think she killed those two men?' Jonathan demanded at last. 'Her father and her friend. You don't think she took a piece of glass that she'd created and smashed it and stuck it in their necks and watched the blood flood out?'

'No!' Matthew said. 'Of course not!'

'Then what possible harm could I do?'

Matthew was about to talk about the importance of rules, procedure, but he could see that the words would mean nothing to Jonathan. Rules had never mattered to him. So instead, they drove back to the coast in silence.

Chapter Twenty-One

THE NEXT DAY, ROSS ARRIVED AT the police station early, but the boss was still there before him, doing the things that most senior officers wouldn't think to do themselves: filling the coffee machine, setting out the chairs in the ops room. Ross knew Venn's willingness to muck in was admirable, but it made him uncomfortable. He liked his boundaries to be clear, to know where he stood. Besides, he was ambitious. One day he'd be a DI and he wouldn't want to be concerned with the trivia of an investigation. He was anxious that Venn might be setting an unfortunate precedent.

Jen Rafferty flew in at the last minute, red hair flying. Ross had got to know her better when they'd worked on the Simon Walden murder, but he still found her tricky. She was too opinionated, too dismissive of his ideas. Too willing to side with the scrotes. Too emotional altogether. Venn stood at the front. Ross always thought he looked like an undertaker. It was the understated dark suits, worn sometimes even in this weather, and the shiny black shoes, the sombre, thoughtful manner. The hair, already quite grey.

Venn had started talking.

'Two murders,' he said. 'Nigel Yeo and Wesley Curnow. Connected through the community at Westacombe Farm.' A pause. 'Of course, the press will have a field day with this – I've already seen one of the national tabloid headlines, *Double Murder on Sunshine Coast* – but we have to ignore that sort of speculation. The victims were individuals and they have families. They deserve our respect. However, we'll obviously be looking for connections. These killings weren't random or coincidental.'

Ross tried not to yawn. He wished Venn would get to the important stuff. His boss was still talking:

'Nigel Yeo worked for an organization called North Devon Patients Together or NDPT. I've checked his diary and on the morning of his death he had a meeting with three individuals who work in the hospital. I've arranged to see them today. There was a possibility that Dr Yeo had found evidence of negligence or lack of care in the treatment of a young man with a mental health illness who went on to kill himself. That man was called Alexander Mackenzie and he provides another link with the second victim, because his sister, Janey Mackenzie, was a friend of Wesley Curnow's. They were together on the evening before Mr Yeo's body was found.' Venn looked round at the room to check that everyone had understood the importance of the information and the complexity of the relationships.

This time Ross did yawn. It was like being back at school.

'We can assume that both men drove themselves to the places where they were found; the pathologist has confirmed that both were killed at the scenes. So, were they lured to some fictional meeting? We still haven't found either man's mobile phone.' Venn looked out at the room. 'Ross, I know you've had information from Yeo's service provider, but can you follow up with Wesley Curnow's? I'd like you with me for the meeting in the hospital, but they can't see us until nine thirty.'

'Sure, boss.' He tried to sound eager.

Jen Rafferty stuck up her hand. 'I've dug up some interesting info on Roger Prior, the CEO of the health trust. Husband to Cynthia who hosted the party on Friday night.'

Venn was interested. 'He's one of the people we've arranged to see.'

'He was forced to resign from a big trust in London after an inquiry following the suicide of a teenager with mental health problems. The report failed to hold any individual responsible, but Prior was blamed by implication in the press and he was hounded on social media. The suicide occurred in the hospital, but you can see why he wouldn't want another scandal.'

'Indeed.' Venn shut his eyes for a moment. It was impossible to tell what he made of this news. 'Thanks, Jen. Can you get all the relevant information across to me? I'll read it before the meeting. And, of course, copy Ross in.'

Oh, great! Ross thought. *An hour of reading boring background information, which will turn out to be irrelevant, and chasing mobile phone records. Just what I joined the police for. Not.*

'Sure,' Jen said. 'I was thinking I'd speak to the mother of the lad who committed suicide in Camden. His name was Luke Wallace. I'm sure I can track her down and get a few more details.'

Venn nodded. 'Good plan. But before that, I'd like you to speak to the Mackenzie family. See if you can talk to them all together. Martha, the actress mother, is home at the moment. Get a feel for what's going on there. I'm not after witness statements just yet. I can't see they'd have motive to kill either man, but somehow they're at the heart of the case.'

'I've been a regular at the Sandpiper, though I'm not close to the family. Are you still happy for me to do that?'

In the moment before Venn answered, Ross held his breath, hoping that he and Jen might be asked to swap roles. Let her do the phones and sit with the suits in the hospital. He wouldn't mind seeing Janey again. He imagined sitting in the bar by the beach, chatting over coffee, getting to understand her better, while picking up a detail vital to the case.

But the inspector only smiled. 'Most of us have been in the Sandpiper at some time or another. I'm sure we can trust you to keep it professional.' He looked out at the room. 'Anyone got anything else to contribute? Ideas? Information? Anything that I might have overlooked?'

Ross stood up. 'When I chatted to Janey Mackenzie yesterday, I asked about the car Curnow saw driving very fast down his lane. She hadn't seen anything when she dropped Wesley off, but she said that when she was walking from the bar to her home, a vehicle drove at speed through the village.'

'Any description?'

Ross shrugged. 'Something big and black.'

Jen stuck up her hand. 'Roger Prior drives a black SUV.'

Venn smiled. 'Useful to know, but so do many of our residents and most of the visitors to the county. Vicki, could you go back through the CCTV? Any other contributions?'

There was a silence and, after a pause, Matthew Venn went on. 'We'll need good routine policing then. Thanks to Vicki, we have a record of Nigel Yeo's car in the service station just outside Instow on the night before his body was discovered. Jen, could you check with the staff there? See if anyone remembers seeing him? And besides checking for our mysterious black SUV in Instow in the early hours of Saturday morning, let's look at the roads coming into Barnstaple yesterday afternoon. If we can find the same vehicle in both places, we might just have hit the jackpot. I'd like to fix a time for Curnow's arrival at the Woodyard and CCTV might give us that answer too.'

He looked up again. 'One more thing. Yeo was in a relationship with a colleague. A woman called Lauren Miller. Thanks for the heads-up on that, Ross. Let's see if you can get an equally speedy result on Wesley's mobile records.' He collected his papers into a neat bundle and walked away to his office.

The hospital was on a slight hill. It was on the edge of the town, but surrounded by trees, so it had the air of being in the country. Ross and Venn waited in a queue at reception, behind a wheezing elderly man and a woman with a screaming kid. Ross thought he and Mel might start a family sometime – Mel mentioned it occasionally in a kind of dreamy, wistful voice – but of course, any child of theirs would be well behaved. It wouldn't scream or have tantrums in public. That sort of thing was down to the parents, wasn't it, and Mel would be a brilliant mother.

He thought they should jump the queue, by flashing their warrant cards, but Venn seemed to have endless patience. At last, they reached the desk and the receptionist pointed them to a square building separate from the main hospital. 'They're in the admin block.'

Three people were waiting for them in a long, airy room with a view of the car park. There was a tall, older, black-haired man and two women, one sleek and middle-aged, one younger, Asian. The group sat at one end of a rectangular table, and looked, Ross thought, like an interviewing panel. It was clear that they had met earlier to discuss tactics, to come up with a shared position. His mother had always given doctors God-like status and Ross felt suddenly nervous, as if he were the one to be interrogated.

Venn introduced himself and took a seat close to the group. 'This is Ross May, one of my team.' Ross nodded and took out his notebook. He wasn't expecting to speak, but the boss would want a detailed record of the meeting.

Ross had anticipated that the guy would take charge, but it was the older woman who stood to greet them. 'Fiona Radley, head of comms. These are my colleagues, Roger Prior, CEO of the trust, and Ratna Joshi. She's the psychiatrist who worked most closely with Alexander Mackenzie, and I understand you have some questions about his care.'

'Of course, we're all deeply upset by Nigel's death,' Prior said. 'He was a valued colleague before he retired to work with Patients Together. He had many friends here and he'll be sorely missed. Please pass on our condolences to his daughter.'

Ross thought this sounded like a rehearsed speech.

'You were a personal friend too, I understand,' Venn said.

The statement seemed to make Prior uncomfortable. 'He was a neighbour. My wife and I supported him after the death of his wife.'

Ross decided Prior was the kind of witness who'd never give a straight answer. He hated that.

'I'm sorry, Inspector,' the head of PR had a shrill voice, 'but I think we should stick to the clinical facts here.'

'The clinical facts are that Dr Yeo was stabbed to death by a person or persons unknown and that the three of you saw him on the morning before he died.'

The room fell silent. Fiona Radley took a tissue from her handbag and sneezed. 'Sorry,' she said. 'Hay fever.'

Venn ignored her. 'What did you discuss at that meeting?'

'I think you know, Inspector. Dr Yeo had asked for the meeting because he was looking into the suicide of one of our patients.' Radley paused. 'I'm sure you won't expect us to pass on details of a confidential conversation.'

Venn ignored the question and asked one of his own. 'Was Dr Yeo aware that Mr Prior had resigned from his previous post in north London following a similar scandal?'

Silence descended again, before Venn continued. 'Because that was a matter of public record and not at all confidential.'

This time Prior responded. 'There was a serious case review, Inspector, and both the trust and I were cleared of any blame.' The words were trotted out as if he'd said them many times before.

'It wouldn't look good, though, if you were caught up in a similar incident.'

Radley came in again, smooth and composed. 'Nigel was concerned that our procedures hadn't been strictly followed. Alexander had been sectioned under the Mental Health Act, after being brought to A&E by one of your officers. He was admitted to Gorsehill, our acute psychiatric hospital. The following morning, we decided that he had capacity to make his own decisions and allowed him to discharge himself.' A pause. 'At the meeting on Friday morning we were able to reassure Dr Yeo that, in fact, the guidelines *had* been strictly followed. He seemed satisfied by the explanation.'

And yet, Ross thought, *that evening he went to a party, held by the wife of the trust's CEO, especially to talk to a detective sergeant about the case. The facts don't quite hang together.*

'Who took the decision to allow Mr Mackenzie to discharge himself?' Venn's voice hadn't changed in tone. There was no judgement, just a mild enquiry.

'I did.' This was the younger woman, Ratna Joshi. She was slight, dressed in black trousers and a gold silk blouse.

'Dr Joshi is a registrar in Gorsehill.' This was Radley again, trying to keep control.

'Newly appointed,' Joshi said. She had a North Country accent and the words were sharp, uncompromising. 'In charge of the unit over the weekend. With two more emergency admissions to process and no beds. Mack had a family who cared for him. I thought it would be safe to discharge him into community support.' She looked up and stared at Venn. 'But of course, the community team was as stretched as we were.'

'So, he fell through a gap in the service.'

'Something like that,' the young doctor said. 'It didn't help that until his eighteenth birthday he'd been treated as a child, so there wasn't a continuity of care. But Nigel wasn't interested in apportioning individual blame. He said the NDPT wanted to check that there was no systemic problem, and that it wouldn't happen again.'

'The family had talked about going to the media.' Radley was becoming impatient. 'The last thing the NHS needs is more bad press, and for a poorly resourced sector to have to pay out huge sums in compensation. We explained to Nigel that we'd improved our service as a result of Alexander's death. I think he accepted that. I hoped that he'd be willing to explain our change of procedure to the Mackenzies.'

'And was he?' Venn asked. 'Was he willing to talk to the family on your behalf?'

'I had the impression that his view on the matter had mellowed a little. He was, at least, listening to our arguments.' She looked at her colleagues. 'I'd say we parted on good terms. Wouldn't you agree?'

Prior nodded vigorously. Joshi said nothing.

'Were minutes taken?'

'No!' Radley again. 'It wasn't a formal meeting.' A pause. 'Are you implying that you don't believe our account of events?'

'I'm not implying anything,' Venn said. 'But a record of the conversation would have been useful.' A pause. 'Did Dr Yeo give any indication of how he intended to proceed with his investigation?'

'No.'

Venn nodded but made no response. Instead there was another question. 'How did Dr Yeo appear to you at your meeting? Did he seem distracted? Anxious?'

Radley thought for a while. 'Not anxious,' she said. 'I can't imagine Nigel being anxious about anything. But perhaps he was a little distracted. I thought that he might have had other things on his mind.'

'His diary showed that he had another meeting at the hospital, later in the day. Would you know who that was with?'

Radley shook her head. 'But of course, I can try to find out for you, Inspector.' A bright, professional smile. She was being *very* helpful, Ross thought, now the focus had shifted away from Prior.

'At the end of the meeting,' Venn said, 'perhaps you talked about other, less formal things. Plans for the evening, for the weekend?'

'No,' Radley said. 'I'm sorry. There was nothing like that.'

They looked at Venn to check that the interview was over.

Roger Prior started gathering together the files on the desk in front of him. Ross thought they were relieved. It was as if this had been less disturbing than they'd been expecting. There was a sense of relaxation, a release of tension.

Venn was already on his feet too. 'Just one more thing.' The words caught them all, froze them, so they posed like statues, waiting for the question. Dreading it, perhaps. 'There were some numbers in Dr Yeo's diary. 8531 or 8537. They were smudged and not quite legible. Do they mean anything to you? Could it be a file number? A patient number?'

Ross sensed relief again. The question hadn't troubled them. Prior answered immediately. 'I'm sorry, no. I have no idea at all what they could mean. Certainly not anything related to Nigel's work here in the hospital.'

They were walking back to the vehicle when they heard foot-steps running behind them. It was Ratna Joshi, the young psychiatrist, light on her feet in black ballet pumps. Her hair was in a long plait down her back and it swung as she ran. They were on a tarmac path leading through the car park, in full sunlight. The heat bounced off the hard surfaces, and in places the asphalt had melted and was sticky underfoot.

The woman was slightly breathless after the run. 'There's something you should know. I didn't want to say in the meeting. Fiona told us only to answer questions, not to volunteer information.'

'Go on.' Venn had stopped and turned towards her.

'I saw Nigel on Friday after we had that meeting. It was early evening. I'd finished for the day and I was on my way out. We bumped into each other in the corridor.'

'So, he'd definitely come back to the hospital? There must have been another meeting?'

'Or he'd stayed on all day to see people in different departments. Something routine. He was here quite often.'

'Of course, we'll check that out. Ms Radley did say that she'd help.' Venn smiled at her. 'How did Dr Yeo seem?'

'He was angry,' Ratna said. 'Furious. I'd never seen him like that. Nigel was usually a calm presence. He said he wasn't going to be silenced. The truth had to be told.'

Chapter Twenty-Two

THE SANDPIPER WAS CLOSED ALL DAY on Mondays. 'Our one day of rest,' George said when Jen called to make an appointment. 'Yes, we'll all wait in to speak to you. Come to the house. That's where we'll be.'

The house was whitewashed and, like the cafe bar next door, it faced the sea, only separated from the beach by the narrow road. There was a wrought-iron balcony on the first floor, and that was where Martha was standing when Jen parked outside. She was leaning against the rail, holding a cigarette in one hand, blowing the smoke towards the shore. Martha Mackenzie had been part of Jen's childhood – the soap she'd acted in for more than thirty years had been required early evening TV viewing – and, despite herself, Jen was aware of the woman's celebrity. There was a thrill in meeting someone so famous.

'You must be the detective.' Martha's voice was deep and it carried. A woman walking past with a buggy turned to stare. She recognized Martha too and gave an excited little wave. Martha waved back. Graciously. 'Just a mo and I'll be down to let you in.'

The young mother looked at Jen with a touch of envy and walked on.

Jen had seen Martha before in the bar, a glamorous presence with a small crowd around her, but they'd never been introduced. It seemed Martha recognized her, though. 'Of course, you're Wesley's chum. Poor Wesley. You must be devastated. We all are.' She reached out and gave Jen a hug, surrounding her with the smell of cigarette and expensive perfume. Jen wondered what Venn would say about an interview beginning with such informality. But then he'd told her to put the family at their ease.

Eventually, Martha pulled away. 'Come on through. The others are still finishing breakfast but I was desperate for a ciggie.'

The kitchen was long and narrow and ended in double glass doors leading onto a patio garden, with terracotta pots and rough stone walls covered with climbing plants. One shelf ran right along the room's longest wall. It had been painted yellow and held strange trinkets, bits of brightly coloured pottery and glass, shells, tiny carvings that might have been made by Wesley. The doors were open, so the kitchen and the garden seemed like one space. George and Janey sat inside at a light-wood table. There was a jug of coffee, a plate with a remaining single croissant.

'We have a late breakfast on Mondays,' Martha said. 'It's become rather a ritual.'

Janey looked up and gave a little smile. Jen thought she might be about to say something, but in the end, she continued to stare into her mug. She seemed exhausted, blank. George stood up and held out his hand. 'Jen,' he said. 'How lovely to see a friendly face. I worried they might send a stranger.'

'This isn't a formal interview,' Jen said. 'That will probably come later because you all knew both victims, and I won't be allowed to take part in that. This is an initial chat to see if you might be able to help.' Her attention was caught again by the yard outside. 'You've made it so beautiful here.'

'That was Mack,' Janey said. 'His design; his work. You should have seen it when we first moved in! We're trying to keep it going for him but none of us has his green fingers.'

George was still on his feet, pouring coffee. 'Would you like anything to eat? That croissant won't be so nice now, but I can make you toast. Eggs, maybe?' Speaking with the Scottish accent that had always set him apart.

Jen shook her head. 'I'm afraid I have questions.'

'Of course you do, darling,' Martha said. 'That's why you're here.'

'Did either of you see Wesley yesterday? You were friends. Perhaps he called in?'

'I didn't see him,' George said. 'One of my chefs was off sick and I was in the kitchen for most of the day. I hardly went into the bar at all, except to cover for Janey when she went off to speak to your colleague.'

'Your staff will be able to confirm that?'

'You're asking if I have an alibi?' He sounded amused, unoffended. 'We close early on a Sunday. There are so many places here serving Sunday lunch and we don't feel the need to compete. So, our regulars come for breakfast or brunch and we close in the early afternoon. I have an alibi until then, and one of your officers came to talk to Janey. After that, no.'

'Where did you go?'

'I drove inland,' George said. 'I wanted to get away from the crowds for a bit. There's a place near Torrington where

Mack loved to walk. He was a great walker. Seal Point was his favourite place, but I knew that would be packed on a Sunday afternoon so I headed inland instead. I got back at about six.'

It seemed a long explanation to a simple question, but George had always been garrulous. Jen turned to his wife. 'You didn't want to go too?'

The woman smiled. All her features were large and her smile was generous, wide. She was wearing lipstick. Jen thought about that: the effort of putting on make-up just to be in the house. Every day a performance. 'Walking's not really my thing. Not in this heat. I went and lay on the bed. Dozed for a while. The idea of a siesta is very civilized, don't you think? I didn't wake until George came back.'

Throughout the exchange, Janey had been silent, unresponsive. Now she looked up. 'I suppose you want to hear about me.'

'Please.'

'When I came off shift, I had a shower, changed, then I headed out. I wanted to escape this place too. It's crazy in the summer. Sometimes, I long for grey days, a storm from the west, just to keep people away. Pouring rain. I wonder why I ever came home. But I couldn't drive. I'd parked in the lane by the side of the bar and some bastard tourist had boxed me in. I was really, really pissed off, wrote a note and stuck it on his windscreen, made a record of his registration number, thinking I'd dob him in to the parking guys. I never did, of course. Couldn't be arsed and it seemed a bit petty. In the end I went for a walk. Out past the cricket club towards Fremington Quay. It was a bit quieter there. Still lots of people about, but not crazy busy.'

'Do you still have a note of the car's registration number?'

171

'Nah,' Janey said. 'At least probably not.'

'You might want to look,' Jen said, 'just in case.'

There was a moment of silence while the implication of that sunk in, but there was no response. No righteous indignation. Janey just nodded in agreement. 'I'm sure I can dig it out.'

'And the family just has two vehicles? You don't have your own, Mrs Mackenzie?'

'No,' the woman said. 'If I need a car, I use George or Janey's.'

'You all seem to have been close to Wesley. How did you meet him?' Jen thought the more general question might put them at ease, start a natural conversation.

'He was a regular in the bar,' George said, 'and he had a way of making you feel like a friend. Of wanting to be his friend. We run a business but I found myself buying drinks for him. Just as well he was one of a kind because we'd have gone under if I treated all my customers as drinking pals.'

'I'm not sure how close we really were,' Janey said. 'I think at heart he was an actor. It was subconscious. Like you, Mummy. He became the person we all wanted him to be. He was great to have in the bar because he could lift the mood. He'd walk in and suddenly he made everyone feel cleverer, more amusing. But what lay under the charm?' She shrugged. 'I don't think we'll ever know now.'

'Had he upset anyone recently?'

Another silence. 'This is going to sound very petty,' Martha said. 'Not something that could ever trigger murder.'

'All the same,' Jen said, 'it would be useful to know. That's why I'm here drinking coffee with you and we're not taking statements. I'm after background, the gossip.'

'He had a way of charming middle-aged women.' Martha

sounded dismissive. Maybe she didn't consider herself middle-aged. 'Perhaps he made them feel younger, though he was no spring chicken himself. Wherever he went, they were around him, giggling, buying him meals and drinks. But he had one special admirer. Cynthia Prior. Of course, you know her.'

Jen nodded.

'Her husband's a dry old stick who doesn't share any of her interests. Cynthia considered Wesley a sort of cultural companion. She'd think nothing of taking him to London to see a show that interested her, or dragging him round an exhibition. All expenses paid, of course. First-class rail and a fabulous meal at the end of the evening. In return for his company. But recently, he'd been seeing a lot less of her. It's possible that Roger finally put his foot down. I don't know him well, but I imagine he's a man who would care about appearances. But I had the impression that Wesley was the one who'd started to keep his distance.' Martha turned to her daughter. 'What do you think, Janey? You probably knew Wesley better than the rest of us.'

Janey shook her head as if she had no answer. 'I don't know what was going on. Like I said before, nobody really understood Wesley Curnow. He was a mystery to us all.'

'Was he close to Mack?' Jen thought that might be another link between their victims. If the two were friends, Wesley could have been supporting Nigel's campaign to investigate the young man's death.

'Wesley didn't really like people who made demands on him,' Janey said. 'It was always the other way around. And depressed people can be *very* demanding. I think Mack was hurt because Wes kept his distance during that last episode of illness. When they let him out of hospital, he got in touch with

Wes, and asked to see him. When there was no reply to his texts and calls, Mack walked up to Westacombe. He was so restless at that time, so impatient. He was pacing, talking to himself, hearing strange voices. Wes just didn't know how to handle a madman landing up on his doorstep. All that real emotion was too much for him. In the end, he phoned me and asked me to take Mack away. Mack was crying all the way home in the car. I suppose it must have seemed like the worst kind of rejection from someone he'd admired and considered a friend. That was the day before he killed himself.'

'You must have found that very hurtful.'

And yet you still hung out with Wesley. You were dancing with him at Cynthia's party.

'Not really. I could understand how Wesley found it uncomfortable. I'd probably have reacted in just the same way if Mack hadn't been my brother.' Janey paused. 'We're all supposed to be open about mental health these days. Very sympathetic. But the *reality* of the bloody thing, the person's self-obsession, the relentless movement, like they're constantly wired, the tedious repetition of paranoid thoughts, that hasn't changed. You can't know just how exhausting severe depression can be for other people until you've experienced it.' She looked up. 'I'm sorry. That sounds callous. But it was incredibly painful to deal with. That was why we needed the health professionals, partly just to take over some of the responsibility, but to give us hope that they could make Mack better and keep him safe. We couldn't do it any more. And the health service let us down.'

'Did any of you feel that Wesley was responsible for Mack's death?'

'No!' George's response was immediate. 'That was the health

service. They mismanaged the whole case. I phoned them when Janey brought Mack back from Westacombe in such a state. I phoned his consultant. His secretary said he'd phone us back, but of course, he didn't. I phoned the community support team. Again nothing. Apparently, my son wasn't sufficiently suicidal to warrant immediate intervention. And he had family support. The hospital had prescribed medication to help Mack sleep and we gave it to him that evening and made sure he was in bed. We thought he was asleep. The next day was Monday – our day off – and the rest of us were later getting up than usual. As Janey said, we were all exhausted. When we woke up, there was no sign of Mack. Maybe he hadn't swallowed the pills or maybe they weren't as strong as we'd imagined. We all went to look for him. Frantic. You can't imagine what it was like. I still have nightmares . . . Then we discovered that he'd taken his car.'

'Who found his note?'

'Some holidaymaker,' Janey said. 'Dad called the police when we realized Mack's car was missing and they found it outside our chalet in the dunes. His body didn't turn up until several days later, washed ashore on the north end of Lundy, pulled out by the tide.'

When George turned to face Jen, there were tears running down his face, and when he spoke, the words were sharp and jagged. 'That wasn't Wesley's fault. He wasn't trained in mental health. It wasn't even the fault of the poor sods who let him discharge himself too soon, and then were too overstretched to respond when he had a crisis. It was the system. And I want the whole world to know how it let my son down.'

Jen didn't know what to say. She'd been in the bar a couple of times since Mack's death. George had been his usual urbane self, accepting the condolences of regulars with a hug of thanks, a few grateful words. There'd been none of this anger. Now, she thought he must be as fine an actor as his wife, to have persuaded them all that he'd accepted the death of his son with grace.

She got to her feet. 'I don't want to disturb you all any further, but I wonder if I could chat to Janey?' Jen turned to the woman. 'It sounds as if you were as close to Wesley as anyone. We could go into Instow. Get a coffee.' She thought there were things she'd never want to say in front of *her* parents.

'Sure,' Janey said. Then after a moment's thought she added, her voice tentative, 'Could we go to Seal Bay? Have a little walk on the point? It was Mack's happy place. I was planning to go this morning. It won't be so busy today.'

Martha put her arm around her daughter's shoulder. 'Are you sure, darling? Won't that just bring everything back?'

Janey tensed under the touch. 'Don't you think these murders haven't brought it back already? The nightmares. The flash-backs? I kept waking up last night. I'd drift back and then be haunted again.'

Her voice was angry, bitter and Jen saw that the young woman's hands were trembling. She couldn't imagine what it must be like, to be reminded over and over of the loss of a brother.

'There's nothing I'd like better than a wander by the sea in the line of duty,' Jen said, 'and we'll get an ice cream. My treat.'

They parked by the Mackenzies' chalet, but they didn't go inside. The building was made of wood and the paint was peeling; it was less grand and impressive than some of the others, but Jen could see how it would appeal to a couple of kids. It would be the best kind of den.

Janey led her through the dunes, across the beach and onto the coastal path. They didn't start talking until they were on their own, facing out to the sea. It was as smooth as oil, glittering in full sunlight. As Janey had said, the path was relatively quiet.

'Tell me a bit more about Wesley,' Jen said. 'How close were you?'

But Janey had stopped where the cliff was closest to the water and was looking out towards Lundy on the horizon.

'This is where they found the note that Mack left for us.'

'What did it say?'

'That he needed to find peace at last.' Janey looked back at Jen. 'I feel like that now. These murders. It's like blow after blow. As if you've been mugged and someone's kicking you, over and over again. Just as you think it's all over, they come back to hit you.'

'You're not feeling suicidal, though?'

There was a moment's hesitation before she answered. 'Nah. Don't worry. I'm a survivor. Poor Mack wasn't.'

'So, tell me about Wesley, if you feel that you're up to talking about it, if it's not one kick too many.'

'Yeah, I'm okay. It's good to get away from the house. We've all been affected by Mack's death in different ways. Mum and Dad are all, like, we've got to keep the show on the road. It'll get to them sometime, though.'

'I think it's already got to them. They just have different ways of dealing with it.'

'Maybe.' Janey was still staring out to sea. Lundy was shimmering in the heat haze on the horizon. 'Wesley was a bit of a drifter. High-achieving parents, with plenty of money, but not much time to give to their son. That was how I read it at least. He always said that his grandmother was more like a real mum.' She gave a little laugh. 'I think she spoiled him rotten. Perhaps that's why he liked her so much. And why he got on so well with all his middle-aged female groupies.'

'How did he seem at the party?'

'Just as he always did. Pretty chilled. Making sure he got more than his fair share of the food and the wine. That was classic Wesley.'

'He didn't seem anxious or worried?'

Janey laughed again. 'Wes didn't really do anxious.'

'Did you notice if Nigel Yeo spoke to him at the party?'

'Nigel spoke to everyone when he first came in.' She looked back at Jen. 'But you were there. You'll have seen as much as me.'

'Ah,' Jen said. 'You were sober. I very much wasn't.'

They walked back to the car then, stopping for the ice cream on the way. In the car Janey started scrabbling in her bag. At last she pulled out a scrap of paper. 'There you are! That guy's registration number. The one who blocked me in.' A brief moment of triumph.

Jen wasn't sure how useful the conversation had been but when she dropped Janey back in Instow, the younger woman gave her a quick hug. 'Thanks,' she said. 'Really, you've helped a lot.'

On the way back to Barnstaple, Jen stopped at the filling station on the edge of Instow. According to CCTV, Nigel had stopped here for fuel on the way to Westacombe after leaving Cynthia's party. She introduced herself to a faded, middle-aged woman, who was perched on a tall stool behind the counter.

'I don't suppose you were on duty on Friday evening?'

'Yeah. The graveyard shift. Eight until we closed at midnight.'

'CCTV shows that a man called in. Dr Nigel Yeo. He was murdered up at Westacombe Farm later that night or early the following morning.'

The woman brightened. This was a moment of excitement, as close to fame as she was likely to get. 'I heard about that on the radio.'

Jen got out a photograph and set it on the counter. 'Do you remember him?'

'Yes! The last customer of the night. He said he was glad we were still open. He hadn't realized how low he was on diesel. I told him it wouldn't do to run out at that time of night and he said especially as he was heading out into the wilds.'

Jen thought that all made sense and it was exactly as they'd suspected. 'Thanks.' She paused, and thought she'd throw the woman a little titbit to make her day. 'You were probably the last person, other than the killer, to see him alive.' When she walked out onto the forecourt she turned and saw the woman was already on her phone, spreading the news to all her friends, basking in a strange sort of glory.

Chapter Twenty-Three

THE PATIENTS TOGETHER OFFICES WHERE Nigel Yeo had been based were in Ilfracombe, not far from Hope Street. That was where Simon Walden, the victim in Matthew's first North Devon murder inquiry, had lived and images of the case – the chaotic, quirky house and its bright, articulate residents – returned as he parked and looked down over the town.

Matthew made an effort to refocus his attention on the present inquiry. He'd been allowed to take Alexander Mackenzie's notes from the hospital and had read them before setting out. He'd found little new there. There was nothing that might suddenly have triggered a need for a cover-up surrounding Mack's death. Nothing to explain a good man's murder. Or the death of an engaging ageing hippy.

Matthew wasn't puzzled by Yeo's involvement in the Mackenzie suicide. Nigel had been friends with the Mackenzie family, and he'd probably have seen Mack's suicide as a test case, an example of how the trust might have mishandled other patients who were suffering acute depression. It could be useful ammunition in his attempt to push mental health further up the agenda.

No, it was Nigel Yeo's dramatic murder which was so start-ling and inexplicable. Matthew couldn't quite see how it could relate to Mack's death. Yeo's investigation had been ongoing. There was nothing in these notes which suggested new infor-mation. If Nigel Yeo had discovered something new, it seemed he hadn't shared it with the medics or the team at the hospital. He might, though, Matthew thought, have shared it with his colleagues at NDPT.

He'd started walking down one of the steep roads leading to the high street when his phone buzzed. An unfamiliar number.

'Inspector Venn. It's Fiona Radley.'

The head of PR, who was so protective of Roger Prior.

'I've checked with my colleagues here. Nigel had a meeting with the end-of-life team last Friday. It started at four p.m., though he was a little late arriving. It was all perfectly routine. They were talking about the transition between hospital and social care. Something we're determined to improve here at North Devon.' Still sending out the corporate message, even in a call to the police.

Matthew continued down the steep street. It was empty apart from a cat sleeping on one of the doorsteps. Tourists didn't wander this far from the harbour. He found the office in a converted domestic house, part of an Edwardian terrace. On one side was a dentist's surgery, on the other a family home. A brass plaque on the door announced its presence and told visitors to walk in. Matthew hadn't made an appointment and wasn't even sure if anyone would be there, but a plump woman in her forties, wearing a sleeveless yellow top and a yellow skirt, was sitting at a desk, fanning herself with a manila file. On the desk was a woman's magazine, which from the front cover had the sole purpose of celebrating the scandals of celebrities. The room was very warm. She seemed surprised to see him. He introduced himself.

'You'll be here about poor Nigel.' She wore large, heavy-rimmed specs, took them off and wiped her eyes. Matthew could see no tears. 'I wasn't sure what I should do this morning, but I thought I should come in anyway. I phoned one of the board members and he said to keep things ticking over until they find a new boss.'

'What's your role, Ms . . . ?' Matthew paused.

'Bull. Steph Bull. Admin officer, they call me. But really general dogsbody. I answer the phone, man reception, do the filing and printing, make sure everyone's diaries are up to date, take minutes at meetings.'

'How many other people are employed here?'

'Three more. Julie, Tony and Lauren. They're all part-time, and nobody else is in on a Monday. Julie and Tony work mostly with community groups. Lauren does the fundraising and finance, but she seems to have become Nigel's right-hand woman, working with him on his pet projects.' From her tone, Matthew guessed that Steph and Lauren Miller were not best friends.

'I'm not entirely sure what the NDPT does.' Matthew sat in the chair on the public side of the desk. 'Perhaps you could explain.'

'We're here to represent the patients' views to the medical institutions.' A pause. 'We work with local authorities and patient groups, as a kind of co-ordinating body, and feed our findings back to the hospitals and primary health trusts.'

'And does investigation into individual negligence cases usually form a part of your work?'

'Not until Nigel arrived.' She snapped her lips shut as if

frightened she might reveal too much. Perhaps she didn't want to appear to be speaking ill of the dead. 'Before he retired, Philip was in charge. A lovely man. He saw his role as different, more supportive to the medical trusts, providing information to improve their services. His style was more . . .' – she paused again – '. . . collaborative.'

'And Nigel wasn't collaborative?'

Matthew thought he knew what was going on here. The previous boss had been after a quiet life in the run-up to retirement. He'd disliked confrontation. Then along came Nigel, with his medical training. More energy and more confidence. Generating more work for the staff, who'd had a very easy life under the old regime.

'He said our role was to shake things up. Look at better ways of doing things, represent the patients more actively. He left Julie and Tony doing the routine community engagement, and took on the more active inquiries.'

'What about Lauren Miller?'

'Oh, she was brought in by Nigel and she was a true believer. I suppose she said all the right things to get the job. Before her, we had Millie. She took redundancy after the first month. She'd been here for years and couldn't adapt to the new ways.' Steph looked over her glasses. 'I did say she should stick it out, because she only had a year to retirement, but she couldn't face the pressure. She said the stress was getting her down.'

'And the stress was about Nigel suggesting the organization take on a more challenging role?'

'No, Millie wouldn't have had much to do with that, except making sure we had the funds to cover it. No, it was Nigel getting an auditor in to look at the books. A legal requirement apparently, though Philip hadn't seemed to see the need.'

Matthew nodded. He suspected that Millie had been incompetent rather than fraudulent, but it wouldn't hurt to talk to Lauren again. 'If you could let me have the other staff's contact details . . .'

Steph looked at her phone and rattled off mobile numbers and email addresses. 'Julie and Tony live locally, but Lauren's out in Appledore.' From her tone, the town could have been at the other end of the country. 'She uses it as an excuse to work from home one day a week.' This was obviously another niggling resentment.

Matthew wondered how Nigel had survived the poisonous atmosphere of the NDPT office. *He* found it tricky enough to manage his own team: Ross May with his allegiance to Superintendent Joe Oldham, and impulsive Jen Rafferty with her flashes of temper. Steph turned her attention back to the magazine and to fan herself again with the file. The flab beneath her upper arm wobbled as it moved. He found himself fascinated by it and forced himself to turn away.

'We came across a number in Nigel's diary,' Matthew said. '8531 or 8537. Does that mean anything to you? Could it be a reference for a case? A file?'

She shook her head. 'It doesn't mean anything to me.' She'd given the matter very little thought.

Matthew persisted. 'On Friday morning Nigel had a meeting in the hospital. He was there later in the day. I understand it was a routine session.'

'Oh yeah. That was another of his particular interests. End-of-life care. I suppose it was personal because of the way his wife died. Tragic.' There was no evidence in her voice that she'd shared Yeo's sadness or his interest in the subject. 'He'd started looking into care homes too. As if we didn't have enough to do.'

So, that confirms Radley's phone call. The later meeting had nothing to do with Alexander Mackenzie. Nigel had bumped into Ratna Joshi by chance in the hospital, just as she said.

'And what was he doing between those meetings?'

'No idea.' She shrugged. 'We were expecting him back in the office but he never turned up. He didn't even bother ringing in.'

Matthew stood up. All the other people in Yeo's life had been devastated by his death, but this woman seemed not to care. He'd reached the door when she spoke again. 'He wasn't a saint, you know. Not the man everyone thought he was. It's all very well having principles, but not everyone's as bright or driven as him. We got the impression that he cared more about his ideals than he did about us.'

Chapter Twenty-Four

ON HIS WAY BACK TO THE police station, Matthew stopped at the Woodyard. The back of the building was still taped off and a constable stood there, red-faced and bored, but the centre was just opening after a morning of shutdown. Matthew went in with the elderly ladies carrying yoga mats. He overheard gossip about the killing:

'Liz said it was Wesley Curnow that got killed. Such a gentle soul. I bought some art from him at the Christmas craft fair.'

'Makes you think, though. Maureen cancelled this morning. Just in case.'

'I doubt if a killer's going to come into the yoga class.' There was a ripple of laughter.

'Well, you never know. I thought twice about coming.' This voice was anxious, almost panicky. 'And after what happened here earlier in the year. It's a strange sort of coincidence, isn't it?'

The women moved on through the building and then the entrance hall was almost empty. Emptier than it should have been on a weekday morning. That was something else for

Jonathan to worry about, Matthew thought. He ran the Woodyard on a shoestring, and couldn't afford for freelance classes to cancel. It had been hard enough recently to keep the place going.

He found his husband in the cafe, chatting to the staff. The night before there'd still been a tension between them, but now Jonathan looked up and gave one of his wide, wonderful smiles. Lucy Braddick was there. She'd been wiping tables and there was still a cloth in her hand. She was anxious, agitated and Jonathan was trying to calm her. 'Nothing bad will happen to you, Luce. I promise. It's not like last time.'

'Wesley was my friend,' she said. 'I'm sad. Not worried about me.'

'When did you last see him?' Matthew knew Lucy well and they too were friends.

'Yesterday. He was in here yesterday, waiting for someone.' She looked at Bob, the cafe manager. 'Wasn't he?'

Bob shrugged. 'I didn't notice him, but it was manic busy until mid-afternoon.'

'Did you see him with anyone else, Luce?' Jonathan asked. She shook her head. 'He went off on his own.'

'How do you know he was waiting for someone?'

Lucy thought about that. 'He often met people in here. He'd sit and wait with the free newspaper and sometimes he'd get a coffee, and then someone would come and buy him lunch.' A pause. 'Or a cake. He liked Bob's cakes.'

Matthew smiled. 'And these people he met, were they all women?'

She nodded, as if the idea was new to her. 'Yeah! All women!'

'Did you recognize any of them?'

Lucy frowned. 'Some of them were regulars, but I don't know their names.'

'If I show you a photo, would you recognize them?'

'I don't know.' Matthew saw that the anxiety was setting in again.

'It wouldn't be like a test,' he said. 'More like a game.' He paused. 'You could have your dad with you, if that would help.'

'I don't live with my dad now.' She gave a beam; for a moment the anxiety was forgotten. 'I've got my own place.'

Jonathan smiled. 'It's in River Bank, isn't it, Luce? Supported living.'

'Home, sweet home.' Another big smile.

'I bet your dad misses you.' Matthew had come to know Maurice Braddick too. He was in his eighties, a widower, and he loved the bones of his learning-disabled daughter. Loved her enough, Matthew thought now, to let her go.

'I sometimes go and stay at his house at weekends,' Lucy conceded. 'He likes the company.'

'So, I might bring in some pictures for you to look at.'

'You can come to my flat if you like,' she said. 'I'll make you a cup of tea.'

After leaving the Woodyard, Matthew drove on to Westacombe. He felt unable to settle, and hated the thought of going back to his overheated office in the police station before he needed to be there for the evening briefing. It was late afternoon now and the roads were quiet, everything washed with sunlight. The fields were so dry after weeks of drought that they were white, as if they'd been treated with lime. Matthew thought of Frank Ley. When Matthew had broken the news of Wesley's death, he hadn't told Ley that they suspected the murder weapon was a piece of glass, which, only the day before, had stood in the comfortable living room in Westacombe House. Perhaps now, it was time to do that.

As he drove into the farmyard, he saw the Grieves twins. They were playing on a swing hanging from a tree beside the family's cottage. One girl was sitting on the swing and the other was standing behind her, rocking, so it jerked from side to side. They were shrieking with laughter. He thought how idyllic their childhood seemed. He'd been an only child, growing up in a family where laughter was in short supply. His mother had usually disapproved of his friends, so he'd grown up with the notion that he was different, even superior in some way. No wonder the other kids in the class had disliked him and stayed clear.

He moved round the house to Ley's front door and knocked but there was no answer. Matthew had asked him to stay in Westacombe for a few days, rather than going to his London home, but of course, that had been a request, not some form of house arrest. The man could be working, visiting one of his other businesses. But his absence made Matthew uneasy, jittery. Again, he couldn't face going back to the police station in Barnstaple, especially while he was so anxious, so jumpy. He thought he'd wait for a while to see if Ley returned.

He walked towards the end of Ley's land. Jonathan would have been able to name the shrubs, the swathes of blooms in the beds, but they were mysterious to Matthew and he felt that he'd wandered into some strange and secret garden. Like the Grieves' cottage, it was the stuff of fiction. The sweet smell of the flowers and the sound of insects had a dreamlike quality and Matthew thought that the police officers in the farmyard seemed to belong to a different narrative altogether. If this was Alexander Mackenzie's work, the young man had been a skilled gardener. Beyond the more formal borders, Matthew came to a wild flower meadow. It was past its best now, but still covered with buttercups, clover and tall, white daisies. There was a path through the middle, where the grass had been flattened. In the distance was the sea, impossibly blue.

He followed the track to a patch of heathland, separated from the meadow by a low dry-stone wall. Matthew assumed that this marked the edge of Ley's land. There was a stile over the wall and he stood for a moment with his foot on the wooden bar, feeling a sense of freedom and adventure that he'd never experienced as a child. The closest he'd got had been the memory he'd shared with his mother of the picnics on the beach, but he'd been closely supervised then and called back if he wandered too far into the rockpools at the side of the bay. He imagined that the two girls on the swing would be allowed at least as far as the meadow by themselves. He pictured them picking armfuls of flowers and taking them home for their mother.

Beyond the wall there was rough open land, covered with huge clumps of gorse, startlingly yellow, but the path led on and was easy to follow. It came eventually to a five-bar gate which opened onto the main road on the outskirts of Instow. A hundred yards away Matthew could see the unmarked turning into the paved track, which led back to the farm. The road was busier with traffic than it had been; it was the end of the working day.

Matthew thought it would be perfectly possible for any of the Westacombe residents to have taken this shortcut the day before. They would have avoided the notice of the police officer at the farm entrance. They'd have needed a lift into Barnstaple or to have borrowed a car to get to the Woodyard to stab Wesley Curnow, but perhaps the killer had an accomplice, knowing or unknowing.

Walking back through the garden to Westacombe Farm, Matthew wondered what he'd do if Frank was still absent from the place and considered the implication of such a disappearance. Might Ley be the murderer? Or a third victim? He knew that planning ahead was his skill and his weakness. He spent too much of his time responding to disasters that never happened. Jonathan said that he had a vivid imagination: *That's why you're such a brilliant detective, but you could be an artist. Or a writer.*

When he emerged from the formal garden and onto the lawn, he saw that Ley was there, and he felt relieved and shocked at the same time. It was almost as if Ley was part of the mirage the garden had created in Matthew's mind, a fantasy figure from a piece of fiction. The man was sitting close to the house on a sun lounger, with a glass in his hand. He wore a straw hat, which had the look of a boater: Billy Bunter in summer issue uniform. He lifted the glass in greeting to Matthew, and didn't seem surprised to see him.

'I hope I wasn't trespassing,' Matthew said. 'I called earlier but you were out.'

'Yes, a meeting with the team in the Golden Fleece in Lovacott; it's one of my businesses. They've just won an award for their hospitality and I wanted to share the good news with the staff.' Despite the celebratory nature of his visit to the pub, his tone was reflective, a little sad. 'It was good to get away from all that's happened here.'

'You're still hands-on then.'

'Well . . .' Ley gave a little laugh. 'I share the glory and they do all the hard work. You know how it is.'

'I've been exploring,' Matthew said. 'I found the shortcut down to Instow. Is it a public right of way?'

'Not across the garden, though I don't mind if any of the Westacombe residents use it. Beyond the wall and the stile, it's common land and free to anyone.' He looked at Matthew. 'Do you think an outsider came in that way and attacked Nigel Yeo?'

Matthew didn't like to say he was more concerned that one of the residents had left by the path to kill Wesley. 'I'm not sure what I think yet,' he said.

Ley swivelled his body so he was more upright and his feet were on the ground. 'Do you have any news, Inspector?'

Venn sat on the low wall which surrounded the terrace. At least now he wasn't looking down on the man and they could have a proper conversation.

'When Eve found Wesley's body, she identified the weapon that killed him.' He paused. 'It was a shard of glass from the vase she'd given you. The large blue vase that held the flowers which were standing in your fireplace when I first came to visit you. Of course, she might be mistaken. You might be able to find the vase for me.'

'I can look,' Ley said, 'but I'm sure I won't find it if Eve has identified it. She's an artist. Each piece of glass is individual. It holds her signature.'

'You said that Sarah might have come in to tidy the house this morning, but she said she wasn't here.'

'Really? I must have been mistaken then.' He gave another little smile. 'I'm getting very absent-minded in my old age.'

'Would you have any idea how the glass came to be in Wesley Curnow's workshop at the Woodyard?'

'Do you think I killed him?' Ley's mood was quite changed now. He was suddenly sharper, more alert.

'I don't think anything. But I need to know how a piece of

glass from your living room ended up in Wesley Curnow's neck.'

'Any of the residents could have got in. There's a door from their side of the house, and the key hangs in their ground-floor kitchen. None of us is exactly security conscious.'

'There were lots of tools in the shed at the Woodyard, potential weapons. I'm wondering why a killer would risk coming into your space and stealing the bowl. It seems unnecessarily complicated.'

'Some sort of message, do you think? Or perhaps the killer wanted to implicate me?'

Perhaps. Or Eve. Or either of the Grieves.

'Is there anyone who might have a reason to do that?'

There was a moment of silence filled with birdsong.

'I've always tried to do the right thing, Inspector. I explained that when we first met. But I haven't been popular. Some of my projects haven't worked out as I would have wished.' He paused. 'There was one scheme . . . It caused a negative reaction. I had hate mail. Threats.'

'What was the scheme?'

'There's a hamlet on the edge of Exmoor called Spennicott. The school was about to close and they'd already lost their shop. The nearest post office is five miles away. The community was dying. So, I bought it.'

'What exactly did you buy?'

'All of it. Well, as much as I could. There were already a number of cottages for sale, too expensive for the locals. Some of them I let out at a reasonable rent to young people from the village. A few I hung on to for holiday lets to provide an income. I took over the pub and put in a manager to bring it back to life. And everyone went along with me. They knew that the new businesses would bring jobs and that would attract families into the area.'

'But things changed?' Matthew could see how the story was moving forward.

'Yes. Perhaps I moved too quickly. Too dramatically. There's a big house on the edge of the village, which had been turned into an old people's home years ago, and it was obvious that the business wasn't viable. Social services couldn't afford to pay the fees to keep the place running and nor could individuals. I put in an offer. A change of management wouldn't make the care home any more profitable – the model just doesn't work – so my plan is to turn it into a boutique hotel.'

Matthew thought about that. Ley had said he was motivated by guilt, not profit, in his development projects.

'Couldn't you subsidize the care home, to save the residents from disruption, at least for their lifetimes?'

'I'm not sure that I could,' Ley said. 'It doesn't meet any of the regs. A recent inspection rated it as excellent on care but in need of substantial improvement when it came to hygiene and facilities. The old people might love staying there, but it's probably not safe.' He paused. 'Imagine how I'd feel if one of them had an accident? Or there was an outbreak of food poisoning? Besides, I don't think it's right to prop up a failing business. It gives a false sense of hope, if it's not going to be sustainable in the long term.'

So, Matthew thought. *Perhaps you're not such a philanthropist after all.* 'And it was the closure of the care home that prompted the hate mail and the threats?'

'Yes, there was a campaign, not just in the village but more widely.'

'Did the campaign have a leader?' Matthew couldn't see

how this could be relevant. Ley hadn't been murdered and he couldn't believe that someone with a grudge would kill two strangers just to implicate the financier. But he was curious.

'Yes, a writer called Paul Reed. His mother was one of the care home's residents. I'm not quite sure why he was so venomous in his response.' Ley paused. 'Guilt perhaps because he wasn't prepared to look after his relative himself.' He looked up. 'As I said before, guilt is a terrible thing. Or he could just have been looking for a good story, another reputation to trash.'

There was a moment of silence. Matthew could tell that there was more to come. 'I should probably have told you this before, but Reed involved Patients Together in his campaign. He said that most of the residents of the care home were NHS patients too.'

'So, Nigel was investigating your role in closing down the home?'

Steph Bull, the admin officer, had said that Yeo had been passionate about the transition from hospital to social care. Matthew could see how he might get pulled in to this project.

Ley nodded. 'Unofficially, I think. I can't see how it was really part of his brief. Perhaps he felt he had to follow up the complaint just because the two of us were friends and he couldn't be seen to show any favouritism. He went to visit last week. The Thursday before he died.'

Venn waited for Ley to give more details, but the man remained silent.

'What were his findings?'

Ley turned back to face him. 'I don't know,' he said. 'How could I? Nigel didn't have the chance to make his report.'

Chapter Twenty-Five

AFTER DROPPING JANEY MACKENZIE IN INSTOW, Jen Rafferty made her way back to the police station. She tracked down the registered owner of the vehicle which had blocked Janey in the afternoon before and gave him a call. He was belligerent, blustering.

'The council should have reserved parking for locals. All those people coming from outside, taking up our spaces, when we just want to take the kiddies to the beach. I didn't know I was doing any harm.'

He had a Brummie accent. Not so local himself. But he'd confirmed Janey's story. She hadn't driven into Barnstaple the day before. Not using her own car at least.

Jen wanted to talk to the mother of Luke Wallace, the teenager who'd committed suicide in London, the lad whose death had forced Roger Prior to resign from his high-profile post in Camden. She'd contacted the woman through the 'Love Luke' Facebook page, and they'd arranged to talk on the phone. Matthew Venn was still out and Jen used his office to take the call. This wasn't a conversation to be had with the noise of the open-plan room in the background.

'Detective Sergeant Rafferty.' The woman sounded calm, normal. Jen wasn't sure what she'd been expecting. A nutter perhaps. Someone hysterical. Or greedy, just desperate for compensation. 'Thanks for getting in touch. How can I help?'

Jen had planned how to approach the woman carefully. It wouldn't do to suggest that Roger Prior was a killer. Or even to link him to the investigation. Jen might not like the man, but she couldn't be the person to ruin his career without evidence. For one thing, Cynthia would never talk to her again and Jen was already missing her support and friendship.

'We had another suicide, much like Luke's, here on the North Devon coast. Our officers were involved. We want to prepare them for any possible future case, perhaps put together a training package to help them deal better with people with severe depression. I hoped you might be able to help, to give the signs to look out for.' And all that, Jen thought, was true. She'd be prepared to put together a training module herself. She knew what depression felt like.

'But that's brilliant!' Jen hadn't been expecting such an enthusiastic response and felt a little uncomfortable. The woman went on: 'Of course, the police have to be at the front line when it comes to mental illness these days. The health service has been cut so much the police have to take up the slack.'

'You felt your son was let down by the NHS?'

'He was! I don't blame any individual, but there just wasn't anyone there when we most needed the support.' She paused. 'There *were* other influences. He'd found his way onto one of those foul suicide websites.'

'What are those?' Jen looked on Venn's desk for a pen to take notes. They were lined in a row next to a neat pile of scrap paper. Of course they were.

'There are chatrooms where people come together to celebrate dying, to encourage members to take their own lives,' Luke's mother said. 'That was how it seemed to us at least, though they *say* they're just offering support.'

'Is there any way I could find out if the local young man who died here had accessed one of those?'

'I don't know.' The woman sounded uncertain. 'I can send you the link to the one Luke used. It was called Peace at Last. You might be able to trace the information through that. But the sites change and move, and they're not illegal.'

'I understand that the head of the trust resigned soon after your son's death. He must have felt some responsibility.'

'He was forced to leave.' Now the woman's words were harsh and bitter. 'And he moved almost straight into another cushy, well-paid post in a different part of the country.' There was no mention of where Prior had taken up his new post. Perhaps she hadn't cared enough about the details to find out.

'Has anyone else been in touch with you?' Jen asked. 'We've been working closely with an organization called Patients Together and their senior officer, Dr Nigel Yeo, was looking into the young man's death here.'

'Yes! Soon after Luke died, we had lots of enquiries, more than I could remember, but that was a recent one.'

'Was Nigel in touch by phone?'

'By email first and then we had a phone call. I told him what I've just told you.' For the first time in the conversation, the woman sounded uncertain. 'If you're working together, can't you just ask him?'

'He died,' Jen said, 'very suddenly. That's one reason for my call.'

There was a silence. 'Oh,' the woman said. 'I'm so sorry. We only had that one conversation, but he seemed such a lovely, caring man.'

Jen wandered back into the main office. There was still no sign of Venn, but Ross was there. Of all the team, he was the most tech savvy. She explained about the suicide forum and Luke Wallace. 'If we get hold of Mack's laptop, would we be able to tell what he'd been into?'

'You think that might be relevant?' Ross, as ever, seemed dismissive of any idea that wasn't his. Or Joe Oldham's.

'Yeah, I do. What if Nigel Yeo had found out, in the course of his investigation, that Mack had been encouraged to kill himself on one of those sick sites? You told me Mack's psychiatrist said Yeo was furious the afternoon before he died. Discovering that Mack had been provoked to suicide might have made him even angrier than if he'd thought it was down to the hospital's negligence.' Jen thought for a moment. 'According to Janey, Mack's suicide note said he was looking for peace at last. That's the name of the chatroom Luke had accessed.'

'It could be a coincidence . . .'

'Yeah, it could. But it does fit in with all the facts.'

'You believe Yeo might have traced this suicide site to someone local?' Jen could tell that Ross was more interested now. She thought if she wasn't careful, he'd claim the idea as his own.

'I hadn't thought that far, but maybe.'

'It'd have to be some nutjob, provoking a kid to kill himself. Can you think of anyone involved who might be that wacko?'

Jen shook her head. She suspected Wesley might have looked at the site, not because he was suicidal but because he'd always been curious about the strange and the perverse. He said it fed into his art. Wesley was dead too, though, and that didn't fit with the theory. 'It'd be great if the tech guys could check Mack's laptop, if I can persuade the family to hand it over to us. Luke's mother sent me a link to the site *he* was using. Wouldn't it be interesting if Mack had accessed it too?' She paused. 'Nigel Yeo had phoned Mrs Wallace the week before he died. One coincidence too many, do you think?'

Ross was just about to answer when Jen saw Joe Oldham approaching. The superintendent was a big man. Once he might have been fit; he was the leading light in the rugby club after all. Now he was flabby, with a florid face suggesting a heart attack about to happen. He could have retired months before, but Jen thought he liked the status, the power. He'd have nobody to bully at home.

'Where's Venn?' The superintendent didn't hide his distaste.

'At Westacombe following up an inquiry with Mr Ley.' Jen paused. 'He'll be back in an hour for the briefing, if you'd like to join us.' Knowing Oldham was on his way out for his first drink of the evening and that it was a compulsion he'd not be able to resist.

'Nah,' Oldham said. 'Don't want to interfere. Don't want it said I don't trust my team. Tell Venn to keep me updated.' He waddled away. His breathing was so poor that Jen almost felt sorry for him. Almost, but not quite, because he was a poisonous sod.

She waited until he'd left the room before speaking again. 'I'll phone George Mackenzie, see if he'll let us have Mack's laptop.'

'I've got a friend in tech. A wizard. You get it, I'll make sure he does it himself and fast-tracks it. We can sort out the budget later.'

She smiled. She enjoyed these moments of collaboration with Ross, thought he might not be such a dick after all. She got out her phone to call Mackenzie. By the time she'd finished, Venn was back and the meeting was about to start.

Venn was unusually informal, with rolled-up shirtsleeves, no jacket. He looked flushed, as if he'd been in the sun. He stood at the front, beside the large whiteboard, and as always, they quickly fell silent. Jen wished she had that authority.

'It's been a busy day,' he said, 'though I'm not sure how far we've got. More questions than answers, I think. Ross, can you take minutes, and get them out to the team as soon as possible? There's too much information to take in at a sitting.'

Ross nodded and got out his iPad. Throughout the briefing, Jen heard him tapping on the keypad, a background rhythm to the conversation.

'Shall I start?' As Venn leaned back against the desk, Jen saw that there were grass stains on his pale summer trousers. She was astonished. She'd never before seen him anything but immaculate. 'Ross and I met the team at the hospital this morning. Their head of comms was very much in charge and she seemed more concerned about the hospital's image than providing any useful information. Mack's psychiatrist, Ratna Joshi, was more forthcoming when we saw her on her own, though, and implied that something had disturbed Yeo later that day. Jen, could you go and see her tomorrow?'

Jen nodded and Venn continued. 'Patients Together, headed up by Yeo, seems to have been pretty dysfunctional. I had the impression he was easing out the dead wood – the woman in charge of finance had taken redundancy – and that Lauren was the only staff member he trusted.'

'Sounds pretty ruthless,' Ross said.

'Maybe. Or maybe he took his role seriously and wasn't prepared to tolerate hangers-on.'

Matthew paused and looked around the room again to check that he had their attention. 'I had a quick visit to the Woodyard. Lucy Braddick says Wesley was in the cafe on Sunday afternoon and waiting for someone, who didn't turn up.' He glanced around once more to make sure they all recognized Lucy's name. They did. Lucy was a hero to the team. 'Usually he met one of his middle-aged lady friends there, apparently. I'd like to get a handle on who those women were. Wesley might have confided in one of them.' A pause. 'Ross, that's for you.'

'Start with Cynthia Prior,' Jen said.

'The magistrate?'

'Yeah, she was his biggest admirer. And of course, she's linked to the case because her husband's head of the trust. And Roger Prior was in charge of the trust where Luke Wallace killed himself. An interesting coincidence.'

'I met Prior at this morning's meeting.' Ross paused. 'A cold fish.'

'Arctic,' she said.

'Finally,' Venn said, 'I went to visit Frank Ley. While I was waiting for him, I found a shortcut to the main road between Barnstaple and Instow. It goes through his garden and over a bit of common land. We can't assume that just because a Westacombe resident didn't pass through the checkpoint at the farmyard, they couldn't have killed Wesley Curnow.'

Jen thought Venn had finished and would ask her to take over, but he went on:

'It seems that Ley has been the target of a hate campaign over one of his developments. I'm not sure how that can be relevant, but if his connection to the murders comes to light, it could be an excuse for the press to start thinking conspiracy theories and cover-ups. I'll check it out.' Now, he did nod towards Jen to continue.

She described her visit to the Mackenzies' house in Instow. 'They're much angrier about the way Mack was treated than I'd realized.' She turned to Venn and again explained what she'd learned from her call to London. 'Dr Yeo had phoned her too, not long before he was killed. Ross and I wondered if Mack Mackenzie had used the same site. In his suicide note, he wrote that he was finding peace at last, and Peace at Last was the name of the group Luke had joined. We wondered if there might be a connection.'

'There were almost five years between both deaths,' Venn said. 'It seems a little unlikely.'

'We don't know how many other suicides linked to the site there have been.'

Venn considered for a moment. 'You think that Nigel Yeo had tracked down someone who was provoking these young people to kill themselves?' He looked out at the room. 'Why would anyone want to do something like that?'

'Power?' Jen said. 'Control?' *Some strange form of art?* She could imagine Wesley dabbling in the site, manipulating the members for his own amusement. But Wesley was dead.

Venn didn't answer and she continued. 'I think it's worth investigation, and George Mackenzie has just given permission for us to take his son's laptop. Ross has a mate in IT who's willing to fast-track it.'

'Let's give it a go, then.' Jen couldn't tell what Venn was thinking, whether he was humouring them or if he thought it was really worth following up. The inspector paused for a beat. 'I want to know where Yeo was on Friday afternoon. We know he had a meeting in the hospital in the morning with Roger Prior and his colleagues and he was there again at close of play, but he seems to have gone AWOL for the rest of the day. Let's find out where he was and what he was doing.'

They drifted away then and Jen walked home, through the evening streets. People had spilled out of the pubs onto the Newport pavements. At home, her children were in their rooms, each on a screen, each preoccupied and scarcely responding when she looked in on them.

How can I tell what they're looking at? Would I know if they were depressed? If some sick bastard was persuading them that suicide is a grand gesture, a final escape?

Chapter Twenty-Six

MEL WAS ON AN EARLY SHIFT but Ross got up before her. He'd seen little of her since Nigel Yeo's murder and he had an ill-defined, worrying sense that she was unhappy. When he'd got in the night before, she'd already eaten and was ready for bed, sitting in the living room in her nightie and the silk dressing gown he'd bought for her last birthday, watching television. There was cold meat and salad in the fridge and she set it out for him and put a jacket potato in the microwave, but seemed reluctant to talk. When he joined her in bed, he tried to take her in his arms, but she turned away, tense and silent. Now, he went to the kitchen while she was still asleep, before the alarm clock had woken him, made tea and brought it up to her.

'That's kind.' She seemed more herself. He loved her like this, tousled, bare-faced. She'd pulled herself into a sitting position and her nightdress had slipped over one shoulder.

'Is everything okay?' He wanted to reach out and stroke the shoulder, but her coldness of the night before made him reluctant. He didn't know how he'd feel if she pushed him away.

'Yeah,' she said. 'Everything's fine. Sorry if I seemed a bit grumpy last night. It was a long day. One of my residents died. We were expecting it, but she'd been with us for years.'

'Oh, I'm sorry.' But still he didn't touch her and still he wasn't entirely reassured.

Ross found Cynthia Prior in the magistrates' court. He arrived just before the morning session ended for lunch and slipped in at the back. Cynthia was chair of the bench and Ross heard her sentence a young woman to probation for shoplifting. He knew the woman and the family she'd come from and thought she was bloody lucky not to have got at the very least a suspended prison term. He stood with the faded solicitor and the scattering of the defendant's relatives, as the magistrates left the court, then went to wait in the lobby.

Cynthia Prior emerged on her own. She was wearing an orange linen dress and carried a big straw bag. She recognized him immediately and wasn't pleased to see him.

'Detective Constable May, do you have a case this afternoon? I thought it was just traffic for the rest of the day.'

'I was hoping to talk to you.' The lobby had cleared of people now, and a shaft of sunlight caught motes of dust. 'About Wesley Curnow.'

'Ah, poor Wesley. I'll miss him so much.' She turned away from him, perhaps to hide her distress, and continued to walk to the entrance. 'I was just going to lunch. I don't have a lot of time. If you must ask your questions, why don't you join me?'

He followed her around the corner of the street and into a little tea shop where she was clearly well known. A small table furthest away from the window had a reserved sign on it and she sat there. When the waitress came, she ordered smoked salmon sandwiches and Earl Grey tea without looking at the menu. Ross was hungry, but he wasn't sure about the etiquette of eating with a potential suspect, who was also a member of the magistracy. In the end he went for coffee and a teacake. He couldn't see a teacake as proper food.

'Wesley was a good friend,' Cynthia said, once the waitress had left them. 'What would you like to know?'

'When did you last see him?'

'The Friday night of my party. He was one of the last to leave. I did speak to him, though, on the Sunday that he died. He phoned me in the morning, obviously upset about Nigel's murder. He asked if we could meet up.'

The waitress arrived with a tray, then had to return with cutlery. She was elderly and slow and Ross struggled to contain his impatience.

'Did you agree to see him?'

Cynthia cut her sandwich into smaller pieces. 'No. Of course, I wanted to. I could tell how upset Wesley was, but Sunday's our family time. Inviolable. And my husband's not finding things easy either at the moment; you'll know all about Nigel's witch hunt. I didn't feel I could desert him. So, I cooked a proper lunch, which we ate mid-afternoon, and we opened a bottle of good wine, and then another, and that was our Sunday.'

'Why did you invite Nigel to your party, and arrange for him to meet Sergeant Rafferty, if you thought his investigation was a witch hunt?'

She shrugged. 'I wasn't sure why exactly Nigel wanted to meet Jen. If he'd seriously thought Roger and his team had committed a crime, he'd have made a more formal approach.'

'What did your husband make of your relationship with Mr Curnow?' Ross knew he would never be able to cope with Mel hanging out with another bloke, trips to London, meals in restaurants where all their friends could see what was going on. Making a tit of him.

'Oh my God, it wasn't that sort of relationship.' Cynthia gave a choking burst of laughter. 'I didn't fancy him! I didn't even like him that much. It was a friendship of convenience. I don't enjoy going to the theatre or to exhibitions on my own. What's the fun in that! And he did know about art. He could be entertaining too if he set his mind to it. Roger was just glad that he didn't have to turn out unless it was really something he enjoyed.'

'What about Wesley's other lady friends?' Ross asked. 'Did they have *friendships of convenience* too?'

'Oh, I think some of them imagined they were in love with him. He could be charming and he had a way of making them feel special. In return for a free meal and a few glasses of wine. He had rather expensive tastes in booze. But it would have taken a very classy offer – a Scottish castle or a New York apartment – to persuade him to give up his freedom. He was genuinely a free spirit and he did love his art and his music.'

'Would he have called one of his other women on Sunday morning, do you think? As you were unavailable?'

'He might have called Eve. They might not have been close friends, but they respected each other's work. Really, he saw the other, older women he hung out with just as meal tickets.'

'What about Janey Mackenzie?'

She gave another little laugh. 'I think Wes was finally coming to realize that Janey was a bit beyond him.'

'She went with him to your party.'

'She did, but she made it quite clear all night that she was bored out of her skull. Wesley's closer to her parents in age and I think she saw him as a family friend, a kind of quite hip uncle, rather than a potential partner.' Cynthia looked at her watch. 'I'm sorry, but I really should get back to court.'

'Did Wesley ever discuss Alexander Mackenzie's death with you? Wes was a friend of the family and he lived and worked with Eve at Westacombe. He must have been curious.'

Cynthia got to her feet. She'd already paid the bill, for his share as well as her own, which had made Ross feel uncomfortable, as if he was playing the role that Wesley once had, of kept companion. He thought Matthew Venn would never have allowed himself to be put in this position. She stopped, poised by the table, for a moment.

'Wesley didn't really do curiosity. Not about things like that. He really only cared about himself, his own interests and his own comfort.' She pulled her bag onto her arm. 'Perhaps we're all like that when you come down to it. But some of us are better at hiding our selfishness than others.'

Chapter Twenty-Seven

JEN TRACKED DOWN RATNA JOSHI TO the psychiatric unit in the grounds of the general hospital, where Matthew and Ross had spoken to her the day before. When she finally got through on the phone, after forcing her way through a series of receptionists and a medical secretary, the doctor sounded busy, distracted. 'Is this really necessary? I talked to your colleagues yesterday.'

'More information has come to light,' Jen said. 'I do need your help.'

'I'm on a long shift today. I won't be free until eight this evening.'

'Why don't I come to you?' Jen could sense Joshi dreaming up excuses and continued before she could speak. 'I'll be there at ten.'

Gorsehill, where Mack had been treated, was a modern building not far from the main hospital building. It was run by the same trust. Jen wasn't sure what she'd been expecting:

locked doors, mad people howling at the sky. Instead it could have been any health centre in the country. There was the same wide entrance, with the trust's logo on a sign outside, the same reminder about parking charges. Outside, a group of men in tracksuit bottoms and T-shirts stood smoking. They ignored her as she walked in.

Ratna Joshi came to reception to collect her, and they walked together along a corridor to her office, past a nurses' station, where a woman in her thirties was in tears, apparently inconsolable. As they passed, grief seemed to turn to rage and the patient started yelling at the staff, her words incomprehensible. Ratna approached her and put her arms around her. 'Hey, Lizzie, take it easy. We'll get you home soon. I promise. But you're not quite ready yet. Let's get you back to your room.' The woman sobbed into the young doctor's shoulder and Ratna held her until she grew calm. At last the patient pulled away and looked around her, blank-faced, suddenly completely unemotional. She walked off, straight-backed down the corridor away from them, without another word.

'What was wrong with her?' Jen had found the encounter, the transformation, shocking.

She didn't expect an answer, but as the doctor stopped to unlock her office door, she responded. 'Postnatal psychosis. She was so unwell that she threatened to stab her two-month-old baby. We had to admit her for her own and the baby's safety. She has a toddler at home too.' She stood aside to let Jen in. 'We have a limited number of beds and community care is stretched. Those are the decisions we have to make every day: do I admit Lizzie or a young man with severe depression and a family to support him?' She nodded for Jen to take a chair. 'I assume you *are* here about Alexander Mackenzie and Nigel Yeo.'

'I am.' Jen tried to order her thoughts, still shaken. 'But not to criticize. I don't know how you do this. People think police officers have it tough, but I wouldn't be in your shoes for a day.'

'I'm going to make coffee,' Ratna said. 'Only instant, but better than nothing. Would you like one?'

'Sure.'

Someone walked down the corridor outside singing. The noise was loud, tuneful and joyous. Patient or carer? Did it matter? Somehow, Jen thought, within these walls, it felt as if they were all in it together, all maybe a little bit crazy and a lot under pressure.

'So, what was so urgent?' Ratna asked.

'Nigel had been in touch with the mother of another young guy, Luke Wallace, who committed suicide. Mrs Wallace was convinced that her son was failed by the medical staff who should have been caring for him. He lived in Camden and at the time the trust was managed by Roger Prior.' A pause. 'Mr Prior was the subject of a social media hate campaign and vilified in the local press there.'

Ratna was listening – Jen supposed a psychiatrist would have to be good at that – but she said nothing.

Jen went on: 'I spoke to the woman too. She'd told Nigel that her son had accessed a website that encouraged patients to kill themselves. I wondered if Mack had admitted to doing that too. If he had, it might explain Nigel's anger when you saw him on the evening before his body was found. Perhaps his fury wasn't directed at you and the trust, but at the people behind the website.'

'You believe that was why Nigel Yeo was killed? Because

212

he'd discovered the identity of the individual who persuaded Alexander Mackenzie to jump into the sea that day?'

'I believe it's one explanation.' Jen took a sip of the coffee. 'What do you think? Might it be feasible? Could Mack have been using a site like that?'

Silence. Ratna was frowning, thinking. Nothing she did was hasty or ill-judged. The office looked out onto a courtyard, with a square of green space in the middle. A group of women sat on the grass, chatting. An older woman with a lanyard and a pass seemed to be leading the conversation. Some sort of group therapy session? Jen couldn't hear the words, but was fascinated all the same. She was glad that Ratna was taking time to consider the question seriously.

'He might have done, but I'm not sure if any of us would know if he'd been getting those kinds of messages through a group on the internet. If he was determined to kill himself, he'd have lied, pretended, made up the stories he thought we'd want to hear so we'd discharge him. Or let him discharge himself.' She paused. 'I was taken in. I honestly didn't think he was so sick. He was severely depressed, but he told me he wasn't having suicidal thoughts. He was lying and I should have pressed him.'

'He could have done that? Pretended he was less ill than he really was?'

This time the answer came more quickly. 'Sure. He could have created a narrative in his head that we were the bad people, the people who were trying to stop him finding peace or rest. Or whatever he'd been persuaded by the group that death would bring for him. If he'd bought into that story, he'd see it as his mission to mislead.'

Jen tried to process that. 'Why would anybody do that? Get other people to kill themselves?'

'Not all the websites are persuasive. Some are there genuinely to give support to people with suicidal thoughts, to take the ideas seriously and not to judge. Others might be more dangerous. They could attract people who are very sick themselves and see it as a God-given mission to help sufferers into another world. A messiah complex isn't unusual in psychosis.' She nodded towards the door and gave a little smile. 'Any number of my patients think they're Jesus. Some might join because they're teetering on the edge of suicide and hope the group will help them find the courage and the means.' Ratna paused for a moment. 'I suppose there might be occasional individuals who get off on the power over life and death. Who aren't ill in the sense that we understand the word. Who are just there to provoke another person's death.'

Jen felt winded, as if she'd been punched in the gut. If you could target a vulnerable individual in that way, wouldn't it be murder? An almost perfect murder. 'That would be evil.'

'Yes,' the doctor said. 'Truly evil. But not, I understand, against the law.'

'Have you come across any patients who have admitted to using one of the suicide forums?'

Ratna shook her head. 'But I probably wouldn't. As I said, if someone's that serious about killing themselves, they're not going to discuss it with one of us. We'd be seen as restrictive, part of the conspiracy preventing them from having the freedom to make their own choices.'

'Did Mack have any special friends while he was here? Any of the staff members he was particularly close to?'

'He was only here for one night before he died, so there

was no real chance for him to make friends. And it's hard for severely depressed people to connect with other individuals, especially if they're ill too.'

Jen remembered Mack as Janey had described him: the restless pacing, the incomprehensible muttering, the isolation in a world of his own. She'd called Mack self-obsessed too. Of course, real friendship with another person would be impossible for someone that ill. If Mack *had* turned to the internet suicide forums, with their wild ideas, they would give an impression of community, permission to be entirely selfish. He could take in the comments and the encouragement without needing to give anything in return.

'Was there a staff member he connected to?' Jen asked the question without expecting any positive response and Ratna shook her head.

'This is an acute hospital. Most patients aren't here for long enough to form useful relationships. We're stretched. Impossibly stretched.'

'One last question,' Jen said. She was starting to sense Ratna's impatience. 'When you saw Nigel Yeo on Friday as you were leaving for the day, did he give you any idea where he'd spent the earlier part of the afternoon?'

The doctor shook her head. 'No idea at all.'

Jen's car had been parked in full sunlight and she got the air con blasting as she got in. She sat for a moment before deciding to drive to the coast and to the Mackenzies'. She couldn't think why they might want to hide Mack's laptop or computer, or delete his browsing history, but she didn't want to take any chances.

Martha was just where Jen had seen her on the previous visit, standing on the balcony, looking out at the beach, cigarette in hand. She waved at Jen. 'You're becoming a regular!' Her tone was ambiguous. It didn't make Jen feel that she was welcome.

'I'm sorry to disturb you again. I'm hoping you might be able to help me.'

'George and Janey are working. They're both busy and I wouldn't want to call them home.' Again, the actress managed to give the impression that Jen was intruding. 'But I'll see what I can do. Just wait there and I'll let you in.'

Once more, Jen was led into the sunlit kitchen, but this time the place was tidy, almost sterile. It was hard to imagine the family together here, eating a late breakfast, as they'd been when she'd visited on Sunday. The found objects on the yellow shelf seemed out of place, relics of former days. Martha sat at the table. There was no offer of coffee. 'What is it?'

'Before he was killed, Nigel Yeo spoke to a mother whose son also died from suicide. We have no exact record of the call, but they discussed a website chatroom where people considering suicide were given tips and encouragement to carry it out. Do you know if Alexander visited a similar site?'

Martha shook her head. 'By the end he'd stopped talking to us, to his father and me. At least, he stopped making any sense.' She was no friendlier, but she looked broken, exhausted. No longer the glamorous actress performing for an audience.

'He *did* have access to a computer? A smartphone?'

'Of course. We all do now, don't we?' Again, it was hard to tell whether the weariness was real or manufactured.

'Do you still have his devices?'

Martha looked up. 'Not his phone. That was lost when he

drowned. He always carried it in his jeans pocket. He was always losing the bloody thing. Or sitting on it.'

'His laptop?'

'That's in his room.'

'Would you mind if I took it away with me?'

There was a pause. 'And that would help your investigation how?'

'It's a theory,' Jen said. 'If someone Mack knew was part of the suicide chatroom, and encouraged him to take his own life and then Nigel found out, that could be a motive for murder.'

'But my son didn't have any suicidal friends. Everyone he'd gone to school with was upbeat.' Her voice turned hard and was tinged with envy. 'Normal.'

Jen remembered Ratna's theory about a participant in the group being turned on by the power over life and death. 'Perhaps one of his friends was curious.' She hesitated. 'Or evil.'

'You think someone might have encouraged Mack to take his own life for *fun*?' The woman looked physically sick.

'As I said, it's just a theory.'

'Of course, take his laptop. It's in his room. The small room at the front on the second floor at the top of the stairs.' She looked at Jen. 'Do you mind getting it? I haven't gone in there since he died. George said we should clear his stuff. Move on. But I can't bear the thought of it.' She paused again. 'I slept in his old rugby shirt for the first week after he went missing. I thought it smelled of him.'

'Of course.' At the door, Jen looked back at her. 'Would you mind if I had a quick look through his things? I won't take anything away without your permission.'

Martha stared at her and Jen thought the woman would

refuse. 'Of course,' she said at last. 'He was a very private person. None of us was allowed up there. But I suppose it's not going to bother him now.'

After the first floor, the stairs narrowed. There were two rooms on the top floor, a bathroom and a bedroom. As Martha had said, the bedroom looked down over the beach. There was also a view of the balcony beneath, and on it, Jen saw an overflowing ashtray besides an old-fashioned striped deckchair. She thought Martha must spend most of her days there, separate from the world, reminded of her glory days, whenever passers-by recognized her. It was a sort of stage.

The bedroom was neater than Jen had expected, certainly neater than her children's rooms, even Ella's, and her daughter was a tidy soul. There was a double bed under the window, with a purple duvet cover. A couple of white-wood cupboards containing folded clothes, a desk and an Anglepoise lamp against one wall. On the desk, a laptop, still plugged in. It was hard to believe that someone with the chaotic mind and racing thoughts described by Ratna would keep his room so ordered, but perhaps he needed that. Perhaps he needed this clear space when he was contemplating taking his own life. The decision would be spiritual, almost religious. Perhaps if he was so convinced that it was the right thing for him, he hadn't needed any encouragement and it was a decision he'd taken in a moment of clarity and reason.

Jen unplugged the computer and put it in her bag. She walked down the stairs and paused at the kitchen door. Martha was still sitting there, her face set, apparently lost in thought.

'I've got the PC,' Jen said. 'I've not taken anything else. Was Mack always that tidy?'

'Yes,' Martha said. 'It was one of his obsessions.' She looked up. 'I hope you get to the bottom of it. All of it. At the moment we're stuck as a family, in the roles we had, before our son died. George is still playing the jovial "mine host", Janey is still the perpetual student with a holiday job, while she should be thinking of a proper career. And I'm still the actress waiting for a new role. We go round and round as if we're on a giant carousel. We can't move on.'

Chapter Twenty-Eight

AS HE DROVE INLAND, TOWARDS THE moor and Spennicott, the village where Frank Ley was considered an enemy, Matthew Venn felt like a wicked schoolboy, bunking off school. As a child he would never have done such a thing, and might even have reported other kids who were behaving so badly. He'd been too scared of the world to be a rule-breaker. But today he could understand the joy, the freedom of running away from everyday responsibility.

The guilt, which was a backdrop to his life, added spice to the feeling of escape, the sense that he was on the verge of adventure. This *was* the place that Nigel Yeo had visited in the week that he was murdered, but Matthew couldn't really justify the expedition. He could have sent one of his team or talked on the phone to the leader of the campaign to keep the care home open.

Spennicott was in a valley bottom; beyond it the hills began to rise into Exmoor and the heat haze. It wasn't very far from the farm where Jonathan had lived with his adoptive parents. At first sight the village was unprepossessing: just one road with a narrow pavement on each side and a line of grey houses. There was nothing obvious here to attract tourists. No thatched cottages with roses round the door. No easy, picturesque footpath leading to the moors. The village centre was more appealing – a slow river was crossed by an ancient stone bridge and the garden of the pub led down to the bank – but Matthew could see why the place had needed Ley's help to bring people in.

Although it was too early for lunch the pub car park was more than half full and a sign outside said it sold artisan coffee. One of the outbuildings had been turned into a shop and post office and there was a queue leading into the street. A woman came out with a basket of fresh vegetables – carrots with the green fronds still attached, courgettes and loose, ripe tomatoes – and climbed into a new four-by-four.

Venn went into the building and ordered coffee at the bar. 'I'm looking for the old people's home. Do you know where I can find it?'

'The Mount? Past the school and then take the track on your right. It's a bit overgrown. You might miss it.' The voice was local, so Frank Ley had provided this man, at least, with a job. His was the only North Devon accent Venn heard when he was drinking his coffee, and Venn was the youngest customer. The others were older, early retirees on holiday, or second-homers escaping the city.

But, after all, what was wrong with that? Matthew thought. He was lucky to have been born here. Why shouldn't other people enjoy the place and sustain the communities which might otherwise die? Still, he understood the permanent residents' feeling that they'd been invaded and that a traditional way of life was under attack. Perhaps Jonathan had been right about the dangers of rural gentrification.

Matthew had decided to visit the care home before talking to Paul Reed, the writer leading the campaign against its closure. It would be good to understand what had led the man to such a violent reaction. He went back to the car and crossed the bridge. It was playtime in the school on the opposite bank, and through the open windows he heard children's laughter.

The overgrown track led up a slight rise through woodland. Earlier in the year there would have been a pool of bluebells, and some of the dying blossoms remained under the trees. The drive ended in a gravel parking circle by the side of a large Victorian house, all gables and chimney pots. At the front of the building there was a paved terrace, where six elderly people were gathered with a carer in a blue uniform. Two of the residents were in wheelchairs and all wore white cotton hats to protect them from the sun. Now that he was here, Venn wasn't sure what to do. He'd thought just to see the place, but his car had been noticed, and he didn't feel he could just drive away. He got out and walked towards the group.

'Hello, my dear!' The woman in the wheelchair waved and shouted across at him. 'What's a handsome fellow like you doing here?'

He was still a little way from the terrace, taking a shortcut across overgrown grass, so didn't feel the need to answer. Through open French windows leading onto the terrace, he saw a shabby lounge with a threadbare rug over scratched wooden floors and sagging armchairs. It would be hard to lever a frail elderly person out of one of those. There was the sound of a hoover from deep in the house.

The carer got to her feet to greet him. 'If you're considering the Mount as a home for a relative, I'm afraid we're not taking any more residents just now.'

'They're trying to close us down,' the woman in the wheel-chair said, 'but we're not bloody having it.'

'This is Viv Reed.' The carer was laughing. He thought she probably laughed a lot. 'She's the Mount's shop steward.'

'Used to be a Labour councillor,' Viv said. 'And there weren't so many of *those* around here. I'm still keeping up the fight. Along with my son Paul.'

'He's leading the campaign against the closure?'

'He is!' She sounded inordinately proud.

'Won't do no good, though.' The speaker was a little, shriv-elled man. 'That Francis Ley will do just what he likes. Folks think he's a saint, but it's all about money with him.'

Venn thought that Steph Bull in the Patients Together office had said exactly the same about Nigel Yeo. He wondered if *he'd* got both men wrong. Had they somehow generated their own propaganda, cultivated the image of being good and generous men, while being as selfish as everyone else?

'I'm not looking for a place for a relative,' he said. 'I'm a detective investigating the murder of Dr Nigel Yeo. I understand he came here last week? He was looking into the closure of the Mount.'

'We heard that he was dead,' Viv said. 'We thought, *That's it. Our last hope gone.*'

'You had the impression that he was supporting your cause?'

'He came for tea,' Viv said. 'He saw how happy we all were.'

Matthew thought that didn't quite answer the question.

Before he could say anything more, the carer joined in the conversation. 'The doctor talked about his wife,' she said. 'The early onset Alzheimer's. He said that he'd been lucky enough to be able to care for her at home, and that she'd lived a full life, even when she was very ill. He said that everyone should

223

have that right.' A pause. 'Unfortunately, we don't have facilities to look after patients with severe dementia here. We couldn't cope. I wonder if that might have influenced his impression of the home.'

There was a silence, broken by the call of woodpigeons in the trees in front of the house.

Venn turned back to Viv.

'Was your son here when Dr Yeo visited?'

'Of course he was here. He'd invited the doctor to visit.'

'Did the doctor come back the following day? The Friday afternoon? Perhaps for another look? We're trying to trace his movements on that day.'

The carer shook her head.

Venn left them then and walked back to the car. He wondered again what he would do if ever his mother couldn't manage on her own. He was the only child and the responsibility would lie with him. Wouldn't she be happier here, with the laughing carers and friendly residents, than in a clinical building with easily cleaned floors and specialist equipment? Perhaps she would, until the winter came and the roof started leaking and the bedrooms were cold at night. In the sunshine, it was easy to be romantic about such things, and besides, his mother had never been sociable, even when she was young.

Reed's house was beyond the school, with a view of the river. It was a rather ugly villa, almost suburban, out of place in the rural setting. Venn had made an appointment and the man was waiting for him. He was unprepossessing too, a grey man in his fifties with strange hairy growths on his face, giving him the appearance of a weasel. His voice was educated, pedantic.

It was hard to believe that the joyous Viv had given birth to him.

This was clearly not a family home. There was no sign of children or a partner. The door opened onto a corridor, stacked on one side with bundles of newspapers and cardboard boxes, everything dusty. There was brown lino on the floor. Reed led him through to the back of the house, to what must have been intended as a dining room, but which was now a large, cluttered office. There was a view over an unkempt garden and the river, but the window faced north and the place was still dark.

'A bit of an overreaction this, isn't it? Sending a detective all the way from Barnstaple. As far as I know, I haven't broken the law. As always, it seems to be one law for the rich and another for the rest of us. Francis Ley makes a complaint and I'm under investigation. He ruins the lives of a dozen elderly people and nothing happens.'

'Mr Ley hasn't made a complaint of any sort. I'm investigating the murder of Dr Nigel Yeo. We're tracing his movements for the last week of his life. You did meet him on Thursday afternoon?'

'Oh!' Reed sounded deflated. It seemed he'd worked himself up for a battle only to be disappointed. 'Yes.'

'Can you explain how Dr Yeo came to be involved with your campaign?' Venn paused. 'I've been looking at the press you've generated. Very impressive. An article in the *Observer*. Even, I understand, a question in the House.'

'That was all very well,' Reed said, 'but our publicity seemed to have little impact on Francis Ley. He was still determined to go ahead with the closure. I thought if I could get a group like Patients Together on board, someone official, Ley might start to take us seriously.'

'This seems very personal,' Venn said.

'Of course it's personal! It's about my mother's future.'

'I visited the Mount before coming here. Your mother seems remarkably adaptable. I'm sure she'd settle perfectly well in another home.' Venn paused for a moment. 'I wondered if you had another reason for taking on Mr Ley.'

'The decision to close the Mount was a final straw,' Reed said. 'He owns this village like some sort of feudal lord. We're not in the Middle Ages.'

Venn thought that still didn't quite explain the antipathy. 'You're a writer?'

'Yes.' Reed looked at Venn with suspicion. 'A travel writer and essayist. I freelance for the press and I've had a couple of books published by mainstream houses. Not huge commercial successes, but well reviewed and the most recent won a rather prestigious award.'

Venn wasn't quite sure where this was going.

'In one of my articles for a Sunday paper, I explored the ethics of a wealthy man buying up a village, changing its character, excluding local people. Of course, Ley took exception to the piece. His lawyers claimed there were inaccuracies and threatened to sue. I would never have been able to fund a court case, so I was forced to make an apology.' He paused. 'It was humiliating.'

In those three words, Venn thought, lay the background to the campaign to keep open the Mount. Reed needed to show that he'd been right all along, that he was a downtrodden purveyor of truth. That Ley was a fat cat who cared nothing for the people of the village.

'What did Dr Yeo make of the Mount?' Matthew asked. 'Did he support your view?'

'I don't know.' Reed turned away. 'I suspect he wouldn't have had the guts to stand up to Ley. The man's all-powerful and he seems to have everyone in his pocket. Planners, politicians, councillors.'

This was starting to sound like paranoia. Venn imagined Reed on his own here in the dark and dusty house, becoming obsessed with Ley, his wealth and his power. Brooding. Jealous. Resentful.

'Dr Yeo didn't feed back his impressions to you?'

'No!' Reed was still bitter. 'He was pleasant enough when we were shown around the Mount. He engaged with the residents. He said he'd call in to see me here the following afternoon to give me his response.'

Venn thought that seemed beyond the call of duty. Perhaps Yeo had felt some sympathy for this sad, lonely little man and had wanted to let him down gently.

'What happened?'

'Nothing! I got a phone call on Friday cancelling the visit. Yeo was very apologetic. Apparently. And very melodramatic. *A matter of life and death,* he said, which was obviously an excuse.'

Venn could sense the conspiracy theories swirling around in the man's mind, and moved towards the door.

'Dr Yeo didn't go into any more details about why he had to cancel his meeting with you?'

'No,' Reed said. 'Yeo had gone through the motions, but clearly he wasn't prepared to waste his time any further on me.'

Venn thought there was more to it than that. Something had happened after Yeo's meeting in the hospital with Prior, Radley and Joshi to make him decide not to make the trip out to Spennicott. Something which might have led to his death.

★

Venn drove back across the bridge and parked by the pub. It was full now with people who'd come to take lunch. They were spilling out into the garden with their drinks. He phoned Lauren Miller.

'Just a quick query. Nigel went to Spennicott to investigate a complaint about an old people's home. Was that normally something he'd get involved in?'

'No,' she said, 'but the whole case was so high profile, and the relationships had become so fraught, so venomous, that he thought a visit might take the heat out of the situation. Reed had made a formal complaint on behalf of the whole community.'

'And of course, Nigel couldn't be seen to be siding with Ley, who was his daughter's landlord and benefactor, without taking the matter seriously.'

'Well,' Lauren said, 'maybe there was something like that going on too.'

Venn thought she sounded faintly amused. 'What was the outcome of the visit?'

'Oh, he thought Frank's judgement had been perfectly sound. The home needed so much work to bring it up to scratch that the residents' lives would have been disrupted even more than if they'd been forced to move to another local facility. He was hoping to mediate. Perhaps to persuade Frank to offer compensation to the residents to make up for the inconvenience. That way it might be possible to bring about some reconciliation.'

'I see.' Matthew thought Reed would just see an offer like that as a form of bribery, but, worded properly, he might view it as a victory. 'When did you discuss this?'

'We met up on Thursday evening,' Lauren said. 'He was planning to visit Paul Reed, the activist behind the campaign, the following afternoon to sound him out. He thought Francis would agree to anything that would speed up the process of converting the place into a hotel, but he wanted Reed's agreement at least to consider the offer first.'

'But he never went,' Venn said, almost to himself. 'Something happened and he had to cancel. You really have no idea what that might have been?'

'I'm sorry, Inspector, I don't.'

Venn was about to drive off when he saw that there'd been a voicemail from Jen. She must have called while he was talking to Lauren. Her voice was urgent, a little breathless.

'I've picked up Mack's laptop and Ross will get it to his techie mate. Roger Prior just phoned for you. He'd like to talk to you. He said he's working from home this afternoon, if that would be convenient.'

Oh yes, that would be very convenient. Matthew looked back at the pub's customers, sitting in the sun, waiting for their meals, and felt only a brief moment of envy.

Chapter Twenty-Nine

THE PRIORS' HOUSE WAS VERY CLOSE to Nigel Yeo's in geography, but grander, larger. Venn thought the couple must rattle around in it. According to Jen, they'd never had kids. But then he supposed that selling a house in north London would have given them enough cash to go for something palatial.

Roger Prior led him into an office just off the hall. He seemed uneasy, pale, his skin almost white against the dark, rather oily hair. Venn could understand his discomfort. If the man had been hounded by the media previously over the suicide of Luke Wallace, he'd be anxious about being linked to another controversial case. This time to a double murder.

The office was functional, but strangely old-fashioned. It seemed designed to give the impression of a library in a country house. One wall was lined with books and there was a low leather chesterfield against another. An impressive desk and chair stood under the window. Venn wondered if the room was supposed to intimidate, but then Prior wouldn't often see colleagues here. Perhaps the man needed reassurance about his own status.

'How can I help you?' Matthew waited for a moment. 'Or perhaps you think you can help me?'

'No, nothing like that.' The man paused, and Matthew saw now that it wasn't anxiety that was causing the pale face, the tremor, but rage. Roger Prior was one of those men who simmer, feed their resentment in the privacy of their own minds and then blow up. 'One of your officers went to see my wife this morning. In court.'

'He did.' Prior might be hovering on the verge of losing control, but Venn felt very much in command of the interview, confident. 'I asked DC Ross to talk to her.'

'That seems like an intolerable intrusion, Inspector. I'd like to know how you can justify it.'

'Mrs Prior was the close friend of a murder victim. Of two murder victims. That makes her a very useful witness.'

'It would perhaps have been polite to make an appointment. Not to appear suddenly at her place of work.' Prior was struggling to keep calm now. Venn could sense the tension like a smell. The man's voice was shrill, fraying at the edges.

'Two men have been murdered. Stabbed and left to bleed. I think we've moved beyond a need for politeness.' Venn kept his voice deliberately calm. Until now they'd been standing, with Prior in front of the desk. Matthew took a seat on the chesterfield. 'Now I'm here, I have some questions for you. Why don't you have a seat? This might take a little while.'

Again, he thought Prior might explode. It hadn't been a conscious tactic to provoke the man, but Matthew wondered now if he'd been hoping for such an outburst since entering the room. Had he taken the lead in the man's house, given him orders, just to goad him to a response? It wasn't his usual way to conduct an interview, but he wasn't often called on to interrogate entitled and wealthy men.

For a moment, he thought Prior would demand that he leave – he stood very still, his eyes wide and staring – but instead the man walked round the desk and sat.

'You were involved in an inquiry into a young man's suicide in your former post.' Venn's voice was low, conversational.

'I was cleared of all responsibility!'

'I think it was suggested that you resign, which isn't quite the same thing.' Venn paused for a moment. 'But the details aren't really important, are they? The point is that, having settled into a new place and with a new role, the last thing you'd want would be more adverse publicity.'

'It was a dreadful coincidence. I felt as if I was being haunted by my past. That the circumstances of the previous inquiry were following me and there was no escape.' He looked directly at Venn. 'I still have nightmares about that time.'

Venn was going to say that he imagined the dead boys' families still had nightmares too, but he restrained himself. He thought now that Prior wasn't just on the edge of fury, but on the edge of a breakdown, and he didn't want that on his conscience.

'Nigel Yeo had found out about the Luke Wallace case?' Matthew made his voice friendlier, more sympathetic.

'Oh yes, Nigel was extremely *thorough*.' From Prior's mouth the word didn't sound like a compliment.

'He brought it up at the meeting you had on the Friday, before his body was found?'

'We'd discussed it a number of times before that. I think I'd convinced him that the connection was coincidental. Except in public relations terms.' Prior half stood in his chair. 'You have to understand, Inspector, that I had no reason to kill Nigel Yeo. He was doing his job and I was doing mine. We'd come to an understanding about changes to the trust's proced-ures around supporting people suffering from mental ill health. It would have cost us money, but nothing is more important that a young person's life.'

Or a prominent man's reputation.

'He hadn't threatened to make your relationship to the Luke Wallace case public? In order to get the trust to change its policy?'

'No.' Prior returned to his seat. 'He wasn't that sort of man, Inspector. Not the sort to stoop to blackmail. We fell out on a number of occasions, but I admired his principles and his courage.'

'At that last meeting,' Venn said, 'did Dr Yeo mention the possibility that Alexander Mackenzie had accessed a website promoting and encouraging suicide?'

'No!' Prior seemed shocked by the suggestion. 'That was never mentioned on any of the occasions when we met, and it didn't appear in any of Dr Joshi's notes.'

'How well did you know Wesley Curnow?'

The change in tack threw Prior for a moment. 'Not well at all. He was an acquaintance of my wife's.'

'But he came to the house at times?'

Prior shrugged. 'My wife's a sociable woman. She works for a number of charitable organizations and hosts many fund-raising events. People come to the house all the time.' He seemed to feel the need to explain. 'We're not the sort of couple who lives in each other's pockets. We live our own lives. It means we have something to say to each other when we finally get together.'

Venn wondered if the man was protesting too much, if Prior had felt belittled by his wife's choice of friends, but he didn't push the point.

There was a minute of silence. Matthew was wondering what this conversation had achieved. He'd gained no new information. But he thought he did have a greater understanding now of this man: powerful, used to authority, but stressed and with the potential to crack and splinter under the slightest further pressure.

Prior had regained a little of his poise, his dignity. Perhaps he realized that Venn was less of a threat than he'd first thought. He pushed himself to his feet. 'If there's nothing else, Inspector, I'll see you out.'

Matthew nodded and followed him to the front door. Outside, the air was still and there was the smell of a barbecue in a neighbouring garden.

The team was gathered in the ops room when he got back to the station, waiting for the evening's briefing. They shared their experiences of the day. Ross described his conversation with Cynthia Prior.

'You really think she didn't have any romantic feelings for Wesley Curnow? It was as she said, a friendship of convenience?' Venn was close to few people outside work. In contrast, Jonathan seemed to have hundreds of friends, people he greeted with joy and hugs, and invited to their house for supper and drinks. He opened his arms and let them into their lives.

'Yeah, I do. She hardly seemed devastated by his death.'

'You know her, Jen,' Matthew said. 'Does that sound right to you?'

Jen nodded. 'You've met Roger. Uptight and wedded to the job. Not an arty bone in his body. She needed someone who could share her interests. Really, I don't think there was any more to it than that.'

'I've just come from their house,' Venn said. 'I was summoned by Mr Prior.'

'What did he want?'

Venn thought about that. 'Honestly? I'm not sure. To find out what we know? To lay down a marker? He's certainly stressed, but that's understandable after the press he got following the Wallace case. It doesn't mean he's a killer.'

He went on to describe his visit to Spennicott and the old people's home. 'So, we have another connection between Yeo and Francis Ley. I can't see how Nigel Yeo's investigation into the closure of the Mount can be relevant to the investigation, but we do need to know where he went on Friday afternoon.'

Matthew looked around the room and saw that they were all as tired as he was. It would be fruitless to rake over the points of the case again. At this moment all he wanted was to be at home, with Jonathan in their house by the shore. A life that was simple and less fraught was overwhelmingly tempting. 'Let's call it a day. Come back tomorrow with fresh ideas. We're exhausted and there's a danger that we'll just go around in circles.'

The light had almost gone when he drove past Braunton Great Marsh and through the toll gate towards Crow Point. There was a red blur on the horizon where the sun was setting, so the gulls and the egrets, disturbed into the air by the sound of his car, were flushed rose. Perhaps because he'd been thinking of friendship, he had a fear, driving to the house, that Jonathan might have friends there. He pictured the house lit up, people spilling out onto the terrace with drinks, but, as he approached, he saw that the only vehicle on the drive belonged to Jonathan.

He'd been gearing himself up to be pleasant, to put on a show, and was flooded with relief. There *was* a light on in the kitchen and he saw his husband sharp and clear, putting a pan into the oven. He was holding it with a bright yellow folded tea towel, and his feet were bare. Matthew opened the French doors from the terrace and went in. Jonathan turned and smiled.

'I heard the car. I thought you'd be starving. I made a veggie shepherd's pie.'

'Could it wait for a while? I wondered about a walk into the marsh. There's still enough light.'

'Sure. Why not? I'll just turn the oven down. It'll be ready when we get back.' Everything for Jonathan was that easy.

They took the track inland, away from the shore and along towards the toll gate. When they came to the marsh they stopped and looked out. There was the silhouette of a heron, tall and stately, dark grey against the paler grey of the water. It stood quite alone.

'I'm sorry I blundered into your investigation.' Jonathan was leaning against a fence that was pockmarked with lichen. 'I should have been more careful.'

'You were just thinking about Eve.'

Jonathan nodded towards the heron. 'Those birds always remind me of you. So patient. Just willing to wait. Entirely focused on their prey.' A pause. 'I wish I could be more like that. But I jump in, all splash and noise.'

'I've never heard one call,' Matthew said.

'That's like you too then. Silent. I'm never quite sure what you're thinking.'

Matthew didn't know what to say. He wanted to tell Jonathan that he loved him just the way he was, but it would have sounded trite, and even now, he wasn't entirely sure that was true. He linked his arm through Jonathan's. By the time they got home, all the colour was gone and the only light came from the moon.

Chapter Thirty

ROSS MAY GOT HOME TO FIND that Mel was out again. He was going to text her, but in the end he phoned. She picked up his call almost immediately. He could hear voices in the background and was aware of his body relaxing. She was out with her mates, nothing wrong with that. Nothing for him to worry about. To obsess about.

'Where are you?' Despite his relief, the tension he'd felt when he'd arrived in the house and found it empty was still there in his voice. He could hear it and was about to apologize. He didn't want to be one of those men who couldn't trust their wives, who wanted to control them.

But she answered before he could explain. 'It's Joanne's birthday. I told you we were all going out straight from work.' There was that hint of resentment, of the defiance that he'd picked up over the weekend.

'Oh, of course. Sorry. It's this case, sending everything out of my mind.' Now the apology sounded forced and lame. 'Have a brilliant time and send her my best wishes.' He didn't think he could ask her now what time she planned to be back.

In the end, she wasn't late. He'd been listening out for her all evening, for the footsteps on the drive through the open window, for the key in the lock. He'd stuck a ready meal in the microwave and opened a beer. He'd finished the meal but was still nursing the bottle when he heard her. He'd limited himself to one, because Mel might need a lift. He'd hoped she might text him, asking him to pick her up, or to come out to join them.

He'd switched on the television before she came into the room. He didn't want her to know he'd been waiting for her. She must have changed at work for the evening out because she looked gorgeous, in a sleeveless cotton dress and sandals, with a small wedged heel. Simple and classy.

'Good night?'

'Yeah,' she said. 'I'm knackered, though. It was another crazy day at work. I might just head up to bed.' She didn't seem drunk. Not even a little bit tipsy.

'Why don't you have a quick drink with me before you go? I haven't seen you properly for days.'

'Nah,' she said. 'I'm on earlies again tomorrow.'

'Just one drink!' That tone in his voice again. Bossy. Controlling. Where had it come from? 'Please.'

She hesitated and he thought she might refuse. He was already feeling the shame of having a simple request turned down. From Mel, who claimed to love him, who, in the past, would have done anything for him.

In the end, she smiled. 'All right then. There's a bottle of white already open in the fridge. I'll have a small glass of that.'

He jumped to his feet and went to the kitchen to pour it for her. When he came back, she'd slipped off her sandals and was sitting with her feet curled under her on the sofa. She took the glass of wine and leaned against him when he sat down beside her. Of course, he was pleased that balance and order had been restored, but there was a seed of anger in his mind, because he was her husband, and she shouldn't have made him feel like that, so anxious and so impotent. So needy. In bed, she put her arms around him, but he was the one to turn away and pretend to sleep.

The next morning, everything seemed back to normal. They had breakfast together and chatted about everyday things: putting the bins out, what he might like for dinner, when they might go to see Mel's family. Ross found himself hyper-alert, though. It was as if he was on a case, looking out for any discrepancy in the evidence. That germ of anger and suspicion was there even when he was smiling and when Mel bent down to kiss him before she rushed off to work.

When he got to the station, Ross found he'd already received an email from his friend Steve Barton. Steve was a digital forensic expert, registered with the police service; he'd worked for a forensic science company in the Midlands on cybercrime, but recently he'd come home to keep an eye on his dad, who had chronic arthritis. They didn't live together – Steve always said he needed his own space to work – but at least he could help out.

Ross was proud to be mates with such a brainbox, happy to bask in the reflected glory of his success. They'd known each other since school. Steve had been a geek even then, a demon gamer and maths nerd. They'd got on okay and had stayed in touch after Steve went to London to university. Now he was back, Ross had put some work his way and when that had turned out well, he'd persuaded Joe Oldham to spread the word county-wide. Barton was known now as someone who could deliver on anything cyber-related. Ross made sure that all the approaches to Barton went through him: *He'll rush it through as a favour. Otherwise you'd be waiting for weeks.* Making himself indispensable.

Barton's email was brief:

I've had a quick look. If you want to meet up, I'll talk you through it. I can do a report but you won't get that until the end of tomorrow. Lots of other work on.

Maybe that was boasting, playing a kind of hard to get, but Ross didn't want to take the risk by saying he'd wait. He imagined standing in front of the room at the evening briefing, passing on a vital piece of evidence. He emailed:

Where and when?

The reply came straight back.

The Dog and Ferret at one. You can buy me lunch.

The Dog and Ferret was classic Steve Barton. Eccentric. An old man's pub where the customers sat with their pints of mild reading yesterday's free newspaper and grousing about the young. Pasties were the only food on offer. Steve had always haunted bizarre places, making friends with people Ross would never be seen dead with.

He was already there when Ross arrived, at a table in a dusty corner. The pub was almost empty. Two elderly women were sitting in the window, drinking big glasses of white wine. One had her little finger raised, a mockery of a posh person drinking tea. They stared through the smeared window into the street, and for all the time Ross was there, neither of the women spoke.

Steve could have been a surfer. His blond hair was too long and he needed a shave. He wore a loose T-shirt so well washed that any logo had faded, and frayed jeans. He had a friendship bracelet on his wrist and sandals on his feet. Anywhere else, Ross would have been embarrassed to be seen in his company, but nobody he knew drank in the Dog and Ferret.

'What have you got for me?'

'At least you can buy me lunch. I'll have a pasty and another pint of the bitter.'

'I thought you were snowed under.'

'Hey! A man's got to eat.'

Ross came back with the pint, an orange juice and two pasties.

Steve started talking while his mouth was still full. 'Your guy never saved much on his system and he deleted everything before he topped himself.' He wiped a spray of pastry from the front of his shirt. 'I suppose you would, wouldn't you? I mean, you wouldn't want your family seeing all the dodgy porn sites you'd been on.'

'It's not the porn sites I'm interested in. Are you saying you can't access his accounts?'

'Course not.' Steve beamed. 'These days we can access anything. Last month I destroyed a defendant's alibi by showing he'd used a smart app to start his washing machine remotely. His neighbour had said he must have been in that evening because she could hear the machine going, but in fact, he was thirty miles away.' He paused, a stand-up waiting for applause that never came. 'Digging around on your guy's laptop was a piece of piss.'

'So, let's hear what you got.' Steve had always been a smart-arse. 'I'm in the middle of a murder investigation. I'm not like you. I can't spend all day in the pub.'

'You said you were interested in the few weeks before Mackenzie died. The man had a Gmail account and from that he sent stuff to his close family and did routine transactions. Pretty boring: happy birthday to his gran, some purchases from Amazon. The day before he went missing, he'd sent a photo of himself in a garden to his mum and his sister.' Steve paused. 'The wider Google account's a bit thin, to be honest, but then most of the family communications would get sent by text these days.' He looked up. 'I could check out his phone if you have it?'

Ross shook his head. 'We think it drowned with him.'

'That's more difficult then. His service provider will be able to give you contacts and the length of calls, but I don't think you'll get much else. Not the content of texts, for example, and he'd probably be sending photos by WhatsApp and that's encrypted end-to-end.' He paused. 'Are you sure the phone is gone?'

'It wasn't at the top of the cliff where he left his note, and the family say it's not in the house. I suppose a passing walker could have nicked it, but more likely, I think, that he had it with him when he jumped.'

'Because I might be able to track it down otherwise.' Steve had already almost finished his second beer. 'I could use cell site analysis. If you give me the details, it should be possible to map any journey the phone's taken too. At least then you'd know the guy's movements on the night he disappeared.'

'Cool.' But Ross thought they already knew that, because they'd found the man's outer clothes and his note, and Venn, a stickler for detail, had had the handwriting analysed. It had definitely been written by Mack Mackenzie. Ross thought about the emailed photo sent to Janey and Martha. 'The picture of the garden in the email attachment. Has it got a house in the background? A red-brick farmhouse?'

'Yeah, that sounds about right. He's standing there with an older guy. Fat. I'll send it across with the report.'

Ross thought about the pictures of Nigel Yeo's contacts, the ones posted on the board in the ops room. It sounded as if Mack had been standing next to Frank Ley. 'When was that photo sent?'

Steve fished in his jeans pocket and pulled out an envelope with some scribbled notes on the back. 'The day before you told me he'd died. It was a selfie. The two guys standing together.'

'Is that it?' Ross was disappointed. When he'd got the call from Steve, he'd hoped for more than that, for revolutionary news to break open the case. They already knew that Mack had worked for Ley as a jobbing gardener and that he'd visited Westacombe to see Wesley Curnow in the days before his suicide.

'No! What do you take me for?' Steve made out he was hurt. 'I told you, I'm the best. Mackenzie had a separate email account, one that he used for a completely different set of contacts. People that he'd met in a chatroom. That was harder to track down. Even for me.'

'A group promoting suicide?'

'Well, supporting people considering it. They use the hashtag PeaceAtLast and that's the name of the chat group.' Steve looked up. 'But within the Peace at Last forum, there seems to be a core group who call themselves the Suicide Club. Pretty sick, if you ask me. Images of people who look as if they're about to do the deed. One picture of a woman, a noose round her neck, claiming she's only minutes from hanging herself. Another giving a list of over-the-counter meds and the amount you'd need to take to finish yourself off. It could all be fantasy. Like, if you're sharing all that stuff, maybe that's enough, you know. You're telling the world, or the members of the Suicide Club at least, how much you're hurting and getting the sympathy in return, so you don't actually need to do it.'

'Alexander Mackenzie did it,' Ross said. 'Late at night or early one morning, he jumped off a cliff into the sea and drowned. His body was washed up on Lundy a week later.'

'Shit. Of course he did.'

They sat for a moment in silence. One of the women by the window went to the bar and ordered two more large glasses of wine. Ross wondered if they were as miserable as Mack, and were killing themselves slowly. Perhaps the booze was giving them Peace at Last.

'Can you send over a list of contacts? The other individuals who were in the same group?'

'Sure.' Steve's mood had suddenly switched, become sombre. He finished his drink and stood up. 'Sure. I'll get onto it now.'

Walking back to the station, Ross phoned Mel. He wanted to tell her that life was too short for misunderstandings, that they needed to spend more quality time together, and to get back to how they'd been when they were first married. That he was sorry. But she didn't answer, and all he heard was a recorded message of her voice.

Chapter Thirty-One

JEN RAFFERTY GOT PERMISSION FROM VENN to go back to Westacombe to visit Eve Yeo. 'I just want to check she's okay. I know a family liaison officer has kept in touch, but she's had such a tough time.'

'Good plan.' Matthew was sitting at his desk, shirtsleeves rolled up, tie slightly loosened. Jen knew Jonathan teased him about the tie. Eventually, Jonathan had told her, he *would* persuade Matthew to come to work without it, but she couldn't imagine it happening anytime soon. Matthew looked up. 'Talk to the Grieves too. It'd be interesting to know if they were friendly with Mack. As we're following the line of inquiry that Yeo was threatening to expose the suicide chatroom, it'd be good to check out all Mack's contacts' browsing histories.'

'Sarah doesn't strike me as suicidal!'

'Nor me. But belt and braces. You know how I like to work.'

Oh yes, she thought. *I know.*

'Her husband seems less straightforward, though,' Venn went on. 'And talk to Frank Ley. I'm the only person he's had contact with so far. I'd like your opinion of him.' Venn paused.

'He might find you less intimidating than me, easier to talk to.'

Jen smiled. She thought there were few people less intimidating than Matthew Venn. It was one of the reasons he was such a good interviewer. Witnesses felt they could confide in him. But he was the boss. 'Okay,' she said. 'Sure.'

The farmyard had been opened again. No tape. No officer on the gate. Jen squeezed her car past the milk tanker and parked by the workshops. Wesley's studio was shut and padlocked, but the door to Eve's was open. Jen knew that Sarah Grieve had been in to scrub the floor and the walls, a sign of real friendship, and Jen could smell a faint trace of disinfectant. Eve was working with her back to Jen, twisting a metal pipe with a globe of molten green glass at one end, shaping it with a gloved hand. Jen could feel the heat of the furnace from where she was standing by the door.

'Hiya!'

'Who is it?' Eve didn't turn around. 'Sorry, this is almost impossible to do on my own. I need to concentrate.'

'Jen Rafferty. I can come back in a bit. Or help?'

'Give me twenty minutes then I'm all yours.'

Jen went back into the yard and walked round to the front of the big house. She knocked at the door. No answer. Ley's garage was open and she saw his flashy Range Rover inside; he couldn't have gone far. The vehicle was black, like the car Janey had noticed racing through Instow. Jen made a mental note to tell Venn in case he hadn't noticed the vehicle's colour, waited a moment then knocked at the front door again. There was still no response, so she walked to the long window and looked in. She'd always been nosy, always loved these glimpses into other people's lives. Her favourite time of year was early autumn, when people put their lights on, but forgot to draw their curtains. She'd walk down a street and each window held a moment of domestic drama. There was still no sign of Ley. Jen thought she'd talk to the Grieves and come back later.

Sarah was working in the long, low building she used as a dairy. She shouted out as soon as Jen opened the door. 'You can't come in! You're not properly dressed for food prep.' She was wearing a white overall and hairnet, and looked very like one of the CSIs in their scene suits. Jen had a glimpse of stainless-steel counters and bowls.

'Sorry!' Again, it seemed that she was intruding, interrupting the useful activities of others. This might be a wasted morning. She took a step back into the yard and raised her voice. 'Have you seen Mr Ley?'

'Not since yesterday evening. He had us all in for drinks. A sort of belated wake for Wesley and Nigel. He invited the Mackenzies along too, because he wanted us to remember Mack at the same time. He said the negligent treatment that Mack had received made his death a kind of unlawful killing too. Look, can you come to the cottage in a bit? I'll be stopping for coffee in half an hour or so.'

'Cool.' Jen thought she might just sit in the sun for a while to catch a few rays, because she hadn't stopped working for days, and anyway, who would know? She was looking in her bag for her sunglasses when Eve stuck her head out of the workshop.

'I'm all yours.'

A low wooden bench stretched along the front of the workshops, and Eve sat there, with her back to the wall. She tapped the top of the bench with her hand.

'This is one of Wes's creations. I helped him carry the plank up from Instow. It was driftwood, washed up on the beach. He found it early one morning and called me down to bring it back.'

Jen sat beside her. 'I just wanted to see how you are.'

'Better now that I can get back into the studio. The work I'm making's crap, but it's an escape. You have to concentrate so hard, especially if you're working solo, that there's no space in your head for anything else.'

'You're okay working there?' Meaning: *where you found your father's body.*

'There was a moment of silence. 'Yeah,' Eve said. 'In a way, it's comforting. There are so many happy memories of us here together. That last image just feels like a nightmare, not real.'

'And you don't mind staying at Westacombe on your own?'

'I'm not on my own, though. Not really. Sarah's like a mother hen and the twins are very sweet. She lends them to me for company and cuddles. Then Frank had us all in to his place last night.'

'Sarah said. A kind of wake. Were you all right with that?' Jen thought it must have been weird, a repeat of the evening before she'd found her father dead in her workshop.

Eve shrugged. 'He did ask me first. And yeah, I was in the mood to get pissed. I thought it was probably better to do it in company than on my own. I wish he hadn't asked the Mackenzies along, but it would have been churlish to object or to stay away. In the end, they were okay, really supportive.'

'Do you know where Mr Ley is now? I need to speak to him.'

'Probably sleeping off a hangover. He had even more to

drink than me.' Eve paused, squinted into the sun. 'And that wasn't really like him. It was quite sweet really. He got a bit emotional, made a little speech about the three dead men.'

There was a moment of silence. Sarah came out of the dairy and looked as if she was about to approach them, then thought better of interrupting and headed for her cottage.

'I have nightmares,' Eve said, 'about finding them both. Every night it's the same. The glass and the blood. And do you know, it's not the bodies that upsets me – in the dream, I mean, of course, not when I wake up. It's the broken glass. The wasted art.'

'We can help you find someone to talk to. Someone who's used to working with victims, people who've been through trauma.'

'I know, the family liaison officer said. And I will take up the offer, but I'm not ready yet.' She nodded towards the workshop. 'At the moment, this is all the therapy I need.'

Jen stood up. 'How well did you know Alexander Mackenzie, the lad who killed himself?'

'He did Frank's garden, so I saw him around and I got to know him quite well over the years. Sometimes I'd take him out a coffee or a cold drink, and we'd chat while he took a break. I liked him. He was a gentle soul. Open. Like a child but in a good way. Wesley knew the rest of the family better than I did, though.'

Something about her voice made Jen ask, 'You don't like *them*? The others? You said you weren't happy that Frank had invited them to the do last night.'

'I just don't think they were as happy as they all made out. They present this image: the devoted couple, arty and a bit glamorous, then there's Janey who went off to Oxford, the perfect daughter, brainy *and* beautiful. But underneath, it feels a bit rotten. Like the image is all that matters to them, and there's something festering that nobody's willing to talk about.' She paused. 'I've always had a vivid imagination, though.' She gave a little smile. 'Perhaps it isn't like that at all.' There was another moment of silence. 'Besides, I shouldn't be so unkind. They've lost a son, a brother.'

In the cottage, Sarah had already made coffee. She slid a mug over to Jen. She was sitting back in her chair with her hands on her belly and Jen felt a moment of envy. She'd loved being pregnant, and the early months of being a mother. It was only as the kids had grown into toddlers, demanding and impossible to keep still, that life had become difficult. Robbie had hated the mess and the disruption to his routine, the fact that he could no longer be the centre of her attention. He'd grown tense and angry and her life had become a battle to keep him happy, to prevent the increasingly frequent outbursts of temper. She wondered for a moment what it would be like to have a child with somebody calmer. Robbie had always called her a crap mother and she'd believed him, but perhaps it *could* be different. Then she remembered the teething and the screaming, the sore nipples and having absolutely no time to herself and she set the idea aside.

'When are you due?'

'Oh, I've got a couple of months yet. I'm just a fat cow.'

'You're not having twins again?'

'Oh God, no! Imagine!' But she didn't seem so horrified by the idea, and gave a little complacent laugh. Jen thought Sarah would never consider herself a crap mother.

'Did you know Alexander Mackenzie, the young Instow man who killed himself?'

'Handsome Mack? When he started working for Frank, I had a few fantasies about him. Of the Lady Chatterley variety. But he was hardly more than a boy and really a very troubled soul. Frank was so fond of him, and desperately upset when he killed himself. I guess that's why he asked the family up last night.' She paused. 'He did kill himself? You're not linking his death with these murders?'

'No, nothing like that. But Nigel Yeo was investigating a complaint from the family, who think he was let down by the health service. We've found out that Mack was using a suicide forum on the internet. You don't know anything about that?'

Sarah shook her head. 'We certainly never discussed anything personal; we weren't on those sorts of terms. He seemed very shy to me. Cut off from the real world. He only came alive when he was talking about plants and the garden. He might have talked more to Eve. He seemed to treat her almost as a big sister.' She paused. 'He was really poorly the last time I saw him. He'd come up to talk to Wesley and he was in such a state. Tears running down his face. He was banging on the door of Wesley's workshop, but Wes was in his flat. Wes did come into the yard to see what was going on, but he was never very good with dramas like that, and in the end, it was Frank who calmed Mack down. They sent for Janey and she took him home.' Another pause. 'It was a terrible tragedy, but I wasn't surprised when he killed himself. He was let down by the service which should have been there to protect him.'

Jen thought this confirmed everything she'd been told by the Mackenzie family. It was useful but it provided nothing new. She changed tack.

'How do you sell your dairy produce, if you don't have a shop?'

'We supply local delis and restaurants,' Sarah said, 'but we'd have a much better profit without the middle man. Hence the idea for the tea shop.'

'I suppose Frank Ley would have been useful providing those retail contacts, though, because he's set up those kinds of outlets all over the county.'

'Yeah,' Sarah pulled herself upright, 'but we don't want to depend on Frank. Like I said before, John's got this thing about us being independent. In the meantime, we're building up a great online profile and we're doing more and more sales by mail order. John's a bit of a computer whizz. He set up the site and spends most evenings in the upstairs spare room, sorting out the orders. I'm not quite sure what he'll do when the baby arrives and we have to use the space as a nursery. He was grumpy enough when I booted him out for a few days to paint it.'

Jen considered that, and wondered what else John Grieve might be doing online. Was he the sort of man who might enjoy power at a distance? She could see that he might, when he was so dependent on a benefactor in his everyday life. Could John Grieve be sitting each night in a cramped small bedroom, listening to desperate people planning to end their lives, pushing them occasionally to make the decision? Could that be his idea of entertainment? Of fun?

'Where's John now?'

'I'm not sure,' Sarah said. 'He went out straight after break-fast. There's always something to do on the farm. He'll be back when he's hungry. It's already gone his usual lunchtime.' She got to her feet, collected the mugs and set them on the draining

board. 'I should get back to work too. I think I've got hours
at the beginning of the day, then in no time I have to rush off
to collect the kids from school.'

Jen nodded. 'Of course. Thanks for the coffee.' She was
wondering if she could find an excuse to go up into John's
makeshift office, but surely there'd be nothing for an untrained
eye to see. Only a room painted ready for a baby, perhaps
with a mobile hanging from the ceiling, and a Moses basket
in one corner.

Once again, she walked round the farmhouse to Ley's front
door. It was early afternoon and the heat seemed to bounce
from the red brick. She thought the man must surely be awake
by now, even if he'd been drinking heavily the night before.
When there was still no answer, she peered through all the
windows she could find. The living room was tidy, so unless
Sarah had been in early to clean for him, he hadn't been in
such a bad state the night before. That was another of Jen's
markers for judging the extent of her inebriation: the ability
to load the dishwasher before going to bed. She moved on
and looked in another of the windows facing the garden. A
large office, very high-tech, jarring with the architecture of the
house. A sleek desk had been built along one wall and it was
filled with devices: computer, printer, scanner. Perhaps Frank
Ley, single, wealthy, entitled, was a more likely candidate for
the person playing God on the suicide chatroom.

Now she was losing patience. She went back to the door
and thumped on it. Then she turned the handle and went
inside.

'Mr Ley!'

The house felt shady and cool after the blasting heat. She pushed her head through the doors of the rooms she'd already seen from outside. On the office desk was a mobile phone. Surely the man couldn't have gone too far if he'd left that behind. She moved on through the house, all the time expecting Ley to appear, angered by the intrusion. There was a kitchen, which must back onto the kitchen used by Eve and Wesley. It was dark, with a small window looking out to the side of the house, but again very streamlined and full of gadgets: a high-end coffee machine, a juicer and a sleek stainless-steel fridge.

Upstairs there were four bedrooms. Three apparently were scarcely used, and had the feel of an upmarket boutique hotel. One had probably belonged to Ley's mother, because here there were a few personal touches. A faded wedding photo. A cross-stitched sampler of the alphabet. Ley's bedroom was big, with long windows looking over the garden and out to a glimmer of sea in the distance. The bed had been slept in but not made. He'd had a shower; there was a damp towel folded on the rail. Clothes had been put on an elegant blue chair, but presumably Ley had been wearing those the day before. There was still no sign of the man himself.

Jen went outside again and walked across the lawn and past the borders as far as the boundary wall. It had occurred to her that someone who'd shared Mack's passion for gardening wouldn't be indoors on a day like this. She found a wheelbarrow half full of weeds, but they were dry and shrivelled, and had obviously been there for some time. Ley himself seemed to have disappeared.

Chapter Thirty-Two

MATTHEW VENN WAS IN HIS OFFICE, chatting to Ross, trying to make sense of the information the DC had gleaned from his techie friend. The space felt like a sauna and he could feel sweat running down his back; he'd brought in a spare shirt and wondered when he might find a moment to change.

'So, Mack *had* accessed one of these suicide sites?'

'Yes, something called Peace at Last.' Ross paused. 'And we know those were the words Mack used in his suicide note. Luke Wallace had been a member too, so it's a well-established forum. The chatroom seems relatively supportive but Steve came across a core group who call themselves the Suicide Club and Mack had been sucked into that too. They seem more actively determined to encourage members to kill themselves.'

'Do we know who pulled him in?'

Ross shook his head. 'Steve says tracking down the other individuals will take time.'

Venn forgot his embarrassment, the heat and the sweat, and felt a wave of pity for the people who'd been desperate enough to consider suicide. He'd had a kind of breakdown after losing his faith. He hadn't just lost his God, but his community, cast out by his parents and the Brethren. He'd even had a fleeting longing for the peace that death might bring, but that had been different from taking active steps to kill himself. He couldn't quite imagine that desperation.

He turned back to Ross. 'It would be most helpful if Barton could give us the names of other people using the site. Especially the person moderating the Suicide Club.'

'He said he'd work on it this afternoon.'

His office door opened. No knock. And a shadow blocked out the light. Superintendent Joe Oldham, Matthew's boss.

'Ah.' Oldham leaned against the door frame as if the effort of walking down the corridor had been too much for him to remain upright. 'Two birds with one stone.' The Yorkshire accent had remained unchanged and was a matter of pride. 'How's it going then? I'm getting pressure from above. Always piggy in the middle, that's me.' His voice was an unpleasant whine.

'Ross has come up with some very useful information,' Matthew said. 'We're about to follow it up.' He'd learned that praising Ross and being vaguely optimistic was the best tactic where Oldham was concerned. The superintendent considered Ross a protégé. And although Oldham insisted that he liked to be on top of a major operation, he'd never been much interested in detail.

'I can tell Exeter we're near to an arrest then?'

'We're hopeful.'

'Grand.' The big man levered himself away from the door frame and walked away, once more letting in sunlight. 'Keep me informed.'

They watched the large back disappear into the corridor.

Ross's phone rang. He listened for a moment then passed it to Venn. 'It's Jen. She's been trying to get hold of you.'

Venn felt for his phone, realized he'd left it in the pocket of the jacket he'd carefully put over the back of a chair in the main office.

'Sorry, Jen. What's the problem?'

'I can't find Ley. The door to his house is open, but there's nobody in.'

'And nobody's seen him?'

'Not today. He had a gathering in his house last night – a kind of wake for Nigel and Wesley, and apparently for Alexander too, because he invited the rest of the Mackenzie family to Westacombe to join them. I've been into the house. He definitely slept here last night, but neither Eve nor Sarah Grieve has seen him since.'

'What about John Grieve?'

'I haven't tracked him down either. According to Sarah, he's out on the farm somewhere.'

'I'll be over.'

Venn ended the call and went to retrieve his jacket and his own phone. There was a missed call and a voicemail. From Frank Ley. It had been made more than an hour earlier.

'*If you're coming to Westacombe this morning, Inspector, I wonder if you'd call in and see me. I'd welcome the chance for a chat.*'

The man sounded very tired, a little old. Venn called him back but there was no reply. He remembered his previous anxiety when he'd not been able to find Ley, the sunlit walk across the common from the Instow road, the strange panic as he imagined some tragedy at the farmhouse. He wondered if he was overreacting again by rushing off to Westacombe, but still he checked that his phone was in his pocket and he hurried to his car.

Matthew found Jen sitting where Ley had been on that earlier encounter. She was flushed from too long in the sun. She had a redhead's pale complexion and her nose was peeling; the skin reminded him of flaky pastry, the remains of a croissant on a plate. 'I had another look round the garden, away from the paths, in case he'd fallen. I haven't been back to the workshops in case you didn't want them knowing that Francis has buggered off.' She paused. 'I suppose he only has one car? He couldn't have driven off in another vehicle.'

'Only one car registered,' Venn said.

'Do you think he's done a runner? He could have hired a car or got a taxi to the station. No vehicle's been into the yard while I've been here, but it could have come earlier or driven up his private drive.' She paused. 'His mobile's in his office, though. Surely he wouldn't have left that behind.'

'He phoned me earlier,' Venn said. 'I missed the call. Can you get on to the provider? Treat it as urgent. Find out who else called him this morning.'

Jen nodded.

Venn tried to think his way through the possibilities. 'Why would he be running anyway? Why now, I mean? What's happened in the last couple of days to spook him?'

'You were sniffing round the old folks' home in Spennicott.'

'But according to Lauren, Yeo had agreed with Ley that bringing the care home up to standard would cause more disruption to the residents than moving them. It was clear to me that Reed, who made the complaint, had his own reasons for stirring up the campaign against Francis.' Venn reran his visit to the model village in his head. Venn couldn't see that Ley would be particularly disturbed by the news that the police had been following Nigel's movements in the week before his death.

'Ley held a wake here last night,' Jen said. 'A celebration of the lives of Wesley and Nigel. And Mack. He invited the remaining Mackenzie family to join them.'

Venn thought that was more interesting. 'How did it go?'

'Frank got pissed and made a sentimental speech about all three blokes, according to Eve. But no rows or accusations. At least, if there were, she wasn't letting on.' She looked at her boss. 'But a bit odd, don't you think? Throwing a party at a time like this.'

'Perhaps none of them wanted to be alone.' Venn considered for a moment. It was too early to panic, to call for a full search. Ley was an adult. He could easily have changed his mind after making the phone call to Venn's mobile when there was no reply. If he was troubled, there were surely other people in whom he might confide. He took out his phone and dialled Lauren Miller's number. It went straight to voicemail. He left a message.

'This is Matthew Venn. If you pick this up, please could you call me back.'

He imagined the two of them, Lauren and Frank, friends from London days, sitting in a smart Appledore restaurant, eating a late lunch. Frank would be leaning forward, earnest, sharing his sadness at the loss of two people close to him. There were, after all, very *few* people close to him.

'Can you check local taxi firms?' he said to Jen. 'See if anyone picked him up?'

'Sure.'

He was walking away from Jen when his phone rang. It was Lauren Miller.

'Inspector. I'm sorry I missed your call. How can I help you?'

'I just wondered if you'd heard from Frank today?'

There was a silence at the end of the line. 'Yes,' she said. 'Yes, I have.'

He was about to ask for more details when she continued talking. 'If it's not too inconvenient, perhaps you'd have time to come and see me. This isn't an easy conversation to have on the phone.'

'Of course. I could come now?'

'Thank you.' She was as calm and measured as when they'd met previously, but he heard relief in her voice. 'That would be very kind.'

Chapter Thirty-Three

LAUREN WAS WAITING FOR HIM. She was wearing a cotton dress that reached to her ankles, and looked as cool as she'd sounded on the phone. Her feet were bare, long and brown. She made him fragrant tea in a china pot, poured it through a strainer and offered little sugary biscuits.

'Thank you for coming,' she said. 'Mother's out with a friend. We won't be disturbed.'

'You said you'd heard from Frank today? Did he come here to see you? He seems to have disappeared and I thought you might have an idea where he might be.'

'No, he didn't come here, though perhaps I should have suggested that we meet.' There was a pause. She looked more uncomfortable than he'd seen her. 'There were two phone calls. The first was in the early hours of this morning. I sleep very lightly and though my mobile was on silent, the vibration woke me. Frank was drunk. It was all very awkward.'

'What happened?'

She looked up, her cup still in her hand, and gave a little smile. 'I suppose it was a declaration of love.' She shook her head as if the notion was ridiculous. 'I told him this wasn't a conversation that I needed in the middle of the night and I asked him, very politely, to call me back later in the morning when he'd had a few hours' sleep and a couple of mugs of strong, black coffee.'

'Did he take your advice?'

'He did.' She took a deep breath. 'The call came at nine o'clock this morning. He was very apologetic for waking me the night before. Very sweet. He told me that he'd always admired me and that Nigel's death had made him re-evaluate things. Perhaps it was time for him to be braver emotionally, to express himself more openly.' She paused again. 'He asked if we might become closer. If perhaps one day, I might consider being his wife.'

She looked up. 'At least I didn't laugh! It took a lot of control, but I managed to keep serious. But really! It sounded ridiculous, like something from a Regency romance.'

'What did you say?'

'I thought the kindest thing was to be clear. I told him I'd always value him as a friend, but that I could never consider him as a partner.' She sipped her tea and replaced the cup on the saucer. 'I told him about Nigel and me. I said that Nigel would always be the love of my life, and I couldn't contemplate the possibility of anyone replacing him.'

'How did he respond?'

'He was very quiet,' Lauren said. 'Rather cold and formal. He apologized for disturbing me and he replaced the phone.'

Venn thought that explained Ley's disappearance. He'd gone away somewhere to lick his wounds. He'd been fantasizing for so long about this woman that she'd become a part of his life. This would feel a little like another bereavement. Would it explain Ley's phone call to *him*, though?

'Would you mind if I ask some more questions, while I'm here?'

'Of course. I'm happy to help in any way I can.'

'Did Nigel discuss Alexander Mackenzie's suicide with you?'

'A little.'

'We think he was interested in Mack's membership of a chatroom that brought together people contemplating suicide. Do you know anything about that?'

Lauren didn't respond immediately. 'I overheard a conversation between him and the mother of another victim of suicide. His side of the conversation at least. Later, I asked him what it was about. He was reluctant to tell me – he was always very careful about confidentiality even where Patients Together was concerned – but I'd picked up most of it anyway.'

'What *did* he tell you?'

'That he'd discovered this group. They called themselves the Suicide Club. He said it wasn't a group where people with severe depression could share their experiences and support each other. It was a place where people were actively encouraged to kill themselves.'

'He was angry?'

'Angry and sad.' She looked at the huge seascape hanging on the wall and Venn thought she was losing herself in it again, remembering Nigel Yeo, the love she'd found in middle age. 'Angry that the major providers refused to close the chatroom down, and sad that people were so desperate that they felt the need to use it.' She looked up. 'I've researched them since and found my way into one or two.'

'What about the one used by Mack?'

'Yes, I found that one. Its official name is Peace at Last, but there's a tight group of a few individuals and a moderator within it. *They* call themselves the Suicide Club.'

Venn nodded. He already knew that much. 'Did you get the name of the moderator.'

'Only the name he or she uses online. They call themselves the Crow.' She paused. 'I didn't have the expertise to track down the Crow's real identity. You'd need a security expert for that, and even then, I'm not sure it would be possible.'

That would be for Ross's friend Steve.

'Did you pass all this information on to Nigel?'

'Of course.'

'Was that soon before he died?'

'Not immediately before. Perhaps a couple of weeks.'

Venn wondered about that. If Yeo hadn't only recently discovered the impact of the Suicide Club, what had made him so angry on the Friday afternoon before his body was discovered? Ratna had described his mood as changing dramatically in the course of the day. Still they had no idea of his movements that afternoon, except that he'd told Reed that it was a matter of life and death. Nothing quite made sense.

'Had Nigel learned anything new about the Mackenzie case on the day that he died?'

'I don't know,' she said. 'I didn't see him. He'd asked if I wanted to go to Cynthia's party. He said he wanted to chat to her friend, the woman who's a police officer. I told him I'd rather wait until we'd told Eve we were a couple.' She looked up at Venn. 'I think I explained all that when you were last here. In the end, Mother and I went out to dinner instead to a rather nice new restaurant in Appledore. I did have a text from him that Friday lunchtime, but there was nothing work-related. It was only catching up, just saying he was looking forward to seeing me over the weekend.'

'We really need to track his movements that Friday afternoon. He had a meeting at the hospital in the morning and then another there at four thirty, but we don't know where he was in between. Do you have any idea where he went?'

Lauren shook her head. 'Sorry, I'm afraid I can't help.'

'Nigel had told Paul Reed, the Spennicott campaigner, that he'd go there that afternoon, but he called him to cancel. Do you know anything about that?'

'Ah.' She looked out of the window and into the garden. 'Nigel got involved in the Spennicott old people's home against his better judgement. In the end, he considered that the decision to close the Mount was justified, though he said Frank could have been less hasty and should have involved the residents earlier.' She paused. 'Nigel was sure he'd be able to negotiate a compromise, some sort of deal which would make everyone happy. He said that the writer, Paul Reed, was a poisonous little man, stirring up trouble out of spite. But really, I have no idea why Nigel cancelled the visit.'

'Do you know why Mr Ley was in such a rush to convert the place?' Matthew wasn't quite sure how that could be relevant to the investigation, but Frank's disappearance made him a potential suspect.

Lauren thought for a moment. 'I think Frank saw Spennicott in the abstract, almost as a mathematical equation: the boutique hotel would benefit the community more than the old people's home, so that was the route to take.' She looked up. 'He was looking at the greater good. If he'd actually visited the home and chatted to the residents, his perspective would probably have changed. He was passionate in his support for the campaign to get justice for Mack's family because he'd known him. I think Frank just didn't have the ability to make the imaginative leap, to put himself in the place of people he'd never met, like the care home residents.'

Venn nodded. There were people like that in the police service, people who understood the abstract better than the personal. *He* could well be one of them.

They sat in silence for a moment. The shadows thrown by the trees in her garden were already lengthening. It would be a little cooler there. Soon, he'd have to go back to Barnstaple to meet up with the team and to see if Ley had reappeared.

'Have you heard that there's been another death?' he asked.

'Yes. Wesley Curnow. I read about it earlier this week.'

'Did you know him?'

'I'd met him a couple of times, when Frank invited me to one of his Westacombe gatherings.' She paused and looked up. 'But really, I can't think why anyone would want to kill him.'

'What did Nigel make of him?'

'Not very much. It wasn't in Nigel's nature to dislike people. He tried to understand them. But I think Wesley rather irritated him.'

'Did Nigel try to understand the other staff at Patients Together?'

Lauren laughed out loud. 'Perhaps not as hard as he should have done. But Steph and her cronies are very set in their ways. A lot of gossip goes on in that office, and not a lot of work. I think Nigel was frustrated because he thought the organization could achieve so much more.' A pause. 'And all the doctors I know have a confidence, a certainty that can make them appear arrogant.'

'What will you do now? Will you continue working for them?'

'I still have to decide,' Lauren said. 'I might even apply to take over as CEO. It's Nigel's legacy in a way. I'd hate it to slide back to the way it was, to become a self-satisfied talking shop again. I couldn't remain in my present role with another boss. I'd find that impossible.' She gave a little shake of her head.

'I do have to ask,' Matthew said, 'because you knew both victims. What were you doing on Sunday afternoon, the afternoon Wesley died?'

'Of course you do, Inspector.' She gave the matter a moment's thought. 'Mother and I went to visit a National Trust garden near Torrington. She might not be able to see, but she loves a garden, the scents and the touch of the plants. We had afternoon tea in the cafe there and arrived home at about six o'clock.'

So, it would be impossible, Matthew thought, for Lauren Miller to have stabbed Wesley Curnow in the shed behind the Woodyard. He was pleased to have the confirmation, but he couldn't imagine the calm, thoughtful woman sitting opposite him as a killer.

It was dark by the time Matthew arrived home. Driving back, he was thinking of his husband, picturing the peace of the house, hoping that the tension of the previous day had disappeared. He found Jonathan just where he'd imagined, sitting on the wooden bench outside the kitchen door, a glass in his hand. He would have heard Matthew's car, and there was a glass of very cold, white wine waiting on the table beside him. The tide must be low, because there was no sound of water from the beach or the river. They sat without speaking, looking out at the stars.

Chapter Thirty-Four

JONATHAN WOKE EARLY AND HAD BEEN for a swim before
Matthew got up. It had become a ritual in these hot, heavy
days, a quick run into the sea, a kickstart to the morning. It
set him up for the meetings that filled much of his time at the
Woodyard. Today, there was a gentle swell, and after ten
minutes of vigorous crawl, he'd lain on his back, held up by
the saltwater, looking at the sky until the cold had eased into
his bones and sent him home.

Back at the house, Matthew had made coffee and seemed
to be waiting for him.

'I thought you might already be in town.' Jonathan knew
how much work, how much this particular murder, meant to
his husband. He'd expected him already to be in Barnstaple,
at his desk.

Matthew didn't answer directly. 'Are you busy this morning?'

So, Matthew didn't want to talk about the investigation. He
was shutting Jonathan out again. Jonathan tried not to care.
'No, I thought I'd go in a bit late. I'm owed masses of time.'

'I wondered if you'd come back to Westacombe with me.

I've just phoned Jen and it seems Frank Ley still hasn't turned up, and there's been no sighting of him. We can't justify a big team to look for him – he wasn't a major suspect in either murder – but I'd like a proper search of the grounds around the house. It was dark before we could do it properly yesterday. You'd be on public ground. A volunteer. We sometimes ask volunteers to help in searches. It would be nothing official.'

'Of course.' Jonathan knew this was a big deal. A kind of peace offering.

'He phoned me yesterday morning and sounded a bit low,' Matthew said. 'I'd hate it if he came back to a major fuss, uniformed officers doing a fingertip search, when all he needed was some time on his own.'

'I understand.'

'I didn't answer his call,' Matthew said. 'Perhaps it was my fault that he went off on his own.'

Dump the guilt, Jonathan wanted to say. *Just dump the guilt.*

Jen Rafferty was already there, waiting for them. Despite the heat, it was still early. The rest of the farm was quiet.

'How far did you go yesterday?' Matthew asked her. 'We can carry on from there.'

'Only as far as the wall. I didn't want to trespass.' She looked sheepish. 'Besides, there might have been cows in the field.'

Jonathan couldn't help teasing. 'You're scared of *cows*?'

'I'm a city girl. Freaked out by any animal bigger than me.'

'It's common land,' Matthew said. 'There's a public right of way and there were no cows when I was there last time.' A pause. 'But you go and check the garden properly. We'll do the common and the wilder areas beyond the wall.'

They waited until she'd made a start before setting off.

'I'll take the path down to the Instow road. Can you check the fields on either side? You find anything, you just call me. You don't touch anything.'

Jonathan nodded. He watched Matthew set off along the path through the garden before following. There was a hedge of lavender and the scent made him giddy, almost faint. In the wild flower meadow, he slowed his pace. The path through was clear, but the clover and buttercups had grown so high that they might hide evidence that Ley had been here. At the stile across the wall leading to the common, Jonathan paused. Standing on the wooden frame, he had a better view. He could see the roof of the Westacombe farmhouse behind him, the ribbon of road below him, and Matthew, straight and purposeful, marching towards it.

On the other side of the wall the grass was shorter. Perhaps animals – sheep or horses – were allowed in to graze, but no animals were here now. The gorse was a sunburst of colour, so bright that it hurt his eyes. Jonathan crossed the common horizontally to his left, following the line of the wall. Soon he came to a barbed wire fence, with a field of cows beyond. This land must be part of the farm. He retraced his steps to the right and came to a crumbling wall, much less well maintained than that separating Ley's garden from the common. On the other side of it was a patch of deciduous woodland, shadowy and inviting.

With the geography of the common fixed in his head, he began a proper search, moving backwards and forwards over the grass, peering into gorse thickets. All the time, desperate to find something. Knowing it was ridiculous, childish, but wanting to prove to Matthew that he could be useful. It almost felt like some sort of weird treasure hunt, with Matthew's approval as the reward.

In the end, the man was lying not far from the footpath, but he was hidden by one of the thickets of gorse. He was lying on his back, staring up to the sky, just as Jonathan had done earlier, when he was floating in the sea. He was about to feel for a pulse but remembered what Matthew had said. And this man had clearly been dead for a while. No need to touch him. Standing upright, he felt faint again for a moment, a little nauseous. It was the heat, the sound of bees on the blossom, the sweet honey smell of the gorse. He made a mental note of the position of the body and ran to find Matthew, shouting down the hill at him until he turned and began to walk back, knowing that nothing he could say to his husband would make him feel better about Francis Ley's death.

They stood together at a distance from the body. Matthew had already been on the phone, calling his team, the pathologist, the crime scene manager. The police officer taking over.

'No glass,' Matthew said. 'If it's murder, it's not the same MO.' He was talking to himself. No intelligent answer was expected.

'Do you want me to go?' Jonathan didn't want to cause Matthew embarrassment by being here.

'Of course, if you're busy, if you should be at work, but you'll probably have to make a statement later.'

'No,' Jonathan said quickly. 'No, there's no rush.'

Matthew kept at a distance from the body, but he began to take photos on his phone of Frank Ley, the surrounding gorse thicket, and a wide shot of the common. He was entirely concentrated on his work.

'He looks very peaceful,' Jonathan said. He'd never been very good at silence.

'Yes.' Matthew turned to look at him as if he'd said something of deep significance. 'You're right.'

Jonathan was about to walk back to the house when Matthew's phone rang. Matthew rolled his eyes as he answered, then put it on speaker phone and mouthed, 'It's the boss.' Oldham's words reverberated around the valley:

'You told me you were close to making an arrest. And now we have another bloody body.' The man seemed to pause for breath. 'And not any bloody body. Some high-profile wanker. The press will be here in swarms. Wasps round a bloody jampot. Mosquitos round a fucking open wound.'

Jonathan had met Oldham a couple of times and had taken an instant dislike. He pictured the man, tomato-faced, with as little self-control as a toddler in the middle of a temper tantrum, yelling into his phone.

Oldham was still shouting. 'So, get on top of it, Venn! When I took you on – which was against my better judgement – they told me you were clever. So, prove it! I need a result.'

The last sentence came out as such a scream that Matthew held his mobile away from his ear. Jonathan heard the line go dead. He felt fury on Matthew's behalf.

'How can he speak to you like that?' *When you're already feeling guilty about missing the call from the man.*

Matthew shrugged and put his phone away. 'He won't be there forever.'

'Good.' Jonathan looked up and saw a white-suited figure heading towards them. 'Good.'

'Brian Branscombe,' Matthew said. 'The crime scene manager.'

'What have we got?' Branscombe was a local, his voice relaxed, easy.

'Not sure yet. I'm not convinced this is murder. Can you have a quick look, check his pockets? See if there's anything that tells us what's happened here.'

Jonathan watched Branscombe bending over the body. He felt like a voyeur or that this was a piece of theatre. He thought again that he should go, that he was only in the way, but something held him at the scene. This was exciting. Distasteful but compulsive.

Branscombe reached into an inside pocket and pulled out an envelope. He held it up so Matthew could see what was on the front. 'I think this is for you.'

In old-fashioned script and written with a fountain pen: *Detective Inspector Matthew Venn.*

'And then there's this.' Branscombe held up a plastic medicine bottle. It was empty. He looked at the label. 'Amitriptyline. Regularly prescribed antidepressants. And I think Sal Pengelly will confirm that taken in sufficient quantity, they can kill.'

They sat together in Jonathan's car while Matthew opened the letter. Jonathan had offered again to go back alone to Barnstaple, to leave his husband to work in peace. He knew Matthew had always lived his life in compartments, and although his worlds had clashed big style in the previous investigation into the death of Simon Walden, his husband hated bringing together the personal and the professional. Asking Jonathan to help him look for Ley had been a gesture of reconciliation, a small step to allow their worlds to mix. Neither of them had expected the search to end like this: with a body and a letter from the dead man. Now Jonathan wanted to be here to offer support – he knew Matthew was obsessed by the fact that he hadn't spoken to Ley the day before – but he hoped Matthew wouldn't later regret the bending of rules.

Matthew slit the envelope carefully along the top and he pulled out a single sheet of heavy, high-quality paper. The letter had been written with the same pen and ink as the name on the envelope. Matthew held it with gloved hands and read it out loud.

'Dear Inspector Venn, I must apologize for confusing your investigation with this act of suicide. I'd hoped to explain in person, but when I couldn't get hold of you writing seemed more appropriate after all. Life isn't worth living. My acts of generosity are no longer sufficient to make me less guilty and the people that I cared for and felt I could help – Mack, Nigel and Wesley – no longer need my support. I'm glad that I have the courage to find peace at last.'

Then there was a signature.

'He doesn't mention Lauren Miller,' Jonathan said. 'You said she'd rejected him. Wouldn't that have been a trigger to his suicide?'

'Of course. But he wouldn't have wanted her to feel the guilt that had haunted *him*.' Matthew was quiet for a moment and the next words were spoken almost in a whisper. 'How will I tell her?'

Then he was out of the car, suddenly strong and decisive again. 'You should go,' he said. 'Of course, you won't discuss this with anyone. I need to make that phone call.'

Chapter Thirty-Five

EVE WAS WALKING FROM THE HOUSE to her workshop when Jen Rafferty appeared around the side of the farmhouse. Something about her face, and the way she was hurrying, made Eve certain that there was bad news. Another blow. After believing that life couldn't get worse than this, she'd be battered again.

'Can we go inside?' Jen's voice was breathless.

So, they were once again in the big ground-floor kitchen, sitting almost exactly as they'd been after her father's death, and the whole episode came crashing back into Eve's head. She was paddling in blood again, staring at the shard of glass, feeling the heat of the furnace.

'What?' she demanded. 'What's happened now?'

'We've found Frank. I'm really sorry, but he's dead.'

At least, Eve thought, Jen had come straight out with it. None of those awful euphemisms people had used when her mother had died. *Passed on. Passed away. Passed.* As if, her father had said dryly after the visit of a particularly gushing neighbour, Helen had been asked to give a urine sample. The image of her father came bright and sharp into her head and she had a brief moment of gratitude. She'd worried that she might lose a clear picture of him.

'Did a piece of my glass kill him?' Eve thought she couldn't bear that. The strange sense that she was somehow complicit. That the victims would still be alive if it weren't for her work.

Jen shook her head. 'We're not entirely sure about the cause of death yet. We don't think that it was murder.' She paused. 'When did you last see him?'

'The night before last. At that peculiar party.'

'You didn't catch a glimpse of him yesterday? Not even in the distance?'

Eve tried to remember. These days, events seemed to run together and felt unimportant, irrelevant, overshadowed by memories of violence. She shook her head. 'Where was he found?'

'Near a gorse thicket on the common.'

'I wouldn't have seen him then. He'd have gone straight from his side of the house, through the garden, and I didn't go anywhere near.'

'Did you see anything unusual yesterday? Any strangers around the place?'

'No,' Eve said. 'Nothing unusual happened at all.' *Except that my father and my neighbour have both died and nothing will be the same again.*

There was a gentle knock on the kitchen door and Matthew Venn walked in. He came and sat opposite Eve. Jen Rafferty got to her feet and muttered something about making tea. She disappeared from Eve's line of sight. Venn sat on the wooden chair across the table from her. Again, Eve braced herself for information she didn't really want to hear.

'I wanted you to know,' Matthew said, 'before the rumours start flying. We're pretty sure that Frank killed himself. He took an overdose. He left a note.'

'Why would he do that? He had all this. His work.' Eve found it hard to imagine jovial Frank being so desperate.

'He was depressed,' Matthew said. 'He told me himself he had a history of the illness. And then all the chaos and the violence here . . . He found it hard to deal with all that on his own.'

'He had us!'

'Perhaps that wasn't quite enough.'

In the background Eve could hear the kettle coming to the boil, the clink of mugs.

Matthew seemed to be reaching a decision to speak again. Eve thought there'd be more information about Frank Ley's death, but the question was quite different.

'Do you know someone called Lauren Miller?'

'Yeah, she worked for my dad.'

Another silence. Again, Matthew seemed to be hesitating, uncertain whether to continue speaking.

'I phoned her about Frank's death. She knew him very well. They worked together in London. Frank introduced her to your father. She and your father were very close. She's here and she'd like to talk to you.'

Eve struggled to understand what the detective was trying to say, then it became clear. A flash of understanding that explained her father's recent moments of light-heartedness, how he'd started singing to himself again, his words when he'd offered to spend that last day working with her: *Something rather wonderful has happened. I want to tell you all about it.*

'She and Dad were lovers!'

'Will you see her?' Matthew asked. 'No pressure at all. She'll quite understand if not.'

No! What does she think? That she can replace my mother? Or that she can possibly feel as deeply as I do about my father's dying?

But then the old politeness and a new curiosity took over. Eve nodded her head and Matthew went off to call the woman in.

Chapter Thirty-Six

AFTER SHE'D FINISHED TALKING TO EVE, Jen made her way
back to the Grieves' cottage. The yard had already filled up
with vehicles. She recognized Sally Pengelly's car and waved
to her. Sarah was standing at the cottage door, looking out.

'What's going on?' She sounded anxious. 'Is there a new
lead? Do you know what happened to Nigel and Wesley?'

Jen shook her head but didn't answer. 'Where are the girls?'

'At school.' As if the answer was obvious. Jen thought she
was losing all sense of time.

'And your husband?'

'He's just come in.'

'I need to talk to you both.'

A van full of uniformed officers drove through the gate,
pulling Sarah's gaze back to the yard, but she turned and went
into the house. Jen followed.

John Grieve was standing at the sink, washing his hands.
He was still in overalls and stockinged feet. The sink was under
the window and he nodded outside. 'What on earth's happening
out there?' He turned away and took a towel from a hook

281

behind the door. 'It feels as if we're under siege. How long do we have to carry on like this?' There was an edge of aggression, even threat, under the voice, which made Jen wary. She recognized the danger signs.

'For as long as it takes for us to catch a murderer.' She wanted to add something sarky. *Sorry for the inconvenience.* But after all, these people's lives *had* been turned upside down and two of their friends had died. Now she had to tell them that there'd been another death. But not yet. First, she needed some information.

'Where were you all day yesterday, Mr Grieve?' Jen kept her voice pleasant, polite.

'Out working. The place doesn't run itself.'

Jen sensed Sarah tense beside her. The woman was worried about the impression John was giving. Jen knew all the excuses. *He's tired. Stressed about the business. It's a bad time.* Jen had had to explain her husband's moods to her friends for years. Before things had become really bad and he seldom let her out.

'Where exactly? Honestly, I'm not being deliberately intrusive. I do have a good reason for asking.'

Grieve looked at his wife and then back at Jen. 'I went for a drive,' he said. 'After milking. I needed to get away for a bit.'

'You didn't say.' This was Sarah, trying not to overreact. She wouldn't want to make a fuss in front of a stranger. Jen knew how that felt too.

'I wanted to look at that farm we had our eye on. The one on the edge of the moor, beyond Spennicott.' He paused. 'I thought if Frank wants to create his grand model village there, he might support us, invest. We'd still be part of his empire, but at least we wouldn't be right in his backyard.'

'It would have been nice to know what you were doing.' No apology now. No anxiety about embarrassing themselves in front of Jen. The words were sharp and fierce.

So, she could fight back when she needed to. She wasn't as oppressed as Jen had been. Go, girl!

'Yeah,' he said. 'Look, I'm sorry. I can't explain how tough I'm finding this. All living on top of each other. No kind of space or privacy. And having the police marching all over the place, the press lurking in the lane, just makes things worse.'

Jen was tempted to ask if he was depressed, if he'd contemplated using a suicide chatroom, but she'd save that question for when she had Grieve on his own. 'Did anyone see you this afternoon?' she asked. 'I mean, did an agent show you round the farm? Or the landowner?'

'No.' A pause. 'I just wanted to get a sense of the place. Its potential.'

'Do you know a writer called Paul Reed, who lives in Spennicott? He's been running a publicity campaign against Mr Ley.'

'I've never heard of him!' Grieve was losing his cool now. 'Why do you want to know? What's going on? Why are all these people turning up in the yard?'

'There's been another death.' Jen watched their faces, tried to gauge if the information was new to them, but they both stood staring at her, blank and impassive. Shock, she thought. Perhaps.

Sarah spoke first. 'Who?'

'Frank Ley. It seems he went missing yesterday and we found his body on the common beyond his house this morning.'

John spoke first. 'I wonder what will happen to this place? To us?'

Jen had been wondering about that too. She'd considered it while she was talking to Eve, though she'd thought the glass blower would be okay. She'd inherit her father's house in Barnstaple and wouldn't be left homeless and without funds. And that might happen to this family. 'I suppose it depends if Frank had a will and who he left all his land and his money to.'

But Sarah was in tears. 'We shouldn't be thinking of that now! We're talking about Frank. I've known him since I was a baby. I loved him.' She turned on her husband. 'How can you be so selfish?'

'Because we have two daughters and soon there'll be another child to feed and clothe. And because we have no savings and no pension plan. I'm just worried that we won't be able to hold all this together.' He made a sweeping gesture to take in the clutter, the piles of children's clothes, the toys in a plastic box in the corner. For the first time since they'd started talking, Jen felt sorry for him.

'Did Frank have any other close relatives?' she asked. 'If not, I suppose at least the house and the farm will come to you.'

'Really, I don't think it will.' Sarah blew her nose and wiped her eyes, with what looked to Jen like a tea towel. 'Frank always said he didn't believe in inherited wealth. It'll probably have gone to one of his charities.'

'Do you know if he *made* a will?'

'No!' Sarah said. 'Of course not. It's not the sort of conversation you have with a relative, especially a relative who's your landlord.'

'Did he have a solicitor?'

'Yes.' This was John Grieve. 'He drew up a contract when we took over the management of the farm for Frank. It's a chap called Mason based in Barnstaple.'

'Thanks.' Jen made a quick note. She couldn't see how the disposal of Westacombe Farm could be relevant to Ley's death. It would have been hugely significant if Francis Ley had been murdered and the first victim, but surely not now. She turned back to the couple. 'Did either of you see Frank yesterday?'

'I didn't,' Sarah said. 'I haven't seen him since his party the night before.'

'John?'

'He was up and about first thing yesterday morning, when I went out for milking. I walked the cows up the lane, but took the shortcut through Frank's garden to get to the field. He was drinking coffee on his terrace. Still in his dressing gown. He looked a bit rough.'

'Did he speak to you?' Jen was thinking this was probably the last time Ley had been seen alive.

'He waved. I don't think he said anything. Nothing important anyway. "Lovely morning." Something like that.'

'Did you see anyone else?'

'No.'

'And later?' Jen thought this was like getting blood from a stone. She wondered if Grieve was being deliberately obstructive or awkward. 'You must have walked back past the farmhouse. Didn't you see Frank then?'

'He wasn't sitting on the terrace,' John said. 'He might have been in the house, but I didn't see him.' He paused. 'And that was when I decided to take off, to head over to Spennicott and get a look at the farm there. I was planning what I'd say to Frank, thinking of the business plan I could put together. It would have made sense for him to invest. Real sense. We could have fed our meat into his shop, the pub and the hotel he was planning. Sarah would have had more space for her dairy. But we'd have had some independence. A proper place of our own, away from the coast and all the trippers. And now it'll never happen.' The anger and depression that had seemed to haunt him when Jen had first come into the house appeared to have returned.

'You don't know,' Sarah said. 'He might have left us something. Enough to buy the place on our own. You know how much he loved the girls. I can't imagine he'd not have remembered them.'

'We need more than an old painting or a bit of costume jewellery from his mother!' Grieve turned and left the room.

The women were left staring at each other. 'He'll be upstairs on his computer for hours now,' Sarah said. 'It's all that calms him down when he's in one of his moods. I'd best get the girls down, so they don't disturb him.'

'Is he always as tense as this?'

There was a slight hesitation before she answered. 'No. It's such a stressful time, isn't it? Three deaths connected to the place where we're supposed to feel safe. He just wants to protect us.'

Jen wasn't sure. She thought again that Sarah was so used to defending him, to herself and outsiders, that it had become a habit. The woman went on:

'I feel it too. It's as if we're in some sort of siege, that there's an enemy just outside, waiting to get us. You know that childhood nightmare, when you wake up, convinced that there's a monster hiding in a cupboard or under the bed? The dream's so scary because it's like something evil has invaded your personal haven, the place you retreat to when you're anxious or upset. Westacombe has always been my safe place, but in the past few days I've gone to bed scared. I get up in the night to check the kids are okay. And whenever I get up, I see that John's awake too, lying there, watchful, listening for strange noises in the dark. I don't think he's had more than a couple of hours' sleep since Nigel died. In the morning, we act as if everything's normal. We get the kids off to school and we talk about work. But it's not normal, is it? And it'll never be normal again.' She paused and looked dry-eyed at Jen. 'John's right. Whatever happens, we'll have to move, even if it means shifting into town and doing something boring just to earn a living. At the moment boring seems bloody brilliant.' She stood up. 'I'm sorry, I need some air.'

Sarah opened the door and a beam of morning sunshine flooded the room with light. Jen wasn't sure what to say now. She thought her own experience of an abusive marriage might be colouring her picture of this relationship. Earlier, she'd been planning words of reassurance and encouragement: *You don't have to stay with him if he's being a shit. Get out while you can. Here's my personal number. Give me a call and I can help.*

Now, she thought things were more complicated than that, or very much simpler. As Sarah had said, the couple were living in the eye of a storm and all around them was tragedy and chaos. No wonder their nerves were frayed and John had wanted to leave for a while, to plan a future away from Westacombe. Which didn't mean, of course, that Jen wouldn't be searching out CCTV records for the roads leading towards Spennicott, to check that his story was true.

The women stood together for a moment just outside the cottage door.

Chapter Thirty-Seven

ROSS FOUND THE WHOLE MACKENZIE FAMILY together in the Sandpiper. Venn had asked him to notify them of Frank Ley's death:

'They were friends and another suicide will hit them badly. It'll bring back the details of their son's death.'

By the time Ross got there, it was late afternoon and the cafe had been closed to the public. Inside, they were preparing for the evening's event. Posters on the wall advertised a play, a performance of *Waiting for Godot* by a small Cornish touring company. Ross had heard of Beckett but knew nothing about him, except that he was obscure. He was put off by anything that reminded him of school. When he pushed open the door, he walked into darkness. There were heavy blinds on all the windows. A loud woman's voice shouted at him from the gloom.

'Sorry. We're not open, not even for the bar.'

It wasn't Janey. Someone older. A loud, confident, superior woman's voice that rankled. Her mother, perhaps.

'It's DC Ross May. I need to talk to the Mackenzies.'

Just as his eyes got used to the shadow inside, a spotlight was turned on and blinded him. He wondered if that was deliberate and, again, he felt awkward.

'Sorry.' This time the apology *did* come from Janey. 'We're just getting ready for this evening's play.'

The house lights came on and he saw that the cafe was being transformed. They'd built a low stage at one end of the room and rows of chairs faced it. The counter which had served sandwiches and cream teas during the day was now set up to provide wine and cocktails. Ross thought Mel might like it here. He should bring her here one evening, though not to see a piece of theatre they would probably both struggle to understand.

Janey was wearing a black T-shirt, with a Sandpiper logo, and frayed jeans. Her parents were at the back of the room, working on the lighting. Ross recognized Martha Mackenzie because his mother was a fan of her TV soap. She shouted out to him again, the voice slightly too loud, slightly patronizing.

'This is really not a good time, Constable. And we've told your colleague all that we know.'

'I have some news.' Then he repeated with more authority. 'I need to talk to you.'

The older couple moved from the back of the room. Janey pulled three of the chairs into a semicircle and they sat, looking at him. Again, he felt a little daunted. Martha was wearing a silver tunic over wide black trousers. Her make-up was dark and dramatic – heavy black eyeliner and mascara, with dark red lipstick – but still she seemed to glow, to pull his eyes towards her. 'Well?' she demanded. 'What do we need to know? Have you found the killer? Is that it?'

'I'm afraid there's been another death.' It wasn't how he'd planned to tell them. He'd put together some words driving from the farm. *I know Mr Ley was a close friend and this will come as a shock.*

'Who?' This was Janey. She seemed horrified by the news. In the strange theatrical lights, her face seemed very pale, her eyes wide and large. Like something from a cartoon. Not real at all. None of this seemed quite real.

'Francis Ley.'

'Not Frank!' George Mackenzie's response seemed the most genuine. 'No.'

'He was found on the common near to his garden this morning.'

'How did he die?' George demanded. 'Was he stabbed like Nigel and Wesley?'

'We won't confirm cause of death until after the post-mortem, but it seems that he committed suicide.'

There was complete silence.

'He had everyone round for drinks the night before last,' Janey said. 'The Grieves and Eve, and us. A kind of commemoration of three lives lost. That was what he said.' She paused. 'But perhaps it was his way of saying goodbye.'

'How did he seem?'

Now Martha did speak. 'Bloody sad! As we all were. We were mourning three people close to us. And now, it seems, he was contemplating taking his own life too. And you ask how he was! Good God.' She stood up, pushing back the chair so violently that it fell over. 'I'm going outside for a fag, and to look out for those actors.'

She left and the room seemed very quiet. 'Please forgive my wife,' George said at last. 'She's very upset.'

Ross was thinking that this whole conversation could have come straight out of a play. Everyone's response seemed stilted and unnatural.

George shifted in his seat. 'Look, we should be getting ready for the evening's performance. You don't think we should cancel? We've got a full house.'

Ross thought for a moment. 'No,' he said. 'No need for that.'

As he was leaving the bar, a battered minivan drew up outside and half a dozen people climbed out. Martha was there, greeting them, hugging them as if they were all old friends. Ross presumed they were the actors. As he walked away, he heard her loud voice carrying down the street. 'Come along in. We've had a bit of sad news today, so we're not quite as organized as usual. But of course, the show will go on.' He thought she sounded desperate, as if she was trying too hard to convince the world that she was in control.

At the evening briefing they concentrated on the possibility that Ley had been a member of the Peace at Last forum.

'We need your friend to come up with that information,' Venn said. As if it was Ross's fault that Steve hadn't yet provided the goods.

'Could Ley have been the killer?' This was Jen. 'His suicide wasn't triggered by a very different kind of guilt?'

'Superintendent Oldham has already suggested that theory.' Venn's voice was bland but they could all tell he didn't think much of it. 'It would be very neat, of course, but really, I don't see it. What motive would Ley have for killing Nigel and Wesley?' He looked up at them sharply. 'And I refuse to blacken a dead man's name without real cause.'

It was just the core group tonight. Venn had bought in pizza, and they'd pushed a couple of desks together and sat around pulling the slices apart with their fingers. No plates and no napkins, though the boss had found a roll of paper towel somewhere. If there'd been beer, it could have been a student party.

'Could Ley have been provoked to kill himself?' Jen asked. 'If he was a member of the Suicide Club?'

'It's something to consider.' Venn carefully wiped his hands. 'I presume the Grieves will inherit his estate.'

'According to Sarah Grieve, Ley didn't believe in inherited wealth,' Jen said. Her mouth was full of pizza. Not a good look. Mel would never speak with her mouth full. 'She wasn't very hopeful that their family would get anything. She thought it might all go to charity.' A pause. 'You might be interested to know that John Grieve claimed to be in Spennicott yesterday afternoon, boss.'

'Very interested. A coincidence, do you think?'

'He wasn't visiting the old folks' home. And he claimed he'd never heard of Paul Reed. He's interested in taking over a farm on the edge of the moor there. He'd hoped Francis might invest in the venture, because he'd bought most of the village already.'

Ross could see Venn considering that. 'So, if anything, that family might actually lose out by Francis's dying?'

'I suppose.' Jen hesitated and Ross saw there was more to come. 'John Grieve seemed very tense to me, jumping between anger and depression. Moody. Sarah says he spends a lot of time on the computer.'

'You think he might belong to the Suicide Club?'

Jen shrugged. 'It's certainly worth checking out.'

'I visited Lauren Miller yesterday,' Matthew said. 'It seems probable that her rejection of Ley was the trigger to his suicide.' A pause. 'She'd learned a little about the Suicide Club from Nigel. She's technically competent and had found her way into the chatroom. Apparently, the moderator, the person who seems actively to be advocating suicide, calls themselves the Crow. Lauren couldn't get beyond the nickname, though.' He looked up at Ross. 'Could your friend Steve do that? It's really urgent that we have that information.' Again, his voice was disapproving, as if Ross was the person causing the delay.

'If anyone can, he'll be the one to do it. I'll call him as soon as we're done here.'

'How were the Mackenzies?'

'I don't know,' Ross said. 'They're a weird kind of family. But maybe it was just shock. I couldn't take to the mother, Martha. She seems like a real drama queen.'

'Didn't you say that Francis had invested in their business?' Jen asked. 'Could that be significant?'

'According to George, it was a loan,' Venn said, 'not an investment and they paid it off after the first year. I'll make an appointment with the solicitor in the morning. We'll have more to go on then.' He stood up. 'Let's get home at a decent time. It'll be a busy day tomorrow. Jen, can you go and see Lucy Braddick, show her some photos of Wesley's lady friends? Try to catch her at home rather than at the Woodyard. She's moved into independent living and wanted to show it off. Ask if she remembers seeing any of them on Sunday afternoon. She thought Wesley might be waiting for someone, and she might have seen him with his killer. I promised to call in but I haven't squeezed in the time.' Venn paused. 'Ross, I'll leave the tech to you. Sit with your mate until we can get an answer.

293

I don't want anyone else to jump ahead of us in his queue. And I'll see the solicitor to find out just how much of a fortune Francis Ley had left, where it's going and who might have a financial motive for killing him.'

Out in the car park, Ross called Mel. She answered immediately:

'Hiya, love. How's it going?' She sounded tired, but it was the old Mel. He'd been letting his imagination run away with him.

'There's been another killing,' he said. 'Another death at least. But we're all done now.'

'Okay then. See you soon.'

And that was all it took. A few seconds' conversation, and his heart was singing. It seemed to him that he could have been taking her for granted, that all they needed was some quality time together.

He phoned techie Steve, but there was no reply and he left a message. 'I'll be at yours tomorrow at eight. It's urgent. I'll bring breakfast.' He set off for home.

Chapter Thirty-Eight

EVE ONLY REALIZED AS SHE ATE supper in her flat that she was alone in the big house. No Wesley and no Frank. Frank had never made any noise at all, but here in the attic the walls were thin and she'd often been aware of Wesley's presence. His music. His women. The very occasional sound of a hoover. She imagined herself as a pea rattling around in a huge drum, surrounded by space. The Grieves were only across the yard in their cottage, but Eve didn't want to see them.

She reran the conversation with Lauren. It had been strained and awkward at first. The two detectives had left them alone to talk. Lauren had sat, gripping a mug of tea that never reached her lips.

'I loved your father very much.' The first words spoken.

'So did my mother.' Eve's words had been cruel and hard. They'd seemed to echo around the empty space like bullets.

'I know. Really, I know.'

More silence. But before Lauren drove back to Appledore, they'd been crying together, and Eve had found comfort in the fact that there was someone to share her grief.

By the time Lauren left, all the police officers had drifted away and Eve had retreated upstairs. So much had happened in less than a week that her brain seemed overloaded, heavy. It was a physical sensation. She could feel the weight of her head on her shoulders, down her back and through to her feet. How could she carry so much without collapsing? She sat by the window and watched the sky become darker, richer, until it turned black. Despite the tiredness, she knew she wouldn't sleep, and still she remained in the chair she'd picked up in a charity shop in Bideford, thinking of the people involved in her father's life and her life, the living and the dead, and what could have strung them all together and brought them to this.

Her window faced east, away from the sea, and she was still sitting there at the first grey light of dawn. She might have dozed a little, but her mind hadn't stopped racing. Snippets of remembered conversation were threaded to images: faces, places. A giant necklace of memories.

And then she thought she knew. It started as a suspicion as faint and insubstantial as the pearly light she could see from the window. A memory of the early morning before she'd found her father. Another approaching dawn. A sound filtered through sleep, forgotten in the shock of discovering his body. She got up and made tea, because tea was real and prosaic, and her ideas were fanciful. She needed to stay grounded. Through her window came the dawn chorus, at first a few stray notes, then the full choir of birdsong, impossibly loud. The noise sounded like a validation of her theories.

Now Eve wondered what she should do next. She couldn't imagine talking to Matthew Venn, with his polished shoes and his perfectly ironed shirts. He'd expect facts and logic. She wasn't even sure that Jen Rafferty, who was much more on her wavelength, would understand. Besides, how could she accuse someone of murder with no evidence at all after a strange wakeful night of dreams and fantasies? It could ruin a life. It occurred to her that Lauren Miller would listen to her theories, and would help her sort through them. She had a logical mind and a clear vision. But Eve was still confused about her relationship with the woman. To confide these midnight ramblings would imply an intimacy that Eve wasn't quite ready for.

Then she thought of Jonathan Church. He was married to the police inspector and he was a friend. A real friend. She remembered him bringing her back to the flat the evening that Wesley had been killed, sitting on the floor and drinking wine with her. That was what she needed, someone she could confide in, who wasn't official, who wouldn't see every word as a formal statement.

She'd make another cup of tea and then she'd text him, ask if it was okay for her to call into the Woodyard for a chat. The idea of sitting in his office with the bustle of the art centre going on all around them, of the man himself, solid and square in his cotton T-shirt and his baggy khaki shorts, was reassuring. Jonathan had always reminded her a little of her father. It was his ability to listen, to take her anxieties seriously, but somehow to take them onto his own shoulders, to share them.

She made the tea and got out her phone. Jonathan must be up early too because he replied soon after. **Of course. Busy all day, but what about coming over to the Woodyard for an early supper. Five thirty?**

She wished she'd been able to see him earlier and felt a moment of impatience. Perhaps she should talk to somebody else? Then she thought that there wasn't really any rush. She'd probably got the thing all wrong anyway, losing perspective after her sleepless night. It would be good to spend some time in the studio making glass. In the meantime, there might be a way to check if her night-time imaginings had any truth in them at all. To prove to herself and to others that she was still quite sane.

Chapter Thirty-Nine

MATTHEW AND JONATHAN ATE BREAKFAST together. Jonathan had already been outside for his daily swim. He'd come back exhilarated, his hair still wet, his sandy feet leaving marks on the kitchen floor. He squeezed fresh orange juice and made coffee, and by then Matthew was up too, amazed that his partner could have so much energy.

'How's it all going?' Jonathan hadn't asked the evening before and Matthew had been grateful for that. When he'd arrived home exhausted, he'd preferred to hear Jonathan chat about normal things: an art exhibition at the Woodyard, the touring theatre company bringing a new play, Maurice Braddick's adaptation to life without Lucy, Bob's new menu in the centre cafe.

'It's muddled,' Matthew said now, drinking the last of the coffee. 'Too much going on. Too many connections. Too many motives.' He paused. 'After the early briefing I'm meeting Ley's lawyer. That might throw a bit of light.'

'Eve texted.' Jonathan was spreading homemade marmalade on thick, brown toast. 'I'm meeting her for supper tonight in the Woodyard.'

'What does she want?'

'I guess a bit of support and a shoulder to cry on. She's lost three people very close to her.' Jonathan paused. 'And even that'll be light relief after the trustees' finance meeting, which is happening for most of the rest of the day.'

Matthew smiled. The arts centre thrived under Jonathan's care, but figures seemed too abstract a concept for him to grasp.

Ley's solicitor had an office in Barnstaple, in an elegant terrace looking out over the River Taw. With its long windows and decorative shutters, it wouldn't have looked out of place in a provincial French town. Matthew had walked from the briefing through the town centre and along the riverbank. Above the tideline the mud had been baked hard and edged white with dried salt.

The solicitor was waiting for him in reception. He had the easy manner of an old-fashioned country doctor, confident and competent. 'We don't open to the public until nine thirty, so there's nobody in to man the front desk. Come along to my office.'

It was upstairs at the front of the building, one of the rooms with the shutters. The long window was open, letting in a little air and the sound of traffic below and exhaust fumes. Peter Mason, the solicitor, closed it and half pulled together the slatted shutters, so the light was filtered through the bars.

'Poor Frank,' he said. 'He was more than a client. He was a friend. I'll miss him.' Mason looked up. 'You said on the telephone that it was suicide?'

'Yes, we're waiting for the post-mortem results but we think it was an overdose of antidepressants. He'd been prescribed them during a previous bout of illness. Does that surprise you?'

'It does rather. I think he might have considered suicide rather an indulgence.'

'You'd known him for a long time?'

'Since we were eleven. We were in school together.' He paused. 'He was an odd little scrap even then.'

'In what way?'

'He was fascinated by figures, patterns. Money, not for what it could buy, but for the way the market worked. He was the only teenager I've ever met who read the *Financial Times*. He didn't go to university. He was bright enough but couldn't see the point, joined a City trader and worked his way up. I was more conventional, and didn't stray so far from home. I went off to Exeter to read law.'

Matthew decided to let him continue without interruption. He found the story of Ley's youth fascinating. There was a gap in the conversation while Mason collected his thoughts and Matthew heard the gulls on the river against the background rumble of traffic below.

'He was an only child, of course,' Mason said, 'and Westacombe seemed a bit old-fashioned even then. The family scraped a living from the land. He was very much a loner. Now, I think you might say Francis was somewhere on the autistic spectrum. He found social contact a bit tricky. He was happier with his numbers and couldn't understand people who were less logical, more emotional in their response to the world around them. I was really his only friend at school, but he didn't care.'

Matthew thought about that. It made sense and perhaps it explained Ley's decision to close the Mount. It was rational, inevitable, and he hadn't quite seen how it would have a personal impact on the residents.

'You kept in touch as adults?'

'We weren't close when he was working in London, but we'd meet up when I was back during university holidays, and he was home to visit his mother.' Mason smiled. 'Perhaps we were both misfits. I was a bit of a geek too. We shared a love of cricket, so we had that in common. Then when we both moved back to North Devon, and he asked me to look after his legal affairs, we saw more of each other.'

'Did he ever have a partner?'

'There were women that he fancied, lusted after at a distance, but he didn't have the confidence or the skills to approach them, to get close to them. I'm not sure that he ever had a proper relationship.' Mason paused. 'There was one woman he'd worked with. She was married to someone else but recently the marriage broke up and she turned up here in North Devon. I think Frank hoped something might come of it.'

Matthew felt a fresh stab of sympathy for Frank. How galling it must have been! He'd worshipped Lauren from afar for years, invited her for a meal in his home and she'd fallen for Nigel Yeo, one of his other guests. And then, when Frank had shared his true feelings, she'd rejected him.

'Had you seen Mr Ley recently?'

'We met up for dinner about a month ago.' Mason paused. 'It was a regular arrangement. Frank was a very generous man. He always took me to his favourite restaurant. It was a treat and I looked forward to it.'

'How did he seem? His usual self? Not particularly low or depressed?'

The solicitor shrugged. 'No. I don't think so.'

'Had Mr Ley made a will?'

'He had.' Mason went to a filing cabinet and pulled out a manila envelope. 'I'm his executor as well as his lawyer.'

'If he hadn't made the will,' Matthew said, 'everything would be left to his next of kin?'

'Yes, a woman called Sarah Grieve, who was the grand-daughter of his mother's sister. There was no other close living relative.' Barton pulled the will from the envelope. 'Would you like me to explain the major points, then I can give you a copy to take away?'

'Please.'

'You have to know, Inspector, that while Frank was still a wealthy man, he'd been a philanthropist since making his fortune, and much of his money had already been given away. However, of course, he still did have considerable assets.'

Now Matthew *was* tempted to hurry him along, but after all, Mason had already given useful information and he might still have more to pass on. Best to let him give the details in his own way and at his own speed.

'Westacombe Farm, the house and all its land, was bequeathed to Sarah Grieve and, in the event of her death, to her heirs.'

'Ah,' Matthew said. He thought the Grieves should be pleased, relieved. 'Francis had told them that he didn't believe in inherited wealth and they were anxious about their future.'

'There is a stipulation,' Barton went on. 'The land should not be sold for commercial development and the family should live in the house and continue to farm traditionally.' He looked up from the desk. 'He'd grown up there and had been very fond of his mother, who died there. He had an uncharacter-istically emotional attachment to the place and was concerned that its character shouldn't change.'

Matthew wondered what John Grieve would make of that. The man had clearly wanted a fresh start away from Westacombe, but perhaps being allowed to farm independently, without an onsite landlord, would be enough for him.

Barton was continuing. 'The freehold of the studios and workshops created from farmyard outbuildings have been left to Wesley Curnow and Eve Yeo respectively, along with twenty thousand pounds each to support their businesses.' He looked up. 'Of course, that's no longer relevant now that Mr Curnow's dead, and that workshop will revert to the rest of the farm estate.'

'Is there any specific mention of the Spennicott project and the properties Francis owned there?' Matthew remembered his visit to the old folks' home and wondered if there would be any reprieve for the residents.

'Indeed, yes. That's one of the more complex and unorthodox stipulations, added relatively recently. Frank left the cottages, public house, shop and the Mount, currently in operation as a care home for the elderly, to a community trust of villagers and stakeholders, yet to be formed.' Mason gave a grimace. 'My firm was charged with setting that up. I must say, I'd rather hoped that Frank would outlive me, or that I would have retired before that became necessary. I'm not looking forward to the inevitable endless wrangles and the committee meetings running into the night.'

Matthew smiled in sympathy. 'And the rest of his investments and savings?'

'A quarter of a million to the Spennicott Trust, seed money to see it through its set-up. After that it would be expected to live off the rents and profits of the various businesses. Any excess to be invested for the good of the village.'

'I suppose that makes sense.'

'Another two hundred and fifty thousand goes to the organization Patients Together.' Mason looked at the paper on the desk in front of him and read the exact words. '*To allow this valuable organization to continue to hold the North Devon health trust to account.*'

'So, another of the inheritors is no longer alive to benefit,' Venn said. 'Nigel Yeo, who ran it, was our first victim.' He wondered what Roger Prior would have made of the bequest and the wording.

'Oh, that sum didn't go to any individual, but to the organization. The money will still go to Patients Together.'

'Had he told any of the beneficiaries that they were mentioned in his will?' Venn remembered his last conversation with Lauren. She'd told him that she was considering applying to run the NDPT. He wondered if the information that she wouldn't have to scratch around for funding, at least in the short term, could have influenced her decision. He thought it unlikely.

'That I don't know.'

'Were you involved in Mr Ley's investment in a family business in Instow, the Sandpiper, owned by the Mackenzie family?'

'Not personally,' Mason said. 'Not my area of expertise. But one of my partners drew up the contract.'

'As I understand it, the money was an interest-free loan rather than a formal investment and it has already been repaid. Could you confirm that?'

'I'd need to check with my colleague, but it's the sort of arrangement Frank might have made.'

'Very generous.'

'As I said before, Inspector, Frank was a very generous man.'

Mason put the will back into its envelope. 'The remainder of his wealth will go to a number of national and international charities, but I don't think there's anything else relating to your inquiries.'

'When will you inform the people who'll benefit from Mr Ley's will of their good fortune?'

'Letters will go out today to the individuals and organizations involved. Of course, probate will take a while and they won't receive the money for some time. But it's important that the Grieves continue to manage Westacombe, and they're more likely to do that if they know they have a stake in the place.'

Venn nodded and got to his feet. Mason walked down the stairs with him to show him out, and shook his hand at the door. Outside, the air felt a little different. The sky was still clear but it was humid and sultry, as if soon the heatwave would break, as if they were on the brink of a thunderstorm.

Chapter Forty

JEN STAYED AT HOME LONG ENOUGH to have breakfast with the kids. Since Nigel Yeo's murder they'd all been working ridiculous hours and no way would the overtime budget stretch to cover it all. She was due a bit of time off, and it felt as if she'd hardly seen them for days.

Ella was up, showered and dressed without any prompting, but Ben was still in bed when Jen had everything on the table. She knocked at the door of his room and went in. It was a small room, always dark. He never drew the curtains. It smelled of teenage boy, unwashed sheets and stale pizza. On the desk next to the bed, his computer seemed more alive than her son. Something was flashing. He'd probably been on it for most of the night. Some game with his friends. Killing people for fun. Or checking out unsavoury chatrooms? She was tempted to look, but he woke, looked at her, grunted.

'You'll be late for school.' She couldn't bring herself to be cross. He looked very young, half asleep. 'Breakfast is on the table.'

★

When they were both on their way to school, Jen made herself more coffee, then followed Matthew's suggestion and arranged to meet Lucy Braddick in her new flat in River Bank, a small complex of apartments for learning-disabled adults. She phoned Lucy's dad, Maurice, to find out when would be a good time to visit.

'Well, really,' he said, 'you should be phoning our Luce. The social workers say that I should be letting her make those sorts of decisions. She should be speaking for herself.' His voice was slow, his accent as rich and broad as his daughter's.

'I don't have her phone number, though.' Jen left a pause. 'I was hoping you might be there, Maurice. She'll be a bit more confident with you around, and I don't always understand her speech so well.'

'She's not on shift at the Woodyard until this afternoon,' Maurice replied. 'I suppose I could phone her and ask her to stay in this morning, warn her that we'll be calling by.' Jen could tell that he was delighted to have an excuse to visit his daughter. 'I was planning to come into Barnstaple to do a bit of shopping anyway.'

While she was waiting until it was time to visit Lucy, Jen pulled together images of the women Wesley Curnow had known. She was reminded of the Simon Walden investigation, another occasion when she'd shown photographs to a woman with Down's syndrome, but then Lucy had been a potential victim, not a witness. Jen found pictures of Martha and Janey Mackenzie; they'd appeared in the local newspaper at the time of Mack's death. Both women were wearing black and looked gaunt. Even Martha was looking away from the camera, not playing up to the crowd. George was there too, and the article used his words, as he'd railed against the system that had let his son down. Cynthia was easy to find. Jen chose an image of her friend wearing a vivid red and pink silk dress. She looked at it for a moment and experienced something akin to grief because the friendship they shared was slipping away. It felt like a kind of bereavement.

Lucy lived in a three-storey block of new flats built on land which had once been owned by the timber factory. The building itself had been transformed into the Woodyard Centre, but the land had been released for development and the independent living apartments were part of the site. They stood next to a small estate of family social housing and looked out over a children's playground. Jen used the Woodyard car park and walked past the centre to reach Lucy's place. Just as she was passing the Woodyard entrance, she saw Cynthia approaching from inside. She was carrying a rolled-up yoga mat. It would be impossible to avoid bumping into her.

'How's it going?' Jen thought no fucking way was Lady Cynth just going to march past with her nose in the air as if they didn't know each other, as if they hadn't once been best mates.

Cynthia stopped and shrugged. 'Pretty dreadful.' It sounded like an admission of failure. This wasn't the old Cynthia of high energy and endless optimism. 'Roger hardly speaks. He's working twelve-hour days and when he's home he locks himself in the office. He seems to be awake most of the night.' She looked straight at Jen. 'I'm worried about him. Even when things were really bad in London, he wasn't this low.'

'You think he's depressed? I mean, clinically depressed?'

'Yeah, I do.' Cynthia was on the verge of tears. 'I've said he should go to a doctor, but he tells me to leave him alone. There's this anger. I mean, if he was just sitting in a corner weeping, I could handle it, but there's a terrible rage. Against the world and me. For some reason he blames me for all that's happening to him.' A pause. 'We were never soulmates, you know. We never lived in each other's pockets. But in a way, that was why it worked. We were so different that we learned from each other, there was something new to discuss when we did come together. But now? I feel as if I've lost him.'

Jen thought this was one of the unconsidered effects of two murders; stress and suspicion were causing individuals, relationships and even communities to fall apart. She looked at her watch. She should be chatting to Lucy. 'Will you be around all morning? I'll call in, shall I? You can make me one of your spectacular coffees.'

A moment of silence. Jen thought that if the offer was rejected, the friendship would be over for good. No way back. But Cynthia smiled. 'Yeah,' she said. 'I'd really like that.'

Maurice was already in the flat when Jen got there, but it was Lucy who let Jen in, proud as punch. She held her arms wide. 'Welcome.'

The place gave out the vibe of a student hall of residence, but Lucy had her own living space – a sitting room with a kitchen at one end – as well as the bedroom and a shower room. She insisted on showing Jen round, before putting the kettle on and carefully spooning instant coffee into three mugs.

'There's a care worker onsite,' Maurice said, 'but Luce manages everything, don't you, maid?'

'Yep.' She beamed.

'We need your help again,' Jen said, 'but there's no danger this time. Honest.' The last statement was aimed at Maurice, not Lucy. 'I just need you to look at a few pictures. Let me know if you saw any of these women on Sunday after Wesley had been in the cafe. If you finished work soon after, you might have noticed someone while you were walking home.'

'Sure,' Lucy said.

Jen thought she was proud to be asked and desperate to help. She worried that Lucy would try too hard, would convince herself that she recognized one of the faces just to please. 'It's not a test, Luce. It's just as important you tell me if you don't see anyone you know. Just as useful.'

Lucy nodded.

But in the end, when Lucy just stared blankly at the pictures, even at someone like Cynthia, who was a regular in the cafe, they all had a sense of disappointment.

'I just don't remember seeing anyone,' she said. 'When I left work, a bus came in to the stop in front of the Woodyard and people got off. I knew two of my friends from River Bank had gone to Bideford to see their families and I was looking out for them. They'd texted to say they were on their way home. I thought I could walk back to the flat with them. I saw them get off the bus and I waited for them to join me. There was a car coming in and for a minute they couldn't see me, even though I was waving. The car blocked their view.' She paused for a moment. 'That's a bit weird, isn't it? Because the centre was closing, so why would anyone come in?'

'What sort of car, Lucy?' Jen tried to keep any sense of urgency from her voice.

'I don't know anything about cars.' Now she was starting to sound anxious and upset. Jen could tell that Maurice was about to call a halt to the whole conversation. He fidgeted in his seat and wiped his forehead with a large, white handkerchief.

'Oh, nor do I.' Jen jumped in before he could speak. 'Nothing at all. But you might remember a colour.'

'Yes!' Lucy was triumphant. 'It was black! A big, black car.'

'I don't suppose you could tell if it was being driven by a man or a woman?'

Lucy shook her head. 'I didn't see. I was looking out for my mates getting off the bus, and then we were chatting.'

Jen left Maurice and Lucy sitting together and drinking more coffee. She was thinking that the father needed the company far more than the daughter did.

Jen went through the garden gate and round to the back of Cynthia's house, so she didn't have to go into the house past Roger's office. Even if Cynthia wasn't outside, she'd be in the kitchen, and Jen could knock on the back door. In the end, Cynthia *was* in the garden, in the chair where they'd had their last conversation. There was a bottle of Pinot Gris in an ice bucket and she'd already poured herself a glass. No chance of a fancy coffee, then.

'You're starting a bit early.' Jen took a seat beside her. She thought this was like being in an entirely different country or continent. The rainforest or some maharaja's garden in India. She'd never been to either, but despite the drought, there was something exotic about the bright colours and the lush vegetation.

'It's lunchtime,' Cynthia said. 'It's civilized to have a small glass with lunch.' On the table, there was a tray of cheese and cold meat, salad, French bread, a bowl of grapes and strawberries. Two plates, two knives and another glass. 'You will join me?'

'Are you joking? Of course! I'm starving!'

Cynthia pushed across a plate and a knife, then poured Jen a glass of wine. She seemed more composed than when she'd bumped into Jen outside the Woodyard, more in control. She'd prepared herself for the encounter.

'I shouldn't have the wine. You know the boss. A stickler.' But Jen took a sip all the same. This was more important than Venn's rules. 'What do you think's going on with Roger?' She pulled a piece of bread from the loaf and cut a slice of oozing brie, gave all her attention to the taste. Re-establishing a friendship was important, of course. But so was eating when you were given a chance in the middle of an investigation.

'Well, I don't think he killed Nigel Yeo and the others.' Cynthia was prickly again. The tension made her voice shrill.

'I'm here as a mate,' Jen said. 'Not a cop.'

'You're always a cop.'

There was no real answer to that and it was Cynthia who spoke next. 'He's so stressed. I'm worried about what he might do. I know he would never harm other people. He's given his life to the NHS, to saving lives. He might not be a medic, but he's supported them, fought for them. Battled with the government for more resources. More staff. It was that passion that made me fall for him.'

'Do you think he might be so depressed that he'd consider taking his own life? Is that what you're saying?'

There was a moment of silence broken by the raucous call of a magpie.

'Yes,' Cynthia said. 'You know, really, I think that he might.'

'Do you know what he's doing when he's spending all that time in the house in his office?'

'What do you mean?' Cynthia had drunk her wine. She poured herself another glass.

'We've been investigating Mack Mackenzie's browsing history. He was a member of a chatroom called Peace at Last. It's a support group for people considering suicide. Within that, there's a core group who call themselves the Suicide Club. That seems to be made up of more desperate members. We're worried that one or more of those people are actively encouraging or provoking people to kill themselves.'

'You think Roger might be a member?' Now soundless tears were running down Cynthia's face. 'That he could be considering suicide?'

'I'm worried that it might be possible. He was in touch with the professionals treating Luke Wallace, as well as those looking after Mack. We know that both young men were members of the group.'

'And they both killed themselves.'

'Yes, they both killed themselves. And Roger might have had access to enough information from the medics treating them to find the site.' Jen paused. 'It could have started off as professional interest, a way of proving that something other than healthcare negligence had contributed to the suicides.'

'I don't know what to do.' The tears were still streaming down Cynthia's face. She'd turned from a confident, competent woman into a child desperate for reassurance, looking for someone to make decisions for her.

'Do you have the passcode for his computer? We could get in and look.' *And I could find out whether or not he calls himself the Crow.*

'No!' Cynthia said. 'The office is his personal space. I never go in when he's not here.'

Jen was forming an argument in her head. *If you're anxious about his safety, don't you think that's more important than intruding on his personal space?* But she didn't have time to speak, because the phone in her pocket buzzed. A text from Matthew Venn, asking her whereabouts and requesting that she come back to the station as soon as possible.

'I've got to go,' she said. 'Work. Sorry.'

Cynthia stood up. 'Of course. It always is work, isn't it? There's no escape for you.' The words sounded like an accusation. She was still crying. It was as if all the liquid in her body was leaking through her eyes, as if she might drown in it.

Jen took the woman into her arms and squeezed her tight. For a moment, Cynthia relaxed enough to allow herself to be hugged.

'See if you can keep Roger away from the office when he comes in tonight,' Jen said. 'If he's found that website, I can see it could become a kind of obsession. An addiction. It's probably as compulsive, as exciting, as it gets: watching someone deciding if they're going to live or die. Then deciding yourself if it's your turn next.' *Or if you can persuade them to take the final step.*

Cynthia nodded, but Jen could tell she wouldn't stand up to her husband and she wouldn't ask him about the website or his mood. The couple had got into the habit of leading separate lives and had forgotten how to talk about anything important.

Chapter Forty-One

TECHIE STEVE HAD A FLAT ABOVE a florist's shop in a lane just off Boutport Street. The smell of the blooms soaking in the buckets outside hit Ross as he waited to be let in. Next door there was a rowdy pub and even this early in the day there were a few people in the beer garden. Ross couldn't think why Steve was still living here; the noise late into the evening would have driven *him* crazy, especially in this weather when everyone wanted to be outside. Steve didn't seem to be bothered by it, perhaps because the flat was long and thin and the rooms got darker and quieter the further in from the street it went. As Ross remembered, it was like moving to the back of a cave.

At the top of the steps that led up from the nondescript door off the pavement, there was a kitchen littered with pizza boxes and foil containers from takeaway restaurants. Empty beer cans. A smell that would set alarm bells ringing with environmental health. This is where Steve was waiting after Ross had pressed the buzzer and climbed into the gloom. The cyber expert was wearing a filthy fleece dressing gown. Nothing else as far as Ross could tell. He stood, blinking.

'Fuck, man, what do you want? This feels like the middle of the night.'

'It's mid-morning and this is urgent. Where have you got with tracing the Suicide Club members?'

'Something else came in,' Steve muttered, still half asleep. 'Something well paid.'

'Well, this is a matter of life and death.' Ross looked at him with something close to disgust. How could someone who was so bright – and so minted – live like this? 'And you promised you'd stay on it.'

'I was up all night on the other case.' Steve turned away. 'That was urgent too. I need some sleep.'

'Get in the shower and put some clothes on. I've been told to stay with you until we have an answer. So, if you want any kind of life, you'd better get one for me.' A pause. 'And we'll pay your going rate for a quick turnaround.'

Ross wasn't sure how he'd be able to honour that promise, but it seemed to have the required effect. Steve disappeared down the corridor and Ross heard the sound of the hot water boiler firing up for the shower. He couldn't bear waiting in the chaos all around him – it made his skin crawl – and he found a black bin bag, began to fill it with the fast-food containers and banana peel. There was a small dishwasher and he stacked that too. By the time Steve returned, dressed in jeans and a black polo shirt, the worktops had been wiped down. He seemed not to notice any change in the kitchen and didn't thank Ross for his efforts. He went to the fridge and took out a can of Coke, offered one to Ross, who, in the absence of tea or coffee, took it.

'Okay then, let's get working.' Steve had always relished a challenge. His focus had shifted back to the Suicide Club and away from his other, possibly more lucrative, project. He seemed almost pleased that Ross was there, pushing him to action.

The corridor led past a living room. Ross had spent boys' evenings of beer and footie on the telly there on previous visits. It went on past a bathroom, and a closed door, which must lead into Steve's bedroom. This was the furthest Ross had ever been in the flat, but Steve walked on and into a room right at the end of the corridor. Inside, there was a dense darkness. No windows and no external sound. Ross thought someone could go in there and disappear forever. Steve probably *did* go in there and disappear for days. Steve switched on a lamp that provided a pool of light on a desk and shone on more tech than Ross had thought could possibly be contained in one room. Unlike the kitchen, it was clinically clean. There was no dust on the keyboards, no smears on the screens. There was only one chair, a grand leather affair, and Steve sat there, looking, Ross thought, like the captain of the Starship *Enterprise*. They shared an affection for clunky science fiction and Ross suspected that the impression was deliberate. There was nowhere for him to sit and he leaned against the wall.

'An officer for Patients Together got into the Suicide Club and discovered that the moderator had a user name of the Crow,' Ross said. 'What we really need is his real name and contact details. The woman couldn't get those for us.'

'Well, an amateur wouldn't know where to start.' A pause. 'Surprised she got that far.' He turned to face Ross. 'Look, I'm on it. Why don't you piss off and come back in a couple of hours? I can't concentrate with you looking over my shoulder.'

Ross looked at his watch. It was already nearly lunchtime. 'An hour.'

Steve was focused on the screen and seemed not to hear. 'Take a key. It's hanging on a hook in the kitchen. This is soundproofed and I won't hear you ringing.'

Ross decided to go home for lunch. On impulse, he bought roses for Mel from the flower shop before leaving the street. They were pink like the ones she'd had in her wedding bouquet. He wasn't given to romantic impulses, but he felt the need to express his feelings for her. He thought again that he'd taken her for granted recently. Perhaps that lay at the root of this strange intermittent tension between them. He didn't dig into the real fear: that she'd found someone else who was giving her more attention, who appreciated her more. When he got to the house, it seemed unnaturally quiet. He switched on local radio, put the flowers in a vase and made himself a sandwich.

That was when he saw that Mel had left her work diary at home. It sat on the worktop, tempting him. He knew he shouldn't look, but it was work, wasn't it? Not private. This wasn't him stalking or being controlling. He'd gone on a course about coercive control before Christmas and then a case earlier in the year had brought the reality home to him. Before that, he'd been inclined to dismiss the new law as an overreaction. He'd understood that physical abuse was evil and hated the pathetic men who beat up women, but weren't women who allowed themselves to be told what to wear and who to see to blame too? After being involved in the case where extreme coercive control had led to violence, to murder, he'd seen how wrong he'd been. All the same . . . This wasn't real controlling behaviour, was it? It was taking an interest. He stood, staring at the diary.

He was about to reach out and pick it up when the door opened and Mel came in. She looked flushed and flustered, surprised to see him.

'I wasn't expecting you to be here.'

'I bought you flowers,' he said.

'Oh!' It wasn't the response he'd been expecting or hoping for. It was surprise, not pleasure. And there was a kind of guilt in there somewhere, as if she thought she didn't quite deserve the gesture. She must have realized that more was expected, because she smiled and touched his shoulder. 'That's lovely. Really lovely.'

'I've just made a sandwich. Can I get you one?'

'No,' she said. 'I'll grab something at work. I must have left my diary behind and I can't function without it.'

He wasn't sure if she'd seen him about to reach out for it, feeling guilty that he'd even contemplated reading it. 'It's there on the bench. I just noticed it.'

'Oh yeah.' She gave him a little peck on the lips and grabbed the book. At the door, she turned back. 'Thanks for the roses,' she said. 'They're beautiful.' A pause. 'There's something I need to tell you.'

'What is it?' He felt suddenly terrified. All that he'd known, taken for granted, seemed to be sliding away from him.

'Nothing dreadful,' she said. 'Honestly. I have to get back to work, but you will be in?'

'Yeah,' he said. Because he couldn't shout at her, could he? He couldn't force her to talk to him now. 'See you tonight.'

'Yeah, see you then.' She gave a little wave and hurried away. Her scent lingered for a moment in the room and then that disappeared too.

★

He let himself back into Steve's flat, glad to focus on work again. The kitchen was as he'd left it. He took a can of Coke from the fridge and carried it through to Steve's office. The man didn't seem to hear him come in. He was leaning forwards, his nose almost touching the screen, muttering to himself:

'Steven Barton, you can bloody do this.'

Ross put the Coke on the desk in front of him.

'Well?'

'He's clever. I've got details of the Suicide Club's membership, but not of the Crow himself. That'll take a bit longer.'

'Oh.' Ross was disappointed. He'd imagined himself standing in front of the room at the evening briefing, the killer already in custody, taking the glory.

Steve looked briefly away from the screen. 'Look. I'll get there. I'm on it.'

And Ross saw that Steve was totally involved in getting a result now. This was a challenge and there was nothing the man liked better. He wouldn't eat or sleep until he'd identified the leader of the group.

'You'll give me a ring as soon as you've got it?'

'Yeah, sure.' His eyes still fixed on the screen, he slid a sheet of paper across the desk to Ross. 'I printed out the members' details for you.'

Ross looked at the list. There were twelve names there. He recognized one of them.

'I've got to go.'

'Oh, all right.' Steve was lost in his digital world again. 'Pull the door to on your way out.'

★

Ross was the last of the group to arrive in the ops room. Even Vicki Robb was there before him, with a ballpoint in her hand ready to take notes.

They all stared at him. They could tell that he had something important to share.

'Steve hasn't got the identity of the Crow yet.' It was best to limit expectations. 'He should have it by the end of the day. But he did find a membership list for the Suicide Club and one of the people involved in the case is there.'

'Who?'

Ross paused for effect then saw that Venn was irritated by the delay.

'Frank Ley.'

There was a moment of silence. 'So, the words of his suicide letter weren't coincidental,' Venn said. 'He must have been considering the act for some time if he was a member of the inner circle.' A pause. 'Perhaps Mack passed on his contact details to the moderator. We know they were close.'

'Could Frank have been provoked by the Crow?' Jen asked. 'As we suspect Mack was provoked?'

'Perhaps.' Venn seemed lost in thought. It was as if he'd known the dead man well. Ross thought he should be more detached. Joe Oldham always said it was wrong to get too emotionally involved with a case, and Ross agreed.

Jen stuck up her hand. 'I know it's a bit left field, but do you think John Grieve could be the Crow? He spends a lot of time on his computer and he seems very stressed, very low. He knew both suicide victims and could have lured them into the site.' A beat. 'He *could* be our killer.'

Again, it took Venn a while to answer. These periods of

silence made Ross uneasy. He felt himself get tense and fidgety, the bad boy at the back of the classroom again.

'I don't know Grieve well enough to tell. Go and talk to him, Jen. It could make sense if Mack killed himself because Grieve goaded him into it, and Nigel Yeo found out and threatened to tell Frank. The man would have a lot to lose: his home, his livelihood. It might be a factor in Ley's suicide too, if the family are set to inherit. Grieve certainly has motive.'

'Sure.' Jen pushed her red hair away from her face. 'I'll go now.'

Ross was left with a faint sense of anticlimax. It was unfair that, yet again, he was being excluded from all the action.

Chapter Forty-Two

Jen drove to Westacombe on her own. Matthew didn't want anyone to go with her, in case they freaked out John Grieve or upset the man's family. He'd sent Ross in his own car to wait in the lane, though, just in case she needed support later. Jen thought that was Venn's style all over. Understated. No dramatics, not overreacting. But assessing the risk, all the same.

All the way there, she was planning scenarios. Would it be better to speak to Grieve on his own, without Sarah present? She thought it probably would. If he was the Crow, he'd be reluctant to admit it to his wife. He'd felt impotent at Westacombe, the subject of her relative's benevolence, unable to take his own decisions about the farm or the dairy. If he *was* the leading member of the Suicide Club, he might have believed he had the power over life and death, and that would have been heady, intoxicating.

Sarah was in the front garden of the cottage, picking mint that had been planted in an old enamel sink, when Jen drove in. A domestic scene, which made her plans for the encounter with Grieve seem an overreaction, slightly ridiculous. Sarah called across to her as soon as Jen got out of the car. 'Hiya. I was just about to put the kettle on if you fancy some tea?'

'I was hoping to chat to John if he's around.'

'He's upstairs in the office doing the accounts.' By this time Jen had joined her, and Sarah lowered her voice. 'At least, that's what he says he's doing.'

'How does he seem today?'

Sarah shrugged. 'Still pretty low. I haven't wanted to leave him alone. He was on his own when I took the kids to school, but apart from that I've been around. I even went with him to bring the cows up for milking. I said I fancied the fresh air and the exercise.' She was speaking very quietly though there was nobody around to hear. 'Come on in. I'll call John down.'

'Where are the girls?'

'It's one of their friends' birthdays. They've all gone to the leisure centre in Barnstaple for swimming and tea.'

One piece of luck.

Sarah switched on the kettle, then stood at the bottom of the stairs and shouted up to her husband. There was no reply.

'I'll go up to him,' Jen said. 'You should be putting your feet up, this stage of the pregnancy. Make the most of having the girls out of the way and enjoy some tea in peace.' She was halfway up the stairs already and pretended not to hear Sarah shouting after her that this really wasn't a good idea.

John was in the little room that they'd already started decorating as a nursery. He was sitting at an Ikea desk with headphones on. As Jen had imagined, there was a mobile hanging from the ceiling close to his left ear. Penguins with bright red beaks. A polar bear. He didn't hear when Jen tapped at the door and only noticed her when she was right inside the room and standing beside him. There was nowhere else for her to sit so she perched on the edge of the desk. He reached out to shut down the computer, but she took hold of his arm before he could touch the keyboard and gestured for him to take off the headphones.

'Who are you encouraging to kill themselves today?' The words were fierce, but her tone was calm, curious, even friendly.

He stared at her.

'I don't know what you're talking about.' The surprise seemed entirely genuine.

She sat on an easy chair and for a second imagined Sarah sitting here, nursing her new baby in the early hours of the morning.

'Have you ever felt like killing yourself, John? There are people who could help, if you have.'

He stared at her as if she were crazy. 'No! I couldn't. I have responsibilities.' Something in his voice made her uncertain, though, and she waited for him to continue: 'Besides, haven't we all felt like that at one time or another?'

'What are you doing up here on the computer all the time?'

He put his head in his hands and she saw he was shaking. He looked up, straight at her. 'I play,' he said.

'What? Computer games?' Trying to keep the judgement out of her voice. Maybe he was one of those grown men who play computer games.

He didn't answer.

'What then?'

Still no answer.

'Perhaps we should continue this conversation at the police station.'

'I gamble!' The words came out as a scream. 'When I'm up

here, I'm betting online. I know it's a problem. I keep meaning to stop, but then I'm sucked back. Bigger prizes, free bets. And I've lost so much. How can I tell Sarah when she works so hard?'

'She hasn't guessed?'

He shook his head. 'She's always left the financial side of the business to me. She always said I was good with money.'

There was a silence. He looked out at the garden, at the swing hanging from the tree where his daughters loved playing. For a brief moment, Jen imagined Grieve hanging there too, his body limp. She wondered if, despite his earlier denial, he'd ever contemplated it.

'It crept up on me.' Grieve's voice was whining, grating. 'It started as a bit of fun. An adrenaline rush after a boring day. It's an addiction. An illness. You don't understand.'

'No,' Jen said, 'I don't.' His self-pity was making her angry now. She knew she should contain it, but she wanted to shake him. 'You've got a lovely wife and two kids. Another on the way.'

'You don't understand.' Grieve said again. 'That was how it started. Thinking I might make enough to give them the sort of life they deserve.'

'You need to get professional help.' She was seriously losing patience. More than losing patience. It was the man's apathy and self-delusion that got under her skin. She imagined slapping him to bring him somehow to his senses and found herself enjoying the image. She nodded to the computer screen. 'Getting caught up in that nonsense is just pathetic.'

She thought he was going to lash out then, but he gripped the sides of the desk until his knuckles were white and he said nothing.

'Did Nigel Yeo find out about the gambling and threaten to tell your wife?'

'No!' Again, the man just seemed confused. 'What would it have to do with him?'

If John Grieve was lying, Jen thought, he was good. He might be a gambler, losing money he couldn't afford, deceiving his wife about his obsession, but she didn't see him as a murderer. She couldn't imagine him sticking a weapon into a person's neck and watching the blood spilling out. And then doing it all over again. He was too weak. He might lash out in a rage, but could he organize all the details around Wesley's murder? Could he have been sufficiently ruthless to lure Curnow to the Woodyard and then send the text to Eve? It seemed unlikely.

'John!' It was Sarah calling from the bottom of the stairs. 'John, what's going on?'

Sarah Grieve was just where Jen had left her. There was anxiety in the tension of her body, the face, which was pale despite weeks of sunshine, the protective stance. Her relationship to Grieve was almost maternal. There'd been no attempt to follow Jen's suggestion to put up her feet and rest with some tea. Now, Jen might not have been there.

'What's happening?' The question directed at her husband.

'Are you going to tell her, or am I?' Jen knew it wasn't her place to interfere, but she hated to see this family falling apart.

'Is it about these murders?' Sarah's voice was squeaky with stress.

'No!' He was yelling. 'What sort of man do you both think I am?'

Neither woman answered.

'I'm going outside,' Jen said. 'I need to speak to a colleague.

I'll be back in a couple of minutes. Give you two a chance to talk.'

She stood outside the fairy-story thatched cottage, with its clematis on the wall, and the swing hanging from the tree, and phoned Ross.

'Grieve's not the Crow. He's been holed up in his office gambling online, not provoking poor depressed souls to kill themselves. You might as well go back to the station.'

She expected him to say something scathing about her having jumped to conclusions during the briefing, but he was almost sympathetic. 'No worries. You had to check it out.'

Back in the cottage, Sarah and John were sitting at the kitchen table. Tension fizzed between them. Jen joined them. 'Do you need to pick up the girls?'

Sarah shook her head. 'They're getting a lift back.'

'Grand.' *One less thing to worry about.*

The question, domestic and ordinary, seemed to relax the situation a little. Sarah looked up at her, glad to be distracted. 'Have you got kids?'

Jen nodded. 'Two. It was a nightmare when they were younger. I felt like a taxi service.' A beat. 'Has John told you about his problem?'

The woman nodded. 'Some problem! Thousands of pounds in debt when I've been working every hour there is.'

'I don't think he's very well.' The two women might have been alone in the room.

'I didn't know what he was doing up there, all those hours on the computer.' The words flashed back. Sarah was flushed. 'I thought it was porn, okay? I'm not up for sex much these days. Not with this weight and this heat. So, I thought, just let him get on with it. Don't ask. Enjoy the peace.' She pushed her hair away from her forehead. 'I thought he was just being moody and I let it go. I had enough on my plate with the dairy and the kids and looking after Frank's house. I thought we were going through a tough time and everything would get back to normal once the baby was born. But it won't, will it? Things will never get back to normal again.'

On the other side of the table John Grieve sat in silence, his head in his hands. It was as if he was trying to make himself invisible and the conversation was going on without him.

'Really,' Jen said. 'There's no reason why not. Now you know and John can get help.' She paused. 'Frank had made a will. He left all this, the house and the farm, to you. But you won't be able to sell it for development. You'll have to farm it traditionally, as you have been doing.'

There was another longer silence as Sarah seemed to be assimilating the news. She looked at her husband, then back at Jen. 'So, the cottage and the farm will be ours?'

'And the big house. As long as you meet those conditions. Eve would still keep her workshop and her flat.'

'You're joking? We'd have all that space?' She seemed astounded. 'John, do you see what this means?'

He lifted his head. Jen wondered if he was thinking he'd never escape from Westacombe now. He'd never have that farm on the edge of the moor he'd been dreaming of. Gambling on.

'It'll be a whole fresh start!' Sarah said.

Maybe. Jen didn't think it would be that easy. She'd never quite believed in simple happy endings.

'You really didn't know what Frank was intending?'

Sarah shook her head. 'No idea at all. Frank was always ranting about inherited wealth: worthless people who had power just because their parents had made a fortune.'

'Perhaps he didn't think you were worthless,' Jen said. 'Perhaps he thought you both deserved it.'

God, she thought, *that sounds like one of those quotes that my soppy friends spread around on Facebook. Along with the images of their perfect families. The ones that make me want to throw up.*

Sarah, though, seemed to buy into the idea and to take the words seriously. She was probably the sort to share deep and meaningful words of calm and meditation all over her social media.

'It's horrible that Frank killed himself. Of course it is. But it's like he's giving us a second chance.' She got up from her seat, walked behind her husband and put her arms around his shoulders. 'We can get through this. Together. Can't we?'

John stood up too and held his wife close to him. But he still didn't answer.

Walking across the yard to her car in the rosy evening light, Jen thought the air seemed heavy. It felt hard to breathe. She reran the conversation with John Grieve in her head. Her response to him had been unprofessional and out of proportion. He was clearly addicted to gambling. Police officers had been trained to be sympathetic, controlled and he'd got under her skin. She'd almost lost it. The memory of the interview triggered another idea, a possible explanation for Nigel Yeo's murder, which was so unlikely that she wasn't sure she could share it yet with Matthew. She'd reached her vehicle and was wondering if she should do some private investigations of her own when the phone rang. Matthew Venn could read minds, it seemed, even at a distance.

'Where are you?'

'Just walking back to the car. Did Ross tell you? John Grieve was spending all those hours on his computer because he was betting online. His wife had no idea. That was why he seemed so secretive and ashamed.'

'Yes. Did you believe his story?'

'Absolutely. He was shit-scared of telling Sarah about it. We can get someone to look at his browsing history, though.'

'Could you go back and check something out for me?'

'I suppose so.' Jen knew she didn't sound enthusiastic, but she thought she'd escaped the farm and its inhabitants for one day.

'Could you go to Eve Yeo's flat and her studio? It seems that she's gone missing.'

Chapter Forty-Three

JONATHAN WAS IN HIS OFFICE, FOCUSED on spreadsheets and the minutes from the last trustees' meeting, and didn't realize that Eve was late until an extra half hour had passed. It wasn't like her not to be on time. Once, she'd described her punctuality as a curse, something she'd inherited from her father.

'Mum always kept us waiting. It drove Dad crazy.'

He'd had his phone on silent and checked it for missed calls and messages. Nothing. He called her mobile and heard it go straight to voicemail. Leaving his office, he wandered downstairs to look for Eve there. She could be waiting in the lobby or in the cafe. The place was satisfyingly full. That evening there would be a production in the Woodyard's small theatre and the audience was already arriving, catching up with friends in the bar, having an early supper. He looked into the cafe but there was no sign of her, at the table he'd reserved for them, or chatting to Bob.

Jonathan went to the counter and called in to the manager. 'Have you seen Eve Yeo?'

Bob was so busy that he barely looked up. 'Nah, sorry, but you can see what it's like.'

'Is Lucy around?' Lucy would recognize Eve.

'Her shift finished at five. She'll be back later just before the play starts.'

That was when Jonathan had a real sense of unease, so he called Eve again and left her a message.

'Hey, love, where are you? Can you give me a ring?'

And that was when he went back to his office to call Matthew.

After the call, he sat for a moment, staring at the blank computer screen, but he knew that it would be impossible to concentrate on work. He'd asked Matthew if he should go to Westacombe to check on Eve.

'No need,' Matthew had said. 'Jen's already there. I'll get her to look.'

So, Jonathan was left, helpless and restless, with nothing useful to do. He locked his office and went back to the lobby. Lucy Braddick was just walking in, dressed in a bright green dress, swinging a big straw bag.

'Hi, Luce. You back to help with the play?'

She nodded. 'I just went home for my tea.'

'I'm looking for Eve Yeo. I don't suppose you've seen her?'

'Eve, who makes the glass?'

'That's right.'

'She was here earlier.' Lucy gave one of her delightful smiles. 'She was waiting for you!'

'Are you sure?'

''Course I'm sure.' Lucy sounded offended.

'Was Eve on her own when you saw her?'

'Yeah, she was just coming out of the ladies' loos.'

'And what time was that? It's really quite important, Luce.'

'It was five o'clock.' Lucy was definite. 'I was just on my way home.'

Back in his office, pacing now, not able to sit, Jonathan was on the phone again to Matthew.

'Is Lucy certain?' Matthew paused. 'You know what Oldham'll say if we shift the whole focus of the investigation to the Woodyard on the evidence of a learning-disabled adult and Eve's car *is* still at Westacombe.'

'Well, she wouldn't be driving if she was going to meet me for supper!' Despite his anxiety, Jonathan allowed a trace of amusement into his voice. 'We always shared a bottle of wine when we met up. I'd already booked a taxi to get me home. And yeah, Lucy was positive.'

'Was Eve with anyone when Lucy saw her?'

Jonathan thought he could sense Matthew holding his breath, waiting for an answer. 'No. Luce saw her outside the ladies' loos, so even if she'd come to the centre with someone else, she'd be on her own in there.' Jonathan paused. 'What do you want me to do?'

'Start a search of the place. We'll be there.'

Chapter Forty-Four

IT WAS NEARLY EIGHT O'CLOCK WHEN Jonathan phoned to
say that Eve had been seen in the Woodyard, and by then
Matthew was frantic. He could feel his self-control unravelling.
Outside, the humidity, which had been growing all day, seemed
unbearable and in the station, there was little light. After the
full blast of sunshine that had lit up the building for weeks, it
felt as if they were suddenly in a different season, a different
world.

Stress had been ratcheting up throughout the evening as
they failed to get news of the glass blower and Matthew had
been left with a sense of failure and fear.

His team had been squashed into his office, their focus still
on Westacombe Farm.

'Jen, you looked in Eve's flat and workshop. Anything?'

She'd shaken her head, looked across at him and then taken
a breath. 'But while I was talking to Grieve in the cottage,
something occurred to me. A sort of theory. I know it sounds
crazy and there's nothing concrete at all, but listen to this . . .'

She'd continued talking and Matthew had listened, because

he recognized listening as his one great skill, and he took confidence from it. The facts of the case had shifted in his head and formed a different pattern altogether, like the coloured pieces in a child's kaleidoscope moving when the cardboard tube is turned.

'Of course,' he'd said. 'We've been asking all the wrong questions. Talk me through the conversation you had with Lucy Braddick again.'

Jen had repeated Lucy's story of seeing the big black car driving into the Woodyard car park as she was waiting for her friends to come off the Bideford bus.

'That would work then,' he'd said. 'Yes, I can see how that would tie in too.'

'What now?' Ross, always eager for action, had already jumped to his feet.

'We don't do anything in a rush. We don't have nearly enough information for a warrant!' Matthew thought that trying to contain Ross was like training an overactive puppy. But his *own* thoughts were overactive too, racing and not fully formed. He hated working like this, making plans on the hoof.

Ross was still standing, rocking back and forwards on the balls of his feet. Matthew wanted to scream at him to be still. *How can I think when you're fidgeting like a toddler? When will you grow up?* He could feel the tension in his back and his neck, and was worried that he might not be able to resist the temptation to let rip.

That was when the call came through from Jonathan, and his husband, usually so relaxed, sounded fearful, overwhelmed by panic. Matthew's team stared at their boss. Even Ross was still as he waited for Matthew to speak.

'Okay,' Venn said at last. 'This is what we do.' A pause. 'We don't waste our resources with another sweep at Westacombe. Round up as many people as we can to canvass people in the Woodyard, and we'll need a proper search there. I know Jonathan has his people looking, but only in the public areas. The Woodyard is where Wesley died, after all, and it's a warren of a place.'

Matthew turned to Jen. 'That night at the Priors' party,' he said. 'I think something must have happened there to trigger all this. You chatted to Nigel. I know I've asked you this before, but looking back, did you notice anything which might have been important?'

She shook her head slowly. 'I'm *so* sorry. It was a party. I was halfway pissed before he arrived. He was very straight. Nice enough but maybe a bit uptight. That's all.'

Matthew thought for a moment. 'Ross, I want you to go to the Priors' house. We've got a sharper focus now. We know what we're looking for. Talk to Cynthia. This is important. If nothing else, it might provide some confirmation of Jen's theory.'

'Sure, boss.' Ross didn't move, though. Now he had something concrete to do, the restlessness seemed to have left him, and this wasn't what he'd been expecting or hoping for. It wasn't a real call to action.

'Go now.' Matthew raised his voice. 'Let's move quickly. Very quickly. I don't think I could stand another death.'

He meant the words literally. If there was another lost life while he was in charge of the investigation, he knew he'd collapse under the weight of guilt and his life would never be the same again.

Ross was already out of the door and sprinting across the open-plan office beyond.

'What do you want me to do?' Jen had finished her call and was on her feet too.

Matthew couldn't answer immediately. He had another moment of panic, caught perhaps from Jonathan; incoherent thoughts followed by a desire to run away. Anything not to be forced to make decisions, to take responsibility. To fail. He supposed this was how Ley and the other members of the chatroom must have felt. Suicide, after all, was the ultimate escape. Then everything clicked back into place. Some measure of confidence was restored. He wasn't good at much, but he was a competent detective. He made decisions all the time.

'We go to the Woodyard,' he said. 'To the last place Eve was seen. And we find her.'

Chapter Forty-Five

THE RAIN STARTED AS THEY WERE running to their cars outside the police station, a couple of huge drops that soaked into the parched ground and disappeared. By the time they reached the arts centre, there was a deluge, and a crack of lightning in the distance lit the Woodyard, making it look Gothic, Jen thought, like a building in one of the fantasy films Ella loved to watch. By the time they reached the entrance hall, where Jonathan was waiting, they were drenched.

'Where's Lucy?' Matthew was talking to Jonathan.

Jen could sense both men's tension. She was shaking the rain from her hair, wiping it from her face with her hands, but the boss seemed not to notice her presence.

'In my office. I thought you'd want to talk to her.' Jonathan reached out and touched his husband's shoulder.

Now Matthew did turn to her. 'Jen, will you do that? You saw her last. I'll get the search organized.'

Jen nodded and followed Jonathan upstairs. Lucy was staring through the office window, fascinated by the rain streaming down the pane and the lightning in the distance.

'My dad's scared of thunder and lightning,' she said, turning back into the room. 'I hope he's okay.'

'I think he'll be fine,' Jonathan said. There was no anxiety now in his voice. 'You know Jen, don't you? Can I leave you to talk to her? You understand that Eve's gone missing and we're trying to find her.'

'Like when you tried to find Chrissie?'

'Yes,' Jen said. Chrissie was a woman with Down's syndrome who'd disappeared from the Woodyard during a previous murder investigation. 'You helped us then, Luce. We're hoping you might be able to do the same thing tonight.'

Jonathan gave them both a little wave and left the room.

Jen perched on his desk. 'How well do you know Eve, love?'

'Quite well. She displays her glass here and comes into the cafe. She likes cappuccino and Bob's carrot cake.'

'Does she? You've got a good memory.'

'Customers like it when you remember stuff like that.' Lucy flashed her a quick grin. 'And sometimes they leave you a tip.'

'Tell me about seeing Eve today.'

'I was just finishing my shift and I needed the toilet so Bob said I could go a few minutes early.' Lucy looked up. 'I'm supposed to be working now. I came back after my tea because there's an event in the theatre and it started at seven.'

Jen could tell Lucy was about to launch into a detailed description of the event, so she broke in. 'You were on your way back to River Bank and went to the toilet and that's where you saw Eve.'

'Yes. Well, just outside after I'd finished.'

'Let's play a kind of memory game.' Jen thought that must sound patronizing, but continued all the same. 'Tell me everything you remember about Eve. What she was wearing and what she was doing. You pushed open the door from the ladies' toilets and what did you see outside? Was Eve already there?'

Lucy shook her head. 'She must have been using the loo, and she followed me out.'

Jen nodded and Lucy continued: 'She noticed me and said, "Hello, Luce," and I said hello back.'

'Anything else you can tell me?'

'She was wearing a summer skirt.' Lucy shut her eyes for a moment. 'It was yellow and white. And sandals.' A pause. 'No cardie and no waterproof. If she's gone outside, she'll be soaking.'

'She will.' Jen tried to picture the scene. 'And you were the only people there, Luce? In the corridor outside the toilets?'

Lucy shook her head. 'We were the only people there *then.*'

'Someone might have been there earlier?'

'No,' Lucy said. 'Later. A man came along as we were chatting.'

'Do you think Eve knew him?'

'I'm not sure,' Lucy said, 'but I think the man knew Eve. As he walked down the corridor, I saw his face. It was almost like he was pleased to see her. Like they were friends.'

'But he didn't say anything?'

'I didn't hear. I was in a hurry, thinking about what I'd have for my tea.'

'Can you tell me what he looked like, this man?'

Lucy hesitated. 'I just walked past him. I didn't notice very much.'

'How about age? Was he the same age as Eve?'

On this, it seemed, Lucy was certain. She shook her head vigorously. 'No! He was much older. He could have been her dad.' She paused for a moment. 'But her dad's dead, isn't he? So it couldn't have been him.'

'No, sweetie, it couldn't have been him.'

Lucy shook her head, disappointed, it seemed, not to be able to help more.

'Thanks, Luce,' Jen said. 'You've been absolutely brilliant. I'm sure it'll be fine for you to go home now. Bob won't mind. We'll find someone to take you across to River Bank safely.'

Back in the Woodyard lobby, people were streaming out of the theatre. Uniformed colleagues were showing a photo of Eve to everyone who passed. Jonathan had found the image on a poster they'd made advertising Eve's glass exhibition and had printed it out. But most people barely stopped to glance at it. They were looking at the downpour, as excited as children, bemoaning their lack of foresight in a failure to bring umbrellas or suitable clothes. Jen paused for a moment, looking around her, and her attention was caught by another image. She had a flashback to one of the briefings, Ross reporting back on one of the interviews he'd done in the early stages of the investigation. Then another image. And a sense, if not of hope, of a resolution, a kind of ending.

She phoned Matthew and when there was no reply, collared one of the PCs.

'Where's Venn?'

'He's searching the empty studios right at the top of the building. Apparently, reception's crap up there.'

Jen left without answering and began to run up the bare wooden stairs, beyond the Woodyard's public spaces, and the offices and meeting rooms, to the giant lofts littered with artists' materials and dust.

Chapter Forty-Six

MATTHEW VENN HAD COMPLETED HIS SEARCH of the attics when he heard footsteps echoing on the steps below him. The Woodyard still felt industrial here, ramshackle and bare, all exposed pipes and untreated timbers. At the same time, he must have come back into phone reception because his phone started to ping.

There was a text from Ross. **Nobody at home in the Prior house. What would you like me to do?**

Venn didn't answer immediately; he wanted to think about that. At almost the same time Jen arrived, red hair falling over her face, cheeks flushed with the exertion, so they were practically the same colour. They were on a narrow landing with a long window looking down over the town, just where there was a twist in the stairs. Jen was breathless. She could hardly speak and, at first, he struggled to make out what she was saying.

'I think I know where Eve might be. I'm sorry. It's crazy, I should have realized before,' she told him, words spilling out like the rainwater pouring down the gutters and the drains.

'You and I will go and check it out.' Matthew paused. 'Phone Ross and tell him to stay at the station until we get back to him with instructions. We'll need someone there.'

They were on their way out of the Woodyard, pausing for a moment to look out at the rain, when Ross phoned again. This time his voice was triumphant. 'Steve's just called and he's got the name of the Crow. It was really well hidden, but he finally dug it out.'

'Well? Is it someone connected to the investigation?'

'Yeah. It's the boss of the health trust. Roger Prior.'

That stopped Matthew in his tracks. He felt all his preconceptions shifting. He'd set aside Prior as a potential suspect, worried that his judgement had been clouded by his antipathy to the man. But after all, Prior could have been the cause of two young men's deaths, not through negligence, but through a cruel and active provocation. Matthew saw his participation in the Suicide Club as an addiction. Prior had become as much of a gambler as John Grieve, punting on who would live and who would die. He pictured the man in his grand office at home, cruel and entitled, with his sleek black hair and his sharp nose, and thought that the nickname Crow suited him well. They would find out later how he became involved in the group. Perhaps his humiliation following the Luke Wallace affair had caused him to claw back power in the only way open to him. Now, they just needed to track down Eve and to make sure she was safe.

'Find Prior,' Matthew said. 'Top priority.'

'You'll be coming back to the station?'

Matthew had a moment of indecision before answering. 'No. You're in charge there.' They had to find Eve Yeo before there was another tragedy, and that was worth a gamble too.

He was just about to run out to the car when he heard Jonathan calling his name. Matthew stopped and turned.

'What's happening?' Jonathan was shouting above the sound of the rain.

'We've got a possible lead on Eve.'

'I want to come.'

For a brief moment Matthew hesitated. 'Sorry. Not possible.' He followed Jen into the storm without looking back to see Jonathan's reaction.

Matthew drove because he said he knew the way better. He'd grown up with the country lanes, wasn't thrown by the tall hedges or the grass growing in the middle of the road. It would have been quite dark now, even without the rain, but still the water came, running in streams across the roads, filling ditches, causing ponds where there had been none before. Flash floods spilled out from drains that had been clogged with dry vegetation and blown sand. He drove as quickly as he dared, but had to slow down when he turned off the road and onto a sandy track.

'We're nearly there,' Jen said. 'I think we should walk from here. Even if they can't hear the engine over the sound of the rain, they might see the headlights.'

Matthew reached into the back seat and pulled out two waterproofs and passed one to Jen. 'This is Jonathan's. It might be a tad too big, but better than nothing.'

'Certainly, it's better than nothing. I was expecting to be drowned before we got anywhere close.'

'You know me, I'm like the Scouts. Always prepared.' He said it lightly, as a joke, but he was thinking that he'd never been as poorly prepared as this in a case. This was all guess-work and intuition, and he hated it.

A minute out of the car, his legs and feet were soaking and rain was seeping into the gap between the collar and his neck. Jen was walking ahead of him, using a torch. Her coat had a large hood and something of the shape it formed reminded him of a monk's habit. They were walking down a narrow path through dunes, which seemed to tower on either side, and he fancied it was like a religious procession in a monastery or priory. Occasionally a flash of lightning would illuminate the scene with a sharp, white light, then everything would be black again. The sand beneath their feet was sticky, and in places deep puddles had formed.

With a flashback to his childhood, which was as clear as the lightning strikes, he remembered playing with children from another family on one of their outings to the beach. One of those random chance acquaintances that kids form when they're playing close to each other. The children were building an obstacle course for their parents, with pits dug deep in the sand and bridges made from driftwood, and when it was completed the adults played along, allowing themselves to be blindfolded and led through. The trips into the holes and the falling off the rickety bridges were accompanied by good humour and laughter. His own parents had sat in their old-fashioned deckchairs looking on, his father with interest and his mother with horror.

Now, he thought, this was a similar obstacle course. They were blindfolded too, and he had no idea where or how it would end. They were at Seal Bay, in the dunes behind the wide sweep of beach, not far from where his parents had brought him to picnic, and the boy and the man seemed to collide, to become one person.

Jen broke into his thoughts. 'I must have got this all wrong. The place is all shuttered and there's no light inside. When I saw the poster at the Woodyard, I was convinced that this was where they'd be. The theatre group put on the same play at the Sandpiper and, according to Ross, the Mackenzies support them all over the county. So, I thought, members of the family could have been at the Woodyard at the same time as Eve. But maybe I got that wrong, and it was just another coincidence.'

'No,' he said, 'I don't think you're wrong.' He'd seen the glint of a brass numbered keypad on the door. It had been installed instead of a padlock or a bolt. He pointed his own torch at the ground, saw that it had been churned up with tyre tracks. 'Someone's been here relatively recently.'

'I was here earlier this week with Janey,' Jen said.

He shook his head. 'I think these are more recent. Let's see what's inside.' He banged on the door; there was no reply but he hadn't expected one. If anyone was there, they'd be silent, hiding. They wouldn't expect a stranger to be able to get in.

'It shouldn't be hard to break down that door.'

'No need for that.' Matthew had the numbers he'd found in Nigel Yeo's diary firmly fixed in his head. He'd been carrying them round for nearly a week, knowing that eventually they'd be useful. 'Yeo had a classic doctor's handwriting, so I'm not sure which combination is the right one, but let's try this one first.' He punched the numbers 8531 into the brass keypad on the door. Nothing happened. He tried again: 8537. This time there was a click and the door opened.

'Eve!' He stood outside and shouted in. The noise seemed to echo around the space. No reply and he moved inside. It was dark and hot. No air. If someone had been in the shack recently, they hadn't opened a window. But there was a lot of noise. The rain beating on the plank roof battered his nerves and seemed to drum into his skull. Without thinking, Matthew felt for a light switch, but of course, the chalet had no mains electricity. In the torch beam, he saw matches and a paraffin lamp. He put a match to the lamp, hung it from a hook in the ceiling, which seemed to be there for that purpose, and the room was lit by a gentle glow, which in any other circumstance would have been warm, comforting.

Matthew saw that there were two rooms. They were standing in the living room furnished by a couple of sagging armchairs, with a folding scrubbed pine table against one wall. On it a camping stove and a small Calor gas fridge. Against another, a dresser, with a cupboard underneath and shelves above. On the shelves a selection of tattered paperback novels and a pile of notebooks and files. Matthew was tempted to look at them, but that could wait. There was no sign of Eve.

Jen had already moved into the second room, which was furnished with a small double bed and two bunks against the wall. Matthew stood in the doorway and looked in. There was no space to join her. For the Mackenzies, this must have been more like camping than staying in a real holiday home.

There was no Eve and no possible place where she could have been hidden. It seemed that this drive through the rain had been a wild goose chase. He should have been more cautious, thought things through more steadily. He should be looking for Prior, and what would he be doing here? They'd have to start from the beginning and search for the man elsewhere.

Matthew tried to bring his thoughts into some kind of order. Nigel *had* found the code to the door. It had been written in his diary on the Friday before he'd been killed. It made sense to believe that this was where he'd spent that afternoon, and that something he'd found here had made him very angry. So perhaps this wasn't an entirely wasted trip after all. When Eve had been found, they would come back here and they'd check all the files. But now they had to find the woman.

'Boss.' Jen's voice broke through his thoughts. 'She's been here. And today.' She leaned across the bed and picked up a silver earring shaped like a fish. 'Eve was wearing these when I saw her yesterday.'

'So, where is she then?' The words came out like a scream.

'When Janey brought me here, she took me up the coast path, onto the cliff. Apparently, that was where Mack jumped off and killed himself.'

'But there's no car here.'

'I don't think Eve was brought here by just one person.'

In the end, Matthew thought, *perhaps it all comes back to the family.*

They were out in the storm again. Biblical rain and distant thunder, but fewer flashes of lightning and those that appeared seemed further away. Matthew couldn't see the beach from here because of the mountainous dunes, but he could hear the waves breaking on the shore. He wondered if Jonathan was home yet, sheltering, anxious. Angry about being excluded again. He'd be listening to the breakers too. He paused for a moment to send Ross a text, explaining where they were and sending instructions – *a force-wide alert to stop that vehicle* – holding the phone under his jacket in an attempt to keep it dry. He was tempted to send one to Jonathan too, something apologetic – and meaningful and sentimental – but that had never really been Jonathan's style, and Jen was moving ahead of him so he had to walk quickly to catch up. She, at least, seemed to know where they were going.

Then there was a view of the beach, lit briefly by lightning well out to sea. They'd left the lunar landscape of the dunes behind them. The path rose more steeply. In places it was like walking on the bed of a stream, as the water flowed over his shoes, rattling with loose pebbles, thick with eroded soil. The rain was easing, though. He could tell that the worst of the storm had passed.

Jen stopped. 'Look.' There was no longer any need to shout against the weather and the word came out as a whisper.

Ahead, so far above them that he could scarcely believe they were on the same path, was a moving pinprick of light.

'That must be them,' she said. 'Who else would be so crazy to go out on a night like this?'

'We need to be as quiet as we can. At least until we can see what's happening up there.' Matthew thought the path was so slippery, so close to the edge of the cliff, that a sudden movement, a shout, would spook the people ahead of them, might send them over. Even if a murder wasn't committed tonight, there could be a terrible accident.

'Okay.' Jen pointed the torch down to the path, so there was less chance of it being seen from above, and he followed.

The rain had stopped altogether now and he pushed back his hood, feeling the force of the wind, and the noise of the sea more strongly.

They climbed slowly. Neither of them was fit. Ross would have run up like a mountain goat, and stood at the top looking back at them, despising them for their slowness. Smug and triumphant. Matthew thought he'd be glad of that speed now.

But because he and Jen moved cautiously, there was no sound. They could choose to put their feet on the cropped grass at the side of the path, to avoid the bare rock and the loose rocks. The small point of light ahead of them came closer. The cloud started to lift and Matthew could make out the Lundy lighthouse beams, even a faint occasional moon, full and pale.

Jen switched off her torch and got very close to him so she could whisper in his ear. He felt her damp hair on his cheek.

'Let's go that way, so we're above them and we can surprise them.' In the glimmer of moonlight, she nodded away from the cliff edge. It didn't look like much of a path.

He nodded back. There *was* no path. They scrambled through the gorse and bramble until they were higher than the people below them. From here, he and Jen could look down on them. Still, the figures below were only shapes, shadows, but they were speaking. Matthew slid down the bank until he was close enough to listen in. One woman and one man, so close to the cliff edge that one step would take them over. A push could send one of them flying. He'd have the other to arrest then, but Eve Yeo would be dead.

He lay on his belly, so if they should look up, there'd be no silhouette on the horizon. The cloud thinned and the moon glinted for a moment on an object in the man's hands. A shard of glass. He could see the colour – as yellow as butter – even in this pale, monochrome light. Then the cloud covered the moon again and everything was still and dark. But in that moment, he'd seen enough to identify George Mackenzie, holding the glass like a dagger against Eve Yeo's neck. The other arm was curved around the young woman's waist, holding her fast. George's face was in profile and his head looked as if it had been carved from hard wood, magnificent and proud.

Matthew slid closer. George was talking. 'Why did you have to meddle?' He sounded very sad, almost heartbroken. It was as if this situation was all Eve's fault and he was just an unfortunate bystander. 'Bad enough that your father had to stick his nose into our business. Really, it didn't need to come to this.'

Matthew weighed up his chances of jumping the man, of taking the glass from him, without both of the people close to the cliff edge falling to their deaths. He'd never been physically competent; he was so clumsy that perhaps he'd fall too. In a moment of black humour, he wondered if he should have written that last sentimental message to Jonathan after all.

He might not be any kind of action man, but he *could* persuade and he *could* listen. Those were the skills he was prepared to own.

He eased himself into a sitting position, aware of Jen, very tense, behind him.

The people on the cliff edge seemed not to notice.

'George, please let Eve go.' He kept his voice boring, ordinary. He could be in one of those planning meetings he so detested.

There was a movement below him, but now it was dark again and he couldn't see exactly what was going on.

'George, this is Matthew Venn. You remember me, don't you? We spoke after Nigel's death. And, of course, you will know my husband Jonathan. He's a regular at the Sandpiper and he runs the Woodyard. You were there this evening, helping out with the Beckett. A very fine production, by the way, so I understand. That was how we knew where to find you. I'm going to use my torch so we can all see what's going on. I hope that's all right with you.'

Still no response. He shone the torch, not directly at Eve and George so it would blind them, but to one side. He saw them in muted monochrome, shadowy, like an early photograph. George was still holding the glass to Eve's neck.

'Please drop the glass, George. You can see that this isn't helping. Another young person dead. Where's the sense in that?'

'I would have done anything to protect my family.' In the strange shadowy light, Matthew saw the man's mouth open in a scream.

'I know,' Matthew said. 'I know. You loved the bones of them both. I could tell that when we were talking that day behind the bar. There are no monsters in this story. We imagined some kind of evil genius provoking the vulnerable to their deaths, but it wasn't like that at all.' Out of his line of vision, he was aware of a movement, but he continued: 'Why don't you tell me what happened, George? Why don't you put down the glass and let Eve come here to me, and then you'll have a chance to explain?'

He moved his torch a little, so it was shining almost directly onto the man's face. He saw the tears streaming down his cheeks, as he blinked against the light.

'Please, George.'

And perhaps the man would have taken the chance to explain, but at that moment, Jen was behind him, grabbing George round the neck, forcing the glass from his hand. Matthew saw the shard fly over the cliff and imagined he could hear the sound of it reaching the water. He slid down to the path and took Eve into his arms. She was shaking like a tiny bird, fallen from the nest, cold and scared. She was still in a cotton blouse, a yellow and white skirt and sandals.

'It's okay,' he said. 'It's over.'

'No,' she said, 'it'll never be over.'

And he could tell that for her that was true.

Chapter Forty-Seven

VENN PHONED ROSS AS THEY WERE walking back down from
the cliff, and by the time they reached the chalet, he was there
to meet them. Jen knew that once she was alone with the boss,
she'd get a bollocking from Venn for jumping the gun and
tackling George Mackenzie without authorization. What could
she say? Tell the truth: that she was cold and wet and she
needed a piss and she didn't want to stay all night on the top
of a cliff catching her death while he tried to have a civilized
conversation with the man? Or lie and say she'd sensed that
George was about to jump and take Eve with him?

Ross got George into his car and stood for a moment. Jen
thought she and Matthew must look an odd couple, in their
oversized waterproofs, Venn still with his suit underneath, his
highly polished work shoes covered in sand. Eve was already
in Matthew's car, wrapped in a blanket they'd taken from the
chalet, the heating on. Before joining her, Matthew made a
call. Jen heard a brief explanation. No real details, just that
Eve was in a bad way.

'I don't think she should be on her own tonight. I wonder

if you could meet us in the station, take her home with you. I'm not sure who else to ask.'

He must have been pleased with the answer because he nodded and smiled.

'They've been to the Woodyard and they've got the vehicle,' Ross said, impatient to pass on the news, to prove, Jen thought, how clever he was. She could tell that he was disappointed not to have been in on the clifftop action. He'd have loved that, playing the hero. 'They're bringing it in.'

'And the driver?'

'Oh yes, the driver too.'

When they reached the police station, a tall, elegant, white-haired woman was waiting for them. Jen recognized her from photos on the board in the ops room as Lauren Miller. For a moment, Jen wondered if she'd got things wrong and this was the other person Ross had arranged to be brought in for questioning, but it seemed that she was the woman the boss had phoned to take care of Eve.

'You know Lauren, don't you?' Matthew said to Eve when they got into the station. The younger woman was still wrapped in her blanket, looking like a victim from some natural disaster – a tsunami or a hurricane – profiled on the television news. She was blank with shock. How could she not be? She'd been hit by so many tragedies in the last week. Perhaps, Jen thought, the friendship of this calm older woman would help her pull through.

Matthew was still talking to Eve. 'Lauren's going to take you home this evening. We don't think you should be on your own and I'll come and see you tomorrow to explain everything.'

'That is all right with you, Eve?' Lauren didn't touch Eve,

or talk down to her, and Jen warmed to the older woman immediately. 'We can go back to your flat if you'd prefer. Or there might be someone else I could call?'

'No.' Eve reached out and touched the woman's arm. 'No, I'd like to stay with you.'

They met in the ops room to make plans. Jen had phoned home and talked to Ella. It had taken her a while to answer.

'Mum, I was asleep!' Doing the classic disgruntled teenager impersonation. 'Yeah, duh, we guessed you were at work.'

It was only then that Jen realized that it had gone midnight, a week after she'd wandered home after Cynthia's party. She wondered how their friendship would survive Jen's knowledge that Roger had been sitting in his grand office in his respectable house, scheming the death of vulnerable young people, watching them die.

Matthew had made coffee and they were sitting round one table. Ross had magicked a packet of chocolate biscuits from his desk drawer. Jen thought she'd need the sugar to keep her going through the interview. The interviews.

'So, it was the Scotsman all the time,' Ross said. 'With his high and mighty wife, playing the star in their tinpot cafe. He made out he was so friendly, so concerned about Nigel, and all the time he was a murderer.'

'Oh no,' Matthew said. 'George Mackenzie didn't kill anyone. And really, I don't think he'd have been able to bring himself to kill Eve. That show on the cliffs was all guilt and desperation. And performance. He'd become a better actor than Martha.'

He left it to Jen to explain to Ross, to take the glory.

★

Matthew chose Jen to be with him on the interview. The woman who sat opposite them in the interview room looked very young and frail. Twitchy and nervy, but still somehow confident. The precocious child, who thought her cuteness would help her get away with anything. Even murder. Who had never grown up, never developed any self-control, who saw life as a kind of game to be played and won. The duty solicitor sitting next to her looked equally young, and as if he'd just been woken from a deep sleep, and hadn't had time to shave. Jen remembered the conversation on the cliff. Matthew had told George that there'd been no monsters in this case, but Jen wasn't sure that was true. Venn might *want* to believe that was true, but this fragile young woman had killed three people and had been very happy to implicate others.

Matthew went through the formalities and switched on the recorder.

'Miss Mackenzie.' He paused. 'Janey, perhaps you can explain what happened the night you killed your brother.'

Jen thought Venn had the knack of sounding interested and the use of the woman's first name made him come across as fatherly, not in the least bit intimidating. He gave the impression that he wasn't there to progress the case, but because he genuinely wanted to understand.

Janey looked up, surprised. It wasn't the question she'd been expecting.

'Sergeant Rafferty here explained it rather well,' Matthew went on. 'She was interviewing an individual with an addiction, a mental illness and she said that suddenly she wanted to slap him. She knew he wasn't well, but that didn't matter. He was so infuriatingly self-absorbed that she was almost provoked to violence. This is a professional police officer, used to controlling her feelings, and the interviewee wasn't even very ill, certainly not psychotic like Mack.' Matthew paused. 'So, I can see how, after weeks of being sympathetic, something might have snapped. Cracked. Shattered like glass.'

He looked at Janey across the table. 'It all happened the day that Mack was released from hospital, didn't it? He went to Westacombe because he wanted to spend some time with Wesley, but Wesley was selfish, a little weak, and he couldn't deal with your brother's restlessness and depression. You were called to go to the farm and bring Mack home. Frank Ley was there too that afternoon. I'm sure you must remember it clearly.'

Janey looked up. 'My brother was very ill. The hospital should never have let him come out.'

'Your family said that later that night, Mack drove himself to your chalet in the dunes, then went up on the cliff path and jumped. He'd left a note in a plastic bag, weighed down by a stone on the cliff path, and a walker found it the following morning. But of course, that wasn't what happened. I could never accept that a man in such distress would be able to drive. Why don't you talk us through it?'

'I drove him to the coast,' Janey Mackenzie said, 'in his own car. I thought he would find it more peaceful in the chalet; we'd both loved it there when we were children. And at least it would give my parents a break. They were asleep by then. But he couldn't settle.'

'The drive didn't calm him?'

She shook her head. 'He had this pent-up anger. *Nothing* would calm him. I'd planned that we'd both stay in the chalet, but he spat out the pills we'd been given to help him sleep. It was cold, but a very clear night. A full moon. Rather beautiful.

He wanted to walk, so I went with him.' She paused. 'You don't know how draining it can be. Those constant demands on your sympathy. You can't see any end to it. You can't believe that the person you love will ever be well again. It's like living with a stranger.'

'What happened when you got to the top?'

'It was so beautiful there. Still and clear, and that sky full of stars and an enormous moon. But Mack couldn't enjoy it. He couldn't see the beauty. He was crying and talking, rambling, telling the same crazy stories about a suicide club and, as you say, something cracked.' She paused and stared up at Venn. 'I pushed him.' Another moment of silence. 'I'm not even sure that I intended to kill him. I just wanted the noise to stop. For him to stop sucking all the life from me. From us all.'

'You were sure he'd fallen to his death?'

'The cliff was in shadow, but it was sheer there. I knew he wouldn't have survived.'

'What happened next?'

'I drove home. My parents were still asleep.' She looked up. 'Mack was always saying he wanted to die. He'd hooked up with those crazies online. He even wrote suicide notes. A number of them, practising the words, trying, I suppose, to explain his despair. He probably shared them with his online mates, like teenagers sharing their crap poetry. I took one from his bedroom and drove back to the chalet and left the car outside. I put his note, wrapped in the clear plastic bag, on the cliff path, weighed down with a stone. I knew it would be found there. Then I walked back to the village and called a minicab from outside the pub. It was late but the pub was famous for its lock-ins. I knew the taxi driver wouldn't think twice about it. Then I went home and to bed.'

Matthew nodded. 'And the next day, you reported Mack missing and the police found his car at the chalet. A few days later, his body was washed up on Lundy.'

Janey didn't need to reply.

At that point, Jen asked a question herself. 'What I don't understand is why you didn't just explain what had happened that night. You could have phoned the police and the coastguard. People would have understood the strain you'd been under. A court would have been sympathetic. Why all this pretence? Two more murders!'

You could even have said that he'd slipped, Jen thought. *He was erratic, unstable, nobody would have questioned it. Why the elaborate planning? Did you need the drama, the control, the lying? Did you even enjoy it?*

Jen had always been less sympathetic than Venn, and now she thought this sad little girl pose was all an act. Janey might be immature like Mack, but she wasn't sad. She'd gloried in the drama and the violence. Throughout their childhood, Mack had been the centre of attention, had sapped her parents' energy and demanded their love. And they'd both been in their mother's shadow. This series of killings had put *her* in control.

'That night I thought my parents had been through enough. Imagine the fuss, the press interest! Martha Mackenzie's daughter charged with murder! You don't know how Mack's illness had worn them down. It nearly broke their marriage. I thought now he was dead we'd all begin to live again.'

But you didn't begin to live. You've all been stuck in the roles you had when your brother died.

Janey stopped short and when she spoke again, her tone had changed, had become bitter and angry. 'And besides, there would have been no more murders if Nigel Yeo hadn't started to pry.'

'Frank Ley asked him to investigate the NHS's role in Mack's suicide.'

She nodded. 'My father encouraged the inquiry. And, at first, I was pleased. After all, the trust *was* to blame really. They deserved to have their negligence made public. Mack wouldn't be dead if he'd been properly looked after. We wouldn't have been put under that stress.'

'But Dr Yeo took the investigation seriously,' Venn said. 'How did he come to suspect that Mack hadn't killed himself after all?'

Janey closed her eyes. Jen thought she was exhausted, but wired. Perhaps she hadn't slept for days. 'Nigel was just so bloody thorough. So persistent. He'd found out about the chatroom Mack was using and he asked my father if he could look in the chalet in case Mack had left anything there; any clue as to who might be moderating it. My parents never used the place. They couldn't bear to after my brother died, so it had become my hideaway, my safe space, just as it had been Mack's. I wrote stuff there, trying to get rid of my guilt. Trying to explain to myself how I felt about it all. Turning it into a kind of Gothic fiction. After all, who would ever go there to find it?'

'But Nigel came across it,' Jen said. 'On that Friday after-noon.'

'He cancelled a meeting in Spennicott,' Venn said. 'He must have phoned from the chalet when he saw your writing.'

Janey nodded. 'My father gave him the door code. I didn't know!'

'Until the night of Cynthia's party?'

'I should never have been there!' Now she sounded again like a petulant child, screaming to the wind that life was unfair. 'I only went as a favour to Wesley.'

'What happened at the party, Janey?' Jen thought again that she could have prevented all this. If she'd been sober, if she'd noticed the conversation between the two, if she'd persuaded Nigel to speak to her.

'Nigel said he needed to talk to me. I'd never seen him like that before. So stern. He said he'd go round to Westacombe, and wait for me in Eve's studio. If I didn't turn up, he'd go to the police in the morning. He'd give me a chance to explain.' She looked at Jen. 'I'd seen him chatting to you so I knew he was serious, that he meant what he said. An hour after he left, I told Wesley I wanted to go home. I dropped him at the bottom of the lane, left my car there and walked to Westacombe, taking the shortcut over the common and through Frank's garden to the farmyard. I knew I'd get there before Wes, going that way.'

'And you killed Dr Yeo.' Matthew's voice was quiet. 'If you could confirm that, Miss Mackenzie. We need it for the tape.'

'Yes, I killed Dr Yeo. I smashed a large green vase on the workbench and I stuck a shard into his neck.' She sounded defiant, almost gloating. *So*, Jen thought, *I was right and she is a monster after all.*

'And had you planned that?' Matthew asked. 'Is that why you dropped Wesley at the end of the lane and walked up secretly? You knew you were going to kill Nigel?' Again, the voice was quiet, deceptively conversational.

'I don't know.' It was a wail and suddenly she seemed like a little girl again. 'It was a nightmare. It was just like with Mack. He was talking and talking at me, giving me this lecture about how people with depression *can* be treated and their families *can* get them back. Yeo said I'd stolen Mack's life when he could have been helped. And in the end, I just wanted to shut him up.'

There was silence in the interview room. Outside a drunk was yelling, and an officer was telling him to be quiet.

'Wesley told us he saw a car, driving very fast down the lane. Did he make that story up? To give you some sort of alibi?'

'No,' Janey said. She gave a little smile. Jen thought now she wanted them to know how clever she'd been. 'That was me. I took Nigel's keys and I drove his car fast down the lane. I almost knocked Wesley into the ditch. I left it on the Instow road and took my own car home. After a nightcap with Dad, and when everyone was asleep at home, I took Nigel's car back.'

'We didn't find any fingerprints other than Nigel's in his car,' Venn said. 'How was that?'

'I had gloves in my vehicle.' Again, she was showing them how she'd thought of everything. 'Left over from walks in the winter.'

'You made up the story about seeing a car speeding through Instow?'

She nodded. 'I thought you might take time looking for it.'

'Then you walked home through Frank's garden and over the common?'

'Yes.' There was that superior smile again. 'It was almost morning when it was all done.'

'But it wasn't all done, was it?' Matthew said. 'Why did Wesley have to die? Did he recognize the car that nearly flattened him once he was sober? Or were you starting to take pleasure in the killing, Janey? Was that it? I've checked with the university. You specialized in Victorian fiction in Oxford and your dissertation was focused on the Gothic novel. There's nothing more Gothic than a series of murders where the victims are found with different-coloured glass in the neck.'

'No!' She seemed shocked. Offended. But she gave the

seductive smile all the same and Jen wasn't convinced. 'Of course I didn't enjoy it.' She paused. 'There was a moon the night that Nigel died. It seemed that Wesley might have glimpsed my face when I almost drove into him. He wasn't sure, he was drunk after all, but he phoned me the next day about it. Just gentle questions: "But that couldn't be right, could it, Janey? I must have been imagining it. It must have been the killer rocketing down the lane like that." Then the nice young policeman came to interview me and said he was going back to talk to Wes, to check out his story, so it seemed wise to make sure.'

'Wesley loved you!' Jen said. 'He would have lied for you. There was no need to kill him.'

Janey stared at her with eyes that were as cool and clear as glass. 'I couldn't take that chance.' Again, Jen thought that after years of being in the background, feeling ignored while her parents cared for her brother, she was loving this starring role.

Matthew continued with his questions. 'So, you suggested meeting Wesley in his workshop at the Woodyard, and you knew that he'd come. As Sergeant Rafferty says, he'd always been sweet on you. According to Eve, you were the only woman he'd really cared for.'

'Really? He was middle-aged. Virtually a pensioner.' She gave a shiver of disgust, and then that smile again. 'But yeah, I knew he'd be there if I asked him.'

'And then it all became very elaborate, didn't it, Miss Mackenzie?' In the fierce light of the interview room, Jen could see that Matthew was getting very tired now, but he kept his focus, his full attention fixed on the young woman who sat opposite. 'Using Wesley's phone to text Eve. A bit of a game, was that? Rather cruel, we thought at the time.'

There was no response from Janey, and Matthew continued. 'The whole transport business was very clever, though. That did throw us off the scent for quite a while. Because your car *was* blocked in – we checked that – and your father was driving inland in the family vehicle. So how could you have got into Barnstaple to meet him? Lucy Braddick who works at the Woodyard gave us the answer to that. The bus from Bideford arrived there just before Wesley was killed. Lucy noticed because her friends were on it. She didn't see you get off, but we've checked with the driver and he's confirmed that he picked up a passenger from Instow who matches your description.'

This time he didn't wait for a response, but looked at her with the same steely focus. 'Why the glass as a murder weapon again? And why the blue glass vase that Eve had made for Frank? Did it appeal to your sense of theatre? Or was it to shift our attention back to Westacombe? To Eve?'

She gave a little shrug. 'A bit of both perhaps. Eve's never been my favourite person, though Mack adored her. He seemed to be comparing me to her. She's so together, so bloody competent. I always had the sense that she rather despised me. My parents were always banging on about how brilliant her glass was, how it had been exhibited at the V&A. But it was easy for her to be creative. Her father believed in her and supported everything she did. Besides, it was a challenge. A dare. I knew where the key through to Frank's part of the house was kept. It was risky to walk up through the garden and steal the glass vase from his living room. I loved the thrill, the excitement, that adrenaline rush at the prospect of being caught breaking in to steal. Life had become so *boring* at home. I'd had so many plans after I left university. I was going to travel, fall in love, write my own novel.'

'Couldn't you still have done all those things?' Jen asked.

'No,' Janey said. 'I couldn't. Everything at home revolved around Mack. You've seen how nothing is changed in his bedroom. My parents are stuck, fixed in time, and I've been sucked into their strange, unhealthy world.'

Serial killing, Jen thought, *is a pretty extreme way to escape, to get the excitement you craved. And by then you were caught up in the fantasy of it. You're much madder than your brother ever was.*

'Tell me about today,' Matthew said, 'and Eve.' He looked at the clock on the interview room wall. 'Or I suppose I should say yesterday. What was all that about?'

'She had to meddle.' Janey had become the sulky child again. 'Really, if she'd just left it alone . . .'

. . . we might never have caught you. But Jen thought they would have caught her. They'd already made the connections. Ross had been sent to Cynthia's to check that there'd been a serious conversation between Janey and Nigel at the party, but even without that confirmation, they'd have brought Janey in for questioning.

'What did she do?' Matthew asked.

'She phoned my father.' Janey paused. 'If she'd just got in touch with me, I could have persuaded her. I could have sorted things out.'

'How did she know you were involved?'

'She didn't *know*. How could she *know*? She guessed. She was asking my father all these questions about where I'd been. She must have heard me bringing Nigel's car back the morning after he died. She recognized the engine sound, but after she'd found his body, she was in such a state of shock that it didn't register, until early yesterday morning. And that got her thinking.

369

She knew Wesley would do anything for me. So, there she was, on the phone, spreading her poison. My father overreacted, came into the cafe where I was working and started asking me for explanations.' Janey looked up. 'I've never been able to lie to my father. We've always been close. He had to be both parents to us, while my mother only cared about her career.'

'George should have contacted us,' Matthew said sadly. 'Now he'll be prosecuted too.' He stretched his arms above his head to relieve the tension. 'You were both going to be in the Woodyard in the afternoon.'

'Yes, we support the Cornish theatre company which put on the Beckett in the Sandpiper earlier in the week. They're doing a mini-tour of the south-west and were in the Woodyard last night. Mum and I had agreed to help them set up, and we'd done all the advertising. Dad said he'd take over at the last minute.'

'I saw the posters in the Woodyard lobby,' Jen said.

And Lucy Braddick saw George with Eve when she was coming out of the loo.

'Did you know Eve would be there?'

'Oh yeah. She'd kind of demanded to see Dad, to ask him all those questions. It was, like, talk to me or I'll go to the police. So, Dad arranged to meet her in the Woodyard before the performance started. We both thought it would be better to keep her away from Instow, away from Mum, who'd make a drama out of the whole thing. Dad wanted to protect Mum, to just make the whole thing go away. And he did it for me, of course. I don't know that Eve *really* thought I could be involved. Maybe she just needed reassurance. But again, we couldn't risk it. I was thinking of Dad by then. Honestly, I was!'

Yeah, right.

'He and Mum hadn't been properly close for ages. I was all he had after Mack died. He wouldn't have survived me going to prison. It would be like losing another child.'

'So, you took Eve to the chalet?'

'Yeah. Dad persuaded her they couldn't talk in the Woodyard. He said he'd take her somewhere quieter. Eve had known him for years, and everyone trusts the lovely George. She thought they were just going to chat in the car, but I was already in the driving seat and set off as soon as she got in. That was a bit of a surprise for her. Yes, you *could* say that she was quite shocked to see me.' Janey gave that smug little smile that had come to define her. 'And I already had the piece of broken glass. Luckily we had a little Yeo vase in the kitchen at home.' She looked at Jen. 'You probably saw it on the shelf when you came for coffee that morning. It was yellow. So pretty. As soon as they got in the car, I gave it to Dad and told him to use it if Eve made a fuss. That soon shut her up. It wasn't part of the plan to kill her with it, but it was satisfying to scare her with her own creation, and it tied the plot together. That's how I would have written it.'

'What happened then?' Despite herself, Jen was finding herself sucked into the narrative. Janey was a good storyteller. Perhaps in prison she'd finally write the novel she'd dreamed of.

'We kept her in the chalet until it got dark. There are always people walking the coastal path. Then I had to go back to the Woodyard for the close of the play, to help the team pack up.'

'And provide an alibi.'

'Well, yes, if it should become necessary. Of course, we'd already taken Eve's phone.'

'And you told your father to kill her.'

Another cruel smile. 'I told you. My father loves me. I believed he would have done anything to rescue me, and to save me from prison.' A pause. 'I thought it would be seen as another tragedy. A bereaved daughter, walking on the cliffs, surprised by the storm. The path made suddenly dangerously slippery. A dreadful accident.'

'But your father couldn't quite do it.'

'No.' A tone of disdain. 'It seems not.'

They sat for a moment of silence. Matthew went through the formalities of the charges. Through the high window, Jen saw the first light of dawn.

Chapter Forty-Eight

THE TEAM ATE TOGETHER IN A cafe by the river. Sausage sandwiches and mugs of coffee. The air was fresher, blowing in from the Atlantic with scudding clouds and occasional showers. Ross found it hard to share the celebration, the sense of relief. The day before, Mel had promised that they'd talk, that she'd tell him what had been bothering her over the past few weeks, but he'd not had a chance to get home. All the same, he hadn't felt able to turn down Matthew's offer of breakfast, because these people were starting to feel like family too.

'I think that heatwave made everyone a little bit mad,' Matthew said. 'Do you reckon Janey would have continued her killing spree if the weather had been cooler on the night of Cynthia's party?'

'Yeah, I think she enjoyed it.' Jen wiped tomato sauce from her chin. 'It's George I feel sorry for. I don't think he had any idea what his daughter had done until Eve phoned him up yesterday morning with all those questions. And then he got swept along with Janey's plan. He couldn't deny her anything.

In the interview, he kept saying that he must have been responsible. "We were their parents. We brought them up. And they were both damaged in their own way. I couldn't lose another child.'"

'Guilt,' Matthew said. 'It's a terrible thing.' He still thought Frank Ley had been weighed down with guilt and that this had contributed to his death. It wasn't just that Lauren had rejected his offer of love.

'They're all a bit bonkers, aren't they, these theatrical types?' Ross swallowed the last of his sandwich and decided it was time to get home.

'Poor Eve,' Jen said. 'All that trauma in a young person's life. Will you go and see her, boss? Let her know what happened.'

Matthew nodded. 'I've already phoned and told Eve that both Janey and George have been charged. I'll head over to Appledore to speak to her this afternoon. I need to go home and change. Lauren and her mother will be looking after her.'

Ross pulled onto the drive and saw that Mel's car was still there. He'd lost track of her shift pattern and hadn't known whether to expect her. She was in the kitchen, still in running gear, stretching, easing the muscles in her legs. Usually she'd have greeted him with a hug, an enquiry about the case, some joke about having to find a lover because she saw so little of him. Now, he wasn't even sure that she was pleased to see him.

She switched on the kettle. 'Coffee?' Her back to him. Just the stance of her body seemed tense and cold. Anxious.

'What's wrong?' he said. 'You told me we could talk.'

'We will. Now.'

'What have I been doing wrong? Whatever it is, I can fix it.'

She turned so she was facing him. 'I'm not sure that you can fix this.'

He ran through his behaviour of the past month. He'd taken her for granted, assumed that because he was the main bread-winner he should decide how they ran their life, how they should spend their money. Perhaps he was like those men he'd read about: coercive, controlling. 'I'm learning,' he said. Then he wondered if that was true. Growing up, his model had been Joe Oldham, a close friend of his father's, an old-fashioned cop and an old-fashioned man. And something about Ross still admired the superintendent for his swagger and his humour. His determination not to be cowed, to get whatever he wanted. Oldham had despised Matthew Venn from the moment he'd been appointed, and Ross had taken his lead from the man.

'Is there someone else?' It had been on his mind for days, that she might have a lover. Not a fling. A fling would be hard, but he thought he could cope with that. But what if she'd found someone she loved better than him? Someone more thoughtful. More gentle.

She looked at him. 'No! Is that what you've been thinking?'

'You've been so distant,' he said.

'I suspected I was ill,' she said. 'Breast cancer. My mum had it when she was in her fifties. I found a lump. I had to go for a biopsy.'

'Why didn't you tell me?' He couldn't believe she would keep something like that to herself. Not a lover, but it felt like a different sort of betrayal.

She shrugged. 'You were so wrapped up in yourself. This case.' A pause. 'You liked me because I looked after you. The house. All this . . . I wasn't sure how it would be if you had to take care of me.'

'I'm so sorry.' He paused. 'I will look after you.'

'I had the result of the biopsy last night.' She smiled. 'Not malignant. I was being foolish, panicking. Nothing to worry about. Just a scare.'

'And a scare for me.' A warning, he thought. 'Sit down,' he said. He didn't want her to see that he was on the verge of tears. 'I'll bring the coffee through.'

Chapter Forty-Nine

WHEN JEN GOT HOME, SHE HAD a moment of panic. There was no sign of the kids and they should be up and getting ready for school. She'd lost all sense of time; this week had been elastic: days had flashed by in a muddle of activity and then seconds had slowed to an eternity. Watching George and Eve on the clifftop, Jen had felt that she'd sat through a whole action movie, but scarcely minutes had passed. Only now did she realize that this was Saturday. A week ago, she'd been in bed with a hangover and she'd woken to Ella's disapproval and news of Nigel Yeo's death.

She switched on the kettle to make tea. The dishwasher had been emptied and the surfaces were clear. *Oh El*, she thought, *I really don't know what I did to deserve you*. There were footsteps on the stairs and her daughter appeared, her phone in one hand. She was texting, but she looked up when she saw Jen.

'Hi, Mum. You must be knackered.'

'Just a bit. The kettle's still hot if you want a brew.' She paused. 'Your brother okay?'

'Well, I think he was late on his computer, so don't expect him to emerge anytime soon.'

'Do you know what he's up to when he's on the computer?'

'Mostly shoot 'em up games with his mates.' Ella still had most of her attention on her phone. 'I made him switch it off when Zach went home at one.'

Jen sighed. Maybe there were worse things than those sorts of games. 'Oh God, El. What will I do next year when you go off to university?'

Ella set down the phone and considered the question seriously. 'Nothing different,' she said. 'You'll never change. You'll always take work seriously.' A pause. 'You know what? We really wouldn't want you to be anything different. We admire what you do.' She nodded towards the ceiling. 'And he'll grow up eventually. You might have to instruct him in the mysteries of the washing machine when I go, though.'

Jen laughed.

'Saturday night,' she said. 'Takeaway?'

'Mum! We've been living on takeaway all week. Or stuff from the freezer.'

'I'll cook then.'

There was a pause. 'Nah,' Ella said. 'No offence, Mum, but your cooking? Takeaway.' She wandered back to her room, taking a mug of tea with her.

The house was quiet. There was the background noise of traffic on the road outside, but Jen was used to that and it didn't register. She was exhausted, but she knew she wasn't ready for sleep. This was like jet lag. Best to keep awake all day and sleep properly tonight. She went through to the small living room. Her phone rang. Cynthia.

'I've just told Roger to go,' she said. 'I said I'd be out of the house for a couple of hours and I wanted him gone by the time I get back.'

'So you know? About the Suicide Club.'

'After you told me about that website, I asked him what he was doing when he was shut up in the office. He was almost boasting. He said he was doing more to help his depressed patients than through his work in the hospital.'

Jen could tell her friend was crying. 'Fancy a coffee? If you don't mind slumming it, you could come here.'

Chapter Fifty

AFTER BREAKFAST, MATTHEW DROVE HOME across Braunton Great Marsh, past the pools rich with wading birds and waterfowl. The grey heron still stood, solitary and motionless, its eyes fixed on the water. Under the huge sky, Matthew felt the tension drain from his forehead and his limbs, and all he was left with was his own guilt. Although there was nothing that he could have done to save Nigel, he should have prevented Wesley's death. He'd become so absorbed with Nigel's work, had taken Mack's suicide for granted, and fixated on the online Suicide Club. He should have realized that family was at the heart of most murders. Janey had played them, revelling in their confusion and her power over her victims. Still, Matthew had lived with guilt for many years, since leaving the Brethren, and he thought he could manage that.

He passed through the toll gate and onto the track that led to Crow Point and home. He parked by the house, and, climbing out of the car, he was surrounded by natural sounds: the long calls of the herring gulls on the beach and the cries of the

380

lapwing in the marsh. The sea must have been wild and the tide must be in because he could hear the waves breaking, even from where he stood. The kitchen door was shut against the westerly breeze and Jonathan was taking a late breakfast inside.

The noise of the wind had obviously masked the sound of the car, because Jonathan wasn't aware of him approaching. Matthew stood for a moment, looking in. He needed certainty, strong boundaries; it was what he'd grown up with. In his last two investigations work and home had blurred and collided and he knew that Jonathan had resented his attempts to keep the two entirely separate. Matthew had phoned home the night before, but the call had been short and he still wasn't sure how things stood between them.

Jonathan turned and saw Matthew. Matthew wasn't certain what the response would be and he waited, wary and anxious. Jonathan waved to him, mimed joy and an offer of coffee. All resentment apparently forgotten, at least for now. It seemed that his husband didn't harbour grudges. Matthew went inside and closed the door behind him. He went up to Jonathan and put his arm around his shoulder.

'I was thinking,' he said, 'that we could invite Eve and Lauren Miller for lunch tomorrow. If you don't mind cooking.'

'Is that appropriate? Before the case comes to court?' Teasing.

'Probably not. But I'm learning to be a bit more flexible. Let's do it anyway.'

'Speaking of lunch, the post came early today.' Jonathan was grinning. He pushed an envelope across the table towards him.

Inside there was a card, with an image of a bunch of flowers on the front and *Thanks* in gold letters. Matthew opened it.

Writing that he recognized immediately, but slightly less firm, less certain than he remembered.

Thank you for a delicious lunch.

No signature, but none was needed.